THE HAUNTING OF EDWARD DRAKE

ANDREW CONRY-MURRAY

This book is dedicated to the memory of my father, Andrew J. Murray. I miss you, Dad.

"...he possessed certain keys by which he could discern things invisible to the natural eye."

— NO MAN KNOWS MY HISTORY

1
BOSTON, 1884

Mrs. Coffin surprised Edward with a séance.

He had come to her Beacon Hill home expecting a dull evening's supper with Mrs. Coffin and her two guests. Instead, the parlor was arranged for a psychic reading. A red velvet armchair stood in the center of the room. The gas lamps were turned low. Shadows dripped from the plaster ceiling and pooled among the heavy window drapes. Mrs. Coffin, elderly Mrs. Greenwood, and a minister sipped herbal tea by the fireplace. A fire snarled and snapped in the hearth.

Edward paused in the doorway. "Why is the room so dark?"

"Come in, Edward," said Mrs. Coffin. "I thought we might enjoy a séance tonight."

"Your invitation didn't mention a séance."

Mrs. Coffin set down her tea and went to him. Unlike many of the pinched and narrow matrons of her class, Mrs. Coffin had a generous bosom and ample hips, which her dressmakers artfully arrayed in chiffon and lace. A pearl-colored shawl draped her shoulders.

She hooked Edward's arm. "You needn't be upset. It's just a little amusement."

No, it wasn't. Edward considered turning on his heel, but he would have to break Mrs. Coffin's grip. Not wanting to wrestle with his patron, he resigned himself to being drawn in.

"Mrs. Greenwood, how delightful to see you again," murmured Edward as he bent over the elderly woman's hand. Years ago, Mrs. Greenwood had been a regular at Mrs. Coffin's séances.

Edward turned to the minister, a ruddy, middle-aged fellow who introduced himself as Reverend Cooke. Edward had never met him before. "Good evening, Reverend. Aren't you and the Holy Ghost already on speaking terms? What use have you for a séance?"

Reverend Cooke chuckled. "I do admit to a personal fascination with ethereal phenomena. As do you, I've been told. You serve Mrs. Coffin as a medium."

"Not for many years. As a boy I imagined I could speak to ghosts. Mrs. Coffin indulged my imagination—and her own. But you're familiar with the passage 'When I was a child, I spake of childish things?'"

"First Corinthians," said the Reverend.

"Precisely. I've put away those childish things."

Mrs. Coffin tsked.

At that moment a woman glided into the parlor on a cloud of incense and a swirl of scarlet and yellow silks. Madame Corbeau, a spirit medium. She wore a headscarf of Chinese brocade. Emerald and ruby rings glittered on her fingers. French by birth, Madame Corbeau had made a name for herself among Boston's upper class as a spiritualist. She invoked departed spirits, guided fingers over Ouija boards, and titillated staid Brahmins with her witchery. Mrs. Coffin adored Corbeau. Edward thought her an accomplished fake.

Madame Corbeau processed to the armchair at the center of the room. "*Mesdames et Messieurs*, the spirits of the dead are here among us. Though invisible to the naked eye, they are ever present." Her voice, warm and low, was spiced with the accent of the French countryside.

"We are linked to the dead by a spirit organ that resides inside each of us. No anatomist can pin this organ to a card, no vivisectionist can remove it with a blade. Yet it exists within us, a delicate instrument for detecting emanations from beyond the grave."

"Through this organ we receive signals from our beloved departed—a sudden prickle on the skin, the glimpse of a loved one from the corner of the eye, the sense of a presence in an empty room. Let us now activate our spirit organs so that we might commune with those beyond the grave."

Madame Corbeau extended a hand to Edward. "Come, sir."

"Me? Surely our hostess should go first." Mrs. Coffin never missed a chance to sit with Corbeau.

"I had a private session with Madame this afternoon," said Mrs. Coffin.

"Then what of your guests?"

"They'll wait their turns. Go sit with Madame."

"I'm afraid I'll make for a tedious subject."

"Not as tedious as you and I bickering. Now go!" The cords in Mrs. Coffin's throat tightened. Irritation ruddied her cheeks.

"Very well."

Mrs. Coffin had taken Edward into her life sixteen years ago because of spiritualism. As a boy he'd shown a propensity for delivering "messages" to Mrs. Coffin from her beloved sister Lilith, who had died of fever in childhood. When Edward was just ten years old, Mrs. Coffin had taken him from his family in upstate New York and brought him to Boston to live with her and perform for her. From age ten to sixteen he had served her as a spirit medium, both in private sessions and in group sittings like this.

But at age sixteen Edward had renounced spiritualism and refused to perform as a medium. There was no communication with spirits. Despite Mrs. Coffin's insistence, he couldn't speak with the dead. He had no "spirit organ." No one did. He'd made up the stories he'd told her, his intent only to appease this odd, wealthy woman who had snatched him out of poverty and pressed him into her service.

He was twenty-six now, with no patience for spiritualism. Yet once again he found himself the centerpiece of a farcical performance. It was embarrassing and undignified, and he hoped it would be done quickly.

Edward sat in the chair, back straight and expression bland. Mrs. Greenwood and the Reverend gawked from the shadows. They wanted something to happen; a shock or shiver to jolt and amuse. A story to collect that they could tell in other drawing rooms on other nights. Or just a hint that mysteries lurked behind the curtain of their quotidian lives.

Edward planned to disappoint them. He would sit calmly and respond politely to Corbeau until this sham sputtered and extinguished like a damp wick. Then he could get on with the evening and return to his own apartment.

Madame Corbeau circled him once, twice, a third time. Her slippers whispered against the carpet. She passed her palms languidly over him, as if she moved through water. Shards of red and green light from her rings slashed Edward's face.

"Ahhhh," she sighed. "His spirit organ is potent, this one. He possesses a clear and open conduit to the dead." She addressed Mrs. Coffin. "*Madame*, you were correct to recognize his gift."

"Flatter your patron," thought Edward. "How original." Yet he saw the effect on Mrs. Coffin; she beamed like a student praised by her teacher.

With the tips of her fingers, Madame Corbeau caressed Edward's lank brown hair, which he wore long to hide a burn scar below his left ear. He ducked from her touch. He wasn't a pet to be scratched.

"Edward Drake, your spirit organ is powerful. I sense it within you, wild and raw. It pulses with primitive strength. Like a beast it prowls, feral and untamed."

"Are you describing a spirit organ or an infection of rabies?"

Mrs. Greenwood tittered.

Madame Corbeau persisted. "A force courses through you, *Monsieur*. It draws the dead to you like a fire in the night. Let us call forth their spirits!"

She held out her hands, palms up in invitation. She closed her eyes and swayed her hips. "I am the bridge across the chasm of death. I am the door between the realms. Spirits come over! Spirits come through! Spirits come over! Spirits come through!"

Her body trembled. She moaned and hummed, an eerie, exotic sound in the formal parlor. Edward crossed his legs and waited for her pantomime to end.

"*Voila!*" She clapped her hands with a crack. "The spirits have revealed themselves. I see them here in this room." She turned to the drapes, as if to acknowledge a flock of ghosts perched among the folds. "*Les enfants mort.* Why are you here?"

She took Edward's chin in her hand and studied him. "A cord of sorrow binds you, *monsieur*. It trails out behind you. It snares the souls of dead children."

Mrs. Greenwood gasped—such gruesome talk!

"I see the fear in their eyes, the bruises on their throats," said Madame Corbeau. "I see their corpses in the forest."

Edward stiffened. How could she know about *that*? Had Mrs. Coffin told her what had happened to him as a boy?

"Their innocent lives taken by cruel hands. *Monsieur*, those children were murdered!"

The mood in the room changed; levity and amusement curdled into something cold and heavy. A current of dread drifted through the parlor. A spoon on the teakwood coffee table quivered, though no hand was near to disturb it.

"Three children, their lives stolen. *Monsieur*, they are drawn to you, bound to you." Corbeau flinched, as if pricked by a thorn. "*Mon Dieu.* He was there as well—*un bête diabolique.* You saw him in the forest."

For a moment Edward was back in the winter woods of his childhood, trembling in the cold. Frigid wind slashed through the holes in his coat. Naked branches groped him. And *he* was nearby, the grinning figure creeping through the trees.

"Alone in the cold," croaked Madame Corbeau. "Alone and frightened. Darkness is falling. *Garcon, il n'y a personne pour vous aider.*"

Clammy sweat beaded the back of Edward's neck. Terrible memories seeped into his head, memories he had worked assiduously to forget. Three corpses in the woods. Three dead children he'd found over several awful weeks. He and his father had carried the bodies back to town. And the grinning figure in the woods who had led him to the corpses.

A porcelain cup rattled in its saucer. The fire choked in its grate.

"Little boy, there's no one to help you."

Curios on the mantle shivered. A vase tipped on its side. It rolled off the mantle and smashed on the hearth. Mrs. Coffin yelped.

"The one you fear!" cried Madame Corbeau. "You saw him with the bodies. He approaches once more!"

Edward pressed his hands to his ears. He didn't want to hear any more. Why had he allowed himself to be goaded into this?

"Broken boy!" cried Madame Corbeau. "He showed you the dead children. He'll do it again!"

"No!" rasped Edward.

Suddenly Madame Corbeau convulsed. Her hands leapt like startled birds and knocked aside her brocade scarf. Rings of auburn hair spilled across her brow. She jerked forward and backward, a hideous bowing doll. Cups and saucers on the coffee table chattered like teeth in shivering skulls.

"Dear God, he's here!" moaned Corbeau. "He's here with me! I don't want him! I don't want him!" She threw back her head. Black foam gushed from her mouth. She made a fist and struck herself on the forehead. "*Sortez de ma tête!*"

Mrs. Greenwood clutched the Reverend, who closed his eyes and whispered a prayer.

"*Sortez de ma tête!*" Corbeau's lips mashed the foam. Her slippers beat against the carpet.

Mrs. Coffin, mouth agape, sat pinned to her chair.

"Get out of my head!" shrieked Corbeau. Another gout of black foam erupted from her throat.

"Enough!" cried Edward. He leapt from his seat.

"Get him out! Get him out!" shrieked Corbeau. Flecks of foam spattered Edward's face. She clawed at her skull. "For God's sake get him out!"

Edward struck her with his open right hand. The blow sounded sharp and clear as a gunshot. Her convulsions ceased. The chattering dishes went still.

Madame Corbeau breathed like a lathered horse. Black spittle ringed her mouth. Her eyes were wet and full of pity. Her lips moved, stiff and rubbery.

"The one you fear," she whispered. "He waits for you, Edward Drake. He waits for you in the dark."

2

PALMYRA, 1868
THE HAUNTED CHILD

Edward Drake, ten years old, waited impatiently for his turn with the stories. His teacher, Mrs. Henshaw, had loaned the family a book of tales by Washington Irving. Some of the stories were dull; long sketches of landscapes and customs in far-away countries. But not the one about the decapitated Hessian officer who chased young men through the forests of New York—forests just like the one outside Eddie's door. *That* story sent delightful shivers up and down his skin.

His brother Fred had gotten the book first. Fred sat on their shared bed, hunched beneath a blanket so Eddie couldn't see the pages, not even the illustrations. Eddie bounced on the balls of his stocking feet. The pine planks of the one-room cabin were cold. A wood stove smoked in one corner of the shack. Eddie got as close to Fred as he could while keeping within the stove's stingy radius of heat.

"Ain't you done?" demanded Eddie.

"Don't say 'ain't,'" corrected Fred.

"You *ain't* my teacher," said Eddie.

"Well how can I be done if you keep interrupting me?"

"Shush!" warned Mama. She had mending in her lap and one anxious eye on their father, who brooded over a hand of solitaire. James Drake couldn't abide bickering while he played solitaire.

Eddie's eldest brother Jim Jr. poked and grabbed at Eddie. Jim wanted to wrestle.

"Cut it out!" Eddie was the youngest and scrawniest of the three Drake boys. He knew he'd end up pinned and bleeding on the splintery floor if he grappled with Jim. Jim favored their father in height and strength. At thirteen he was already six feet tall, and nearly strong as a grown man.

"Cut it out," mimicked Jim. His quick fingers caught the skin on Eddie's upper arm and pinched. Eddie yelped.

Then Pop's big hand swung down, hard and callused. Eddie shrank, expecting a blow. Instead, Pop snatched up Eddie, bundled him into a ratty coat and hand-me-down shoes, and dragged him into the cold.

James Drake was a money digger. He believed treasure was hidden in the earth—a chest of Spanish coins perhaps, or a cache of precious gems, or a horde of silver that British soldiers had plundered and buried during the War of Independence and never retrieved. If a man with a talent for money-digging could recover such treasure, he'd live a life of ease and security.

James Drake wasn't alone in this belief. A loose fraternity of money diggers and treasure hunters roamed the hills and gorges of western New York. They burrowed into drumlins, dug pits in empty fields, and excavated Indian middens. They swapped tales of well-diggers who found gems instead of water, and homesteaders who unearthed silver spoons and golden cups while digging out cellars.

Eddie had met a few of these money-diggers. They seemed a rascally bunch, full of grandiose talk about fortunes soon to be found. They made sly claims of occult knowledge and theorized about ley lines and the azimuth of the sun and the moon. They wielded instruments of finding—divining rods and plumb bobs and cracked hand-mirrors in tarnished frames. These instruments were supposedly attuned to precious metals buried in the earth, and would guide their operators to hidden treasure.

If so, Eddie wondered, how come all these men were so poor?

Eddie's father had his own instrument: a pair of seeing stones. One stone was white, bisected with a vein of prickly pink quartz. The other was midnight black and smooth as glass. Pop had dug them from the foundations of an old manse that had burned to the ground a long time ago. Pop carried his seeing stones in a brown felt sack. He consulted them by putting his face into the mouth of the sack. He said the stones projected visions into his eyes, visions only he could perceive.

James Drake enjoyed a bit of success as a money-digger—no treasure yet, but items of modest value or practical use: An axe buried beneath a drift of leaves, the head still sharp. A wagon wheel in a tangle of underbrush, which he rolled into town and sold to the wainwright. A tarnished copper bracelet dug out from an Indian barrow and traded for pork shoulder and a quarter-wheel of cheese. Three jugs of moonshine, wrapped in burlap and secreted beneath a log, which Pop drank on a two-day bender that ended with him in jail until he'd dried out.

Last summer, when a mare ran off from the paddock of a farmer named Tom Hollings, Pop had gazed into his stones, gathered Eddie, and found the beast cropping grass in a meadow. Neighbors talked about how James Drake had walked more than a mile in a straight line, no deviation, from his shack to the horse, as if a string had been tied between him and the animal. Tom Hollings had paid James two dollars cash for the horse's return. The incident secured James' reputation in Palmyra as a man of peculiar talents.

Pop enjoyed his notoriety as a money-digger. It was an improvement on his reputation as a drunk. Folks all over Palmyra knew the name of James Drake—in the Bottoms where Eddie and his family lived, and even in the good parts of town. People were curious about his strange abilities. Perhaps they were a little afraid of him. Eddie understood; he was afraid of him too.

On this day, Eddie and his father traipsed for hours through the woods. Flakes of snow dusted dead leaves on the ground. Barren oak and maple branches clawed the sky with witchy fingers. A pickpocket wind slipped through the holes in Eddie's coat and stole his warmth. His fingers and toes ached with cold.

Eddie wanted to go home. Surely it was his turn with the book by now. Yet he daren't ask if they could go back. A thunderhead had settled on Pop's brow. If they went home empty-handed, that thunder would fall on Eddie. His father would slap and punch him. Or whip him with his belt. Or knock his head with a chunk of firewood. For good measure he might beat Mama, too.

"Been out here awhile now," rumbled Pop. "You see anything, or you just wastin' time?"

Eddie did see something. Mr. Jangles lurked behind a clutch of maples. Mr. Jangles was an elderly man in a faded tartan waistcoat and old-fashioned black suit. He wore big leather boots, creased with age. Wispy silver hair hung past his collar. He had green eyes and crooked yellow teeth.

Only Eddie could see Mr. Jangles. The old man appeared on a whim, like a cloud that obscures the sun. If Eddie and his father were on a treasure hunt, sometimes Mr. Jangles showed up and helped Eddie find things. Eddie would follow Mr. Jangles, and Pop would follow Eddie, utterly unaware of the creeping old man. And whatever Eddie found—wagon wheel, copper bracelet, that farmer's horse—Pop always claimed the seeing stones had guided them. It wasn't true, but Eddie didn't dare gainsay his father.

Eddie supposed he should be grateful to Mr. Jangles. The items he revealed kept the family from starvation. But Eddie didn't like Mr. Jangles. He moved like a mantis, long-limbed and predatory. Dread and sorrow trailed him like an odor. Some nights Eddie woke in his bed to find Mr. Jangles peering through the window at him, his bloodless face waxy in the moonlight, his long nose pressed against the glass. He would tap the pane with a fingernail, tack tack tack. *Let me in*. Eddie would pull the blanket over his head and burrow into the tangle of Fred and Jim's limbs.

Eddie didn't know where Mr. Jangles came from. He wasn't even sure what Mr. Jangles *was*. He wasn't a witch. Witches were warty old women. Neither was Mr. Jangles a devil. Mama said devils had cloven hooves, hairy goat legs, and horns on their heads. The chief devil was called Old Scratch. He appeared in a flash of blue fire and a brimstone stink. Naughty boys who didn't mind their mothers were apt to be snatched up by Old Scratch and carried down to hell.

The best Eddie could figure was that Mr. Jangles was a ghost. It explained the silence with which he moved, and why no one else could see him.

Eddie didn't know why this ghost had attached itself to him. He worried it meant there was something bad inside him, something foul or rotten that drew Mr. Jangles like a crow to carrion. Maybe there was a mark on Eddie's soul, like the mark that God put on Cain. Or it might be because of bad thoughts in Eddie's head. Like last year, when a few men had dragged Pop home, drunk and stinking. They said they'd found him passed out on the train tracks. If a train had come, it would've cut him in half.

"Shoulda left him there," Eddie had thought. The words had popped into his head from some down-deep place. Shock and guilt followed immediately. How could he think such a thing? It was terrible to wish someone dead, especially your father. Only a bad child could wish such evil.

Perhaps this badness drew Mr. Jangles to him. Perhaps Mr. Jangles fed on it, like a tick on blood. So Eddie tried to be good, to never have bad thoughts, in hopes he might starve Mr. Jangles and make him go away. It was hard, but Eddie tried and tried. So far, it hadn't worked.

Now Mr. Jangles beckoned with a crooked finger. His green eyes glittered with mischief, like he wanted to play a trick.

"Go away," whispered Eddie. If he was alone, he'd run for home.

But Pop was here. Pop's eyes roved among the trees, clambered over roots and ridges, traced the dip and rise of the terrain, seeking but not finding.

"Well?" demanded Pop. "You see anything?" His left hand closed into a fist.

Mr. Jangles crept deeper into the forest, long-limbed and silent. He glanced back and jerked his head, encouraging Eddie to come on.

Eddie didn't want to come on, but decided he must. Whatever mischief Mr. Jangles might be up to, it couldn't be worse than a beating from Pop. And maybe the old man would show them something good. Something they could eat or sell.

"That way." Eddie pointed to the maples where Mr. Jangles had passed.

Pop considered the direction. He opened the sack that held his seeing stones and put his face to it, as if consulting a compass.

In the distance, Mr. Jangles paused. Eddie sensed his impatience like a man rapping on a door.

"Yes, that's the way," said Pop. "Go on."

They passed through the trees and came to a narrow, frozen creek. A tangle of roots formed a hollow on the opposite bank. A swatch of fabric was caught in the hollow. Eddie strode toward it, his excitement rising. It might be a tinker's bindle, packed with pots and knives and utensils they could sell. Or a sack of corn meal; they might eat hot corn bread tonight, sweetened with a bit of borrowed molasses. His stomach rumbled in anticipation.

It was no bindle. It was the hem of a dress. Eddie crept closer. Two bare feet poked out from the hem. Mr. Jangles had led him to a body.

It was a girl. Her eyes were closed, her hands folded in the lap of her gingham dress. Her lips were blue. Hideous purple blotches ringed her throat.

She was Katie Cooper. Ten years old, same as Eddie. Katie had gone missing two weeks ago. Her disappearance was the talk of Palmyra. Search parties had scoured the woods, including the

Cooper family's hound dogs, to no avail. After days of searching, word was the hound dogs had crawled under Katie's bed and wouldn't come out, not even to eat or drink. They just lay in the dark and mourned.

"Good Christ, we found her," said Pop.

"What do we do?" Eddie trembled beside his father. Someone had *killed* poor Katie. He wanted to run away. He wanted to dash to his mother and climb into her arms.

Pop stroked his chin, weighing the consequences of leaving or taking her. At last he said "Let's bring her to her kin."

Reluctantly, Eddie followed his father across the creek. Their shoes cracked thin sheets of ice. They knelt by Katie. Crystals of snow adorned her hair. Grownups said she played piano almost as good as the choirmaster at the Episcopal church. Now her hands curled inwards like claws, stiff and ugly. Those hands would coax no more music from a piano, nor stroke her hounds' soft ears. Eddie choked back tears, afraid to cry in front of his father.

"Help me get her," said Pop.

Eddie recoiled—a boy from the Bottoms didn't dare touch a town girl. But no one could see his transgression. And Katie was beyond caring.

He turned his head away as he slid his hands beneath her narrow shoulders. The cold of her corpse leeched into his palms. He was touching a dead body! His throat hitched. He struggled not to spew his meager breakfast.

They lifted her from her bed of roots. Dead leaves clung to her hair and dress. Then his father took her. She sagged in his arms, heavy and dull as a sack of ingots. Sorrow and foreboding filled Eddie's heart.

"Get my things," said Pop.

Eddie retrieved the bag and shovel from the ground. As he did, Mr. Jangles peeked from behind an oak. The apparition pointed a long finger at Eddie, and then at the corpse in his father's arms. Mr.

Jangles wanted Eddie to understand something. Something to do with Katie.

Inside his head, Eddie cried "Go away! Leave me be!"

Mr. Jangles did not go away. He gestured to himself, then to Eddie, miming a connection. Then he raised an index finger. It stuck in the air like a crooked twig.

One.

He raised a second finger.

Two.

Then a third.

Three.

Mr. Jangles was counting. Katie Cooper was the first, but more children would be killed. And Mr. Jangles would show them to Eddie.

Eddie's bladder let go. Warm urine fanned his crotch and trickled down one leg. Inside his head he pleaded with Mr. Jangles. "I'll be good! I swear I'll be good! Please don't hurt no one else!"

Mr. Jangles wrinkled his nose, as if disgusted that Eddie had wet himself. Then he turned and ambled into the forest. Winter's hush lay heavy and solemn. Eddie stood in the woods with his father and a corpse.

3
BOSTON, 1884
THE HAUNTED MAN

Leeds gymnasium smelled of sweat, low tide, and old tobacco. A former warehouse near Boston's Central Wharf, the gym had once stored hogsheads of tobacco leaf from plantations in Virginia and North Carolina. Now it was home to a motley mix of amateur pugilists. As Edward Drake stepped through the door, the raftered ceiling echoed with the thud of fists pounding heavy bags and the whipcrack of jump ropes against the floor. Cold October gusts rattled the building's frame, sifting dust from the roof and causing the gas lamps to flicker.

Edward's affiliation with Mrs. Coffin gave him access to better-appointed gymnasiums with choicer amenities: soaking tubs, masseuses, and clubrooms where you could relax with a drink and the day's papers. Edward preferred Leeds. Its members came from all strata of Boston society: gentlemen idlers, prosperous professionals, and thick-necked tradesmen. You might take turns at a heavy bag with a city councilor, then shadowbox next to a stevedore. The editor of the transcendentalist journal *The Dial* had once knocked Edward to the canvas with a crafty right hook. Three nights ago, Edward had sparred with a man who drove the cab that had brought him to the office the next morning. Edward relished the gym's democratic spirit. Inside Leeds, your social rank didn't matter; only hand speed, footwork, and grit.

A boxing ring dominated the open floor. It was a raised square of canvas 24 feet by 24 feet. Three lines of scratchy hemp ropes marked the ring's perimeter. The ropes were threaded through posts, one in each corner, mounted with turnbuckles to keep the lines taut. As Edward crossed the room, two men in the ring jabbed at one another. They were watched by a squat, tough Englishman named Michael Sykes, the gym's owner. "Nah, nah!" he exhorted in a broad Yorkshire accent. "Keep yer gloves up. Up, I say!"

Around the ring were heavy bags, speed bags, jump ropes, juggling clubs, dumbbells, a pull-up bar—stations of the cross for boxing's faithful. Men sweated and puffed at their exercises, concentration fixed as they pursued the synthesis of muscle, tendon, and intention.

Edward threaded his way to a narrow changing room, a dusty chamber with a pair of benches and stacks of wooden cubbies where members stored their street clothes. He yawned mightily as he unbuttoned his shirt. After the debacle in Mrs. Coffin's parlor last night, he'd returned to his own apartment and switched on every lamp in every room. He'd sat up until dawn, too afraid of nightmares to risk sleep.

Today he'd had a long day at work. As a newly minted site supervisor for the landscape architect Frederick Law Olmsted, Edward had spent hours tramping through a mucky marsh with a surveyor and a gang of workmen. The marsh was to be drained and filled as part of a grand project to create a series of public parks that would stretch several miles from downtown Boston to its outlying neighborhoods. Edward had sloshed around the marsh with a theodolite, survey maps, and stakes to mark the site. Tomorrow the digging would begin in earnest.

Tonight, Edward hoped a bout of vigorous exercise would clear his mind. That foolish Corbeau woman had uncorked a vial of rotten memories—the dead children, and the ghost that Edward had imagined as a boy. He wanted those memories out of his head. He folded his good clothes and placed them in his cubby, then changed into a long-sleeve wool shirt and a pair of short pants. He laced up thin leather boots with rubber soles. The gym was cold. Gooseprickles dotted his legs.

As Edward emerged from the changing room, one of the boxers in the ring called out "Hallo, Ed! Get up here, would you? It's only pitiful old men in here tonight and I need a workout."

Edward jogged over to the ring. His friend Thomas Connelly had addressed him. Tom was a lawyer in his mid-twenties. He was a mediocre boxer, but had the shoulders of a bull. The son of a quarryman, he'd grown up cutting and lifting granite. Though years had passed since he'd worked a quarry, he retained a prodigious strength.

Tom took a playful swipe at his opponent, a white-haired, heavyset fellow who lectured in history at Harvard College. "The professor might frighten his undergraduates, but he's hardly a match in here," said Tom.

"Stick it up your bum, Connelly" said the professor.

"I haven't warmed up yet," said Edward. "Can you two give me five minutes?"

"He won't last five minutes," said Tom. "I'll drag him 'round this ring like Ajax dragged Hector around the walls of Troy."

"Achilles, not Ajax," corrected Edward—just before the professor could. "You're lucky it's not a battle of wits in there."

The professor chortled.

"Bookworms," growled Tom. He dropped into a fighting stance. "Make haste with your calisthenics!"

Edward limbered up with windmills and deep-knee bends. He wrapped his knuckles with strips of cloth and hit the heavy bag to warm his waist and shoulders. He skipped rope to wake up his legs. When he returned to the ring, Tom was leaning on a post, watching others at their exercise. Sweat matted his dark hair and stained the underarms of his shirt.

"Ready now?" asked Tom.

"I am. Are you? You look done in."

"Been sparring an hour already, but I've enough wind for the likes of you."

"You lawyers are all wind," said Edward, climbing through the ropes.

"Sauce is it? Let's see how witty you are with a fat lip."

They tapped gloves, then separated and circled one another. Tom moved with the easy confidence of a powerful man. Edward, smaller and slighter, bounced on his toes, wanting to stay away from Tom's left hand. The two men traded jabs, then Tom darted inside Edward's guard, firing blows. Edward slipped the first punch, but the second struck his ribs. He grunted.

"That's for the Achilles crack," said Tom. For the next two minutes he bullied Edward around the ring. But soon Edward began to assert himself. He'd been boxing for two years now, and his technique and speed began to overmaster Tom's raw strength. Patiently he targeted Tom's ribs and belly until Tom began to drop his hands to protect his mid-section. This exposed Tom's head to Edward's jab. By round five, Edward was getting the better of his friend. The lawyer's nose was swollen, the left side of his face puffy.

Finally Mr. Sykes broke in. "Enough, lads, enough. I think you're finished for the night, Tommy."

"Indeed I am," said the lawyer. "Well fought, Ed." They tapped gloves again.

"Go towel off," said Sykes. Then he turned to Edward. "And you, son. I can see your hook comin' a mile away. I'll fix that." Without bothering to glove up, he worked with Edward for the next fifteen minutes. Sykes was smooth and precise. His limbs meshed like gears: ankle, hip, waist, and shoulder perfectly synchronized. Sykes never touched his pupil, but Edward was reminded he wouldn't last five seconds against the Yorkshireman in a real contest.

When they were done, Edward finished with a bout of rope work. He liked skipping rope. His mind went quiet as he fell into the rhythm of the exercise, his breath in his ears, the rope clapping time against the plank floor.

A voice broke in. "Good work tonight," Tom said. His face was red and blotchy. "Are you finished? Let's get beefsteaks."

Edward hadn't planned to dine out, but he gladly accepted the invitation. He toweled off and changed quickly. Outside, the wind off the harbor was pungent with salt and tar. It snapped the hem of Edward's coat and chilled the damp hair that hung past his collar.

It was a short walk from the gymnasium to Durgin-Park in Faneuil Hall. The restaurant was dim and noisy, a bubbling clatter of cutlery and talk. Smells of brine, molasses, and roasting meats drifted through the smokey air. Diners ate communally, seated elbow to elbow at long wooden tables, dockworkers and sailors alongside merchants and shopkeepers. Edward and Tom shouldered through the press and found two empty places at one end of a rough-hewn table. They nodded to their table-mates, fishermen in heavy sweaters who barely glanced up from their mugs of ale and heaping platters of steamed clams and mussels.

Tom shouted an order for two steaks and two beers to a grey-haired matron in a stained apron. She clutched six foaming mugs in her hands, never spilling a drop as she weaved among benches and boots. Edward preferred wine or spirits with his steak, but he was thirsty from his exercise and beer would go down better.

Tom rubbed his eyes. "God I'm tired. I spent the day drowning in documents. I'll spend tomorrow that way too." He tipped his head at the working men who shared their table. "D'you ever think about throwing it all aside and going to sea? Escape the tedium of the office for good honest work on the deck of a ship?"

"I thought you became a lawyer to avoid honest work."

Tom kicked him under the table. "This project of Mr. Olmsted's is a dog's dinner of property claims. Almost every acre you and your crew are supposed to dig up is in dispute. Some joker showed up today brandishing a parchment. He declared it was a royal land grant to his great-great-great grandfather."

"A King's grant? Did he have a good claim?"

"Complete forgery. He'd written it himself, then dunked the parchment in tea to age it."

"A forgery? How'd you know?"

"Because the tricksy bastard wrote in street names. There weren't any streets here in 1629! I grabbed him by his collar and threw him right out onto the road. The whole time he's waving his paper and shouting 'King Charles decreed it! King Chaaaarles!'"

Tom and Edward had met several months ago at one of the interminable planning meetings required of Mr. Olmsted's great project. They'd been salted in among the clerks, secretaries, and factotums around the perimeter of a grand conference room. They'd recognized one another almost immediately—two unlikely lads who had leapt barriers of class and circumstance to gain access here. They might be standing against the wall instead of seated at the table, but they'd made it into the room.

Tom Connelly was Irish Catholic. He'd taken pains to file down the Galway accent of his parents, who had emigrated to Massachusetts in the 1850s, but his surname was a dead giveaway to the Protestant gatekeepers of Boston's professional class.

Tom had grown up poor, his father a quarryman and his mother a domestic. As the oldest son from a family of seven, he'd been expected to follow his father into the trade. A priest in Tom's parish school had spotted the boy's intelligence and pugnacious ambition and taken a hand in Tom's education. Tom had eventually won a scholarship to Boston College, a modest school in the South End founded by Jesuits to educate Irish-Catholic strivers like Tom. After college, he'd gone to work for a small law firm in the city.

As they carved their way through slabs of medium-rare steaks and mugs of malty brown beer, Tom nattered about politics. He'd become involved with the campaign of a city alderman named Hugh O'Brien, who had ambitions of becoming mayor.

Edward knew an Irish-Catholic would never run Yankee-dominated Boston, so he only half-listened to Tom's chatter. He didn't mean to be rude, but the cramped, crowded restaurant made conversation a chore. And the growing lateness of the hour wore on him. Would he sleep tonight, or would the old bad memories chase him in the dark, leaving him even more exhausted tomorrow?

When the meal was done, Edward paid the bill as a kind of apology for his poor companionship. The two men exited into the night. A long row of shuttered market stalls lined the cobbled lane of Faneuil Hall.

"You all right?" asked Tom. "You were distant at supper. Did I brain you during our bout? Should we get some smelling salts and a head bandage from Sykes?"

Edward wondered how much he could say to Tom. He'd revealed bits and pieces of his upbringing to his friend, but had never said a word about the murdered children, nor the lurking specter in the woods.

A wind came up from the harbor. Something rattled down an alley, half-seen in the dim moonlight. It might be a scrap of newspaper. Or the hem of the dress of a murdered child.

"Did you ever see ghosts when you were a boy?" The words tumbled from Edward's mouth before he could stop them.

"Ghosts?"

Edward blushed. Why had he said anything? "Never mind."

"Oh I won't leave that one alone. Do you see ghosts, Ed?"

"I did, a long time ago. That is, I thought I did. But it couldn't have been real."

"What did it look like? A figure draped in white, floating around a room?"

"He looked like an old man. He followed me in the woods. But leave it, Tom. The hour's late, and perhaps you did rattle my head."

Tom patted Edward's shoulder awkwardly. "Listen, Ed. Children imagine all sorts of rubbish. I used to think I could talk to crows."

"What?"

Now Tom looked sheepish. "Well, just one crow. He roosted in the eaves of our tenement. Soot-black he was. When I cawed at him, he cawed back. I called him Pebble. I told my brothers I could talk to him. I said Pebble would fly into their hair and peck their eyes unless they did as I said."

"You thought you could talk to a bird?"

"Well now, here's the thing about childhood. It's a bit hazy, isn't it? Did I, at age nine or ten, believe I talked to Pebble? Perhaps I did. I certainly wanted my brothers to think so. But it was nonsense. A game of make-believe."

"Make-believe," agreed Edward. "You're right, Tom. Children imagine all sorts of rubbish."

"There you are." Tom knuckled Edward in the ribs. "It's no good dwelling on the past, Ed. You and I both came up rough. You more than me, I think—which is saying something. But that's all behind us." He swept his hand to encompass Boston, shrouded in mist and coal smoke. "Put your eyes to the horizon. We're men now, making our names and fortunes. In five years' time, we'll have the city at our feet."

Edward liked that. He raised an invisible glass in a toast. "At our feet. But you're mad if you think your man O'Brien will be mayor."

"Oh ho!" Tom took up a boxer's shuffle and jabbed at the shadows. "There's more of us Irish than you Yanks. I've been up and down every ward in Boston with Mr. O'Brien—our lads are ready. The next election's going to be ours."

"Put a wager on it? A dollar?"

"Make it a fiver. I'll happily take your money." They shook on it.

"Goodnight Ed. Beware of ghosts on your walk home."

"And you of crows."

———

Edward lived by himself on the fifth floor of a brownstone in Back Bay. Twenty-five years ago, this land had been tidal flats on the

Shawmut peninsula. City planners had shipped in immense quantities of dirt and gravel to fill the flats and create a new parcel of ground on which to build. They set down a grid of five broad, straight avenues, modeled after Haussmann's imperial boulevards in Paris. Next had come blocks of opulent row houses, rising four and five stories and fronted with tall, multi-paned windows. Greek and Romanesque flourishes adorned the facades: columns and arches, pointed pediments, carved pendants. Elegant stone steps lifted the entrances above the streets, allowing ladies and gentlemen to sweep grandly down from their homes and out into the city.

Mrs. Coffin owned the building where Edward lived, as well as the brownstones on either side. She didn't live in any of them. They were an investment suggested by one of her business managers. Edward opened an iron gate and walked down a narrow alley to the back entrance. He paused at the coal shed to fill a bucket to take up with him. The stairwell was narrow, musty, and pitch dark. Edward took the stairs at a jog—not, he told himself, because something might grab his ankle as he climbed, but because it was good for his boxing.

His rooms were on the fifth floor. This was the servants' quarters, meant for domestics who would attend the family on the lower floors. Two neighbors lived below him, spinsters called Ms. Cutler and Ms. Hewes. They often climbed the front stairs to ask Edward to move a chair or table from one sitting room to another, or hang a painting, or hammer a loose nail. Afterwards they served him tea and digestive biscuits. Now and then they groused to Edward about having to give up the top floor, but their complaints were perfunctory. The ladies shared four floors between them and had more space than they knew what to do with.

The back stairs opened onto a plain kitchen with a linoleum floor and a hulking iron stove. A skylight overhead allowed a bit of light during the day. Service bells were fixed to one wall, connected by ropes and pulleys to the lower floors. Soon after he'd moved in,

Edward had disconnected the bells to stop Ms. Hewes ringing him like a butler.

The kitchen was silent, the stove dead. His own housekeeper, Mrs. Penney, must've gone home already. He left the coal bucket by the stove. The rooms beyond were neat but plain, the plastered walls bare of wainscoting, the floorboards unvarnished. Edward didn't mind. Mrs. Coffin charged him no rent, and he had the floor to himself—four rooms, plus a bath and the kitchen.

He bathed quickly, then changed into his nightclothes. As was his habit before bed, he went to his study to write letters and read. The study was his favorite room in the apartment. He'd dressed the pine plank floor with a red and gold carpet he'd purchased in Istanbul. He had a sideboard with a brandy snifter and a pair of cut crystal glasses. A fireplace stood on one wall, braced on either side by shelves of books.

Over the mantle hung a landscape by the Dutch painter Aelbert Cuyp—a print, not the original. The foreground was a high hill where shepherds played pipes amidst their sheep and kine. In the distance, watery polders drowsed beneath an immense blue sky hazy with cloud. If reading or correspondence grew tiresome, Edward could lift his eyes and wander the landscape.

In front of the fireplace sat a stuffed leather armchair, modeled after the chairs in the reading room of the Boston Athenaeum. The chair was solid and comfortable, the leather supple and soft.

He yawned as he built a fire, then sat and laid a writing board across his lap. He'd been neglecting a letter to Evelyn Forrest, a childhood friend who still lived in Palmyra where he'd grown up. The Forrests were a Negro family. Race-mixing was unusual in Palmyra, but a peculiar circumstance had joined Edward and Evelyn, as well as her younger brother Luke. They'd had a strange adventure in a cave—a perilous experience that had bonded the three children.

After Mrs. Coffin had removed Edward from Palmyra to Boston, he'd tried to stay in contact with his mother, as well as with Evelyn and Luke. For months he'd written home, but had never received any replies. Eventually he'd stopped writing. It wasn't until years later that Mrs. Coffin revealed a cache of almost two hundred letters that she had kept from him. Mrs. Coffin had intercepted them and hid them away. Edward had been furious; for years he'd thought his mother and friends had abandoned him. "How could you do such a thing?" he'd shouted. Mrs. Coffin refused to apologize; she said she'd only wanted to protect him from homesickness and melancholy.

After reading through those letters, Edward had written a brief note to Luke and Evelyn to explain what had happened. Given that more than a decade had passed since they'd corresponded, he presumed he wouldn't hear back.

To his delight, he'd received a reply about a week later. Luke and Evelyn had each written to him on a shared sheet of paper. He learned that Luke was helping their father run the family's dairy farm, and that Evelyn was a school teacher. Encouraged by their friendly tone, Edward began to write once or twice a month. Over time, Luke's messages got briefer while Evelyn's got longer. Soon he stopped addressing his letters to brother and sister, and wrote to Evelyn alone. He and Evelyn had been corresponding regularly for two years now.

Tonight, however, Edward found it hard to concentrate. Evelyn was a link to his childhood, and his childhood wasn't something he wanted to dwell on. After several false starts, he abandoned the letter and decided to read. He chose a collection of Sherlock Holmes stories and brought the book to his bedroom. He'd read the stories before, but Conan-Doyle's tales of meticulous logic would be the perfect antidote to Madame Corbeau's foolish spiritualism. Thus armed against the supernatural, Edward settled himself comfortably beneath the blankets and opened the book.

4

The next morning, Edward tramped across the worksite. Mud squelched beneath his boots and spattered his trousers. He stifled a yawn and discretely checked his pocket watch. Only 9:30. "Good Christ," he muttered. He'd slept poorly again last night, and a long day of work stretched out ahead of him.

A cold October drizzle pissed down from the gray sky. Dampness seeped into his wool coat. The stench of human feces wafted from the fens, into which the town of Brookline emptied its sewers.

As an assistant supervisor for the firm of F.L. Olmsted & Company, Edward's task was to drain several hundred yards of these marshy fens. Once drained, the marsh would be filled with rock and soil. Gardeners would plant dogwood and willow trees, green lawns, flowering shrubs, and rose bushes. A walking path of cinder and crushed stone would link this reclaimed land to the Emerald Necklace, a string of parks and greenways designed by Mr. Olmsted. When complete, the seven-mile necklace would adorn Boston and its outlying neighborhoods, from the Commons downtown to Franklin Park in Jamaica Plain.

On drizzly, stinking days such as this, Edward doubted a park could ever emerge from this sopping ribbon of miasmic fens.

A gang of Irishmen, Canuks, and Negros dug a trench to drain these fens. They shoveled mud and excrement into wheelbarrows. Their spades bit the mire in a queasy rhythm; slursh-plop slursh-plop. Each turn of their blades fouled the air.

Edward hid another yawn behind a hand. God, he was tired! Despite his plan to clear his head with exercise last night, he still hadn't found any sleep. He'd read until well past midnight. Yet even as his eyes had blurred and his head drooped, unpleasant visions had seeped into his mind: Winter corpses with blue lips. A man, silent and shadowy, stalking through a snow-dusted wood. Three dead children, their empty eyes staring up at him in accusation as he and his father lifted their bodies from the ground. Instead of sleeping he'd sat up all night, electric lamps burning to throw back the dark. He hadn't switched off the lamps until he'd heard Mrs. Penney tromping up back stairs this morning, coming to make his breakfast.

A young man squished across the fens with papers for Edward to sign; his clerk, Robert Bacon. Bacon was a gangly lad of twenty, with blond hair and a spray of freckles across his nose. Bacon had secured the clerkship after his uncle donated five hundred dollars to the project.

Edward didn't begrudge the nepotism; he himself had been given a place because of Mrs. Coffin. When the great architect Olmsted moved from New York to Boston last year, Mrs. Coffin had welcomed his wife, Mary, into New England society. At charity events and fund raisers for the project, Mrs. Coffin had impressed on Mrs. Olmsted Edward's industriousness and availability. In turn, Mrs. Olmsted had pressed upon her husband. Orders traveled down the company's hierarchy to make a place for Edward.

Edward had started as a clerk. He'd vowed to make the most of this opportunity. Six days a week he'd been first to the office in the morning and last to leave each night. He'd performed unglamorous but essential chores, including the tedious shepherding of forms, permits, and site surveys demanded by various municipal bureaucracies.

He'd logged hundreds of miles traipsing among various city and county offices to obtain the seals, stamps, and signatures that allowed the project to move forward. He attended planning meetings. He caught errors in budgets and blueprints and offered humble suggestions for improvements.

His work caught the eye of the project's director, Elijah Sprague. The director invited Edward to accompany him on tours of potential sites. Edward, a competent draftsman, sketched the sites. One of Edward's planning drawings stood on an easel in Mr. Sprague's office.

Three weeks ago, Sprague had asked him to supervise this dig. Edward had no illusions about the promotion to supervisor—shoveling shit should be within the capabilities of a rich benefactor's ward. Yet Edward took his duty seriously; he meant to see the fens drained ahead of schedule and under budget.

Edward signed the papers Robert presented, then massaged his right wrist. His father had broken it when he was a boy and it ached in damp weather. "I could use a cup of tea. How about you, Robert?"

"I could, sir." At the mess tent, Edward let Robert pour him a mug. The brew, though of poor quality, was hot and strong. The heat felt good in his chest and belly.

Across the worksite, a trio of Canuks jabbered together; two burly fellows in newsboy caps, and a squib of a man in a battered derby. They joshed and japed as they worked, their Quebecois French drifting over the wet smack of their spades.

Edward's own people, as much as he knew of them, had been Huguenots from France—a Protestant sect in a Catholic land. French Catholics had hunted and murdered Hugenots. His ancestors had fled some two hundred years ago, first to Canada, and then down across the border into Maine and New York. Edward had grown up hearing a few tattered French phrases from his father—mostly commands to shut up or fuck off—but that was the extent of his heritage.

Edward wondered if he shared any ancestors with the Quebecois at the worksite, but he knew better than to strike up a conversation. The men would fall silent and stand stiffly until he moved on. After all, Edward was *le chef*. He wore a suit. He worked with this mind rather than his back. He might have come from similar stock, but he was no longer *of* them.

If Edward was an outsider among the laborers, he wasn't quite within the circle of the fellows at the office. They were Harvard, Yale, and Bowdoin men. Edward hadn't been to college. Mrs. Coffin had paid for him to be tutored in her home by an old gentleman called Mr. Bollen. Though he'd excelled under Mr. Bollen's instruction, when he came of age for university Mrs. Coffin instead arranged for him to serve as a junior clerk in the Coffins' shipping business. She felt it was a position more befitting his station. He'd worked there for several years before joining Mr. Olmsted's project.

Edward believed himself to be as well-educated as his colleagues; he only lacked the degree. That lack could be overcome (so he'd thought) by demonstrating his effort, intelligence, and wit. But after striving for months to show he could stand with the college men, he realized it didn't matter if he could conjugate Latin verbs, calculate the angle of a slope, or quote Coleridge and Yeats. His mind wasn't the issue. It was school colors on a tie, fight songs, university sporting rivalries, and alumni-only supper clubs where relationships were forged. These were boundaries he simply couldn't cross.

A cry of alarm interrupted his thoughts. The workers clustered around a section of the trench. They leaned on their shovels and pointed.

Edward stalked over and found the foreman, an Irish fellow called Feaney. Feaney was a bulldog of a man, with stumpy legs and a thick neck. His left cheek was plugged with tobacco.

"Why have the men stopped working?"

"They've dug up bones, sir. Human bones." Feaney pointed to the trench. White bones huddled in the filth. A child-size skull sat atop a knuckled strand of vertebra. The vertebra linked to a slender pelvis and long, thin femurs. Dirt and muck occluded the remainder of the skeleton.

"Jesus, Mary, and Joseph," said Feaney. "We've dug up a child's grave." He removed his hat and crossed himself. "Tis a sin to disturb consecrated ground."

A Negro said "Trouble a grave, you trouble its spirit. You fellas gonna need charms to keep the haunts away." The man executed a complicated movement with the fingers of his right hand. Edward recognized the gesture: a ward against vengeful spirits.

The sight of the bones unnerved him, but he didn't want superstitious twaddle delaying his schedule. "This isn't consecrated ground. There's no record of a cemetery or churchyard anywhere nearby."

He took a spade and eased himself into the trench. "We'll dig a perimeter around the bones." Gently Edward shifted mud away from the skeleton. Other men obeyed, though a handful stood at the edge of the trench and only watched, their eyes hooded.

As they worked, someone whispered "Old bones. What to do with old bones?" Edward scanned the men to see who it was. He glimpsed a gaunt face with green eyes, a terrible face he hadn't seen in years. A face he'd hoped to never see again. Then it was gone. "Get ahold of yourself," he muttered.

Soon the men opened a wide, shallow pit that revealed the entire skeleton. Bony fingers clutched at the muck as if trying to dig itself out. The skull's empty sockets stared accusingly at its exhumers. The lower jaw, still dotted with baby teeth, hung open in a cry.

Edward wiped his forehead with a sleeve. His hands were filthy, his trousers fouled with mud and shit, his leather boots a ruin. Dull pain throbbed in his sinuses.

The rain changed from a drizzle to a downpour. Susurrating sheets of water kicked up plumes of mud. Raindrops slapped the bones, making ghoulish music. The workers bunched together against the rain.

"What now, Mr. Drake?" asked Feaney.

"This must be an unmarked grave. My guess is it's very old; maybe an Indian, or perhaps a Puritan child. I need to inform the director. We'll leave off digging for now. Get these men under the mess tent." Edward took a coin from his wallet and gave it to Feaney. "Send someone for a bottle of spirits. Every man gets a drink—one drink. When the worst of the rain passes, we'll start a new trench over there."

"Very good, sir." Feaney pocketed the money. "Are you well, Mr. Drake? You look peaked."

"I'm fine," said Edward. He wasn't. His head pounded and he shivered beneath his wet wool. The excavation of the bones unsettled him. He recalled Madame Corbeau's words about a cord of sorrow that trailed out behind him and snared dead children.

The workers abandoned their spades and hurried to the mess tent. As they dispersed, one man remained. He stood with his back to Edward. Rain plastered his lank white hair to his skull and dripped beneath his coat collar.

"You there—go get your drink," said Edward.

Slowly the man turned. His head moved in the cradle of his neck as if it wouldn't stop. He grinned at Edward, an old friend paying a call. Mr. Jangles.

Edward cursed the Corbeau witch and her damned seance. Her talk of childhood terrors had him hallucinating at ten o'clock in the morning. "You're not here," Edward hissed. "It's just a lack of sleep."

Mr. Jangles held Edward's eye. A voice slipped into Edward's ears, thready and faint. *Come home. We've work to do.*

Edward grimaced. How could see someone, hear someone who wasn't there? Rain pounded on his hat and sluiced off the brim, half-obscuring the apparition. The pit became a pool. The bones huddled in dank water.

"Sir, get out of the rain!" called Robert.

Mr. Jangles pointed to the skeleton. *This one's of no use. Old bones are no good.* His green eyes blazed with intent. *I need living children. And I have them!*

"No," moaned Edward.

Come home. We've work to do.

"I won't! You're not real!"

Mr. Jangles hopped into the pit. His boots squelched in the mud. He lifted the skull and held it out to Edward.

Come home. We'll finish what we began.

"No!" screamed Edward. "I won't go through it again! I won't, damn you!" Edward snatched up a spade and swung at the specter. Mr. Jangles danced away. Edward swung again and nearly toppled into the muddy hole. "Damn you! Damn you to hell!"

"Sir, what are you doing?" It was the foreman, Feaney. The Irishman took Edward's shoulder.

"Get him out of there!" shouted Edward. He broke Feaney's grip and surged for the pit, wanting to bash the specter, smash him to bits. "Get out of there!"

"Help!" cried Feaney. Men rushed from the tent. Hands pulled Edward away from the pit. Edward kicked wildly and shouted curses. Mr. Jangles toyed with the skull, mocked its open-mouthed grin.

"You bastard! Leave it be! And leave me alone!"

They wrestled Edward into a wagon. Robert and Feaney held him down. Edward fought them.

"You won't have me!" he screamed. "Do you hear? I'll never serve you!" From the wagon he saw Mr. Jangles hop out of the pit, saunter across the fens, and vanish behind a curtain of reeds.

"Go!" shouted Feaney at the driver. "Get him to a doctor!"

As the wagon lurched away, Edward shrieked. His pitiful cries carried across the work site. "Not again! Please God not again!"

5
PALMYRA, 1868
THE HAUNTED CHILD

Eddie worked an arithmetic problem, his tongue resting in the pocket of his cheek. Around him, chalk squeaked on slate, bottoms wriggled on wooden benches. February gusts rattled the school's windows.

Eddie's feet and fingers were cold, but his belly was content. Just minutes ago, his teacher Mrs. Henshaw had lifted a checked cloth from a plate of ginger snaps. "Look, children," she'd said. "I baked too many for myself. I wonder if anyone could help me eat these?" The tray passed up and down the rows. Eddie, who'd been given no breakfast at home, took two.

This happened often in winter: Mrs. Henshaw baked too many ginger snaps, too many biscuits, too many molasses cookies. The heat of the ginger still in his mouth, Eddie wondered how Mrs. Henshaw could be so sharp at arithmetic in school, yet so slipshod in her kitchen. He loved her for it.

The door banged open. As one, the children's heads swiveled toward the sound. A man strode into the room carrying the cold with him. He made directly for Mrs. Henshaw. He bent to her ear. Mrs. Henshaw's face shifted from surprise and irritation to alarm.

"You children go home," said the man aloud. "Gather up your things and get." He departed, leaving silence in his wake. Then a boy whooped and a racket of questions followed.

"Hush!" commanded Mrs. Henshaw. "Our school has been ordered to close. Leave your slates at your places. I will dismiss you by rows. You are to go straight home—no dawdling and no foolishness. If you walk home by yourself, come stand at my desk and I will accompany you."

"But Mrs. Henshaw, why are we..."

"No questions. Row five, collect your things from the cloakroom."

Once dismissed, the children clumped together outside the schoolhouse and swapped theories about the closing. Mrs. Henshaw came out and scattered them homeward.

The Drake boys walked shoulder to shoulder, Eddie tucked between Jim and Fred. Mischievous wind blew ice crystals into their faces. "I know why they sent us home," said Fred. A teacher's pet, Fred had been at Mrs. Henshaw's desk when the stranger had spoken to her.

"No you don't," said Jim.

"I heard that man with my own ears. He's the sheriff."

"I know who he was."

"He said two children were taken from their beds last night. No one knows where they are. They just vanished." Fred spoke solemnly. He wasn't one to make up stories.

"Took from their beds?" asked Jim.

"Yes. He said there's men and dogs in the woods right now looking for them."

A cold finger traced gooseflesh along Eddie's spine. When he and Pop had found Katie Cooper, Mr. Jangles had signed to Eddie that more children would be hurt. Now two had gone missing. Was this his doing?

Ever since that terrible day, Eddie had tried everything he could think of to banish the ghost. He'd passed a handful of salt over himself three times and threw the salt into the fire. He'd turned his head and spit in the road. He'd made various warding signs with his hand and fingers, the same that grownups did to thwart the evil eye or dispel ill fortune. He'd even tried calling on Mama's saints. Unlike her husband and children, she'd been raised Catholic. Mama often asked St. Anthony to help her find lost things, and St. Jude for hope and strength. Despite Pop scoffing at her Papist superstitions, Mama held to her saints. But these invisible guardians had not helped him. Maybe he hadn't said the right words. Or perhaps Anthony and Jude couldn't be bothered with those who didn't bow to the Pope.

Whatever the reason, Eddie had resigned himself to dealing with Mr. Jangles alone. But he didn't know how. He was powerless against this spirit. And now two more children had gone missing. Those children might get hurt. They might die. And it was Eddie's fault because he hadn't been able to make Mr. Jangles go away.

Sorrow and despair weighed him. He whipped his head around, expecting to see the long-limbed apparition sauntering through the pines toward him, to lead him on some dark errand or lay corpses at Eddie's feet.

Eddie wanted to dash home, but Jim and Fred would call him a baby. He leaned into Fred and tried to hold his nerve.

The news must've reached the Bottoms ahead of the boys; Mama waited in the door, heedless of the cold. She drew them inside and pulled them to her bosom. Jim and Fred wriggled free of her grasp, but Eddie stayed.

Pop stood at the window. He glanced at his sons but said nothing. He nursed a bottle of spirits, something clear and eye-watering from a neighbor's still.

For the next two days search parties tramped through woods and fields. Sometimes the wind carried the cries of men calling the names of the lost. Hunting dogs and yard dogs were set loose in hopes they might catch a child's scent. At the close of each day the dogs bayed their failure, a mournful chorus that pricked tears in Eddie's eyes. He prayed fervently that the children would be found.

Then a storm came and dropped several feet of snow on Palmyra.

Snow draped the pines in white shrouds and leaned in man-high drifts against the shacks in the Bottoms. But there were no snowball fights, no sledding, no snowmen. Palmyra's children were kept indoors. That was all right with Eddie. He dreaded to go outside.

He did keep his ears open to news and gossip. The mood in Palmyra was grim, even vengeful. Accusations were flung. Some blamed a drifter called Red Padraig. Red Padraig had blown into Palmyra that fall, traveling with a toothy dog and an old long rifle. Half Irish and half Mohawk, Red Padraig had copper skin, long black hair, and a foul mouth. He knew Indian hexes. When Tom Hollings caught Padraig and that dog sleeping in his barn in October, the farmer had driven them off with a shotgun. On his way out, Red Padraig had sketched a hex sign in the air and muttered a curse. The next day, two of Hollings' sheep died.

Then the drifter had troubled the virtue of several white women on Main Street, making lewd suggestions and snatching at their petticoats. He'd slipped into the woods before a gang of men could correct him. He'd lurked around Palmyra ever since. He stole food, vandalized property, and skulked through the woods with his vicious mutt. Hollings and others blamed him for the children's disappearance.

But some people muttered the name of James Drake. Folks had been suspicious of James's recovery of Katie Cooper. How had a shiftless drunk found her body when dozens of good men had failed? Did his peep stones truly show him visions? If so, that smacked of black magic and sorcery—nothing that good Christian people should tolerate. Perhaps something ought to be done.

Eddie knew Mr. Jangles was to blame, but didn't dare speak of it. Who would believe him? And if they did, folks might blame Eddie for setting Mr. Jangles among them. They might drive off Eddie in hopes that the ghost would follow. So Eddie kept silent.

But the secret ate at him. His stomach hurt. His sleep was broken by awful dreams. His cheeks hollowed and his eyes sank into his skull. Mama fretted that he'd caught a fever. She made him drink birch bark tea, and rubbed his chest with a camphor oil made by Tante V, an old midwife who lived in the Bottoms. But these things had no power to banish Mr. Jangles, and Eddie grew wan and listless.

Four days after the school closed, a man banged on the door of the Drake cabin. He wore a heavy coat and thick gloves. He carried a rifle. Dirty snow slid off his boots onto Mama's clean-swept floor.

Pop stood stiff and wary. Knowing the mood of Palmyra village, Pop too had stayed indoors, forgoing his treasure hunts and keeping his head down. Eddie and his brothers watched from a corner, a handful of wood soldiers scattered among them. Mama placed herself between the intruder and her children.

"My name's John Stone," said the stranger. Eddie knew that name. John Stone was father to Emily, one of the missing children. The Stone family owned a lumber mill and lived in a two-story house on a good lot near town. John Stone wasn't the richest man in Palmyra, but he swung weight. He was a deacon in the Presbyterian church and captain of the fire company. He certainly wasn't a man who would pay a call to anyone in the Bottoms. A neighbor had told Pop that John Stone had been deputized by Sheriff Winston—the same man who had closed Eddie's school. As a sworn deputy, John had the power of the law behind him—to detain, to arrest. To shoot a man if necessary.

"He's come for me," thought Eddie. "Somehow they found out Mr. Jangles is my fault, and he's here to jail me—or hang me dead." Eddie didn't want to die, but maybe if he was dead, Mr. Jangles would leave Palmyra's children alone.

"My wife," started John. Then he stopped. He tugged his beard and furrowed his brow, as if he'd prepared a speech and then forgotten it. His lips and cheeks were chapped raw from days of tramping in the cold. "My wife sent me. 'Cause of them stones of yours." John tilted his head at Pop.

Pop didn't speak. He stood stiff as a dog ready to fight or flee.

"My kin and I been searchin' the woods every day," said John, "even in that storm. But we haven't found Emily. Someone saw Red Padraig skulking 'round my barn just before she went missing."

"What's he to do with me?" snarled Pop. "I don't associate with half-breeds."

"I don't say you do. My wife's been speakin' to the Cooper family. You found their Katie. Mrs. Cooper's grateful to you. You brought Katie home so they could lay her to rest. Mrs. Cooper says you found Katie with your stones."

Pop shrugged.

"I don't know what else to do," said John. He pushed a hand through his hair, standing it at wild angles. "I'm at my wits' end. I search and I pray and I search, but I can't find her. So I've come to ask...can you look for my little girl?" His voice cracked.

"He can't help you," thought Eddie. But he watched his father's face—the crease in his brow, the muscles twitching in his whiskered jaw, his brown eyes skipping between John Stone's face and John Stone's rifle. There was risk here, but also the chance of reward.

"If I do it," said Pop, "people need to know I got your blessing. You tell folks it was *you* who asked me to search."

"I'll tell 'em. I'll tell the sheriff, my kin, everyone in town. Just find her if you can."

Pop unclenched himself. He stood a head taller than John, who was not a small man. He placed a hand on John's shoulder. John glanced at it, but did not remove it nor duck away.

"I'll look for your Emily," said Pop.

"I'd be grateful. My wife and I both. Do you think...do you think you can find her alive?"

"Don't know," said Pop. "But I'll do my best for her. I need solitude to begin."

"'Course. I'll leave you to it." He touched his forehead to Mama and hurried out.

When the man had gone, Pop turned to his family. He didn't bother to hide his eager, hungry expression. "You see that? John Stone came hat in hand to my door and asked my help." Pop flung an arm toward the other shacks outside. "I bet they were watching. They thought they'd see John Stone put me down. But I'm standin'. And John Stone begged my aid. 'Cause he knows. They all know. I got the gift."

Even as Pop spoke, his eyes slid to Eddie. Eddie said nothing. Pop fetched his stones from atop their shelf. He fetched Eddie as well.

"Let's go, boy."

"Must you take him?" asked Mama. "It's so cold and he's not well."

"He'll be fine."

"But maybe it's not right to put him through this?"

Pop turned on her. "What'd you know of it? Huh?"

"I'll go," croaked Eddie. He didn't want to go. He didn't want to find more dead children, nor see Mr. Jangles prancing over their corpses. But he didn't want Pop to hit Mama. And he had no choice. This was his fault, after all. Some badness inside him had let Mr. Jangles into this world to make mischief. To make murder. Eddie couldn't stop it, so he would have to face it. He shrugged into a coat and shoes, wrapped his face in a thin scarf, and followed his father into the snow.

6

BOSTON, 1884
THE HAUNTED MAN

Edward dressed for dinner, then inspected the results in his bedroom mirror. His bespoke trousers sagged at the hips. His favorite brocade waistcoat, which should button snugly across his torso, hung slack. A yellow cravat drooped from his neck like a wilted flower. His cheeks were hollow, his color pallid.

For the past six days he'd been abed, struck down by a fever after the incident at the fens. He had no clear memories of his illness other than a rank fog of foul dreams, the stinging odor of camphor oil, and sweat-stained sheets. His housekeeper Mrs. Penny said he'd wrapped himself Moorishly in his blankets, and perspired so profusely she'd had to change his bedding twice a day. He'd taken little nourishment while ill save cups of tea and spoonsful of a beef consommé sent up by Ms. Cutler and Ms. Hewes. Already slender of build, his clothes loose slack on his frame.

He fussed with his hair, which was the color and texture of dirty straw. He wore it long to hide the ugly scarring just below and behind his right ear, where his father had thrown burning fat on him as a boy. It tended to stand at wild angles and required no end of brushing, hair oil, and pomade to lay it flat. He spent a few minutes pulling a wet comb through it, then gave up. It would have to do.

He went to the parlor, where Tom Connelly sat reading a newspaper. Tom had dropped by to check in on his sick friend.

"You look like a scarecrow done up by Saville Row," he said.

"I should've made friends with a physician instead of a lawyer. I could get medical advice instead of smart remarks."

"You don't need to be a doctor to see you've lost weight. Those old ladies downstairs should've fed you steak, not broth. You'll need some iron in your blood before you get back in the ring. It wouldn't be fair for me to hit you in your current state. I'll bring some of my mother's pot roast next time I visit."

Edward's stomach growled.

"I'll take that as an offer accepted."

Edward checked his watch: half-past six. He was dining with Mrs. Coffin at seven.

"Is that my hint it's time to leave?" asked Tom.

"Fraid so. Mrs. Coffin will tut at me if I'm late for supper. But thanks for looking in on me."

"Going back to work tomorrow?"

Edward nodded.

"Are you sure you're well enough?"

"Now you sound like the old ladies downstairs. I don't need to be fussed over."

"Very well, old chum. Come by the office tomorrow and I'll take you for a proper lunch." They shook hands and Tom departed.

Edward retrieved his coat from a rack. As he passed through the kitchen, electric lamps burned in the sconces. Edward clucked; Mrs. Penny must've left them on. Edward had offered her countless demonstrations of the lamps' safety—safer for sure than gas—yet she would not touch a switch. She was convinced a mischievous surge of current would leap out and stop her heart.

He turned off the lamps and went down the back stairs and out into the October evening. The silver scythe of a moon hung overhead. It had rained earlier in the day, but the dusky sky was cloudless now.

He traveled down Newbury Street and through a wrought-iron gate into the Public Gardens. He drank deep draughts of clean air, rinsing sickroom murk from his lungs. The Belgian elms were shedding leaves, making damp carpets of red and orange. He strode briskly, pleased to exercise his limbs after so many days in bed.

He did intend to return to work tomorrow, but he wondered what his reception might be. Feaney and the other men had seen him screaming and flailing at the empty air. They'd watched him get carted off like a lunatic. Could he still command their obedience? Would they mock him behind his back—or to his face?

Edward decided the first man to make a crack would get a swift correction, with a fist if necessary. The workers might take him for a lace-curtain sop, but they were mistaken. If they dared twitch the lace aside, they would find something steely behind it.

And what of the hallucination? He hadn't been troubled by visions for years. Not since that incident with the Howlands when he'd...hurt himself. Instinctively his fingers touched the scar on his left wrist. Why had the hallucinations returned? How could he see Mr. Jangles so clearly, hear his voice in his head?

Well, the answer was simple. Madame Corbeau's séance had exhumed frightening memories from his childhood. Then he'd spent two days tramping through malarial fens and gone two nights without sleep. Likely he'd caught a fever. By the time the workers had dug up that skeleton, the sight of the bones had triggered a fit. His addled mind had conjured the illusion of Mr. Jangles.

It was a tidy explanation, and reasonable enough. Yet the fact that he'd hallucinated at all still concerned him.

From his boyhood through age sixteen, Edward's life had been steeped in ghosts and spiritualism. Mr. Jangles had been a regular presence, both in Palmyra and in Boston. But at age of sixteen, after a seance with the Howlands, Edward had severed himself from spiritualism. It had been a deliberate act—an act of self-preservation.

He'd trained his mind to shut out all thoughts of ghosts and spirits, to extinguish any spark of imagination or fancy. It had taken an immense effort of will. To police one's thoughts, moment by moment, hour by hour, day by day, was more exhausting than any physical labor.

His task had been made more difficult by Mrs. Coffin, who had bullied and cajoled and pleaded with him to perform as a medium. But he had rebuffed her requests with a fierce, silent refusal. Like a bulldog against a bull, he'd fastened his jaws to the neck of her demands and clamped down until they went still. He didn't like to go against her—it had caused several years of unpleasantness between them. But his own sanity had been at stake.

And from age sixteen until now, it seemed to have worked. Through grinding daily practice, he had snuffed out supernatural thoughts. And in that period he'd suffered no more hallucinations, received no more visits from Mr Jangles. The success of this regimen gave him the confidence to assert that, after all, Mr. Jangles was imaginary. Of course he was.

But now Mr. Jangles had returned. What did it mean? Was there, after all, some supernatural force at work in his life? And was it making itself known to him again?

No! It was a lapse of will, that was all. He must avoid conditions that evoked the unpleasantness of his past. He must redouble his efforts to strengthen his mind. Rest was key. So was clean air and wholesome occupations—reading, writing letters, practicing boxing, studying landscape design. He would regain control of his imagination. Whatever phantasms Madame Corbeau had unleashed during the séance, he would collar them and shut them behind an iron door. He wouldn't allow them out.

The winding path through the Gardens emptied onto the intersection of Beacon and Charles Streets. Edward followed the broad avenue of Charles. He turned right to climb the steep slope of Mt. Vernon Street, which led to the crest of Beacon Hill.

The slope was lined with arc lamps on slender metal poles. The electric glow pushed brightly against the gathering dark. As he ascended the lane, tendrils of mist chased his ankles. The mist diffused the lamplight, scattering a heavenly radiance on the red brick townhouses, as if God made visible His favor for the prosperous Brahmins on Beacon Hill.

Mrs. Coffin lived at the crown of the hill, on the corner of Mt. Vernon and Louisburg Square. Her four-story Greek Revival row house looked out on a slender oval park fenced with iron. Unlike the broad, public Commons down below, this park was held in private by Beacon Hill's homeowners.

Edward knocked at the back door. The housekeeper Mary Sullivan greeted him. Middle-aged and stout, Mary had strong hands and graying copper hair tucked under a white serving cap. Her face and neck were red from the heat of the kitchen. She was one of the few servants who had shown him kindness when he'd lived here as a boy, sneaking him extra helpings of cake now and then, and wrapping him in her arms when homesickness overwhelmed him.

"Tis Edward Drake!" she cried. "I'm pleased to see you on your feet, young sir. The missus said you've been abed with fever." She appraised the loose fit of his garments. "You look in need of feedin'."

Edward took her hand. "Run away with me, Mary, and you can fatten me up all you like!"

"You rascal! Give me your things before Mr. Stephen sees your foolishness." Stephen Spencer was a Negro who ran the Coffin household. A fiercely correct old man, he'd never liked Edward. He'd made no secret of his disdain for the ill-bred wretch who had threatened the order and dignity of the household.

"Pay no mind to that old stick," said Edward. He'd come to the back door specifically to avoid Stephen at the front of the house.

"That old stick could put me out in the street," said Mary. She took Edward's coat and hat and gestured to the hallway. "Go through to the parlor. You can wait there while the Missus finishes dressing." She appraised him one last time. "I'll put extra dinner rolls on your plate."

Edward touched his forehead, then passed down the narrow hall. The parlor had been restored to its finicky order, all traces of Corbeaus's chaotic performance whisked away. A fire was laid in the grate. Edward went to the hearth to borrow its warmth. He leaned against the mantle of Italian marble where Mrs. Coffin displayed her curios. A Viennese crystal decanter stood in place of the vase that had shattered during last week's séance.

An oil portrait of Tristam Coffin, Mrs. Coffin's husband, hung above the mantel. Tristam had died before Edward came to Beacon Hill. The portrait had always unsettled him, especially as a boy. If he was anything like the painting, Edward was glad not to have met him. Tristam wore a stony, humorless expression. His hard white face hovered above the stiff collar of his black frock coat. His spine was rigid as an oaken mast. Gold flecks gleamed in cold blue eyes, as if generations of wealth had seeped into his blood.

But that wealth and that blood would not carry forward. Mrs. Coffin had not borne any children of her own. The family fortune would pass to Mrs. Coffin's brother-in-law when she died. Edward guessed her failure to produce an heir had been a bitter cup to Tristam. And a ragamuffin boy brought in from the wilds of New York to indulge his wife's spiritualist fancies would be no recompense.

Mrs. Coffin had yet to arrive. Edward compared his watch to the Chippendale clock in the corner. A local artisan came once a week to attended its gears. The clock and Edward's watch agreed: Mrs. Coffin was five minutes late.

At six minutes after, Tilda Coffin sailed into the room on a gust of rose-petal sachet. "Edward. How delightful to see you. Do you mind if we take supper in here tonight?" She ensconced herself in a French Provencal settee. "It's just you and I, and the dining room is drafty."

"By all means, Mum." Ever since he was a boy, Tilda had insisted Edward call her Mum—in private.

"You look thin, dear. You need a good meal. I fed you broth while you were ill, but you wouldn't take more than few mouthfuls."

Edward had no recollection of her ministrations, but he thanked her.

"I hold myself responsible," said Tilda. "I'm afraid that excitement with Madame Corbeau precipitated your illness."

"The fens are the culprit, Mum. The air is miasmic, and I was soaked with cold rain. It's no wonder I caught a fever."

"It wasn't just a fever. Madame Corbeau shook you. I saw your face that night—you looked as if you'd been bled."

Edward frowned. "I'll admit her histrionics were disturbing. Particularly her foaming at the mouth."

"She was possessed by the spirits," said Tilda.

"She was possessed of a packet of tooth powder, hidden up her sleeve."

Tilda humphed. "That was no trick, Edward. And you can't explain away her words. She spoke of him. 'The one you fear.' You and I both know who she meant—the spirit who's haunted you since you were a boy. You had terrible nightmares about him when you were a child. You woke the whole house more than once with your screams."

Sitting in this fussy parlor bright with lamplight, Edward marshaled his arguments—as much for himself as for his benefactress. "Mum, listen to me. Corbeau's a masterful manipulator. She makes vague pronouncements that could mean a hundred different things. And as she speaks, she watches and listens to how you respond. Your own reactions guide her to the mark. A clever performer like Corbeau can trick people into revealing information while making them think she's pulled the knowledge out of thin air. My father did it all the time."

"Madame Corbeau is nothing like your father! She's a powerful medium—as are you. Remember when you were a boy, how you used to tell me about my dear Lilly? How you delivered messages from her? Couldn't you do it again? I wouldn't bother with Corbeau if you performed for me. When you channeled my sister, it was as if Lilly herself sat by my side."

"Mum…"

"Yes, yes. You're too old for such things."

"It has nothing to do with age. It's simply not possible to speak with the dead."

"You used to."

"I've told you before—I made up all those things."

"You couldn't have."

"Certainly I could. We spent hours every day having our 'sessions.' You revealed bits and pieces of your life with Lilly like crumbs. I picked them up and fed them back to you. When I did well, you praised me and gave me sweets. But many stories I got wrong. I remember I told you how Lilith locked you in the outhouse. But that wasn't possible because you grew up with a water closet. I told you how you and Lilith used to sing hymns together while you plucked a chicken for supper. You've never plucked a chicken in your life."

Mrs. Coffin sniffed.

"I concocted those stories from my own experiences," said Edward. "I didn't realize how different your upbringing was from mine. You've simply chosen to forget how wrong I could be."

"I forget nothing. It's you who's twisted up the truth of your abilities. And what about when you performed for my friends? You'd never met Mrs. Greenwood's husband, but you knew he'd been fond of persimmons, and that he'd brought her a silk robe embroidered with cranes after his voyage to Japan. How could a child know such things if not from her husband's spirit?"

"Mum, how often did I sit quietly in the parlor while you had company? I listened to all your conversations. When it was time for a performance, I just parroted stories I'd already heard. I was a child, Mum. I thought it was a game."

"So I play games when I sit with Madame Corbeau?"

Edward sighed. Tilda raised her hand. "Very well. Let's not chase each other around this tree all evening."

Stephen, in a black jacket and white gloves, entered the parlor wheeling a cart. On it was a cloisonné tray covered with a silver dome. He placed two china plates on the coffee table, laid silver utensils on linen napkins, and poured two cups of herbal tea, all while fastidiously ignoring Edward.

He uncovered the dome to reveal baked cod and green beans cooked with slivered almonds and yellow raisins. Oven-warm Parker House rolls sat on a plate with a pot of fresh butter. Edward inhaled the toothsome scent of the rolls. His stomach growled.

"That's fine, Stephen," said Mrs. Coffin. "We'll serve ourselves."

Stephen bowed himself from the room.

"Go on," said Tilda. "We won't stand on formality tonight."

Edward served a portion of fish and some green beans to Mrs. Coffin. He buttered a roll for himself and ate it in two bites. He ate another roll, then took a piece of fish. The cod had been boned, seasoned with lemon juice and pepper, and lightly breaded. The briny flesh made his mouth water. He forced himself to take small bites, not wanting to gobble his plate in front of Mrs. Coffin.

"I remember the day I brought you home," said Tilda. "Your stomach seemed bottomless. I had to send someone to the market twice a day to keep up with your appetite."

"The way I recall, I was so nervous I could barely eat." He took a second piece of fish and a helping of green beans. "But I've since become more comfortable at your table."

"I'm glad. Now tell me truly—how are you?"

"Much improved. I'm returning to work tomorrow. If I spend another day in bed, *I* shall foam at the mouth." He winked, but she didn't respond to his jest. "Is something wrong, Mum?"

Tilda fidgeted with her fork. "My dear, I have to confess...I've behaved rather shamefully. While you were ill, a pair of letters came for you. One from your brother Fred."

"Oh?" Fred was a minister now. He had a congregation in Rochester, New York, a few miles up the road from Palmyra where they'd been born.

"The other was from that Negress you correspond with in Palmyra."

"Her name is Evelyn, as I've told you. And she's not a girl. She's a grown woman. A school teacher."

Tilda flicked his words aside. "The letters arrived the day after your episode in the fens. You were laid up in bed, delirious with fever."

"Where are these letters? I've looked through my mail since then."

"I have them."

"You took my letters?"

"That's not all. I read them."

"Mum! My private correspondence?"

"Don't scold. I know it was wrong, but I did it for you. News from home upsets you, and you were already unwell—in and out of consciousness, wracked by fever and chills. You thrashed beneath the bedclothes as if you were running from someone."

"That's no excuse! And this isn't the first time you've interfered with my letters. Have you no boundaries? No propriety?"

Mrs. Coffin ignored his protests. "You spoke of *him* while you were ill. You said he'd come back."

"Who?"

"You know who. Your phantom. The one Madame Corbeau spoke of. He was...haunting you."

Edward shifted uncomfortably. "I was fevered."

"That's why I didn't want you to see the letters until I was sure you were fit. I feared they might send you spiraling back into delirium."

"Please, Mum, what's in the letters? Is Fred all right? Is one of his children sick?"

"It's Jim," said Tilda.

Edward's chest tightened. His eldest brother Jim still lived in Palmyra, in the same tumbledown shack in the Bottoms where the Drake boys had been born. Jim had grown from a mischievous, ill-behaved child into a mischievous, ill-behaved man. The last Edward had heard, Jim had taken up Pop's old grifts: money-digging and speaking to the dead.

"What's he done?"

"He's been arrested."

Edward blushed with shame. "Why?"

"I'm afraid it's started again, Edward. And they think your brother is responsible."

"What's started?"

"Three children have gone missing. Little girls named Liza Ames, Becky Deaver, and Cassie Brown. They disappeared more than a week ago. Then Liza Ames was found in the woods. Murdered."

Edward remembered his boyhood, a creek sheathed in ice. A girl with the blue lips and a necklace of bruises. How he'd found her nestled among the roots of a tree. He'd found two more bodies that winter, a boy and another girl.

And now it was happening again. He wiped his brow with a handkerchief. The health and vigor he'd felt earlier began to bleed away as if from a slit vein.

"Jim was discovered with Liza's body," said Tilda. "The sheriff accused him of murder and jailed him."

"Jim? A child-murderer?"

"There's more. A mob came to the jail. They had rope. They meant to hang your brother. Then a fire started."

"Good Christ! What happened?"

"Somehow Jim escaped. He's gone missing. No one knows where he is."

"Mum, please. I must have the letters."

Tilda went to a console, opened a drawer, and returned with two folded pages.

Edward opened the first page and recognized Fred's graceful script —his brother had always been proud of his penmanship. Tilda had related the story accurately: Three Palmyra girls had gone missing. Then Jim had found Liza Ames's body and been arrested under suspicion of murder. A mob attacked the jail and Jim had escaped. Fred wanted Edward to return to Palmyra to look for Jim. He wrote *"You know our brother is no killer. He must be hiding nearby. You can find him and help him. You can find the missing girls. Your family needs you, Edward. Come home."*

Edward trembled. Come home? He didn't want to come home. Not ever.

Next he scanned Evelyn's letter. As he read the words, his heart crumpled. Cassie Brown, one of the missing children, was Evelyn's niece. Evelyn and her family were frantic with worry. They had gone into the woods day after day but hadn't found the girl. Between the lines of her hurried note Edward understood Evelyn's unspoken request—can you help?

Edward folded the pages and slipped them into an inner pocket of his jacket.

"What will you do?" asked Tilda.

"I can't go back there. I have to return to work. There's a great deal to do at the site. I'm sure the project has fallen behind in my absence."

"Edward, how can you say that?"

"Mr. Olmsted and Mr. Sprague entrusted me with this responsibility. I don't want to let them down."

"But your brother," said Tilda. "Your friend Evelyn. And the girls who are still missing. Can you imagine what those poor children must be suffering?"

He could imagine their suffering all too well. His supper threatened to come up. "I can't help them."

"But you can! If you implore the spirits, they'll come to your aid. You have a gift, Edward. You perceive things others can't."

"Mum..."

"Listen to me! I'm no philosopher but I'm also no fool. I know when something's real. When you use your gift, it makes the hairs on the back of my neck stand up. I feel a charge in the air like a gathering storm. When you call the spirits, they answer."

"They don't! None of that is real, Mum. Not like my work in the fens. The blueprints, the trenches, the mud—that's real. What's false is this psychic twaddle you cling to!" Edward banged his fist on the coffee table. The plates jumped.

Tilda's eyes widened. Edward pinched the bridge of his nose, chagrined at his outburst. He left his own chair and sat beside her. "Forgive me, Mum. I shouldn't have done that."

Tilda took Edward's hand. He nearly pulled away in surprise—in the all the years he'd known her, she'd rarely touched him.

"My dear. I don't say it often, but I'm proud of you. You carry yourself with such grace despite everything you've been through. I still shudder when I think of the day I came upon you: a ragged little boy, stick-thin and living in filth, bruises on your arms and legs from that brute of a father. No prospects for anything but a life of squalor. Yet here you are, a man of intelligence and accomplishment. I wish I could claim credit, but I can't. It comes from your own character."

She patted his knuckles. "I know you're proud of your work with Mr. Olmsted. Your dedication to his project is commendable. But there are lives at stake in Palmyra. The missing girls. And Jim—Jim's your family."

"But he isn't, Mum. Not since you took me away."

Tilda released his hand and sat apart from him. Edward returned to his own seat. They sat in silence. The food went cold on its plates.

Edward shivered. He felt the parlor tilt, as if to tip him out of his chair and roll him back to Palmyra. Back to where it had started. Worms of dread wriggled in his belly. He heard a scritching sound, like yellowed fingernails picking at the wallpaper. Corpse memories flicked through his mind; a child's cold skin stippled by bruises, hollow eyes that stared into oblivion.

"I can't go through that again," he told himself. He thought of the vow he'd made on his walk over here, to strengthen his mind against morbid thoughts, to preserve his equilibrium by avoiding situations that would trigger old hallucinations. To go back to Palmyra would surely knock him off his axis, send him spinning into delirium.

A draft blew through the parlor. The fire coughed in the grate. Mrs. Coffin hugged herself.

Edward walked to the sideboard, his gait clumsy. With shaking hands he poured a double measure of tonic water and gulped it down, wishing Mrs. Coffin had something stronger.

Tilda fretted with a handkerchief. The vitality had seeped from her skin. Her fleshy face sagged. How old she looked. And how disappointed. Edward couldn't bear to see it.

"You're a grown man," she said. "You'll make your own decisions. Go back to work if that's more important. Myself, I believe Fred and Evelyn were right to reach out to you. Jim needs you. Cassie Brown and Becky Deaver need you. You could use your gift for all their sakes. But you must make up your own mind."

Edward squeezed the water glass. He didn't want to go back. Yet Tilda's words seared his conscience, just as she knew they would. What's more, Fred had placed an obligation on him to help their brother. And Evelyn had reached out in a moment of terrible distress. Could he turn his back on them?

The truth was, he was afraid to go back. He was afraid of what he might find, what he might see. Yet to stay in Boston was to admit that his fear held power over him. What kind of man would that make him, so frightened of his own imagination he would refuse to help children in distress, or come to his family's aid? There was nothing to be afraid of in Palmyra. Wasn't there?

He squeezed the water glass until it cracked in his hand.

"I'll go."

7

A porter in a peaked cap and neat black coat moved through the first-class train car. He opened chintz curtains, lighted chandeliers, and proffered the latest issues of *Harper's Weekly* and *The Atlantic*.

Edward took one of each, but left them in his lap. He drummed his fingers on the upholstered armchair, anxious for the train to depart. Mid-morning sun honeyed the car's mahogany panels but failed to sweeten his mood.

Earlier today he'd requested a leave of absence from the dig. He told Mr. Sprague that a family matter required his attention, and he would be away for a few days. Mr. Sprague granted the leave, but warned Edward that he would be replaced if he didn't return soon. He also docked Edward's salary.

The loss of pay didn't matter. Edward had a generous annuity from Mrs. Coffin that saw to his needs. He wanted the job because gave him a reason to rise from bed, an opportunity to exercise his talents, and a chance to make his mark on the world. The Emerald Necklace might adorn Boston for a hundred years or more. His fingerprints, however faint, would be impressed on this jewel, and would remain long after he was gone. The low boy inside him, born without prospect or hope, was proud to help create something magnificent for a great city. Without the work, what was he? A useless appendage dangling idly from someone else's fortune. Edward resolved to spend as little time in Palmyra as he could.

After taking his leave from work, he'd stopped at the law firm where Tom worked. He'd told Tom, briefly, about his eldest brother's entanglements. Tom was swamped with work at the moment, but he promised to come to Palmyra as soon as he could—perhaps a day or two. If Edward was able to track down his brother, Tom would serve as Jim's lawyer and ensure he received proper representation. Edward was grateful to his friend, but also embarrassed to have to draw Tom into such an unseemly family situation.

And as for Evelyn Forrest and her missing niece, all Edward could do was add his eyes and ears to the search. Yet search he would, and offer what little comfort he could to the Forrest family. He'd telegrammed Evelyn to inform her of his impending arrival.

A family entered the train car: husband, wife, two young children, and their governess. The governess coaxed the children, a boy and a girl, into their seats. Their blond hair was fine and soft as cornsilk. The boy was still in short pants, with high wool socks and polished shoes. His herringbone jacket was cut precisely to his size. The girl wore a blue silk dress with a ruffled hem and sleeves. The children whined and groused. They kicked at the upholstered seats until the governess produced lollipops from her handbag.

Edward remembered his first train ride. He'd traveled alone from Palmyra to Boston in the emigrant car at the back of the train, his ticket pinned to his shirt. The car had been unheated, poorly ventilated, and equipped with only hard wooden benches. Fourteen hours he'd ridden, cold, hungry, and afraid—a far cry from these pampered goslings with sweets in their mouths and a pretty governess to attend them.

The train departed. Edward opened *Harper's*, but he found it hard to concentrate. His mind refused to latch on to the meaning of the tiny black letters on the white paper. He closed his eyes and gave himself over to the rocking of the car.

He awoke some hours later, muzzy-headed and unrested. "Tea," he thought. He went to the dining car. The car smelled of fresh-baked bread and percolating coffee. Cutlery chimed against porcelain plates. Edward spotted an empty table at the far end. He walked down the swaying center aisle with the exaggerated care of all train passengers, not wanting to topple into a stranger's lap.

He sat alone by the window. The wooded hills of western Massachusetts sped past. Leaves of red, yellow, and orange flickered like tongues of prophetic fire. Whether those tongues spoke of salvation or perdition, Edward could not discern.

A Negro in a waiter's jacket set out china and silver, his deft brown hands hidden inside white gloves. The menu included oysters, duck confit, and beef bourguignon but Edward had no appetite for such rich fare.

"Tea please. With milk. And toast with butter and jam."

During his second cup, a conductor came through to announce the train had crossed into New York state. Anxiety rippled in Edward's belly; he was in home territory now. Or was he? Sixteen years he'd been away; he'd lived more of his life in New England than New York. Could he really call it home?

He'd had little contact with his family since Mrs. Coffin had removed him to Boston. His mother had written letters, but Mrs. Coffin had intercepted them and locked them in a drawer. When Edward had pleaded to read them, she would only say "Your mother sends her regards. She encourages your studies and reminds you to be on your best behavior."

Edward had written his own letters, begging to go home. Boston was tight collars, oppressive decorum, and hostile stares from strange faces. Why had Mama sent him here? He wanted to shed his stiff coat and pinching shoes and run barefoot back to Palmyra. He missed his mother desperately. He longed to hear her sing while she made bread, feel the touch of her lips on his forehead after she bundled him into bed with Fred and Jim, see her smile as he read aloud to her from some borrowed book. He'd spent hours staring out the parlor window onto Louisburg Square, hoping to see Mama in her plain brown dress and blue shawl. But she never came.

As the months passed, Edward drew a thick curtain against memories of the crowded cabin and its familial chaos. There was only pain behind that curtain, as sharp and deep as a driven nail.

At the same time, he grew accustomed to his life in Boston. He'd always been a good student in Palmyra, and he found that with some effort he could win praise from his tutor, Mr. Bollen. He excelled in composition, spelling, and mathematics. He cut his way diligently through thickets of Latin, Greek, and French.

The mental labors he took up were offset by the bodily labors he put aside. He no longer had to gather wood, tend fires, pluck pigeons, make his bed, pitch lime into the pit beneath the outhouse, or do any of the other smelly, messy chores of home. He moved through clean, warm spaces as if that was the natural order of things, and not the persistent work of hidden hands.

Every day he ate fresh-baked bread with pots of butter and jam. The loaves were never burnt nor stale, and he was never stuck with a hard, dry heel. He sucked the juice of sweet oranges from Spain and spooned up mouthfuls of tart grapefruit from Florida, his tongue fizzing with flavor as if he'd licked the sun. At dinner he gorged on roast beef and new potatoes, tender lamb with mint, and his new favorite—suckling pig roasted with apples. The skin of the pig and the juice from the apples formed a fatty-sweet glaze that crackled in his mouth.

He wore clothes that, while itchy and constraining, were tailored to his size. Shirts didn't billow and drape because they'd been handed down from his bigger brothers. The woolens were finely spun, and unmarked by the sweat and odors of Jim and Fred. He wore shoes without holes, and didn't have to stuff them with newspaper to make them fit or keep his feet warm.

And there were books! Mrs. Coffin's library, which stood just off the parlor, held more books than you could find in all of Palmyra. Dickens, Irving, Swift, Cooper, Hawthorne and more were ready to hand. He was allowed, even encouraged, to take down the leather-bound volumes from their shelves. Edward spent hours curled up in an overstuffed wingback chair, a book in his lap and a fire in the grate, finding solace in other worlds and other lives.

As he grew into manhood, he became a keen observer of the mores and manners of high-born Bostonians. He found he could display his learning in subtle and amusing ways in the salons of New England. His impoverished childhood made him a curious specimen for the spiritualists, suffragettes, and social agitators who traipsed through Mrs. Coffin's parlor.

He steamed across the Atlantic in first-class cabins to tour Europe with Mrs. Coffin. He strolled the magnificent gardens at Kew in London, marveled at Napoleon's self-congratulatory arch in Paris, and contemplated the arch's forebearers in Rome.

All these experiences furthered the distance between his present life and his home and family. Now and then he felt an impulse to visit Palmyra, but he never acted. He'd grown into a different person—someone his family wouldn't recognize. He would be a stranger to his kin, even his mother. The rough, rude shack would embarrass him, and his embarrassment would shame him and his mother. So he kept the curtain drawn tight—there would always be time to open it when he was ready.

And then his mother died.

Edward, age twenty-two at the time, was in Greece when Fred telegrammed the news: Mama had succumbed to pneumonia. Would Edward come home?

The telegram was four days old, having first arrived in Boston, then zig-zagged under transatlantic cables in search of him.

Edward and Mrs. Coffin were on the Greek leg of their tour. They had departed from their planned itinerary (Athens - Delphi - Thebes, as laid out in Baedeker), to take advantage of clement weather in the Cyclades. They sailed among the islands on a hired yacht and traipsed dusty hillsides to explore denuded Apollonian temples. In the evenings, they rested on the yacht's deck and drank white retsina and coffee. Greek servants brought plates of fresh-caught mullet, grilled squid, pungent olives, and sharp salty cheese.

The telegram fell into Edward's hands on the island of Delos. After reading it, he rushed to the island's cramped telegraph office. Communication with the clerk was a near Sisyphean exercise. Though Edward could read classical Greek with some fluidity, he did not speak the contemporary tongue. The telegraph clerk had a smattering of Italian and Turkish, but no English or French.

At last, Edward composed a response: Just now received news. In Greece. When is the funeral?

The reply came several hours later: Yesterday.

Edward stumbled out of the office, telegram in hand. The Mediterranean sun flung daggers in his eyes. For years he'd told himself "I'll go home someday. I'll go home to see her." But his mother was gone now, and with it any chance of reunion or reconciliation. The pain was excruciating as surgery without ether.

In Delos's town square, Edward came across a church domed and crenelated in the grand and alien Byzantine mode. He hadn't meant to find such a place. He didn't give much thought to religion, but perhaps some instinct had guided him here.

He'd been baptized in a Methodist church in Palmyra. Its whitewashed planks and gabled roof seemed juvenile compared to the hoary, sun-bleached stones of this thousand-year-old structure. But surely the God of Christian Greeks must be the same as the God of Protestant Americans—or similar enough to admit him.

He passed through heavy wooden doors and into the cupola. Cool shadows were broken by shafts of daylight that streamed from the high, narrow clerestory. Smoky incense lingered in the air. Ceiling mosaics in gold and Aegean blue depicted Christ and a retinue of saints.

He found an apse with a kneeling bench. A fresco of the Virgin

Mother, with a solemn and dusky Christ Child in her lap, watched over a metal rack of tall white candles. Mother and child.

He wept. Hand shaking, he dropped a few drachmae into a strongbox, then struck a match and touched the orange tip of the flame to a fresh candle. He kneeled and bowed his head.

"Mama," he whispered. "Your son remembers you." Memory was all he had—all he would ever have. His tears wet the hard, lacquered wood of the kneeler. "Oh Mama, I miss you. I'm so sorry."

Grief welled up. Edward had borrowed days and months and years in not going to her, and presumed more would be extended. But the debt of days had been called. He felt the weight of it settle on him, a weight perhaps equal to the stony church in which he kneeled. He would pay in regret. He would pay for the rest of his life. His body shook; years of confusion, resentment, and anguish overwhelmed him. Strange sounds ejaculated from his throat, barks and keenings that scattered among the alcoves like broken glass.

His tears seemed bottomless, a hidden aquifer that would spill without end. He thought he might kneel here forever, a weeping foreigner to be adopted by the congregation as a lunatic holy man.

But he stopped crying long before the candle burned down. He wiped his eyes, then stood and walked silently from the church. As he passed into the street, the daylight caused him to stumble. He righted himself and made for the harbor.

Mrs. Coffin waited for him on the yacht, genuine sadness on her face. When she held out her hands to him, the gesture nearly tipped Edward back into his abyss of tears.

Then resentment swelled in him. Mrs. Coffin was the agent of his sorrow. She had taken him from his mother to serve her own grief. She had encouraged Edward to distance himself from his people, to turn his back on his own mother!

Yet his resentment quickly subsided. Tilda Coffin was the cause of his sorrow, but also the source of his great good fortune. He couldn't despise her.

"Dear Edward, you have my deepest sympathies. Such terrible news."

"Thank you," he croaked.

"Can I do anything for you, my dear? Shall we return to the mainland? You might be more comfortable in a proper hotel."

"In truth, I want to go back to Boston."

Over the next two days Mrs. Coffin arranged his voyage; passage on a sailboat from Delos to Syra, a first-class berth on a steamer to Liverpool, then another to Boston.

When the day of departure arrived, Mrs. Coffin worried a lace handkerchief with her fingers. "Edward, I know you don't like me to speak of it, but have you considered using your gift? To communicate with your mother?"

Edward hadn't performed as a medium since he was sixteen, not for Mrs. Coffin nor anyone. He would not engage in such antics on his own behalf.

"My 'gift' is not real," he growled.

"It might bring you comfort."

"Comfort?" Edward still bore scars, figurative and literal, from his final performance as a medium. At sixteen he'd teetered on the edge of insanity. Only the fiercest act of will, and an utter rejection of spiritualism, had enabled him to claw his way back. "There's no comfort to be had."

"Edward..."

"Please. Don't pick that old wound. Let us part without argument."

Mrs. Coffin sighed. "As you wish. You might wire me when you arrive in Boston. Mrs. Greenwood is touring the Rhone valley with her grand-niece, Lucy. I've arranged to meet them. Lucy had hoped you might join us. In any case, I'll likely be in Arles when you dock."

"Yes Mum."

"Will you go home? To Palmyra?"

"I suppose I should."

The train jounced on its rails, shaking Edward from his reverie. He hadn't gone back to Palmyra. There was no point. His mother was already gone and he had no interest in seeing his father or brothers. When his steamer had arrived in Boston, he'd wired some money to Fred to pay the funeral expenses. He'd sent a separate message to Jim, a formalized acknowledgement of their shared loss. Jim hadn't replied, and Edward hadn't expected him to.

As for his father, Edward wanted no communication. And when Pop had died two years later, Edward again stayed away.

8

The train arrived in Rochester just after 10:00 p.m. Edward, cramped and weary, searched for his brother Fred outside the station. The depot was busy. Passengers squabbled over luggage. Tired children hung like simians from their mothers' skirts. Porters shifted goods from the freight cars onto wagons and carts. Edward squeezed through the press, followed by an elderly Negro who wheeled Edward's two enormous trunks on a handcart.

Where was Fred? Back home, Edward would be reclining in his study, the evening papers in his lap and a brandy close to hand. A drink seemed the best antidote for the long train journey, but Edward knew he wouldn't get one tonight. Fred, a minister now, didn't drink alcohol, smoke tobacco, or take any stimulants—other than bracing doses of moral superiority.

He spotted his brother standing by a horse cart. Edward raised a tentative hand in greeting, then beckoned the porter to follow. He stopped an arm's length from Fred. The siblings nodded to one another, but did not embrace or shake hands. A strange force held them apart, like the negative poles of two magnets.

Lean and tall, Fred loomed over Edward. He wore a brown

corduroy suit and a weathered black derby. A starched white collar cinched his throat. Fred had their father's high forehead and deep brown eyes, and their mother's graceful nose and dimpled chin.

Edward was surprised at how old his brother looked. Time had redrawn the child's face he remembered. Crows' feet tracked the corners of Fred's eyes. Hints of grey lurked at his temples. The cares of fatherhood and ministry were inscribed on Fred's skin.

What hadn't changed was Fred's expression—aloof and imperturbable, as if he gazed down on the world from a high stone tower. Edward remembered this look all too well. You couldn't change it no matter how hard you yanked Fred's hair, pinched his arm, or called him 'frog legs' for his bandy knees. Even when Pop beat him, Fred had taken the blows in stoic silence. He'd never winced, grunted, or cried. He'd simply withdrawn to his high place.

Fred's ability to vanish up that stony height had beguiled and frustrated Edward. As a boy he'd longed to be welcomed inside, to climb up and find refuge with his brother. But Fred's tower only had room for one. He'd abandoned Edward below.

"Load my trunks, please," said Edward to the porter. The cart springs groaned as the man heaved the luggage into Fred's buggy.

Fred raised an eyebrow. "What on earth have you brought?"

"Clothes, shoes, boots, toiletries. Several books." Edward thought two trunks suitable for an expedition of unknown length.

"Did you bring a valet as well? Someone to help you dress for dinner?"

Edward decided not to be baited. "Just thinking ahead. If I find Jim, I can stow him in a trunk and ship him to you." He thumped a lid. "We'll split the freight."

A hint of a smile creased Fred's mouth. They had found the track of brotherly banter, shaggy and overgrown but still familiar beneath their feet. Now they could move forward.

Edward tipped the porter and the two brothers climbed into the cart. Fred clicked his tongue and snapped the reins. The aged horse clopped away from the station.

"How is your patron?" asked Fred.

"Mrs. Coffin's well. Still agitating for the vote and pretending to talk to ghosts. She sends her regards." In fact, Mrs. Coffin was also Fred's patron. She had funded Fred's education, including correspondence courses from a Methodist divinity school in Baltimore. When he was certified as a minister, she'd staked him several hundred dollars to establish a church—a loan Fred had only paid back a few years ago. That patronage had been part of the deal that sent Edward to Boston.

"You'll stay at the house with us tonight?"

"Yes, thank you." Fred, his wife, and their six children lived in a modest house near the church where Fred preached. Edward guessed he would be installed in a child's bed, lately occupied by a nephew or three, who would crowd in elsewhere to make room for their uncle. Edward preferred a hotel, but he wouldn't give Fred the satisfaction of judging him too high-handed for the hospitality of plain folk.

The wagon jounced over Rochester's cobbled roads. Street car rails bisected the avenue. Muscular buildings of brick and granite rose nine and ten stories high around them. Scaffold skeletons in empty lots promised more construction to come. Even at this late hour, sawmills along the Genesee River whined and shrieked.

As they neared a bridge, a great stink assaulted Edward's nostrils—the effluvium of the tanneries and rendering plants that lined the riverfront. Edward placed a handkerchief over his nose.

"Something wrong?"

"The odor," said Edward.

"We're accustomed to it. I suppose foul smells aren't tolerated on Beacon Hill?"

Edward recalled the stench coming off the dig at the fens and put his handkerchief away. "How's your ministry?"

"Growing. The mills and tanneries draw workers and their families to the city. My Sunday service counts 200 souls. I have an assistant pastor now, and there's talk of building an extension to the church. The Reverend Dwight Moody has come once or twice to hear my sermons."

Edward had heard of the evangelist. Moody had a reputation as a dynamic speaker and was said to draw crowds of thousands in the United States and England. "Has he? You must be proud." Fred would never confess to the sin of pride.

"I'm grateful God blesses my work."

Silence carried them another few hundred yards. Then Edward raised the subject that had brought him here. "So. What happened to Jim?"

Fred blew air from his lungs, as if preparing to lift a heavy weight. "He fancies himself a medium. You remember Pop's seeing stones? Jim uses them now. He says he can talk to the dead."

"Good Christ," huffed Edward. Then he blushed under Fred's raised eyebrow. "So he's take up the same old nonsense as Pop?"

"Apparently, he's made a bit of name for himself in Palmyra. He'll talk to your departed loved ones, tell your fortune, undo a hex, that sort of thing. About a week ago, he found the body of a young girl in the woods. She'd been strangled."

"Liza Ames," said Edward, remembering her name from Fred's letter.

"Yes. Jim brought Liza's body back to town. He said the seeing stones showed him where to find her. I think he expected a reward. Instead, they threw him in jail."

Edward grimaced. Why had Jim taken up Pop's schemes? What had they ever gotten the old man but a handful of pennies and a reputation as a shiftless folk magician?

"When they searched Jim," said Fred, "they found a yellow hair ribbon in his pocket."

"A hair ribbon? Was it Liza's?"

"No. It belongs to one of the girls who's still missing. Becky Deaver."

"What on earth was Jim doing with it?"

"I don't know. But it doesn't look good. And there's the third missing child—Cassie Brown. She's the niece of your friend Evelyn Forrest."

"Yes, Evelyn wrote me."

"There's something else. Rumors spread that Liza Ames had been...violated." Fred let the word hang in the air. "You take my meaning?"

"I understand."

"The murder was bad enough. Emotions were already raw in Palmyra. So when *that* rumor spread, Liza's father, uncles, and male cousins marched on the jail. They meant to drag Jim from his cell and hang him."

Edward could see it in his mind: a pack of angry men, ropes and lanterns in hand, shouting and cursing as they descended on the jail. "What happened?"

"The sheriff tried to hold back the mob. There was a scuffle and then a fire. Part of the jail was set alight. Somehow Jim escaped in the confusion. He's gone."

"Gone?"

"He's vanished from Palmyra. No one knows where. He's evaded every search party, every hound dog."

"How do you know all this? Has he been in touch with you?"

"No, I haven't heard a word from him. I'm getting all my information from newspapers in Palmyra and Rochester. And Evelyn Forrest has been writing me."

"How are she and her family holding up?"

"She hasn't said. I expect they must be in terrible distress. But they don't hold Jim responsible for Cassie's disappearance, nor the other girls."

"Do you?" This question had troubled Edward from the start.

"What? Of course not. How could you ask such a thing?"

"Because Jim's a brute."

"He's not a brute."

"No? How many black eyes did he give you when we were boys?

How many bloody noses? How many times did he dunk your head in the creek and hold you under?"

"We were young. We roughhoused."

Edward batted Fred's hat from his head. It fell between Fred's feet. "That's roughhousing. Beatings and near-drownings are brutality."

Fred scoffed. "You just couldn't handle yourself. You had to run to Mama and tattle." He snatched his hat from the floor.

"I never tattled. I ran to Mama because Jim would've killed me otherwise."

"Oh, spare me your exaggerations."

"I don't exaggerate! Jim took pleasure in tormenting me. Do you remember when I won a ribbon for the school spelling contest? I beat everyone in the schoolhouse, even the older children. Even you."

Fred shrugged.

"I cherished that ribbon."

"I'm sure you did."

"Then Jim stole it. For days he wouldn't tell me where he hid it, no matter how much I begged. It drove me mad! Jim just laughed—he practically rolled on the floor. Finally, he told me where he put it. Do you remember?"

"No."

"Down the outhouse, Fred. So he could shit on it! So the whole family could shit on it!"

"Mind your tongue, would you?"

"Have I offended your prissy preacher's ears? Shit shit shit! Our brother was a shitting brute!"

Fred yanked the handbrake on the buggy. "That's enough, Eddie! If you think Jim's rotten enough to stoop to kidnapping and murder, tell me now. I'll take you back to the train because there's no reason to help him. Is that what you think?"

Edward clenched his fists. His list of grievances against Jim was long and comprehensive. But Jim's abuses had always been directed at his siblings—mostly Edward. Jim had scrapped with other boys in the Bottoms, but nothing beyond a fistfight or two. He might be mean and callous, but a child killer?

"No," said Edward. "That's not what I think."

"You certain?"

Edward felt the scalpel sharpness of Fred's scrutiny. He was glad he wasn't a sinner in his brother's congregation. "I'm certain."

Fred held his brother's eye for another moment, then released the brake and clucked the horse into motion. They crossed a steel bridge. On the other side, the cobbled street gave way to roads of cinder and gravel, and then to rutted lanes of packed earth. The dense grid of the city was replaced by modest homesteads and open tracts of farmland.

At last they came to Fred's place, a two-story, wood frame house. A porch ran the length of its front face. The house was white-washed and trim, the yard neat. Behind the house stood a small barn and a low shed.

Fred drove the cart to the barn. Edward made a point to help Fred unhitch the horse and bed it. He even tossed a few forks of silage into its trough.

"You pitch much hay in Boston?" asked Fred. "I thought your hands might be too tender."

"My hands? How many calluses do you get from reading a Bible all day?"

"I chop my own wood and draw my own water."

"And lift up your labor to the Lord, I'm sure."

The brothers lugged Edward's trunks across the yard and through the back door of the house. The door opened on a plain, clean kitchen where a middle-aged Negro woman dried dishes. Plaited braids were piled high on her head and bound in a bright yellow scarf. "*Bonsoir*, Reverend," she said. She dipped her head at Edward. "*Bonsoir, Monsieur*."

"Hello, Marie," said Fred. "This is my brother, Mr. Edward Drake. You remember I told you he's staying the night."

"*Oui*. The bedroom ready with clean sheets 'n all."

Edward touched his forehead. "*Bonsoir, Madame. Merci pour l'hébergement.*"

She smiled to hear him speak French. "*Mais non, monsieur. Bienvenue a la maison.*"

"Yes, all right," interrupted Fred. He gestured to the trunks. "We'll take these up later."

Edward followed Fred through to the main rooms. "Who is that, and where is she from?" he whispered.

"Marie Baptiste is her name. She's from Haiti. I hired her as a housekeeper last year. She's teaching the children French."

"La di da!" teased Edward. "Tell me, *mon frere*, will you visit Paris this spring?"

Fred ignored him. They came into a small parlor furnished with a couch and a pair of armchairs, all three pieces sturdy and unfashionable. A braided Shaker rug lay by the fireplace. Oil lamps on the mantle shed pale yellow light. A wood stove warmed the room.

A daguerreotype of a child in a white funeral gown sat on a small table by the hearth. Her eyes were closed and her hands folded in her lap. Next to the photo was a lock of dark hair twined with ribbon. It was flanked by a withered carnation and a candle stub.

Edward turned to his brother.

"Charlotte. She died six months ago, from fever."

Edward was aghast. He'd had no idea. "Oh, Fred. I'm so sorry."

"The same fever nearly carried away little Daniel, but God saw fit to spare him." For a moment Fred's face shivered, as if his glacial equanimity might calve. Edward held his breath. Was his brother going to weep? Then Fred mastered himself.

"Why didn't you tell me?" asked Edward.

"What was there to say? You didn't come to Mama or Pop's funerals, so I assumed..."

"I was in Greece when Mama died."

"You were in Boston when Pop passed. And you haven't once visited Mama's grave."

Edward felt the lash of Fred's words. He had no defense. "But...

your daughter. Do you think me so callous I wouldn't come to your daughter's funeral?"

Fred tugged at his collar. "I thought to send a letter or a telegram, but after she passed a heaviness came over me. For weeks I could barely rise from bed and attend to my duties. I struggled to put one foot in front of the other. By the time I had the strength to do more than just get through each day, many weeks had passed. And there was so little correspondence between us as it was."

"Fred..."

Before Edward could go on, a noise came from above. Fred's wife Lydia came down the stairs with sewing in her hands—a pair of child's britches. She wore a homespun dress, dyed black for mourning. She went to Fred's side. She was a pretty woman with a sensuous mouth and luxuriant pile of raven-dark hair, but she carried herself with such sternness that it made her beauty seem frivolous.

"Good evening, Lydia. Thank you for letting me stay with you."

"Hello Edward. You're welcome in our home." Her tone was more dutiful than honest, but Edward accepted her words with a bow.

"Are you hungry? Supper's finished, but I can fix you a plate of cold roast and a slice of pie. Or Marie could warm some milk while you and Fred sit awhile." Lydia moved toward the kitchen.

"Thank you, but no. I've had a long journey and I think I'll go to bed." He didn't have the strength to sit in the parlor and make small talk amidst the shrine to his dead niece.

9
PALMYRA 1869
THE HAUNTED CHILD

Eddie helped his mother pluck a pair of squab that Fred had caught. Mama would roast them for supper. Eddie was glad for the meat, but he didn't like this job. The birds' heads dangled dumbly from broken necks. Their raw skin was cold and greasy. The birds grew uglier and uglier as he pinched away their soft white feathers.

Fred lay on the pallet, reading aloud from a coverless copy of *The Columbian Orator*, a book of speeches and dialogues he'd scrounged from somewhere. Fred loved to recite from the book, particularly the passages on moral rectitude and the temperance of pleasure. Mama nodded approvingly at Fred's delivery as her fingers worked a bird.

In the loft above, Jim Jr. scratched at a board with a rusted pen knife he'd found in the woods. Pop played solitaire at the table.

Three prim knocks sounded.

"I'll get it!" cried Eddie. He dropped the squab into his mother's apron and sprang to the door. His feet dashed a drift of feathers.

A woman entered the cabin. Fresh spring air followed her. The woman wore a black high-collared dress with puffed shoulders and long sleeves. Lace spilled down her ample bosom. A wide-brimmed hat with bright peacock feathers perched on a head of brown hair shot through with gray. She carried a furled parasol with a pearl handle. She had a handsome, authoritative face. Eddie thought she must be a queen.

"Good day. Is this the residence of James Drake?" Her voice filled every corner of the little shack. Her diction was crisp as a polished apple. Eddie thought Fred could learn a thing or two from her.

Eddie's mother set aside the squab and sketched a curtsey. "I'm Teresa Drake. This is my husband, James."

Pop left his cards and stood. Though taller than the stranger, he seemed reduced in her presence. With one hand he buttoned the top two buttons of his shirt.

The woman spoke loudly and slowly, as if to a foreigner. "My name is Tilda Coffin. I've come from Boston for a suffrage meeting in Rochester. I've been told that you, Mr. Drake, are a man of ethereal qualities."

"'Scuse me?"

"You speak with the dead. Is that so?"

After last winter, when Eddie and his father had recovered the bodies of the three murdered children, folks had visited the shack to hear Pop tell how he'd done it. Pop said his seeing stones allowed him to peer beyond the grave, that the spirits of those poor children had come to him and told where their bodies were laid. And the stones had told him who done it—Red Padraig, the half-breed. Pop said Red Padraig had fled far beyond Palmyra, and used villainous Indian magic to hide himself from Pop's sight. But if he ever came back, the seeing stones would catch him for sure.

Pop also let it be known that the stones allowed him to communicate with other spirits, including the souls of loved ones who had passed on from this life. In exchange for small gifts—a few pennies, a pie, a plate of hotcakes—he peered into his stones and transmitted messages from the dead to the living. Soon this new racket eclipsed money-digging as Pop's primary occupation. Folks came from all over to sit with the man who had found Palmyra's murdered children.

And as with the money-digging, Eddie had found himself dragged into Pop's scheme. It was Mr. Jangles' fault. The specter continued to plague Eddie, stalking him silently wherever Eddie went. Thankfully, no more children had been hurt since the winter, for which Eddie was desperately relieved. Maybe it had been Eddie's prayers. Or maybe Red Padraig had really been the villain, and now that he was gone Palmyra's children were safe.

But something about the ghost was different. Mr. Jangles seemed agitated or frustrated. He also seemed more furiously intent on communicating with Eddie. Signs and gestures were no longer enough. When Mr. Jangles stared at him, it felt as if a buzzing wasp burrowed into Eddie's ear and crawled toward his brain. It made Eddie want to stick a hot poker through his head.

With the buzzing came snatches of words and flickers of images. He saw objects—a teacup or a pocket watch or a decorated china plate. Sometimes it was a room he'd never been in, or a patch of ground he didn't recognize. And there were faces. Strangers' faces. All of it was dim and flickery, like pictures from a magic lantern projected onto a sheet.

Over time, Edward realized they were ghost memories from people who had died. Mr. Jangles was putting the memories into his head. And Edward was powerless to stop them. They crawled around inside his skull, restless and insistent. The only way to make them leave was to tell his father. At first, Pop had growled at Eddie to shut up. He wasn't interested in his boy's odd mumblings. Then one day, a man knocked at the door to ask to sit with Mr. James. His wife had died some months ago, and he was lonely for her.

As Pop directed the man to the table, Eddie had tugged his father's shirt and whispered "Tell him about the daisies in the green vase." Earlier that morning, Mr. Jangles had put that image into Eddie's head. Pop had shoved Eddie aside. But during the sitting, the man mentioned that his wife had loved flowers.

Pop had glanced at his son and said "It was daisies she loved best."

The man nodded.

"She kept them in a green vase."

The man's mouth fell open. "She did. I have it still. But how could you know?"

Pop had glanced at his son again, then gestured to his seeing stones, which sat between him and his supplicant. "These stones give me the far-sight." He instructed the man that once a week he should lay daisies on his wife's grave. That when he did so, he would know her presence and need not feel lonely. The man shook Pop's hands gladly. What's more, he left two dimes for Pop. After that, Pop paid attention if Eddie spoke to him.

For his part, Eddie tried to shut out Mr. Jangles and the ghost memories. He didn't want them in his head. But Mr. Jangles wouldn't relent. What was worse, he sensed that Mr. Jangles wanted something in return. Eddie didn't know what it was, but Mr. Jangles was putting Eddie in his debt. Eddie did not want to owe anything to this spirit, but he was helpless before him.

Today's visitor was clearly a person of quality, but she wasn't the first visitor to request a sitting. Pop began his patter. "Why, yes m'am. I speak to the dead. And they to me."

"If you aren't otherwise occupied, I thought I might request your services." Mrs. Coffin's eyes ranged disapprovingly over the squalid cabin. When they fell on the half-plucked squab, she wrinkled her nose. "There's someone with whom I wish to commune."

"Ma'am, you come to the right place, and you found the right man. I was born at the seventh hour of the seventh day of the seventh month. I got the second sight. My eyes see what no others can."

"If you say," said Mrs. Coffin.

"Please sit down," said Teresa, smoothing her oft-mended house dress. She escorted the visitor to a chair, then fetched a broom to sweep the feathers.

"Fred, get on up in the loft," said Pop. "Eddie, bring my stones."

Fred scurried up the ladder, jostling past Jim Jr., who gaped at the outlandish figure at the table. Eddie took a cigar box from the shelf, carried it to his father, then stood at his side like a footman.

Pop removed a felt bag and tipped out two round stones onto his palm. One stone was white, the other black. "These are my seein' stones. I dug 'em from the earth beneath the light of a full moon."

He placed the stones on the table, one beside the other, his movements easy and confident. He traced the pink vein of quartz in the white stone. "See this? It's like the blood in our bodies. This is the day stone. The life stone."

He touched the black. "Here is the night stone. It gathers darkness and shadows to itself. It represents the *afterlife*."

Pop whispered the final word. Eddie knew it caused visitors to shiver when he said it that way, but Mrs. Coffin sat stiffly. Eddie sensed a tension between his father and this woman, as if they strove against each other. The contest made him anxious.

Pop pressed on. "Light and dark. Life and death. With these stones, I see things invisible to the naked eye. I peer through the veil between this life and the next. I find those who is departed." Then he reached across the table. Eddie stiffened; it was wise to watch Pop's hands.

"Will you join me so that we might summon your beloved?" said Pop. He opened his rough palms to his guest. Mrs. Coffin took his hands—without removing her gloves.

"Close your eyes, m'am. Concentrate on the one you want to speak to. Picture the face. Hear the voice."

Mrs. Coffin closed her eyes. As she did, Pop glanced at Eddie. He raised his eyebrows as if to say "Well? You got somethin' for me?" Eddie shrugged. Today his head was empty.

Pop scowled. He fixed his attention on the woman. "Do you see the person?"

"I do."

"Picture 'em clear now. Clear as you can. See them as they once was in this life."

Now Eddie felt the buzzing sensation in his skull. He hunched his shoulders against it. A face appeared in the window. Mr. Jangles had arrived at last. The specter leered at Eddie. A word came into Eddie's head, faintly, like a voice whispered from the other side of the glass. *Lilly.*

"Flowers again," thought Eddie.

Pop continued his routine. "We're risin'. Risin' into the heavens. I see white clouds and a golden light. A figure is there, hidden in the mist. Give me a name so I can call them forward."

Mrs. Coffin opened her eyes. "I presumed you would know."

Pop smiled falsely. "The stones shall show me, never fear." He released her hands and swept up the stones. He glared at his son again, then dropped the stones into their sack and peered inside. The woman watched closely.

"Come now, spirit. Come now and show yourself. Come now and let us speak." He repeated the incantation twice more. "Yes. Somethin' coming through," he said. "I see...I see a man. Are you widowed?"

"I am."

"Ah! It's your husband I see. John or James. No? George. No, that ain't it. My mind was clouded. The letter 'D' or 'T' comin' through. Do either of those letters mean somethin' to you?"

"My husband's name is Tristam."

Pop smiled. "Yes, Tristam. The stones have revealed him to me."

Mr. Jangles tapped the window. Now an image flitted through Eddie's mind. It was foggy and hard to make out, but Eddie thought it might be a brook. Perhaps that was where the lilies grew? Is that what this woman wanted to talk about? Certainly she didn't seem interested in her husband.

"Tristam," said Pop, as if tasting the name. "Tristam. I sense he was an important man. A wealthy man?"

"Indeed," said Mrs. Coffin. "He made his fortune in shipping."

"So he did. So he did. I hear gulls cry and smell the salt air of a great harbor. Boston harbor. Cargo's bein' unloaded under your husband's eye. There's an account book, and great sums recorded in it. He gave you a good life. A prosperous life. Oh! He speaks to me now. I hear his voice. It's faint, but I shall listen carefully."

Pop tipped an ear to the sack. Mrs. Coffin adjusted her gloves.

"Tristam has moved on from this world, but he watches over you."

"I'm sure he does. He counted every penny I spent while he was alive."

"Those pennies don't matter. Not pennies or dollars. They don't matter to him, for he rests in the arms of the Lord. He wants you to know he's at peace. And now I sense...I sense he's being called back. Angels draw him back. Do you have a message before he goes?"

"I do not."

"Tristam wishes you well. You needn't fret about him. He's at peace, and he bids you to be at peace also. He raises a hand to say farewell. His great affection for you persists. He watches over you. He sees you always and is glad."

Pop set the sack on table and eased back in his chair. He folded his hands across his lean belly.

Mrs. Coffin sniffed. "That's all very well, but my husband wasn't the person I wanted."

Pop sucked his teeth. "Miss, the stones show what they show. It was a vision from Heaven."

"Heaven for Tristam would be the customs house." She rose. Pop also stood. Eddie noted the tightness in his father's jaw—this wasn't how it was supposed to go.

"I'll leave you now," said Mrs. Coffin.

Teresa stepped forward, hands wringing. "We're always pleased to welcome a guest."

The queenly woman took up her parasol and made for the door.

"Miss," said Pop quietly. "What about my fee?"

"Fee? You wish to be paid for that farce? I told you I did not want to speak to my husband."

"And I told you, it was Tristam who answered my call."

"Then take up your fee with him. Good day."

Mrs. Coffin exited.

Pop slammed a fist on the table, then turned on Eddie. "Dammit boy, why'd you sit there like a stump?" He raised a hand, but Eddie fled before the blow fell.

He burst out the door and practically ran into the woman. She was mounting a carriage with help from a driver. One boot perched on the runner.

"Your father's a fraud," she said. "If he sent you to plead his case, you needn't bother. I shan't pay him one cent."

"Lilly," said Eddie.

Mrs. Coffin gasped.

"Push off!" shouted the driver. He raised the buggy whip, but Mrs. Coffin stilled him with a finger. "What did you say?"

"I said lily, your majesty. Lilies by the brook."

She stepped down from the runner. "How did you know my sister's name?"

"Who?"

"You spoke of a brook," said the woman. "And my sister Lilith. You said Lilly's by the brook."

Eddie shrugged. He'd thought of flowers growing by the water, not a girl. But he kept his mouth shut.

The woman pressed one gloved hand to her mouth. "Oh! Oh, I remember now! Lilith and I were visiting grandfather in Hingham; we went outside to escape the adults and their tedious conversation. We took off our shoes and played in the brook behind his house. Lilith found a frog and showed it to me. How we shrieked!"

"I play in the creek," said Eddie. "Sometimes my friends Evelyn and Luke come. Evelyn's a girl, but she ain't scared of frogs."

Mrs. Coffin gripped Eddie's arm. She bent over him, blocking out the sun. Eddie smelled lavender and talcum. Her blue eyes seemed wide enough to swallow him.

"Is there any more? Did she send anything more?"

"No ma'am."

"Can you summon her back? I'll sit with you. I'll concentrate."

"No ma'am. That's all."

"Are you sure, boy?" She shook him, as if it might dislodge another message.

"Yes'm."

Mrs. Coffin straightened, lost in recollection. She still gripped his arm. Eddie waited.

"I'd forgotten that day," she said. "And now it's come back to me. The brook was cold and clear. We made little boats out of leaves, and gathered rocks to build a dam. We played until the sun went down. Nanny scolded us when she found us in our wet petticoats."

"Mama scolds me if I soak my trousers," said Eddie.

"Child, you've given me a most precious gift," said the woman. "I can't tell you how much this memory means to me." She dipped into a small bag that hung from her wrist. "Take this. You've earned it."

It was a silver half-dollar, with an eagle raised on one side. The coin splashed droplets of sunlight across Eddie's face. He'd never held so much money in his life.

"That's for you," said Mrs. Coffin. "Just you."

Eddie heard Mr. Jangles' voice.

In my debt.

The specter sat atop the carriage, one leg crossed over the other. He peered down at Eddie like a raptor.

"No," thought Eddie. "No."

You'll serve me.

"Never!" hissed Eddie.

"What did you say?" asked Mrs. Coffin. "Speak up, child."

"Uh...nothing, your majesty."

Mrs. Coffin took Eddie's chin in her hand. "Could you do it again sometime? Bring me memories from dear Lilith?"

Eddie shrugged. He'd thought the woman wanted to talk about flowers, not her sister. And the wants of this queenly woman meant little to him. He was confused and troubled by Mr. Jangles' message. Serve him? How? And why?

"Well. I suppose that's enough for today. But perhaps I'll return." She patted him absently, then dusted her gloved hands and ascended into the carriage. The driver closed the door and pushed past Eddie. He mounted the high seat and whipped the horse. Mr. Jangles had vanished. The coach drove quickly from the Bottoms.

Pop waited in the dooryard. Eddie placed the coin in his father's hand. He knew Pop had caught the glint of silver. That was all right; the money had come because of Mr. Jangles. Eddie wanted nothing to do with it.

Pop spat at the departing coach. "Take it up with your husband, huh? Looks like I got your money." Then he cuffed Eddie. "Remember —you ain't special. Whatever you have, it came from me."

"Yes Pop." Eddie slipped past his father into the house, wondering what he might owe to Mr. Jangles, and how that debt would be paid.

10

ROCHESTER, 1884
THE HAUNTED MAN

Edward woke in a strange bed. He sat up disoriented and cold, and then remembered where he was: in his brother's house in a child's bedroom, trying to sleep on a thin mattress under scratchy blankets. A massive chest-of-drawers loomed in one corner, a slumbering beast of old worn pine. Three pairs of children's shoes were scattered underneath like the bones of its prey.

Oily shadows oozed from behind the curtains. The color of the dark told Edward he'd woken in the restless hours before dawn, when anxious minds gnawed their worries and slithering things made their secret errands.

The soft sounds of sleep drifted through the house; Fred's snores, the rustle of bedclothes, a child murmuring dream-speak. Edward rubbed his eyes. He'd come uncoupled from the other sleepers and their night's passage. He was alone and stranded in his wakefulness.

He looked to the window. Palmyra was a few scant miles away. Edward was on the border of his childhood now, and at daybreak he would have to cross over. He didn't want to go back to that place; a place where a little boy had felt responsible for the deaths of three children, had been utterly powerless to stop it. And now it was happening again, and the grown man was still helpless.

Edward gripped the blanket. "It's not my fault. It never was."

Outside, wind skittered through the trees. Ragged branches clicked like pincers. A board creaked. Something shuffled in the hall. The bedroom door was ajar. Hadn't he closed it? A figure, small and gowned, passed by the door. Edward's blood went cold. He thought of the shrine downstairs, of Fred's dead daughter Charlotte. Oh God, was it her? Or one of Palmyra's murdered children come to condemn him? The figure crossed back again. It hesitated in the doorway, then stepped through. Edward clenched his teeth against a scream.

It wasn't a ghost. It was his little nephew Daniel, the youngest of Fred's children. The boy's faded sleeping gown hung to his shins. Daniel padded on silent feet and stopped at the head of the bed. He looked up at his uncle with calm curiosity.

"That's my bed," the child whispered. His words were soft and sibilant. He patted the mattress. "Me and my bruvers sleep here."

The air Edward had drawn for a scream leaked out as a whistle. Daniel had his mother's thick dark hair, but Edward saw Fred's stubborn mien in the child's face. The boy must've woken up in a strange bed and wandered back to his own room.

"I know, lad. I'm just borrowing it for one night."

Daniel blinked sleepily. "Just one?"

"Just one."

The child nodded. Then he climbed up and crawled over Edward.

"Here now," whispered Edward. "Wait a moment."

Daniel snuggled against his uncle's shoulder. He popped a thumb into his mouth. Edward sat stiff and awkward. The boy was already half asleep. His breath grew long and even, and his body softened. He was a warm coal at Edward's side.

Edward sat up for a time and watched his nephew. When he was sure the child was deeply asleep, he got carefully out of bed and lifted the boy in his arms. Quietly he stepped into the hallway. The floorboards were chilly against his bare feet. He followed the hall to a bedroom and saw bodies in a tangle of limbs and bedclothes; Daniel's brothers, their sleep undisturbed. He slipped Daniel among his siblings and arranged the blankets warmly around them.

The boys' faces were slack, their lips parted, their narrow chests rising and falling. Edward wondered if he and his own brothers had looked like this once, vulnerable and precious in their communal bed. Had his mother had ever stood over them in the night, watching? The thought of it brought tears to his eyes. He touched Daniel lightly on the cheek, then crept back to his room.

Somewhere in the house a wooden beam groaned the woe of its burden. Edward pulled the bedclothes around him, hoping to get warm. His mind fixed on the tasks ahead: Find his brother. Find Cassie Brown and Becky Deaver. Suddenly the missing girls were more than just names in a letter. They were tiny and precious. They should be tucked safe in theirs beds just like his nephews, not lost in the dark and the cold.

Where could they be? And what could Edward do that hadn't already been done? Mrs. Coffin's words came to him—Use your gift. Implore the spirits to come to your aid.

Foolish woman. There was no help from the spirits because they didn't exist. And yet—he was returning to the place where a spirit had often visited him. He understood now that those visitations were hallucinations, likely sprung from childhood traumas. But his homecoming was sure to exhume old hurts and fears. He must keep a tight rein on his emotions lest they get the best of him.

Edward bunched his limbs together and secured the blankets tightly around him. He dozed fitfully until the first shards of daylight pierced the darkness. Slowly, the house came to life around him.

11

Edward sat at his brother's breakfast table, tired from his night of broken rest. Fred's children buzzed around him. They fetched his napkin, laid out his utensils, and set his plate. Daniel climbed into Edward's lap and burbled happily about a little toy horse his father had carved. The boy galloped the horse across Edward's shoulders and through his tousled hair.

Fred said grace over a breakfast of eggs and fried ham. The eggs had come from the family coop. Edward had been awake to hear the rooster greet the dawn. Day-old bread, sliced and toasted, sat on a cutting board with a jar of Lydia's blackberry preserves. A jug of mild cider passed from hand to hand.

Edward searched the table for tea or coffee. His foggy head needed clearing. He opened his mouth to ask about a hot drink, then closed it again, remembering where he was.

"We don't take stimulants in this house," said Fred, who had noticed his brother's questing eye. "They sap the natural vitality and breed dependence."

"Of course," agreed Edward. Privately, he grumbled over Fred's rectitude. Edward had tea in one of his trunks, but it would be rude to flout his brother's prohibition. He fixed his attention on the toast and grumpily applied blackberry jam. The toy horse stuck its face in Edward's eggs and made munching sounds. Edward sighed.

"However, Lydia bought some tea at the market for your visit."

"Did she? How thoughtful!"

"Go and get it," said Fred to William, his eldest child. The boy ran to the kitchen and emerged with a tray laden with a steaming pot, a white cup, and a brick of black tea. Marie the housekeeper followed close behind. Proudly, William set the tray before his uncle.

Edward recognized the brand stamped on the brick of tea: a third-rate product of poor quality. Ah well. "This is lovely," he said aloud. "Thank you, William. And thank you, Lydia."

Edward broke a section from the brick and dropped it into the pot. The children watched intently, as if witnessing a secret ritual. The hunk sank to the bottom. Hot water seeped in and loosened the compacted mass. The clear water turned dingy brown. Soggy bits of leaf floated to the surface.

William, standing at Edward's elbow, leaned his head into the steam. "It smells good," he said. The other children cried out to sniff the forbidden brew. Fred glanced at Lydia, who assented with a barely perceptible nod.

The children lined up to inhale the scent of the tea. Four of the five pronounced it delightful. Only Daniel said "Yuck." Silently, Edward commended his nephew's discernment.

He poured himself a cup. The tea was weak and slightly sour, but better than nothing. "Very good," he said. Breakfast resumed. Edward drank the whole pot to acknowledge his hosts' good graces.

After the meal, he made to help clear the table but his nieces and nephews swarmed him and whisked his dishes away. Then came a bustle of preparations. Three of the five children attended school, and there was much to do: face washing, teeth brushing, hair combing. Edward was drawn into the maelstrom. He helped Frances Ellen tie her shoes and William find his slate. He chased Daniel into the parlor and cajoled him into his stockings. The rush and ruckus tumbled him into a memory of his own frantic minutes before the school bell: his mother scouring his face with a cloth, Jim dallying at the stove and dirtying his clean hands, Fred halfway out the door hollering to hurry or they'd be late.

Before the children departed, Edward gathered them. He placed a nickel in each of their hands and congratulated them on being such fine young Drakes. The children gaped at their good fortune. Lydia pursed her lips.

Frances Ellen wrapped herself around Edward's leg. "Please Uncle, won't you stay?" As Edward bent to remove her, she put her arms around his neck and kissed his cheek. Daniel rushed in and nestled his head on Edward's shoulder. The other children swarmed. Bundled in their innocent affection, Edward blinked back tears. Why had held himself apart from his family? How much poorer was his life because of it? He clutched the children to compose himself, then returned them to their mother.

"Out you go," said Lydia, shooing her three oldest through the door. "Drakes don't miss the school bell."

"Goodbye Uncle! Goodbye!" They dashed down the lane, lunch pails swinging in their hands.

"We should be off as well," said Fred. He was going to the church office, but first he would take Edward to the depot to catch a local to Palmyra.

Edward thanked Lydia for her hospitality, bid *adieu* to Marie, and walked to the barn with his brother.

"You have lovely children," he said, helping Fred hitch the buggy. "I hope I didn't get you in trouble with the coins. I thought it an avuncular privilege."

"A nickel each is extravagant, but that's all right. I'll speak to them tonight about the value of thrift. And speaking of children, I know you'll have your hands full looking for Jim, but there's also Cassie Brown and Becky Deaver."

"I know."

"They've been gone awhile already and... ."

"You don't have to say it. I know what happens to the ones who go missing."

"And I know what it's like to lose a child. No parent, no family, should have to suffer that."

"I'll do my best. But finding Jim will be hard enough. Which raises a question. What am I do with Jim if I track him down?"

"Bring him here."

"To Rochester?"

"To my house."

"Fred, is that wise? He's a wanted man. His presence could bring the law down on you. It could jeopardize your position as a minister. What does Lydia say?"

"Lydia is a Christian woman. She'll do what's right."

"But harboring a fugitive?"

Fred tightened a strap. "They tried to hang him once already. If they catch him again, they won't scruple a trial—they'll string him up from the nearest branch or gun him down where he stands. You have to find him and the children. Their lives are in your hands, Eddie."

"My hands? That's not fair, Fred. And why did you put this on *me*? Palmyra's two train stops away—you could've looked for Jim days ago instead of summoning me from Boston."

"You're a bachelor, Eddie. I have a house full of children."

"And a wife and a housekeeper. Surely they could spare you for a day or two."

"There's also my congregation. I have obligations and responsibilities."

"You think I don't? I have a job, Fred—a job I'll lose if I'm away too long."

Fred ran his hands along the harness, checking its fit. "I suppose I had another reason. You remember how Pop used to dig for money? You were the only one he took with him. Never me, never Jim."

"You needn't be jealous. Mostly I got blisters on my feet and his belt across my back."

"I'm not jealous. But I recalled that Pop usually came back empty-handed if he went out alone, even when he brought his seeing stones. He only ever found things when he took you."

Edward didn't like the direction of Fred's words. "What are you driving at?"

"To be honest, Eddie, I don't know. I just remember you and Pop coming home with little treasures—a copper bracelet, mash liquor. That horse. And then you found those three children. You and Pop—never Pop by himself. You were always there."

"What then? Should I get Pop's seeing stones? Should I recite his incantations and stick my face in a sack?"

"Don't be foolish. I know that was humbug. But when word came of Jim's trouble, I couldn't help but think on the curious things that had happened back then. It put me in mind to summon you."

Fred pulled himself into the wagon. "Besides, it's about time you did your duty to this family. Climb up, little brother. Drakes don't miss their trains."

12

The train deposited Edward and his luggage at the Palmyra depot. He hired a coach to take him to Jim's house. The old carriage jounced and jolted along the rutted road. Inside the cab, Edward bounced like a loose coin in a purse. He braced himself as best he could on the thinly upholstered bench. Outside, drooping pine and scabby white birch hemmed the lane on either side. A dreary sky cast a pall over the woods.

Something moved among the branches and brambles. Edward pressed his face to the window. It was small and quick, whatever it was. A fox or a wild dog? It kept pace with the coach, slipping through the underbrush with uncommon grace.

It was a child, not an animal. A little girl dashed through the woods. Edward glimpsed a faded gingham dress and dirty bare feet. What was she doing out here in the cold? Did she need help? Edward drew breath to stop the driver when the girl darted into the lane and leapt onto the coach's runner. She put her face to the glass. It was Katie Cooper.

Edward jerked back, his breath caught in his throat. This was the child whose corpse he'd found when he was ten years old, the first of three he'd discovered that awful winter. Terror crackled along his nerves.

Katie peered through the window. Her skin was translucent, her pale eyes mournful. Straw flecked her long brown hair. Freckles smudged her cheeks. A pair of bruises tattooed her windpipe where a murderer's thumbs had shut her throat.

"Good Christ!" croaked Edward.

Katie placed a hand on the window. It seemed a gesture of profound loneliness. Despite his terror and disbelief—surely this was a hallucination—Edward placed his own hand over hers. A mote of cold touched his skin, like the tip of an icicle.

Katie moved her mouth as if to speak. All that emerged was a faint wheeze. She furrowed her brow and tried again. The cords in her neck quivered. With jagged effort she barked a command.

Go back!

The words careened in Edward's skull like frightened sparrows.

He's here. He got plans for you. Go back!

Delivering the message seemed to exhaust her. She dropped from the carriage and vanished.

An invisible corset drew tight around Edward's lungs. His heart kicked against his ribs. A hammer of pain bashed against his forehead. *This* is why he didn't want to come home; Palmyra triggered his hallucinations, conjured up delusions. He'd suffered too much here as a boy, and the weight of it threatened to crack open his skull and spill his sanity all over the ground.

He struck the cab's roof with his walking stick. "Stop!" he cried. He pounded the shabby bench and stomped his boots. "Driver! Stop the coach!"

The cab lurched to a halt. Edward flung open the door and nearly fell out. He sucked in deep draughts of cold air. The corset around his lungs loosened.

The driver, a grizzled fellow with whiskey breath, craned his neck around from the high seat. "Enough with your damned thumping! I won't have my upholstery damaged."

"Turn around," panted Edward. "Take me back to the train depot."

"But I've only just collected you from there."

"Take me back I said!"

The driver scowled. "And how am I meant to turn around? We're hemmed in by trees!"

"I don't care how. Just do it!" Edward slammed the door against the man's complaints. He flopped back against the seat. Sweat streamed from his brow. A headache thudded behind his eyes. He mopped his forehead with a handkerchief. Coming home had been a mistake. Somewhere in his coat was a train timestable. Once he was back at the station, he could catch a local from Palmyra to Albany, then find an express to Boston. With a little luck, he would sleep in his own bed tonight. And he would never set foot here again.

But as the coach made its ponderous turn, the pain in his head receded. His breath returned, as easy and natural as if it had never left him. His panic drained away, leaving him clear-headed enough to reconsider. He'd only just begun this task; could he abandon it so quickly? What would he tell Fred or Evelyn—that a hallucination had frightened him away? Fred would call him hysterical. Evelyn Forrest would think him cowardly. And Jim. Jim might hang.

"Goddammit," he muttered. He swung open the door and stuck his head out again. "Never mind, driver. Take me to my first destination."

"What's that?"

"Take me to the Bottoms."

"So I'm to turn around *again*?"

"Yes. I apologize. There'll be a tip for you."

A shower of invective poured from the driver. Edward retreated into the cab. The horse, now doubly confused, balked in its traces. The driver whipped the beast and cursed Edward as a bastard and a fool. After a great deal of trouble, they were on their way again.

Inside the cab, Edward pulled his coat around him. "There was no ghost," he told himself. "My nerves are wound tight is all." Surely that was the explanation. Some natural feature had caught his eye—an old tree stump animated by the coach's jouncing, or the interplay of sun and shadow through wind-blown branches. His anxious mind had transformed it into a phantasm and played him a trick. It could happen to anyone.

"Just keep your wits and you'll be fine," he told himself. "You'll be fine." He clung to this assertion like a bit of flotsam over a bottomless sea.

The coach rolled along a narrow lane that led to the Bottoms, a bad patch of land at the eastern edge of Palmyra. The town's poorest whites collected here like leaves in a gutter. Shabby, weather-beaten shacks hunched cheek-by-jowl with their neighbors. Cook-stove chimneys coughed brown smoke. Washing hung on lines strung between staked poles. Hens picked among rubbish middens. Orange pumpkins and yellow squash grew in bedraggled kitchen gardens.

The coach crossed a weedy parcel of open ground that bisected the collection of shanties. This patch of land was called 'the common,' a pathetic cousin of Boston's grand public green-space. The common here was boggy and malarial. In the summer months, gnats and mosquitos rose at dusk in whining clouds from dank puddles to bite flesh and drink blood. As a boy, Edward's father had lit smokey fires in a vain effort to keep off the insects. As night fell and the Drake brothers retreated to the hot sheets of their shared bed, they'd scratched their bites until skin and blood clumped beneath their fingernails.

From the carriage, Edward regarded the Bottoms with loathing and pity. He recalled sitting quietly in Mrs. Coffin's parlor while her cadre of wealthy busybodies had discussed the plight of the poor.

Like medical students peeling open a cadaver, they'd taken turns identifying the malignancies in places such as the Bottoms: ignorance and indolence, drunkenness, violence, sexual incontinence. The debates in her salon had spun on a single axis: Did poverty cause such defects, or were these defects inborn, making poverty inevitable?

A few progressives in Mrs. Coffin's circle argued for the plasticity of character. They insisted that the poor were not irredeemable. They could be positively shaped under firm, benevolent hands. (Their eyes often slid to Edward, clean and well-behaved, as if they wished to brandish him as proof). But that argument typically ran aground against the stony bedrock of New England Calvinism—God had determined the elect and the preterite, and no action of man could alter it. Places like the Bottoms were a manifestation of God's ordering of the universe.

The carriage drove to the farthest end of the Bottoms and stopped in front of a dilapidated shack that backed up against a stand of scraggly pine. Pop had built this place with his own hands before Edward had been born. Never one for neighbors, Pop had set the place as far from the others in the Bottoms as he could. The nearest house was a stone's throw away.

Edward wrestled his trunks down from the coach. The driver did not help. Edward paid the fare and added a generous tip for the trouble he'd caused. Payment was accepted in surly silence, and the cab departed.

The shack looked near to falling down under Jim's indifferent ownership. Moss furred the tin roof. Bare planks showed through a slapdash coat of whitewash. The windows were nearly opaque with grime. Lank weeds and rust-colored pine needles sulked in the dooryard.

Edward clucked. Mama had never tolerated a slovenly facade. She'd made her sons scrub the windows once a week, rake the dooryard every day, and pluck weeds and dandelions that sprang up alongside the house. If she rose from her grave and saw the place now, she'd die all over again of mortification.

He made for the shack and then stopped. A face peeked through the small front window, then vanished. Fear brushed the nape of Edward's neck. Was someone inside? Could it be Jim? Or another hallucination?

His heart began to kick again. "Steady now," he told himself. He gripped his walking stick. The smooth oak shaft was solid in his hand. It was topped with a heavy brass knob. If someone inside meant him trouble, the stick would give them trouble right back. What effect it might have on a phantasm he couldn't say.

The door was unlocked. Edward pushed it open and leapt across the threshold, brandishing the stick like a club. The shack was empty. The face in the window must have been a trick of the light. Edward released a long, anxious breath. "Welcome home," he told himself.

Home was a single square room with walls and a floor of planked pine, and two lead-glass windows, one by the door and one in the back wall. The place smelled of pipe tobacco, fried ham, and bachelor.

The shack was smaller and shabbier than Edward remembered. He could cross from one end to the other in a few long strides. How on earth had two adults and three boisterous children lived in this tiny space and not gone mad? His apartment on Boylston Street must be ten times as big, and he had it all to himself.

A hearth of unmortised stone dominated the north wall. A shelf ran above the hearth. It held sacks of flour and corn meal, a jar of oil, tins of salt and pepper, and a half-empty whiskey bottle. A fry pan and dirty dishes rested in a washtub on a three-legged stool near the hearth.

In the middle of the cabin was a rough wooden table and two chairs. A small bag of black felt rested on the table.

At the south wall squatted a barrel-shaped stove. Its grate hung dumbly open, revealing ashy teeth of half-burned logs. A bed with a straw mattress was pushed against the east wall. This was new: Edward and his brothers had slept in a pallet, the three of them jumbled together like cats in a sack. The body warmth had been unbearable in summer and utterly necessary in winter.

Three cotton shirts and two pairs of trousers hung from pegs over the bed. The clothes were homespun and unfashionable, but neat and clean. Jim might not be keeping up the house, but he seemed to be taking care of himself.

Next to the bed, a short ladder was nailed to the wall. The ladder led to a loft, a narrow space beneath the eaves where his parents had slept. Pop had built the loft just after Fred was born, to give himself and Mama a little privacy.

Edward thought of the face in the window. Had someone spotted him and scuttled up to the loft? Could it be Jim? Were the local authorities so dim-witted that Jim had simply slipped back home to hide?

Edward tiptoed across the floor and climbed the ladder. Cautiously he poked his head through the opening. "Hello?"

No one was there. Edward climbed all the way up. He hunched beneath cobweb-draped rafters. His parents' bed and mattress were gone. Jim must've sold them after Pop died. All that remained were a stack of old newspapers and bushel basket filled with books. Edward looked through them. Among novels and histories he was surprised to find *A Stellar Key To The Summer Land,* by the spiritualist Andrew Jackson Davis. The book posited the existence of a belt of stars and planets where humans would live after death. Mrs. Coffin had a copy in her library. He'd tried to read it once, and found only bogus astronomical observations and dense thickets of ethereal claptrap. Jim must be cribbing passages to beguile folks who came to his seances. He tossed the book back into the basket and climbed back down.

He went outside and dragged his trunks into the cabin, grunting with effort. Perhaps Fred was right; he'd overpacked. He shoved the trunks next to the bed. Jim had no wardrobe nor closet, just a battered chest already crowded with shirts, undergarments, and a mothy quilt. Edward would have to live out of his trunks like a traveling salesman. Ah well.

He sat at the table and stretched out his legs. The cabin was chilly and slightly damp. God, he could use a cup of tea! It wasn't even noon and he already felt done in. He decided to get a fire going in the stove. He would heat water and brew some tea. Once refreshed, he would pay a visit to the Forrest farm and let Evelyn know he'd arrived. And then he would start his search for the missing girls.

The felt bag on the table caught his attention. He knew what was inside. He loosened the drawstring. Two stones fell into his palm, one white and one black, each about the size of an egg. A narrow vein of prickly pink quartz bisected the white stone. The black was smooth and glossy. His father's seeing stones.

Edward jounced them in his palm. They were heavier than he remembered, and cold to the touch. The white stone wasn't pure white; more the color of dingy snow. It reminded him of a comet he'd once seen through a telescope. Mr. Bollen had set up the scope on Mrs. Coffin's roof for an astronomy lesson. To the naked eye, the comet was a single bright point, but the lens revealed ragged clusters of dirty ice swathed in dust. The stone in his hand looked as if it had strayed from its celestial course and fallen to earth.

Its companion stone was pure black, inky as midnight in a starless sky. Its oval surface was flawless. The stone stared from his palm like the baleful iris of a basilisk.

No wonder his father had been drawn to these stones. Edward had to admit their appeal, like totems chipped from a heathen idol. But they weren't magical. They had no powers. They did not grant visions or pierce the veil of death. Pop had turned them into cheap props for his spiritualist swindles.

And yet—a sense of disquiet crept over him. He imagined shadowy figures outside, drifting across the grass to gather at his door, drawn by the stones and by the blood-warm palm that held them. He dropped the stones in the sack and pushed the sack away.

"Let's see to that fire," he said aloud. He stood and slapped his thighs, a busy and practical man with a task to complete.

A banging startled him. Someone pounding at the door. Edward peered through a cloudy pane. A man stood in the yard, a rifle in his hands.

"You in there! Open up!"

13

"Who's there?"

"Sheriff Cole. Open the door!"

Hell, thought Edward. What was a lawman doing here? Could he refuse him entry?

"Open up, I say!"

Edward lifted the latch. A tall, broad-shouldered man bulled his way inside. He wore a long duster and Quakerish hat. He planted himself in the center of the room and pointed his rifle at Edward. "Who are you?"

"I'm Edward Drake." He was suddenly conscious of how far he was from Beacon Hill and the protective aura of Mrs. Coffin. He was back in the Bottoms, a place of rough, thoughtless violence.

Sheriff Cole inspected Edward perfunctorily, then he sat uninvited at the table. He removed his hat and ran a rough hand through a mane of sandy blond hair. He gestured for Edward to sit.

"I got word that a fella who looked like Big Jim showed up at the train station," said Cole. "Reportedly he made some trouble in a coach on the way to this shit-burg."

This place was a shit-burg, but Edward thought the insult unnecessary. "That was me," he said coolly. "I'm Jim's brother."

"I see the family resemblance—excepting the height. I suppose no one's ever called you Big Edward. Little Edward might do."

A second insult. Edward clamped his lips against a retort.

"You've come all the way from Boston, yes?"

"How did you know?"

Cole twisted his mouth into something between a smirk and a snarl. "Because I've had to make the Drake family my business. And a nasty business it is. There's another of you in Rochester. Freddy's his name. Is he little like you?"

"He's the *Reverend* Frederick Drake."

"Reverend? Huh. I wired the Rochester constabulary to keep an eye on Freddy, in case Jim showed up. But now you're here, which makes me think so is Jim."

"I don't know. I've only just arrived."

"For what purpose?"

Edward didn't know how to respond. What does one say to a lawman about helping a fugitive?

Cole sneered again, as if reading Edward's hesitation. "I suspect you're here to look for your brother. Big Jim's charged with murdering Liza Ames and kidnapping two more children."

"Jim didn't do it."

"No? He showed up on Main Street with Liza's corpse in his arms!"

"Just because he found her doesn't mean he killed her."

"The girl had been *strangled*," said Cole.

"So? What does that have to do with Jim?"

"What does it have to do? I guess you forgot what Jim did to me."

"You? What do you mean?"

"When we were kids," said Cole. "At Red Creek. You were there when it happened."

Red Creek wound through the woods nearby. Palmyra's children gathered there in spring and summer, wading in shallow pools, sailing paper boats, skipping stones, and hunting crayfish and frogs. Edward and his brothers had played at the creek, but he had no memory of Cole.

"It was just after the fourth of July," said Cole. "I was seventeen. Probably too old be messin' around at the creek, but it was a scorcher that summer and the water was cool. I liked to go there and wade with my shoes off. I started a bit of horseplay that day. I got a little rough with you—might've pushed you under. You started crying. So Big Jim came at me."

"He did?"

"Oh yes. Told me to leave you alone. Called me a few names. Your brother was big even then, but I wasn't a small fella myself. And I sure didn't take lip from Bottoms trash. I threw a haymaker. Jim ducked and then...pow!" Cole smacked a fist into his palm. "Knocked me right in the dirt. One shot was all it took. Even my Dad never hit me so hard. You don't remember this?"

"No," said Edward. Jim had knocked down a lot of people back then, including him. The memories blurred.

"Your brother jumped on top of me," said Cole. "Straddled my chest and locked both hands around my throat. Then he *squeezed*. I'll never forget his eyes—red with hate they were. He would'a choked me to death if a bunch of boys hadn't dragged him off."

"But that was years ago, Sheriff. You can't use a boyhood tussle as proof that Jim murdered Liza Ames."

"It was the same year those three kids were killed. They were strangled to death."

"You're saying Jim killed those children back then?"

"Wouldn't surprise me."

"No," said Edward. "It's just coincidence."

"Coincidence; the refuge of the scoundrel." Cole leaned forward and picked up the sack with the seeing stones. He weighed the bag in his palm, then emptied the stones onto the table. They sat between Edward and the sheriff, blank and dead as taxidermy eyes. "These your brother's peep stones?"

"They belonged to my father. I suppose they're Jim's now."

"Some say Big Jim got the gift. They say he can use the peep stones to talk to the dead. That'd be quite a thing, to call up spirits and speak to them." For a moment Cole's aspect softened, as if he were caught up in an emotion other than belligerence. "I'll admit, I've been tempted to sit with your brother—before all his trouble started, that is. I lost someone very dear to me and I miss her terrible. My heart would be easier if I could speak to her again. You think Jim could summon her spirit?"

"It's not possible to speak to the dead," said Edward.

"Oh? Big Jim said the ghost of Liza Ames told him where to find her body. What do you make of that?"

"The most rational explanation is he found the Ames girl by chance."

"Then who killed her? And who took the other children?"

"How am I to know? Isn't that your job?"

"You're impertinent for a Little Edward. But you're correct. It is my job. And if I'm to do it, I must question your brother. I never got the chance because a few hotheads made a ruckus at the jail."

"Ruckus? They came to murder him!"

"Well. I didn't anticipate the situation getting out of my control like that. But a rumor spread that Liza Ames had been... interfered with. In a vile manner. You take my meaning? Someone had..."

"I understand."

"When the menfolk in the Ames family heard, they went mad with rage. They whipped up some of their neighbors and marched on the jail, wanting to get their hands on Jim. Someone even set a fire to my jail! Jim managed to slip away in the smoke and confusion. Hell, one wall is still all blackened and scorched."

Edward had no sympathy for Cole's structural damage.

"I don't tolerate mobs," said Cole. "If someone needs hanging, I'll deputize a few men and we'll do it lawful. But I also don't tolerate fugitives. Your brother needs to answer for Liza Ames. And if he took the others, or knows their whereabouts, it might be we could find them alive."

"My brother's neither a murderer nor a kidnapper," said Edward.

"So you keep saying. Yet your father found three dead children all those years ago. I talked to a few old-timers about it. They said none of the victims' families wanted to go after your father. Just the opposite—they were grateful to him. If it wasn't for James Drake, they might never've had bodies to bury. Besides, a drifter had passed through at the time, some nasty half-breed. The crimes got pinned on him."

"But the drifter was never caught," continued Cole. "And some people in Palmyra weren't satisfied. Maybe it was true that James Drake had a talent with them stones. But he was also a foul man with filthy habits. He'd drink till he was blind, start fights in the Bottoms, or stagger off to Main Street to howl and cuss at respectable folk until he passed out and pissed himself. And everyone knows how he snatched your mother out of a whorehouse in Buffalo. Never even bothered to marry her—just locked her in this shitbox and put his seed in her belly."

"That's a damn lie!" cried Edward. "My mother was a good woman!"

"And see what their blessed union produced—a drunk and a brawler who plays at sorcery, just like his father. Then one day he shows up with Liza Ames's body. Not only that, he's got Becky Deaver's hair ribbon in his pocket. Who killed Liza? Where is Becky Deaver? Where's the little Negro girl? Jim says he doesn't know. Yet Drake men keep turning up with dead children. Do you see why Jim's got to answer for himself?"

"And how is he meant to do that?" demanded Edward. "If he's caught again, he won't last an hour. He has the right to representation and all the protections of the law. But it seems he won't get that here."

"You impugn my office?"

"I impugn vigilantism."

Cole drew a tobacco pouch from his coat. He stuffed a plug in his mouth. His lower lip bulged grotesquely. "Let's speak plainly, you and I. You're here to find your brother. Likely you have some half-baked plan to sneak him out of Palmyra."

"I'm here to ensure my brother gets a fair hearing," said Edward. "I've retained the services of a law firm in Boston." This wasn't precisely true. He and Thomas Connelly had a gentleman's agreement that Tom would help if he could, but that was all. He certainly didn't have an entire firm behind him. Yet Edward hoped the words "law firm," "retain" and "Boston" might intimidate this simpleton.

"Get all the lawyers you like. Bring the Supreme Court if you can. It doesn't change the fact your brother's a fugitive. And my gut tells me he done it. I'm usually right."

"Your gut speaks, does it? Are you sure it's not just gas?"

A muscle in Cole's cheek twitched. He spit a brown globule onto the floor. "You listen now, Edward Drake. Your brother's a bad seed, squeezed out of a whore's cunt and raised like an animal."

"How dare you!" hissed Edward.

"And now comes little brother to snatch him up and hide him away. You think just because that old widow took you to Boston that you're any better than Jim? Yes, I know about her. She schooled you up and dressed you like a gentleman, but blood don't lie. Bottoms-born and Bottoms-bred, nothing good will ever come of a Drake."

Edward made a fist. "That's enough of your insults! I won't have it!"

Cole leaned full across the table. His long hair bristled. His hot breath stank of tobacco. "You'll have whatever I give you. A murderer is loose in my town. One child is dead, two others missing. The newspaper chides me. A gaggle of mothers honks at me relentlessly. And now you strut into Palmyra full of plots and schemes. But you're just jumped-up trash who's forgotten his place." Cole placed a hand on his rifle. "Do I need to teach it to you?"

Edward's blood roared. He was sick of this man's denigrations!

Cole might be surprised to learn that Jim wasn't the only Drake who could knock him down.

But Cole had a gun, wide-bored and well-oiled. What's more, Cole had the law. Around here, he likely *was* the law. With a furious effort, Edward contained himself. He spoke through clenched teeth.

"No. You needn't teach me."

Cole held Edward's eye for a long moment. Then he leaned back, almost disappointed. "Well now. I thought you and I were about to see what we're made of. But you've decided not to test me. I suppose that's for the best. I've decided you can be of some use to me."

"What do you mean?"

"I mean, I give you permission to look for your brother. But you'll do it under my terms."

"What terms?"

"First, if you uncover any sign of Jim, you'll inform me. Second, if you actually find your brother, you'll bring him to me. I'll lock him away safe while you fetch all the lawyers you want. Third, if you don't find him and decide to go home, you'll clear it with me first."

"I'll do none of those things," scoffed Edward. "You have no right to order my comings and goings."

"Around here, I have every right. I have the ultimate right. Do you understand?"

Edward scowled.

"Accept my terms," said Cole, "or I'll ship you back to Boston right now—in irons if I must. If you want Jim to have a trial, my offer is your only chance. If somebody else finds your brother, it'll be a rope and a tree. And no one will say a word against it. Certainly not me. So decide."

Edward wanted to leap across the table and thrash this bully. How many insults could Cole deliver through a mouthful of broken teeth? But a brawl would accomplish nothing. No one would be helped. Edward took long, deep breaths, damping the furnace of his anger. "Very well," he said.

"Very well what?"

"We have a deal."

Cole flicked his hair back from his face. "Good. That's good. You've made the correct decision." He picked up his gun, seated his hat on his head, and stood. As he rose he knocked his chair over. He didn't trouble himself to right it.

"One other thing," said the sheriff. "The Drake name ain't loved in Palmyra. Folks won't be pleased to see you snooping around. The only reason I allow it is because I have a hunch you'll find Jim. Kin knows kin. And there's something spooky about you Drakes. So have your look. But do it quiet."

"And know this: I'll have eyes on you. I'll know every move you make. If you fail to heed my instructions, I shall fall on you like God's judgement."

Final instructions delivered, Sheriff Cole departed.

When the man had gone, Edward snatched the seeing stones and flung them at door. They thunked against the wood. He kicked over his own chair and stomped around the room, cursing Cole with every pox he could think of—boils, hives, shingles, syphilis, lice, fleas, tapeworms, maggots. Who did that swaggering bumpkin think he was? Edward snatched up his cane and swung it like a bat, imagining the shock of the wood in his palms as he cracked Cole's skull.

But soon his anger cooled. In its place was an iron determination. He would find Jim. He would find the missing children. He would summon Tom down from Boston and prove Jim's innocence. He would humiliate Cole in court and in public. And then he would put Palmyra behind him for all time.

Edward flung on his coat. It was time to go to work.

14

PALMYRA, 1868
THE HAUNTED BOY

Eddie and his brothers played a noisy game of tag with the other children in the Bottoms. Their shouts rang in the autumn air as they dashed and darted around the water pump that served as home base.

Mr. Jangles lurked nearby, perched like a raven on the branch of an oak. He watched the game with unseemly interest. Eddie hated when Mr. Jangles watched. The specter's attention clung like spider threads on the back of his neck. He wished Mr. Jangles would go away.

Then Fred charged, reaching to tag him. For a few moments Eddie was absorbed in the game, dashing away from his brother's touch. When next he glanced up at the branch, Mr. Jangles was gone.

Then the cobwebby feeling came back. Now Mr. Jangles stood by the water pump. He splayed his hands like a net. No one else could see him, but children unconsciously swerved away from his long, horn-nailed fingers.

Then Mr. Jangles walked towards Eddie. His booted feet left no trace in the grass, yet on he came. Eddie wanted to run to his house and hide, but lassitude flooded his limbs, leaving him limp and helpless. Mr. Jangles loomed.

A door banged open and a voice cried out. Tante V rushed out of her house. She was kin to Eddie, his great-aunt from him father's side of the family. Tante V had been married twice; first to a man named Vorhees, then to a fellow named Vaughn. Rather than keep the surnames straight, most folks in the Bottoms called her Miss V, but in Eddie's house she was Tante.

Tante V was a midwife and medicine maker. Many of the children in the Bottoms, Eddie and his brothers included, had passed from their mothers' wombs into her hands. She had plucked them from the birth canal, patted their tiny bodies clean, and set them at the breast to suck. She grew sarsaparilla root and asphodel, and knew the curative properties of herbs, willow bark, and wild plants. She could tame rooks and crows.

Tante V minded everyone's business, scolded everyone's children, and distilled a liquor potent enough to fell a horse. She called the liquor her 'steady,' and she drank it every day of the year.

Now she stormed towards Eddie and the other children. Her grey hair stood at wild angles and her unbelted dressing gown flapped like wings. If Tante V had a headache, she wouldn't hesitate to scatter the youngsters with a few lashes from her tongue.

But something was odd. In her right hand she held a bundle of dried juniper and holly leaves. In her left she carried an ash shovel with hot red coals from her stove. She touched the leaves to the coals. The juniper and holly caught fire at once.

Tante V thrust the burning bundle at Eddie. Smoke stung his eyes and sparks singed his lashes. He flung up his hands and stumbled backward.

"Get out!" she shrieked. "Get the fuck outta here!"

Jim and Fred gaped. The other children fled.

Tante V brandished the smoking sprigs. "Go on, get out! You got no place here!"

Eddie coughed and sputtered. Why was his great-aunt trying to burn him? What had he done to her?

And then his mother interposed. She shouted and cursed at Tante V, who cursed right back. Eddie wrapped his arms around his mother's waist and pressed his face to her apron.

His mother called Tante V a drunk old cow, then drew Eddie across the commons and into their house. She sat him in a chair and wiped his face with a damp cloth.

"Did she scare you, Eddie?"

Eddie nodded.

"Pay no mind to that old witch."

"Is she a witch? Truly?"

"No Eddie. Not truly."

"Why did she want to burn me?"

"She didn't mean no harm. She's just been at her steady. I can smell it on her." His mother stroked his cheek. "But you keep your distance. If she bothers you again, come tell me."

"Okay mama."

She set down the cloth and went back to kneading dough. Outside, the commons were empty. Tante V had retreated into her house. And Mr. Jangles was gone. For now.

15
PALMYRA, 1884
THE HAUNTED MAN

After his interview with the sheriff, Edward strode into the woods. He intended to visit Evelyn Forrest and her family. He could aid them in their search for Cassie Brown while also keeping an eye out for Jim.

The Forrest farm was several miles away, separated by acres of woodland. As Edward followed an old deer trail, he contemplated all the ground he'd have to cover in his search. Of the thirty or so square miles that made up Palmyra's boundaries, much of it was hilly forest: a significant amount of land for one person to cover. Edward dredged from his memory places where he and his brothers had played as boys that might serve as either a hiding place for a kidnapper or a refuge for Jim.

There was the abandoned mill, and the foreman's shack at the quarry. But Edward's money was on a cave that stood a couple miles from the Bottoms. The cave was full of tunnels that burrowed deep into a rocky hillside. The tunnels were dangerous, but a man could find shelter there if he was desperate enough. And Jim was desperate.

Edward didn't relish having to search those tunnels—they were narrow, maze-like, and pitch black. He'd dared them once as a boy and almost not come out. He hoped he wouldn't have to risk them again.

As he walked, he wondered about Sheriff Cole's accusations against his brother. How *had* Jim found Liza Ames's body when dozens of searchers hadn't? Was it a coincidence Jim had also found Becky Deaver's hair ribbon—or evidence of his guilt? And what of the sheriff's claim that Jim had strangled him fifteen years ago, the very same year the three children had been murdered?

Jim *was* violent. Edward knew it. As a boy, Jim had punched and pummeled him and Fred for imagined slights, or no reason at all. He'd written rude words in Fred's book of oratory; pinned Edward to the ground and spat in his face; hid Pop's tobacco in Edward's clothes, then smirked as Pop whipped Edward for stealing.

Did those torments hint at darker aspects of Jim's character? Was Jim a predator? A child-killer? The thought was terrible to consider. Edward needed to stand face to face with Jim and ask—Was it you? If he could look into Jim's eyes, he would know the truth. And if Jim said "No," then Edward would do everything he could to get Jim free of Palmyra.

But what if Jim said yes?

A cry interrupted Edward's thoughts. Edward stopped and listened. Squirrels argued in the canopy above him. A wash of wind teased leaves in their boughs. Then the cry came again, a man's voice raised in hurt and alarm.

Edward raced toward the sound, wondering if it was Jim. Had he been cornered by vigilantes? He dashed through the woods and came to a small clearing. He saw three lads peering up into the branches of an oak. They laughed and pointed. A hound dog paced at the bottom of the tree, its eyes fixed on something overhead.

An old man crouched on a branch perhaps twelve feet off the ground. He had gray hair, a white beard, and shabby overalls. His boots balanced precariously on the limb. He clutched the trunk for dear life.

One lad threw a stone and scored a hit. Blood bloomed on the old man's forehead. He yelped and drew his head into his shoulders. The young men snatched up more stones and pine cones and pelted their captive. The hound scrabbled at the tree, gouging the trunk with sharp claws.

"Stop!" shouted Edward. He ran towards them, one hand raised like a policeman's. "Stop at once!"

The three lads spun and gaped. They were perhaps fifteen or sixteen, weedy young fellows on the verge of manhood. Certainly they were old enough to know what they were doing was wrong. Red shame slunk into their cheeks. For a moment Edward thought they might break and run. Then the dog turned on Edward. It raised its hackles and bared its teeth. The dog's aggression emboldened the young men. Their spines straightened and their chests puffed as they realized their advantage—three against one.

"Let him alone," said Edward gruffly. Could he bluster his way through this?

"What's it to you?" asked the tallest of the three. He had sandy hair, a pimply face, and a threadbare brown coat. He gestured to the old man. "He a friend of yours?"

"No, I don't know him. But that's no way to behave toward an elder."

"Elder? He's a filthy old coot."

"You've not right to treat him that way. Go on and get out of here."

The youth bared his teeth in unconscious imitation of the dog. "You ain't my father. You don't tell me what to do. Now push off before I set my dog on you."

"Let him down and we'll all part ways," said Edward.

The youth looked Edward up and down. "You got money?"

"What?"

"Them's good clothes. You look like you got money."

Edward did have money. A wallet, thick with bills. How stupid to carry so much cash around here. "That's none of your business."

"Maybe you ought to pay us somethin.' We'll let the old man go for a dollar. No, two."

"Three!" said the lad to Edward's left. "He should give us three dollars, Joe. One for each of us."

"That's right," said the one called Joe. "Three dollars."

"You'll get nothing from me."

"Then maybe we'll take it." Joe took a buck knife from his pocket and opened the blade with a practiced flick. "And that coat. I like that coat. Take it off."

Edward brandished his walking stick. After his humiliating interview with the sheriff, he'd be damned if a few pimply thugs pushed him around. "I'll do no such thing."

"We'll see about that." Joe sidled forward, knife held out in his right hand. He stabbed at Edward. Edward swung his stick and knocked the knife away. Then he stepped forward and hit Joe in the jaw with a hard left. Joe stumbled backward, but another youth came in low, catching Edward at the knees. Edward toppled and the three lads were on him, punching and kicking. Edward punched back. The dog darted in and bit Edward's calf. He cried out and kicked the animal with his boot.

"Don't you hurt my dog!" shouted Joe.

"Get his coat!"

Rough hands yanked his coat down his shoulders and stripped it free. Edward tried to get to his feet. Someone kicked him in the stomach, driving the breath from his body. Joe leapt on Edward's back and pinned him to the ground.

"Now his pants!" Hands yanked at his trousers. "Strip'm down. Take it all!" Edward struggled wildly, trying to buck his attacker, but the lad held fast.

"I ought to cut your fucking nuts off," hissed Joe.

Then bodies were flying and Edward was free. He scrambled to his feet, hiking up his trousers. A huge dog had appeared, bigger and fiercer than Joe's. Saliva dripped from its chops. It growled deep in its chest, then lunged at the hound. The hound fled.

A rock flew through the air and struck Joe in the head, staggering him. An old woman with a shock of white hair had thrown it. She chucked another stone and hit a second lad.

"You bitch!" shouted Joe. Blood streamed down his face. He snatched up his knife and made for the old woman. The huge dog barred his way. It growled ferociously, hackles raised and legs stiff. It looked big enough to take off Joe's head in one bite.

There was a whump and a clatter of leaves. The old fellow in the tree had jumped down. He held a shovel like a weapon, ready to bash skulls.

The lads drew together and tallied the forces arrayed against them. For a moment Edward thought they might try another charge —their blood was up, their pride wounded. But the monstrous dog lunged again, eyes burning, fangs ripping the air. Their spirit broke. They sprang into the brush and vanished.

"No-account Bottoms trash," said the old woman. She clucked her tongue at the dog. The giant beast loped to her side and sat, its pink tongue lolling. It leaned its massive head against her hip. To Edward it looked like a cross between a mastiff and a horse.

"Linus Goodword, you all right?" asked the old woman.

"Aye," croaked the man who'd been treed.

"And you?"

Edward nodded dumbly. He brushed at the dirt and leaves stuck to him, trying to mask his anger and humiliation.

"Come over here and let Sherman get a sniff of you." She gestured to the dog.

"Sherman?"

"Named him for the general that whipped them rebs down in Georgia. My youngest boy Bill marched with the general to Savannah. Some Johnny shot and kilt him. Anyways, come say hello. I won't let Sherman eat you."

Gingerly, Edward held out his left hand, wondering if it would end up in Sherman's gullet. The dog sniffed his palm, then licked it with a thick wet tongue.

"Sherman says you alright," said the woman. Edward wiped his hand on his pantleg.

"Well, let's get you sorted." She picked up Edward's coat, brushed the leaves from it, and handed it to him. Then she went to the fellow named Goodword.

The old man stood by a trench about five feet long and nearly as deep. It was recently dug. The fresh-turned earth smelled damp and loamy. A pick axe lay on the ground, crusted with dirt. Next to it was a cone-shaped brass weight, about the size of Edward's fist. The fat end of the cone was tied with a length of twine to a wooden rod.

Edward recognized the device. It was a plumb bob, a tool used by money diggers. The brass cone was supposedly attracted to metals buried in the earth. His father had mucked about with plumb bobs when Edward was a boy, but the seeing stones had always been Pop's preferred instrument for treasure hunting.

"Any luck?" The old woman gestured to the trench.

"Not as yet," said Goodword. "Them boys interrupted me." The man was thin and stooped, but he possessed a wiry vitality. His grey hair was bushy and unkempt. Bits of tree bark flecked his snowy beard. A thin line of blood ran down from his forehead to his cheek.

As Goodword bent to retrieve his plumb bob, Edward remembered who he was. This old man had once run the tannery near the school. The tannery was a noxious place of bloody animal hides and urine-filled curing pits. The stink had drifted into the schoolroom on warm days. Sometimes at recess, Edward and his brothers had crept to the tannery to spy on Goodword. He'd been a frightening figure in those days, draped in a filthy leather apron, a scraping knife in one hand, his scabby arms stained to the elbows in gore. Jim had teased Edward and Fred, saying if Goodword ever caught them snooping, he'd peel them raw and sell their skins to Apaches.

Goodword was also known as an avid money digger. Supposedly

the man had dug trenches and tunnels all over Palmyra in search of gold, silver, and gems.

"What are you digging for?" asked Edward, his tone solicitous. Clearly the old man was a crank, and perhaps touched with monomania. But he felt a kinship with him; they'd both been set upon by those ruffians.

"What's it to you?" snapped Goodword.

"It's nothing. I was just curious."

"Do I know you?"

"My name's Edward Drake. I grew up here, but I've been away for a time." He held out his hand. Goodword didn't take it.

"Drake? You kin to Big Jim?"

"He's my brother."

Goodword scowled. Muttering under his breath, he snatched up his tools and implements. Then he spat at Edward's feet.

"Here now!" cried Edward.

"Your father was a liar and your brother's a thief! Big Jim stole from me. And now you come to share the loot."

"I have not."

"I put a curse on Big Jim. He'll get what he deserves." The old man made a twisting motion with the fingers of left hand, then gestured at Edward as if flinging a dart. "And now I curse you. Let all Drakes go hang!" He marched into the woods, his plumb bob and other tools slung over one shoulder.

Edward gawked. He'd risked his neck to help that fellow and what was his thanks? Spittle on his brogans and a curse on his life. He rubbed the tip of one boot in the dirt and muttered a few curses of his own.

The old woman chuckled. "I see you remember Goodword. You remember me, Eddie?"

Eddie. Only his family called him that. The woman had weather-roughened cheeks and striations of wrinkles in her broad forehead. A thick mane of crinkly white hair waved in the wind. Her eyes were hazel-colored and sharp as cut glass. Her eyes sparked his memory.

He knew her. She was his great-aunt—the one who tried to burn him when he was a boy.

"Tante V," he said.

"I'm glad I run into you, Eddie. You and me got business. Come on."

16

Tante V lived in the Bottoms, which was back the way Edward had already come. He protested that he had an errand elsewhere, but Tante V told him it could wait. Given that his great-aunt had come to his aid, Edward obliged.

Tante V kept a neat kitchen garden behind her little cottage. Orange pumpkins and crook-necked squashes grew beneath shoulder-high bean poles. Sherman led Edward and his great aunt along a short row of gourds, the dog scenting for the nibbling presence of rabbits and squirrels. Medicinal hops laced a trellis against the cottage's back wall.

Inside, tidy bundles of dried herbs and strands of cured sausage hung from a beam. Cucumbers and beets marinated in pickling jars on a shelf. The plank floor was clean-swept, the corners of her ceiling free of cobwebs. A stew simmered in squat black kettle over red coals in the fireplace. The savory scent brought water to Edward's mouth. He hadn't eaten since his breakfast at Fred's house.

"Sit," said his great-aunt. She hung her coat on a peg, then rummaged in a rickety hutch that served as her pantry. Sherman laid down with a grunt on a blanket by the fire. Tante V joined Edward at the table, echoing the dog's grunt as she sat. She carried a clay jug, two tin cups, and a pipe. She unstopped the jug and poured two fingers of clear liquid into each cup. Edward smelled fermented juniper berries and a hint of fennel.

"*Bonne sante*, Eddie." She drained the cup with a tip of her wrist, then shivered with bitter pleasure.

Edward sipped. The liquor raked his throat and watered his eyes. He coughed and sputtered, then ran his tongue against his teeth to scrape away the foul taste. "Good Christ, that's awful."

"It's not made for sippin'," said Tante V. "You got to take it all in one go. It's steady medicine." She tapped her chest. "Look at me—seventy-three years old and I can still put in a day's work. Buried two husbands. Sometimes I think about gettin' a third, but the pickins are slim around here." She struck a match against a table leg and lit her pipe. She puffed on the stem and exhaled with satisfaction.

Edward had never set foot in his great-aunt's house until today. Pop had had no use for relatives, so he'd kept the family apart from kin in Palmyra. Tante V had sometimes brought ointments and tinctures to the house when he and his brothers took sick—or if a beating had been particularly ferocious—but Edward's mother had banned her after the incident with the burning herbs.

That hadn't stopped Jim from sneaking to Tante V's place. He was a regular visitor, and each time he came home he'd tantalized his brothers with mouth-watering descriptions of apple cake, doughnuts, and other delights he'd wheedled from their great-aunt.

"You said we had business," said Edward. He felt uncomfortable at her table. Though they were related, she was practically a stranger, and had once threatened him with fire.

"We do," said Tante V. "I expect you come home on account of Jim. We'll get to your brother, but answer me a question first. Do you see him?"

"Who?"

"Does he come to you in dreams, Eddie? Do you hear his voice in the dark?"

Edward's skin prickled. She was talking about Mr. Jangles.

"I sensed him near you when you was a boy," said Tante V. "Hoverin' like a hawk over a rabbit. Never over your brothers nor your father—not even when your father used his peep stones. Just you. I felt it."

"What did you feel?"

"Coldness. Malice. Wrath."

Edward drank the rest of his liquor. Fire poured down his throat and juniper vapors scoured his nostrils. He slid the cup across the table for a refill.

"Guess I got my answer," said Tante V. "You the one Old Bill picked."

"Old Bill?"

"That's what we called him. Me and mama and my *mémère*." She went to a chest by her bed and returned with an enormous book. She dropped it on the table with a thump: a Bible, bound in amber-colored leather.

Tante V opened the Bible, releasing the musty vanilla scent of old paper. Handwriting crawled down the blank face of the inside cover; names and dates inscribed in ink. Many hands had written in this book, some with blocky thickness, others with slender grace. The inscriptions recorded births, marriages, and deaths. It was a family tree. Edward's family tree.

"This belonged to your great-great *grand-pere*, Etienne Cloud. He was born in Quebec."

Edward nodded. Somewhere in his childhood he'd gleaned that his father's people had fled France for Canada long ago, and then come down from Canada into the American colonies. But he'd never had any formal instruction in his history. The family tree in Tante's Bible intrigued him.

She drew her finger along the limbs that branched out from the root of Etienne Cloud. She stopped briefly at her own entry, made by her father in 1811, and then onward to Edward's father, and then his brothers and himself.

"I wrote you in," she said, tapping Edward's name. "Your brothers, too. See here—Fred and Lydia and their children." She waggled a finger at Edward. "When you gonna add a branch?"

"I'm sorry to say you'll have to amend your record." He told her that Fred's daughter Charlotte had passed in April.

"Oh Lord," she said. "I hadn't heard. How terrible." She rummaged in her hutch for a pencil, then solemnly marked a "d" beneath Charlotte's name with the month and year of her death.

This act of care and recording awakened a curious feeling in Edward. For many years he'd felt himself a man apart, solitary and self-contained, uniquely individual and completely alone. But the lines and threads in Tante's book stitched him to a family and a heritage. He belonged to a place and a people, and here was the proof. He struggled to reconcile this new sense of self.

Tante V went to the cast-iron pot and spooned up two dishes of stew. She brought the dishes to the table with some stale bread. "Eat up, now."

"Thank you," said Edward. He realized he was famished. It was a pork stew with chunks of potato and onion in a rich, fatty broth. He ate with pleasure, and sopped the bread in the broth. Jim hadn't exaggerated their great-aunt's cooking.

"Good?"

"Very good."

"Damn right. That's my granny Lizbet's recipe. Now eat up and listen while I tell you 'bout Etienne Cloud and Old Bill."

17

"Etienne Cloud was born on his family's farm up north over the border," said Tante V. "They lived near the village of St. George on the Chaudière River. That's in Quebec, *oui*?"

"*Oui*," said Edward. "*Parlez-vous Francais, Tante?*"

A shrug. "I picked up a little from my grandmother, but my sisters and I were raised with English."

"And me," said Edward. "I didn't learn until I was an adult."

"Better late than never. If you ever see your great-great-grandfather, you can greet him in his own tongue."

"No chance of that," said Edward.

Tante crooked her head. "No? From all I was told, Etienne was a spirit-man, somewhat like your father. Etienne believed angels spoke to him, and brought him messages from the dead."

"Mmm." Apparently, his family's spiritualist delusions had a long heritage.

"People in St. George came to Etienne to hear messages from their beloved departed. He made charms and talismans to protect against witchcraft and ill fortune. Touched by the spirits, he was. T'were this that led to his trouble."

"*Quelle surprise,*" murmured Edward.

"You a Catholic, Eddie?"

"Me? No." He'd been raised a Congregationalist, but he no strong affiliation to any church. As a boy, his parents had rarely taken him to services. In Boston, Mrs. Coffin had dragged him to the Unitarian church at Brattle Street, but he'd stopped going after he moved into his own apartment. He certainly wasn't a Catholic.

"That's right. Our people are Protestant. Etienne's family were Huguenots from France. You ever hear about them?"

"They were persecuted by the Catholic Church, yes?"

"Indeed. Beaten and murdered. Had their lands stolen. Many were driven from France by fire and sword. A small community of Huguenots settled in St. George. The region was mostly Catholic, but a small community of Hugenots held to their faith."

"Then one year there came to St. George a new priest for the local Catholic parish. He was a Jesuit, lean and tall in a black cassock, and full of Papist arrogance. This priest soon learned how the people of St. George respected Etienne. Catholics and Protestants alike came to Etienne when they desired to hear from their dead. Many wore charms and talismans made by him."

"This angered the priest. If he saw a charm around a parishioner's neck or pinned to their coat, he would snatch it off, stamp it underfoot, and make them pray a penance. He warned his congregation against going to Etienne to speak with their dead. He called such practices diabolic."

"For his part, Etienne ignored the priest. The Jesuit had no authority over him, and many whose talismans had been stomped came back to buy another."

"But the priest continued to speak out against Etienne, calling him a godless heretic who would bring ruin to St. George. One spring, when the river overran its banks and caused great flooding, the priest said it was a sign of God's anger. He declared that if Etienne was tolerated in St. George, even greater misfortune would befall the town."

"At last, the priest himself confronted Etienne as he reaped a field of wheat. The priest demanded that Etienne cease his devilish behaviors. Etienne turned his back on the priest and carried on with his reaping. The Jesuit accused Etienne of being in league with Satan. Etienne decried the priest and called his pope the Anti-Christ. The priest threatened to rouse the village against him. He would drive out Etienne, along with his parents and sisters and grandparents and cousins. His Huguenot devilry would not be tolerated!"

"Etienne grew furious. He had grown up hearing stories of the violence his people had suffered in France—beatings, hangings, burnings, exile. He would not be driven off his own land."

Tante V paused in her story. She poured another finger of her steady and drank it down, then stared into the bottom of the cup.

"What happened?" asked Edward. Despite himself, he'd been drawn into the old woman's tale.

"As the two men argued, the priest slapped Etienne across the face. Without thinking, Etienne struck back—with his scythe. A killing blow."

"Good Christ," said Edward. "He killed a priest?"

"He killed a priest. After that, there was nothing for it. Etienne fled. He went south, crossing the border into Maine. Then he traveled further, hoping to put distance between himself and St. George. He walked for many weeks, hungry and afraid. What's more, Etienne was sick in his heart. He had not meant to kill certainly not a man of the cloth, even if he was a Papist. Etienne felt a stain on his soul. His angels fell silent, leaving him in profound silence. Surely this was a sign he was damned."

"After weeks of walking, Etienne had made his way into the lands around Lake Ontario. He took a day's work when he could, often in exchange for little more than a meal and a barn to sleep in. And always he looked over his shoulder, anxious of the pursuit that must follow: lawmen or agents of the Church."

"Then one morning his fortune changed. He came upon a cart stuck in the mud. It had rained heavily the night before, and the boggy ground had swallowed a wheel. A man pushed at the cart while a woman whipped a straining horse. The woman was queenly, with coal-black hair and flaming eyes. She lashed the horse and shouted at it. Beside her was a child, dark-haired like her mother but plain-faced and shy."

"Etienne joined the man at the back of the cart. The man wore fine clothes, now ruined by mud. Etienne put his strong shoulder to the wagon. With great effort they managed to free the wheel and push the cart onto better ground. The effort left Etienne winded and filthy."

"The man he'd helped was thin and tall. He had long grey hair, a sharp face, and the same haughty air as his wife. He scowled at the mud on his trousers, as if the earth had insulted him. But he was not too proud to acknowledge Etienne's aid. The man stuck out his hand. He spoke to Etienne in English, of which Etienne had only a few words."

"Then the woman said, in excellent French, 'He's come down from the north. *Un Quebecois.*'"

"Etienne wondered how she could know. Perhaps he had muttered an oath while struggling with the wagon? Before he could ponder this, the man spoke again, this time in Etienne's own tongue. He said his name was William Jongold. He owned some land nearby, and could use a strong fellow. He offered to pay wages and put a roof over Etienne's head if Etienne came to work for him."

Tante V paused. She took Edward's empty bowl and filled it again. "You're too stringy for a Drake. You need a wife to make you fat."

Edward accepted the second helping and gestured for his aunt to continue.

"When Etienne heard his own language—for the first time in weeks—it moved him. He suddenly felt less alone. What's more, the offer of work, a place to live, was a balm to his spirit. He had helped these people in their time of need, and they had reciprocated. Perhaps he was not, after all, irredeemable."

"Jongold said he had pressing business and must be off, but he told Etienne where to find him, on the outskirts of a little village called Palmyra. If he wanted work, come and see him. Then the man climbed into the driver's seat and snapped the reins. The cart went around a bend and was gone."

"Etienne wasn't sure what to make of these strange, lordly people and their silent daughter, but he was weary of wandering. Perhaps it was a good idea to stay somewhere for bit, to gather himself and think on what to do next."

"So Etienne pointed his feet toward Palmyra. He arrived a few days later and found Jongold's land. Jongold owned a hundred acres of alfalfa, an apple orchard, a greenhouse. He kept cows and sheep and a flock of geese. He lived in a great house of timber and stone. And as promised, Jongold took Etienne into his service. Etienne lived in a modest cabin on the property. He worked in the fields, he tended the orchard, he cared for the livestock.

"At first Etienne thought only to stay a week or two. But as the days passed, the urge to move on faded. Perhaps the labor appealed to him. He was made for work, not wandering. And when the season turned, winter would be upon him. It would be hard to be alone on the road when the snows came. So he stayed."

"Jongold and his wife, whose name was Gisela, spoke French to him—if the Lady spoke to him at all. Jongold's little daughter Rose taught him English. Etienne missed his family and wished there were some way he could let them know he was safe, but he began to find companionship among the other servants on the property, and at the Protestant church in the village."

"As he settled into his new life, Etienne undertook a kind of penance. He gave half of his monthly wages to those more poor than him. He went to church daily, even though the service was in English and he understood little of it. He fasted on Sundays, taking only water for the whole day. When his own tasks were finished, he would help others around Palmyra—raising a barn, birthing a calf, bringing in a crop. He became known in Palmyra for his kindnesses and helpfulness. After two years in Jongold's service, the angels returned. Their voices brought him messages from the beyond."

"Slowly, shyly, Etienne began to share those messages with his neighbors. Over time, as in St. George, Etienne grew a reputation as a man of curious gifts. People came to him to speak to their dead. He began to fashion talismans, but now he took no money for them."

"Then a new servant came to the house, a lovely woman named Hester. Etienne was smitten. He undertook a patient courtship. He was a handsome, you see. Tall, well-made, and a good man. The courtship blossomed, and Etienne received Jongold's permission to marry."

"The night before the wedding, Jongold called Etienne to his study. The master slid a piece of paper across his grand desk. On it was Etienne's name, and a crude but accurate sketch of his face. It was a wanted notice, with a reward for Etienne's capture.

Etienne gasped—his master knew of his crime! Would Jongold turn him in? Send him away?"

"Instead, Jongold removed the glass cover from an oil lantern on the desk. He gestured to the flame. Etienne took the notice and touched it to the yellow tongue of fire. The paper caught at once. Etienne dropped the burning paper in the fireplace. The fire consumed the notice, leaving only ash. He turned back to his master."

"I care not about your past," said Jongold. "No harm will come to you here, if you are loyal to me."

"Etienne understood. Jongold knew his secret, and this knowledge bound him to Jongold more than any indenture or contract. Etienne felt as if invisible ropes tightened around him. How might his master hold this over him? What price might Jongold extract for his silence? A voice spoke to Etienne. It told him to leave. To walk out of Jongold's study, gather up Hester and their few belongings, and vanish into the night. To go now and not look back."

"As if Jongold knew Etienne's mind, the master said 'Do not risk all that you've gained. You have a good life here. Tomorrow you will be a husband. A year from today you will be a father. Under my protection you will never have to run again.'"

"Despite his misgivings, Etienne agreed. He did have a good life here. Jongold had given him the chance to build it. With Hester at his side, he could make it even better. So he touched his forehead to his master and departed the study. As he went, Jongold left him with a word. 'I waive my Lord's right to your bride. Consider it my wedding gift.'"

"Lord's right? Even as a jest it was in bad taste," said Edward.

"I doubt it was in jest," said Tante V. "Etienne should have listened to the voice that told him to flee. But he didn't want to cast himself and his new bride onto the road. And for a long time, it seemed he'd made the right choice. As Jongold foretold, by the next year Etienne was father to a baby girl. They named her Elizabeth, and called her Lizbet."

Tante V tapped the family tree in the Bible. "Lizbet is my grandmother. I knew her as Granny Lizbet. As you can see here, she was the only child Etienne and Hester ever had—Hester miscarried many times. So they were fierce protective of Lizbet."

"Around the time Lizbet was born, death came to the Jongold house. The lady Gisela and her daughter Rose fell ill. Some malady in the lungs. Jongold summoned doctors from Rochester, from Manhattan, even as far as Philadelphia. Village healers came with herbs and poultices and tinctures. It was even rumored that Jongold tried some black art to save them; a sheep had gone missing, and burnt entrails were later found in a kind of crucible. But no herb, no physic could save them. They died abed, first Rose and then her mother."

"Jongold buried his wife and daughter in Gisela's flower garden. Etienne offered to dig the graves, but Jongold refused. The master himself wrapped the corpses in their winding sheets and laid the bodies in the earth. It was Jongold who covered them with dirt and set the headstones. Jongold wanted no minister. His spoke his own words alone at the burial, while the servants gathered on the great porch to await him."

"Etienne felt sorrow for his master. To lose his wife and his only child, and so close together—what a terrible blow! But he did not spare much thought for Jongold's loss. Etienne had his own daughter to raise. Lizbet grew up working at her mother's side as a house servant. She tended the stove, washed clothes, and cooked and cleaned for the master."

"When Lizbet came into her womanhood she was a beauty, even more lovely than her mother. She had deft delicate hands, hazel eyes, and a figure that swiveled men's heads. That included Master Jongold. He had never re-married. And as Lizbet blossomed, the master began to dote on her, pay her attention. Unwanted attention. You understand?"

Edward nodded. "He wanted to have his way with her."

"Yes. And it seemed only a matter of time before he did. His gaze lingered on her. His hand might brush her waist or her bottom as she passed. When she bent to serve him his dinner, his eyes crawled into her bodice."

"Did your granny speak of this to her father?" asked Edward.

"Ah, no. Jongold told Lizbet he could make trouble for her father —terrible trouble—if she were to complain. So she bore his pinches and fondles in silence."

Tante V paused to draw deeply from her pipe. "Now, in the years Etienne was in service to Jongold, strange tales fell to his ears about his master: that Jongold was a baron from Westphalia who had fled to the New World to escape accusations of sorcery. Or Jongold was a Carpathian prince, banished from his lands for trafficking in black arts. That his lady wife Gisela, each solstice, had taken demon lovers in the forest. That Jongold was a thousand years old, and had kept himself alive through diabolic forces."

"Nonsense," said Edward.

"Etienne thought the same," said Tante V. "Jongold was wealthy and prideful and foreign. Besides French, he knew German and Latin and an old Slavic tongue. He collected books and spent hours a day reading. He held himself apart from village life, and never bothered to hide his scorn for those he considered beneath them—which was everyone, as far as Etienne could see. Such behaviors were certain to spur rumor and speculation among village folk."

"Of all the books Jongold owned, there was one he treasured above all. He kept it in his study, close to hand. When Jongold visited the graves of his wife and daughter, he often brought this book with him. Sometimes the servants heard him talking, as if Gisela and Rose were present. Or he'd sit with his back against his wife's headstone and study the pages."

"What was this book?" asked Edward.

"Granny Lizbet called it *le livre rampant*. The 'creeping book.' As a servant in Jongold's house she saw it often. It was old and heavy, and it made her shiver to look on it. No one besides the master was allowed to touch it, not even to bring it to him nor put it back on its shelf. That was fine with her. She despised that book. She believed Jongold studied it so that he might gain power over men and nature. Unnatural power, eh?"

Edward said "So Etienne made talismans and talked to angels, and Jongold had a sorcerous book—two peas in a pod."

"No, Eddie! They were nothing alike. Etienne did what he did to help people, to ease a hurt or bring healing. But Jongold? Granny Lizbet told me his aims were foul—domination and pain."

Tante V recounted what happened next. As she spoke, Edward sensed this tale had been told many times. Her words had the contours of an heirloom, passed down through the generations from parent to child and polished by long handling.

"One day, Jongold decided he wanted more from Lizbet than a squeeze or fondle. The master called her to his study. He put his hands on her. He meant to ravish her. Granny Lizbet would not submit. She struggled against him. She clawed his face and cried for help."

"The master struck her, a blow that knocked Lizbet to the floor. Her mother Hester heard the commotion. She came running from the kitchen to find Jongold looming over her daughter and rucking up her skirts. With a cry she snatched up Lizbet and bolted from the house. Etienne was returning from an errand in the village. The moment he saw them, he knew what had happened. Red with rage, he ran into the study and confronted Jongold. Etienne declared he was taking his family and leaving."

"You daren't!" the master said. "I know what you are. I'll see that you're hanged. And I'll have that damned girl!"

"Etienne spit at his master's feet. He cared not for Jongold's threats. He turned and made for the door, determined to leave that very moment. But Jongold fell on him. Though old and crooked, the master was strong. Perhaps the strength was granted by his devilish book. The two men grappled like wrestlers, cursing and yowling as they crashed into walls and shelves and knocked bric-brac to the floor."

"As they battled, a lamp overturned and smashed. The lamp oil caught fire. Flames skittered across a rug and climbed woolen drapes, yet still the two men fought. The fire rushed from room to room, climbing rafters and running along roof beams. Quickly the house was engulfed. Somehow Etienne escaped. He dashed outside and watched in horror as flames devoured the house. The fire burned so hot and for so long, the only thing left were the stone foundations."

"What happened to Jongold?" asked Edward.

"He died in the fire. Rumor was Etienne killed him—strangled him or beat him to death, and then set the fire to cover it up."

"Is that true?"

"If it was, my granny never said. And the truth didn't matter. Once again, Etienne had to run. He knew he'd be hung whether he was guilty or not. He left his wife and daughter and fled west. He told Hester and Lizbet to stay and wait—he'd send for them once it was safe. But they never heard from him again. They were never sure if he was caught and hung, or drowned crossing a river, or what."

"As for Jongold, he had no relatives and no will, so the county auctioned the land and cast the servants to the wind. A minister in

Canandaigua hired Lizbet and her mother. But Lizbet was sent back to Palmyra after just a year. By that time, she had a husband at her side—my granddad Nathan Cooper—and an infant in her arms. That infant was my mother, Mercy."

"Why was Lizbet sent back?"

"The minister said Lizbet was...peculiar. That is, peculiar things happened around her. A dish might leap off a shelf and shatter on the floor. A lamp would blow out in a room with no draft. At night, rappings and creakings sounded behind the walls and in the eaves, loud enough to wake the whole house. The minister's five children had nightmares of a skulking, scowling figure. At last, the minister couldn't take it; he paid off Lizbet and sent her away."

Tante V tilted her chin at Edward. "Now we're coming to your part in this, so mind what I say."

Edward wanted no role in this narrative. He pushed his bowl away, his appetite gone.

"Granny Lizbet said it was the spirit of Old Bill who'd made mischief in the minister's house. And when she came back to Palmyra, Old Bill followed."

"Old Bill. You mean William Jongold, her master. The one who died in the fire."

"Yes, Eddie. Old Bill is the ghost of William Jongold. He troubled my grandmother for the rest of her life. And when Granny Lizbet passed, Old Bill fixed on my mother. Then on me and my sister, Juliette. That's your father's mother, Juliette Drake. She died giving birth to your father, God rest her. Old Bill troubled all of us. I've heard his footsteps in the night, felt his cold breath on my neck. More than once I woke screaming from horrible dreams of him. And then you come along, and somethin' in you drew Old Bill to you."

Edward cleared his throat. He couldn't look his great-aunt in the eye.

"Eddie, Old Bill hates our family for what happened. His hate follows us down the generations. He wants to make us pay."

"A broken dish, a creaking floor, a bad dream—that's not proof of a ghost."

"He's real, Eddie. Old Bill is real, and full of rage against the children of Etienne. His spirit won't move on 'til he has his vengeance."

Edward frowned.

"You ever seen Old Bill, Eddie?"

Yes, thought Edward. I call him Mr. Jangles. I could tell you of my childhood visions, or his recent appearance in Boston. But he didn't say those things aloud. It would only encourage his great-aunt.

Instead, he experienced a kind of clarity---and with it a sense of relief. Here was the source of his morbid defect, that crack in his psyche where apparitions slipped from his imagination into waking life. He had grown up among a people steeped in folk magic and superstition. They had crafted a tale of a malicious spirit and passed it down the generations like an inheritable trait. Stories of William Jongold must've been swirling around him his entire life. He'd breathed them like air, eaten and drunk of them at the family table. No wonder he'd imagined a ghost haunting him.

What's more, his boyish mind had turned 'Jongold' into 'Jangles,' and used those stories to account for the terrible, inexplicable things that had happened to him, especially the ghastly shock of finding those poor dead children.

"I'm not mad," he told himself. "Not at all. I did the most rational thing a child could do to account for his suffering. I told myself a story."

Tante V watched from behind a skein of pipe smoke. "You don't believe me. You think I'm a foolish old woman."

"I don't think you're foolish, Tante. You've just given too much credence to old wives' tales."

Tante V clucked. "Or maybe you too proud to heed old wives. The spirit of William Jongold is real. He hate our family for what happened. For generations he been tryin' to strike at us. He did it once, when your Dad found them murdered children. Now he's doin' it again."

"What do you mean? You say Old Bill killed those children?"

"Yes, Eddie. He kilt them and set their bodies like a trap, so that a Drake would be blamed and hung. It nearly worked against your father. Now he's lured Jim into the same trap—and he's hopin' to catch you, too."

Edward shook his head. "Your logic's at fault, Tante. If Old Bill can commit murder, why didn't he just kill Granny Lizbet? Or you? Or me?"

"'Cause we got protection. Etienne Cloud saw to it. He made a shield against Old Bill so his spirit can't strike us directly. Old Bill got to come at us cross-ways, with mischief and sly plots. That's what Granny Lizbet told me, and I believe her."

A clever rationalization. He suspected his great-aunt had a whole store of rationalizations to affirm her beliefs, no matter how illogical they might be. "So when Jim found Liza Ames's body two weeks ago, that was that a trap laid by Old Bill?"

"Yes, Eddie. That poor child was a snare set for Jim. And Jim was a snare set for you—to draw you back here."

Edward rubbed his eyes. When his great-aunt had showed him his family tree and served him a meal at her table, he'd felt a sense of kinship awaken in him, like the tingle that creeps into a sleeping limb when it wakes. But as she'd spooled out her ridiculous tale, the limb had gone dead again, leaving him cold and numb.

"You think I'm telling lies, Eddie."

"No, Tante. You believe what you say. But a man has committed these crimes, not a ghost."

She rapped her knuckles on the table. "Old Bill gonna trap you if you keep thinkin' that way! He's a devious spirit. He broods on his vengeance like a spider in its web."

Edward held up a hand. "Please, enough of Old Bill. We need to talk about my brother."

Tante V frowned. "Alright. *On parle.*"

"Have you seen Jim? Do you know where he might be hiding?"

"He come over and fix a leak in my roof, but that was three, four weeks ago. I ain't seen him since. I think Jim's long gone. That's for the best. If the sheriff catch him, he gonna hang your brother. You should go, too. I know you want to do right by Jim, but it's dangerous here."

"I know it," said Edward. "Those boys who attacked me were proof. And I met Sheriff Cole today. He made it clear I'm not welcome in Palmyra."

Tante V nodded. "Keep away from Cole. He got that badge, so he think he can make his own laws—especially in the Bottoms. And maybe he can."

"I'll steer clear of him." Edward gathered the dishes and cups from the table and set them in a washtub. "Thank you for intervening with those lads, you and Sherman both. And thank you for the meal. I'll take my leave now."

"Where you goin'?"

"I have to meet a friend. Her niece is Cassie Brown, one of the missing children. I'm going to help search for her, and for Jim. I suspect you're right that Jim has fled Palmyra, but there's one or two places he might be hiding. I feel obliged to look."

As Edward made for the door, Tante V grabbed his wrist. "Be careful, Eddie. You think Old Bill is just a story, but I know better. Old Bill got somethin' planned, and you part of it. For better or worse, you part of it."

18

The cave mouth gaped dumbly in the cold afternoon light. It tunneled into a high ridge of schist and shale. Edward paused beneath the cave's overhang to let his eyes adjust to the gloomy interior. After his curious conversation with Tante V, he'd made the long walk out to the Forrest farm to see Evelyn Forrest and her family to offer his services in the search for Cassie Brown. No one had answered to his knock on the farmhouse door, and he'd seen no one around the barn or pasture. He supposed the family must be out looking for Cassie. He hadn't thought to bring pencil or paper so he didn't leave a note. He would have to try to contact them tomorrow.

He'd decided to use the remaining daylight to check this cave. Jim might be hiding inside. He ducked beneath the threshold and went in. Dry sand and mineral grit crunched beneath his shoes. He and his brothers had played in this cave as boys. The rocky ceiling was high enough to stand upright, even for a grownup. It was an ideal bolt hole for a fugitive; you could pass a night or two here, hidden from searchers and sheltered from the elements.

Edward lit the wick on a candle he'd borrowed from Tante V and held it aloft. In the flickering light he scanned for signs of Jim: footprints, food scraps, the remains of a fire. Nothing. The cave was barren.

He moved deeper inside. He and his brothers had been forbidden from playing here, so of course they'd flocked to it. Sometimes they'd pretended the cave was their Indian longhouse, where they held war councils and planned raids. Other times it was a robbers' den, heaped high with plunder. Mostly it was a refuge from Pop.

At the back of the cave the ground fell away in a sheer drop, as if cut by a giant axe. Below was a shallow, spring-fed pool. The drop was a good twenty feet, far enough to grievously wound or even kill anyone who toppled over. Cautiously, Edward peered over the ledge. Stalagmite spears bristled from the placid water.

If you scaled down the precipice and sloshed across the pool, you'd come to a narrow crack in the far wall. Through the crack was a warren of passages leading underground. How far they went, no one could say. Locals called the crack 'the Devil's Smile,' so named for its power to lure people inside—money diggers, explorers, and foolish children. Most of them never came back out. When the moon was high, it was said you could hear voices whispering "Come in, come in! Come in, come in!"

Edward himself had passed through the Devil's Smile many years ago. Beyond that crack was a darkness so black it almost had weight. He'd nearly died in there. At the memory of it, a clammy sweat dampened his forehead.

Edward stepped back from the precipice, then mopped himself with a handkerchief. He shivered at how foolish he'd been to go in—and how lucky to come back out.

He wondered if Jim was hiding in those passages. Even as a brave and reckless boy Jim had never dared the Devil's Smile. Would he now, desperate as he was? Edward hoped not; he couldn't bear the thought of worming his way in there again.

A squeak echoed overhead. Edward raised the candle. Hundreds and hundreds of brown bats hung like wrinkled fruit from the craggy ceiling. They appeared to be asleep, but tiny movements rippled through the colony: twitching noses, quivering wings, yawning mouths. Edward held his breath and backed out of the cave, not wanting to wake the bats and set them swarming.

Outside, he wandered down a narrow track that led to an abandoned orchard. Weeds and brambles cluttered the arbor. The hoary trees, unpruned for years, still bore apples. Edward wasn't tempted; the fruit looked mealy and worm-ridden. Fallen apples littered the ground, and the orchard stank of sour rot. Late-season wasps, not yet killed by the cold, ambled among the windfall and buzzed sluggishly from one deliquescing pile to another.

Beyond the orchard he came to the fieldstone foundations of a sprawling manse that had toppled over long before he'd been born. Thorns and strangling vines climbed a massive hearth and a stub of stone chimney, its geometry still visible beneath the green and brown drapery.

Shallow pits scarred the ground. Money diggers had dug these pits, come to try their luck among the bones of the estate. Earthen mounds of dirt slumped beside the pits, shaggy with crabgrass and dandelions.

Pop had found his seeing stones among these old foundations. He'd dug them out of the ground many years ago, and incorporated them as glittering props into his spiritualist humbug. Edward wondered which pit was his father's—a hole and a moldering pile of dirt the only marks James Drake had left on the world.

A mournful wind skulked among the mounds. This place had the air of a derelict cemetery, the pits the unkempt graves of disappointed men. Gooseprickles dimpled Edward's arms. Did Pop's shade still linger here, nosing through the grounds for some treasure to change his fortune?

"Don't be foolish," Edward scolded himself. "No slipping into your ghostly habits." Nevertheless, his blood was cold. Tiny hairs on the back of his neck stiffened in alarm. If Edward turned around now, would he see his father? Would the old man drift through the weeds, a whiff of pipe tobacco on the wind, one hand reaching to catch his son?

Head down, limbs stiff, Edward marched quickly from the abandoned lot, embarrassed to be chased off by his own imagination, yet unwilling to test it.

19
PALMYRA, 1869
THE HAUNTED CHILD

Eddie Drake woke to golden sunlight spilling through the window above his bed. Specks of dust drifted through the sunbeams. He drifted with them, pleasantly suspended between sleep and waking. The morning unfurled bright and clear and hot.

Then a hand shook him. It was Fred, already up and dressed. At the front door, Jim was slipping outside. Fred pointed to the loft where their parents slept. A low groan came from above, then a rough clearing of the throat. Pop was waking up.

Eddie understood. Pop had just put in a month's work at the sawmill to earn some cash. Six days a week he'd unloaded logs from carts, trimmed knots and burls from the trunks, swept floors, and cleaned and oiled the machinery. He'd come home each night powdered like a dumpling: sawdust on his neck, sawdust in his hair, sawdust in his ears and throat. He'd sneezed dust into his booger-rag and hawked it up in his spittle. For weeks Pop had been too tired to do more than duck his head in a basin of cold water, swallow some supper, and climb up to the loft to sleep. Those had been good days.

Then yesterday Pop had gotten his wages. He'd returned home at sundown and put some money into Mama's hand for flour, cooking oil, dried beans, and salt pork. The rest he'd already spent on bottles of beer and a big jug of mash whiskey. He took a chair out to the dooryard, set his bottles and jug in a half-circle around him, and began to drink.

Most times Pop liked to carouse while he drank, whooping and hollering with other men in the false conviviality of liquor. But now and then he took to his drink like a monk in a cell, silent and solitary. This was one of those times. He'd started with the beer, sipping from the bottles as the dusk spread its skirts around the Bottoms. After the beer was gone, he'd switched to the jug. He drank methodically, using his elbow like a lever to tip the jug up to his mouth. He stopped only to piss behind the house. If a neighbor sauntered over to share a remark and cadge a drink, Pop ignored them until they left.

Dusk gave way to dark. The moon climbed over the treetops and stars came out. The jug rose and fell. Between sips he stared into the middle distance, face blank. At last, near midnight, he'd toppled unconscious off his chair. Mama woke the boys. Together they dragged Pop inside and laid him by the stove. He'd come around long enough to find his way up to the loft and bed.

This morning, Eddie knew what came next. Pop would rumble around the house woozy and ill-tempered, his eyes bloodshot, his head wrecked. Smart boys stayed out of Pop's way after a bender. Jim was already gone. Fred was leaving now. He'd woken Eddie, but he wouldn't wait while Eddie dressed. Eddie was alone on the ground floor. He heard his father sit up in bed, groaning and coughing.

Eddie leapt from the pallet and pulled on trousers. If Pop made it down the ladder before Eddie left, he'd growl "Where you think you're goin?" and Eddie would be trapped. And he would irritate Pop no matter what he did; help Mama with chores, sit quietly with a book, fidget in the corner—it made no difference. Eventually Pop would clobber him for some minor infraction, or no reason at all.

The boards overhead creaked. Fear spurted into Eddie's muscles. He found a shirt on the floor and, not caring whose it was, flung it over his head. He raced barefoot across the cabin and dashed out the door. Outside he wriggled the shirt down over his torso. It hung near his knees. The sleeves draped down past his hands. Must be one of Jim's or Fred's. Too late to change it. Eddie pelted for the woods, shirt-sleeves flapping. He wanted to get out of sight of his father's eye, out of earshot of his voice. The sweet June air lent him wings. He flew through the tall cool grass behind the house and into a belt of green pine and blue fir.

As he ran, he felt a sting of guilt for leaving Mama behind. She would be alone with Pop all day, exposed to the gales of anger that would blow from his hangover. Eddie wished he were big enough to keep Pop from hitting Mama. Big enough to give Pop a taste of his own medicine. But he wasn't. And he knew she would tell him to go, to slip into the daylight and sunshine. To stay away until dusk while she tried to temper her husband's mood with biscuits, coffee, and various hangover remedies sent over by Tante V. Mama was protecting her boy and he loved her for it.

He'd run from the house with no direction in mind. Safe now, he angled toward the abandoned orchard. He'd had no breakfast and he was hungry. He might find apples growing in the trees. Most of them were bad, but with careful inspection you might pick one or two you could stomach. And there was a blackberry bramble near the orchard. The bramble was wild and thorny and usually full of birds, but Eddie could scare off the birds and maybe get enough of the fruit to quiet his belly.

As he traveled, he wondered where his brothers had gone. He guessed Fred was at the creek. Fred liked to sit up high in a tree, silent and watchful as a catamount. Fred said he enjoyed the sound of the water running over the stony bed. Jim might be anywhere. On long summer days like this, Jim might not come back to the Bottoms 'til the moon was up.

Eddie's route took him past the cave where he and his brothers sometimes played. As he passed the entrance, he heard crying. He was alarmed but not surprised—folks heard all kinds of voices in the cave: moans, weeping, and whispered invitations to come in, come in. Everyone knew it was Mummer Ben. Mummer Ben was a money-digger who'd braved the Devil's Smile and the tunnels beyond it. Skinny and scabby with rotten teeth and a cracked smile, Mummer Ben told anyone who'd listen about his discoveries in the cave: passages that burrowed deep into the ground, glittering caverns of mica and pyrite, toad stools tall enough for a man to sit under.

Even more wonderful, he said that after a long journey that took him deep underground, he'd come across fiery crack in the earth. Out of that crack crawled fearsome salamanders the size of dogs. The salamanders glowed red, orange, and violet, and blew fire from their nostrils. They guarded wonderful treasures—diamonds as big as your fist, glittering emeralds and rubies, and a vein of gold so rich the man who mined it could make himself a Senator.

Mummer Ben carried a silver dish on his expeditions. No one knew where he'd gotten good silver. The dish was his instrument for treasure-hunting. When he poured clean water into the dish and prayed to the Holy Spirit, he said a map appeared on the surface of the water to lead him through the passages. With his silver dish to guide him to the lair of the salamanders, all he had to do was tame the beasts and collect their wealth. But the last time he'd gone through the Devil's Smile, he hadn't come out. That was a year ago.

Sometimes when Eddie and his brothers played in the cave, Jim told them Mummer Ben was still alive, worming his skinny body through narrow passages. The old treasure hunter crawled around in the dark hoping to snatch a child. If Mummer Ben caught you, he'd tie you up and carve you like a roast to feed to the salamanders. He'd cut you bit by bit—first a toe, then your tongue, then a chunk of meat from your leg. You'd be alive while he sliced you up, and you'd have to watch the salamanders eat you piece by piece.

Eddie assumed the crying he heard must be Mummer Ben's, leaking up from the opening at the back of the cave. He paused at the overhang and peeked in—if it was Mummer Ben, he wanted to see. Then he'd run to the creek to tell Fred.

It wasn't Mummer Ben. It was a Negro girl. Her black hair was pulled tight in a pair of pigtails. Eddie guessed she was about his age. She stood by the precipice at the back of the cave and looked down at the pool. Her shoulders hitched as she cried. Then she called out "Luke? Can you hear me? Luke, come back!"

Come back? thought Eddie. Had someone gone *into* the passages? His curiosity overrode his apprehension. He crept into the cave. The girl heard his footsteps and spun around. Her eyes were wide and red.

"You all right?" asked Eddie.

The girl turned away. She wiped her eyes and nose on the sleeves of her dress. Then she rounded on Eddie, her expression fierce. "Get out!" she commanded. "This ain't your business!"

"Is someone lost?" asked Eddie. "Did someone go into the tunnels?"

The girl's fierceness crumpled. Her lips drew down and her shoulders sagged. She covered her face and sobbed. "My brother Luke. He went in a long time ago and hasn't come out. I'm scared for him!"

She was right to be scared. Grownups said those tunnels were dangerous—narrow and dark and twisted all around like entrails. Eddie wasn't even supposed to be at the cave. Mama forbade it. He suspected this girl and her brother weren't supposed to be here either. And now she was in bad trouble.

"Why'd he go in?" asked Eddie.

"We were telling stories about Mummer Ben's treasure. I said I wished I could get a diamond. Luke said he didn't care about diamonds or gold. He wanted to catch a salamander and take it home. He wanted it for a pet. It could live in the hearth."

Eddie's jaw fell open at the magnificence of this idea. A giant salamander for a pet! He pictured a brightly glowing amphibian, big as a dog, curled up in his own fireplace. It would wrap itself in its long tail and radiate heat like a stove. Eddie would feed it bits of his supper, or catch mice and squirrels for it. On cold nights it could crawl under the blankets with him. He could teach it to blow jets of fire at Jim. It could protect him and Mama from Pop. Maybe it would even scare off Mr. Jangles! No one would hurt him with such a fearsome friend at his side.

"Your brother knows where the treasure cave is?" asked Eddie.

"He said he did. I said he was a liar. He said he wasn't, so I dared him to go in. I dared him and he went! It's my fault." She sobbed again. "What am I gonna do?"

"We could rescue him," said Eddie. He surprised himself by saying this. He didn't want to go into those tunnels, but he was strangely moved by this girl and her plight. He wanted to help her. And he wanted a salamander. A red one!

"How?"

"Look," said Eddie. He went to a section of the cave where a narrow hole had eroded in the rock face. He and his brothers stowed a few supplies in the hole for when they played here: a bit of thread, a tin cup, an old jackknife, a candle, and a matchbox with a few matches. He removed the candle and matchbox and showed them to her.

"Oh!" she said. "Me and Luke brought a lantern, but he took it in with him."

An idea came to him. "C'mon!" He led the girl out of the cave to the old orchard. Shaggy vines had grown up around the trees. Eddie began to pull at them. "We can tie vines together, like a rope. We can lay them out behind us, to help us find our way back!"

Immediately the girl helped Eddie pull down long strands of green vine. They dragged a bundle back to the cave to untangle them and knot the ends together. As they worked, their hands and fingers turned slimy and greenish. Sometimes the knots broke and they had to start again. But after fifteen or twenty minutes of concentrated effort, they had a longish strand. Eddie wasn't sure how long, but it seemed like a lot.

As they regarded their work Eddie's stomach growled loud enough for the girl to hear. Eddie blushed. The girl reached into a pocket of her dress and took out a cloth napkin. A square of cornbread was folded inside. She offered it to Eddie.

"I already had my breakfast," she said. "I brought it for the salamanders, but you can take it."

Eddie hesitated. His father never took charity—certainly not from Negros—and he demanded the same of his sons. But the cornbread looked good. It was moist and crumbly, with one edge crisped brown where it had touched the side of the pan. Sheepishly he accepted the food. The cornbread was sweet and delicious. With an effort he saved the last couple of bites. They would need something to coax a salamander to come back with them.

"Thank you," said Eddie, handing her the napkin with the remaining morsels "It was good."

The girl nodded. "My momma's the best cook. My name's Evelyn." She held out a brown hand. Here was another of his father's taboos—Drakes didn't associate with coloreds. Then again, he'd already broken that rule by talking to her and eating her cornbread. And to hell with the old man! Eddie took her hand. "I'm Eddie."

"E and E," said Evelyn. "Both our names start with the same letter."

"That's right," said Eddie. "E and E." He took this as a good sign.

"I'm eleven," said Evelyn. "How old are you?"

"Almost eleven," said Eddie. This was stretching the truth. His birthday was months away, but he didn't want to yield any authority to a girl.

Introductions concluded, they gathered up their vines and walked to the precipice. The bottom seemed very far.

"How did your brother get down?"

"He climbed. That way." Evelyn pointed to a spot. Eddie studied it, lips pursed. He thought he could make out little cracks and protrusions that would serve as handholds and footholds.

"Can you climb?" he asked. He had little experience with girls, Negro or otherwise.

Evelyn scoffed. She dropped to her stomach, not caring about her dress, and put her legs over the side.

"Hey wait!" cried Eddie. He'd meant to go first, but she was already over the lip and scrambling down. She went quickly but carefully, testing handholds and finding places for her feet. In less than a minute she was at the bottom. Her brown shoes splashed in the shallow pool.

That didn't seem so bad. He leaned over and tossed down the coil of vines. "Catch!" Evelyn caught it neatly.

Now it was his turn. Eddie patted his pockets to check that the candle and matches were safe, then got down and eased himself over the edge. His bare toes found a crevice. The rock was rough and damp, but the foothold felt secure. He began his descent.

Soon he was next to Evelyn at the bottom. The pads of his feet were scratched and stinging. He dipped them in the sandy, shallow pool. The water was cold! Around them, cone-shaped stalagmites rose from the water. The air was damp and musky. A droplet of water fell from the ceiling and plinked into the pool.

It was dim and shadowy down here, the light from the cave's mouth barely reaching. Across the pool rose a slight embankment. A crack in the wall grinned in the gloaming--the Devil's Smile. It was a sideways grin, maybe six feet from bottom to top, and very narrow. Eddie guessed that once they passed through, it would be pitch black. He shivered.

Evelyn studied the opening. She bit her lip. If she wasn't here, Eddie would've turned around and climbed back up.

"You got the candle?" Her voice was trembly.

Eddie patted his pocket. "Right here."

"Let's go then."

20

Evelyn stuck her head into the crack. "Luke!" she called. "Luke, can you hear me?" Holding their breath, they waited for a response. None came.

"Give me the candle," said Evelyn.

Eddie thought he should carry it. It was his, after all. But if Evelyn was going first, it made sense for her to take it. Reluctantly he handed it over.

"Matches," she said.

"I'll do it," said Eddie. There were five matches in the box—four, once he lit this one. He struck it against the rough strip on the side of the box, hoping neither the match head nor the strip was too damp. His hope was rewarded. A pinhead of orange fire ignited. Quickly Edward touched it to the wick. Then he blew out the match and put the dead stick back in the box. He wasn't sure what good it would do, but he didn't want to waste anything.

Candle in hand, Evelyn turned her body sideways and slipped through the Devil's Smile. Eddie followed. God it was dark! The candle threw barely any light. Evelyn was a shadowy blob just ahead of Eddie. Fear squeezed his heart.

"Don't forget our trail," came Evelyn's voice.

She meant the vines. Eddie had forgotten. He dropped one end and let the strand pay out behind him. They crept forward slowly. The passage was just wide enough to walk single-file, but the rock ceiling began to slant down. After five or six steps they had to stoop, then crouch. Finally they were forced to crawl.

The ground was damp and hard. The passage smelled musty. Dank air kissed his brow.

And it was dark! He'd never known such dark. It hung like a weight around his neck. Eddie tried to fix his eyes on the tiny candle flame, but Evelyn's body often blocked it. How had this boy Luke gone in here by himself?

Evelyn stopped. "Luke!" she shouted. "Luke, can you hear me?" Her voice was flat and dull. The candle guttered as fetid air drifted up the passage.

"We should go back," whispered Eddie. He wanted to get out. They would have to crawl backwards because there was no room to turn around.

"Not yet," said Evelyn. Eddie considered backing out anyway. But no, it would be cowardly to leave the girl by herself. The awful dark had yet to overthrow his pride.

They inched forward another ten paces when Evelyn stopped again. Edward bumped into her. In the meager candle light he saw that the passage cinched to narrow gap in the rock face. They would have to squirm on their bellies if they wanted to go forward.

"I don't wanna go in there," whispered Eddie. What if he got stuck? He imagined tons of rock wedging against his ribs, pressing his head, cracking him open like a chestnut.

"I don't want to either," said Evelyn. "But I can't leave my brother." She drew a deep breath and wriggled through the crack. Now even the tiny glow of the candle was gone. Utter dark fell. Even with his eyes peeled there was no light. Eddie could see nothing. He had never imagined such a darkness could exist. It was horrible! Panic pressed him. Go back or forward?

He chased after the light, squeezing into the crack like a blind snake. The stone was rough against his belly. Rock scraped his scalp and cheeks. He slithered and slithered. The passage was so narrow it was hard to breath. He felt himself getting light-headed. How long was this tunnel? Where was Evelyn? What if the passage opened on some bottomless hole and she'd fallen in? What if Mummer Ben waited on the other side? Jim said Mummer Ben was lonely. And hungry.

No no no. Eddie started to wriggle backwards. He was ashamed to leave Evelyn, but he needed to get out. He needed to breathe! Once free he would run home and tell what happened, even though it meant a beating. He would run home and tell Mama. Then grown-ups could come and get her.

A tiny glow appeared, perhaps a yard ahead of him. It was Evelyn. She was shining the candle for him. Eddie crawled forward again, desperate to reach the light. He pulled himself from the cervix of the passage and into an open space. Evelyn helped him to his feet. He sucked in great deep breaths, greedy for air.

"Where are we?" he whispered.

"Look." She held the candle aloft.

They were in a chamber bigger than Eddie's house. Overhead, dimly visible, was a dome of rock buttressed with columns of limestone. Mineral flecks caught the meager flame and threw it back. Protrusions bulged from the walls like the bones and teeth of buried giants.

A churchly silence hung in this space. Uncounted ages had gathered in this pocket of time. Eddie felt a compulsion to kneel. He sidled next to Evelyn until their shoulders touched, wanting human contact in this inhuman place. She leaned into him.

Yet even as he boggled at this chamber, his panic eased. He was standing upright now. His chest and belly weren't being squeezed. He had Evelyn for company and a burning candle. He almost felt bold. Even Jim had never dared the Devil's Smile!

They crossed the chamber. At the far end, a new passage gaped.

The opening was surprisingly wide—they could walk upright through it. The passage traveled an unknown length, bending rightwards and sloping gently down before being lost in the darkness. The passage looked man-made, the walls and floor smooth.

"Who dug this?" whispered Eddie.

"No one," said Evelyn. "Water did this."

"There ain't no water here."

"I'll bet there was a long time ago. My Daddy reads about geology and such. He said if lots of water flows long enough, it can carve through anything. Even rock."

Eddie doubted this, but he wasn't inclined to argue. Evelyn got down on one knee. "Look!" A faint shoe print was impressed in the dust. "Luke must've gone this way!"

A clue, thought Eddie. They had a clue!

"Luke!" called Evelyn into the passage. "Luke, are you there? We comin' for you!"

The only response was a faint echo.

"C'mon," said Evelyn.

"Hold on," said Eddie. He began to gather up the strand of vines that he'd trailed out behind them.

"What are you doing?" gasped Evelyn.

"There's not much left," said Eddie. "And we don't need it just now. The tunnel we came through only goes one way. When we make back to this chamber, we'll know where to go."

Evelyn considered this, then nodded.

Together they crossed into the new passage. The candle's light was weak. In a few steps the cathedral chamber was lost behind them. The passage smelled like a root cellar. It was cool down here, almost cold. Eddie thought of the hot morning sun and wished even a single beam could come down and light their way.

They shuffled forward. Now and then Evelyn called out her brother's name. Her voice bounced off the smooth walls. When the echoes faded, only silence remained. Where was Luke? How far had he gone?

Then Evelyn yelped and dropped the candle. A dribble of wax had burned her hand. The flame traced the arc of its fall before hitting the ground and going out. Monstrous dark rushed in and swallowed the children. Eddie shrieked and nearly bolted. That would have been the death of him, but Evelyn gripped his wrist.

"Hold still! The candle's got to be near my feet. I can find it, but you got to stay right here! We daren't get separated. Understand?"

Eddie nodded. Then he realized she couldn't see him nod. She was right in front of him but she couldn't see him, nor he her. God, he hated this darkness! The fabric of her dress whispered as she bent to the ground. He heard the soft patting of her hands probing the dust. She patted for a long time. Eddie stood perfectly still, his whole body clenched against panic.

This is what it's like to be dead, he thought. This is what it's like to be buried. All the dead of the world might be down here. Smoky terror slipped inside him. It pooled in his belly and filled his lungs. It drifted up the ladder of his spine and clouded his skull.

"Eddie, you're dead," whispered the smoke. *"You're dead but you ain't realized it till now. You ne'er even made it out of the house. Pop caught you, Eddie. He caught you and beat you so bad he killed you. You knew it would happen someday. That's what Mr. Jangles was trying to tell you. That's why he showed you the children. Because you'd be killed too.*

"No," whispered Eddie. "No."

Your body's goin' cold on the floor. You're a ghost now. It was your ghost that ran through the grass and found Evelyn in the cave. She brought you here 'cause it's where you belong now. You'll never see Mama again. Nor Fred nor Jim nor anyone. You're here with us in the dark. You'll never leave."

He began to cry, a mewling pathetic sound. He forgot Evelyn, forgot her brother, forgot everything but his terror and despair. He was dead and he would never leave this terrible place. He pressed his dirty hands to his face and sobbed.

Then arms wrapped around him. He felt a cheek press against

his. Coils of springy hair tickled his face. He smelled sweat and dust and a kind of spicy scent, like pepper and cinnamon. It was Evelyn.

"It's OK," she whispered. "It's OK, Eddie. I found the candle. It's OK."

21

With trembling hands he lit another match. It took several tries, but finally the match came to life. He lit the candle and then let the match burn as long as he could before blowing it out. The light that remained was pathetic, almost comic, against the ravening dark. But to Eddie it felt like mercy. He and Evelyn shuffled forward, holding hands in the wide passage. Eddie let the vine trail out behind him.

They found their way to a second chamber, smaller than the first but also girded with limestone columns. Above them hung jagged stalactites, sharp-tipped as spears and likely as deadly should they fall. As the passage had only gone one way, Eddie again stowed their length of vine.

Carefully they crossed the chamber. At the other side they ducked under an overhang and found themselves on a kind of stony porch. The ground sloped steeply down, the rock humped like a whale's back. They sat and slid down together. Their feet raised puffs of dust when they landed. Eddie wondered if they'd be able to scramble back up. But he set that worry aside as a new problem confronted them.

Two passages opened before them, one bending right, the other left.

"Which way?" breathed Eddie.

Evelyn frowned. She squatted down and scanned the ground, looking for tracks. If Luke had come this way, there was no sign. Eddie fretted. "What do we do?"

Evelyn shouted down the left-hand passage. "Luke? Can you hear me? Luke? Where are you?"

Again they waited. The echoes died away. Then Eddie thought he heard something. "Listen!" he hissed. He leaned into the opening. The sound came again, faint and distant. He wasn't sure if it was a voice or just his mind playing tricks. He'd noticed as they traveled that he was seeing things: eyes, a face, a flashing figure stalking their progress, a gnarled hand reaching to grab. The voice could be his imagination—or a lure.

"Hello?" Eddie yelled into the left-hand passage. "Is anyone there?"

Again the faint sound. "Did you hear it?" he asked Evelyn.

"I...think so. Let's try it."

They passed through the opening. The walls and floor were craggy and rough. The passage twisted and turned on itself. It branched and then branched again, forcing them to choose the direction. Edward was dearly glad for the vine that trailed out behind them.

They stopped every few feet to call out. Given the way the passages branched, it was hard to tell if they were hearing someone else's voice, or just their own voices coming back to them. But they both agreed—they heard *something*.

The passage narrowed, like giant hands squeezing them in its grip. Soon they were crawling. The air grew damp again. Moisture leeched from the walls and ceiling. Drops of water fell in his hair and on his neck. Eddie hated when the slimy drops splashed him. They were cold, like the touch of a witch's finger. One drop nearly extinguished the candle. Eddie held his breath as the flame hissed and guttered. If they were plunged into pitch dark again, his will would break.

Evelyn stopped. There was a clang, like metal scraping rock. "Found something," she said.

"What is it?" Eddie was gasping for air. The closeness of the passage was a damp blanket wrapping tighter and tighter around his head.

Evelyn handed something back to him. It flashed in her hand. A silver dish.

Mummer Ben had carried a silver dish.

Oh God. Oh God it was true! Mummer Ben had come down here—the very way he and Evelyn were going. Mummer Ben had gone down into the tunnels and never come out! Eddie's deadly stupidity, his incalculable foolishness, were revealed to him in this dish. He would die down here too.

A hideous shriek filled the passage. It went on and on, louder and louder until he thought it would shake loose the bedrock and the whole tunnel would come down around them. It was Mummer Ben screaming. It was Mummer Ben wailing 'God please find me! Someone please find me!'

It wasn't Mummer Ben. It was Eddie. He was screaming and screaming. His jaw was unhinged, his mouth agape. He screamed his throat raw. Then a hand slapped his face. The back of his head smacked against hard wet stone. His jaw snapped shut. Evelyn had hit him.

"Stop it!" she cried. "Eddie stop it and listen!"

Shocked by the blow, Eddie did stop.

"Help me! Is someone there? Help me!" The voice was weak. It sounded far away. It was a boy's voice.

"Luke!" cried Evelyn. "I'm here! I'm coming!" She scrambled forward. Eddie crawled after her, not wanting to be left alone.

"Keep calling!" shouted Evelyn. "Luke, keep calling!"

"I'm here! This way! This way!"

Now the voice was louder. Evelyn scrambled faster. Eddie

crawled after her, paying out the vine. The boy's voice sounded closer and closer. Suddenly they came to a tiny pocket of space, a little hollow notched in the stone. A figure unfolded itself, a skinny Negro boy in filthy clothes. He flung himself at Evelyn.

"Evy you found me! You found me!"

"Luke! Oh Luke!"

The siblings hugged and cried. Eddie cried himself. Then came an awkward introduction between the two boys. Luke grabbed Eddie's hand in both of his and squeezed. "Thank you!" he wept. "Oh thank you thank you!"

"Where's the lantern?" said Evelyn. "We got matches."

"Lost," said Luke regretfully. "I hit my head and dropped it. Couldn't find it. I got all turned around in the dark. I thought I was goin' the right way, back to the entrance. But it was so dark…" His voice broke.

"We know," said Eddie. He'd tasted a portion of that dark, but not the portion this boy had had to swallow. The thought of being alone down here without light made him quake. "We better go quick. Candle's burnin' down."

It was true. The candle had been half-used at the start of the rescue. Now it was barely a stub. The rising hope that Eddie had felt began to dip again.

"You know the way?" asked Luke.

"We marked the path," said Evelyn. "With some vines. It was Eddie's idea." She passed the candle to Eddie. "Go on," she said. "You go first."

It only made sense; as the last one in, Eddie was now pointed in the direction out. He took the candle. He drew strength from the faint nimbus of light in his hand. He crawled forward, hissing as hot wax dribbled onto his skin but bearing it. He followed the vine back along the twisting passages. It had broken in places, but after a few moments of panicked searching he was able to find the ends. He was dearly thankful he'd marked their trail. There were several turnings down here that could have taken them who knows where.

They came upon the silver dish. "Should we take it?" asked Evelyn.

"No," said Eddie. Let it stay down here forever.

At last they emerged into a chamber where they could stand upright. Before them was the humped porch of stone. They'd have to scramble up it. Luke went first, quick and easy. Evelyn tried several times, but her shoes slipped on the rock's smooth face. She took off her shoes, tied them around her neck, then clambered up. Brother and sister were out of sight now. For a moment Eddie quailed. What if they'd abandoned him here? But no—he had the light. They wouldn't leave the light.

"Hurry," came Evelyn's voice from above. It echoed among the crags. Hurry urry rry.

Eddie stepped back two paces and ran at the stone. His bare feet slapped against the rock. Encumbered by the candle, Eddie found it hard to climb. Toward the top he lost his balance and tottered. Luke grabbed his wrist and pulled him in. They ducked beneath the overhang and crossed the small chamber in file. Next came the long wide passage. They jogged along this tunnel three abreast, breath loud in their ears, their slapping feet raising dust.

They came to the cathedral chamber and passed beneath its majestic vault. Next was the crack where they would have to hunker down and squeeze through on their bellies. The candle flickered in Eddie's hand. His palm was damp with sweat, his thumb and fingers coated with wax. His heart thrummed.

"Just through there," said Eddie, pointing to the narrow mouth. "It only goes one way. If the candle goes out, we just keep going, OK? Just keep going forward." Brother and sister nodded.

Eddie went first, Luke behind him, then Evelyn. The tunnel seemed closer than before, as if it didn't want them to leave. It was hard to crawl while holding the candle. Hot wax dripped, and the flame drew closer to his hand. Eddie gritted his teeth, trying his best to endure the pain. At any moment, fire would touch his skin. With growing dread, he realized he would have to get rid of the stub before they could make it out of the squeezing tunnel. They would have to crawl in the dark, completely blind.

He turned his head and called back "Candle's burning me. I have to drop it."

"No!" screamed Luke. "No you can't!"

Eddie yelped as fire touched his skin. On instinct he flung away the stub. Now they were in perfect dark. Luke howled in despair.

"Just keep going," cried Eddie, grappling with his own terror. He felt pinned down by darkness, by miles of rock over him and under him. The tunnel cinched like belt, stealing his breath. He crawled forward blindly. Eyes opened or closed, it made no difference.

Behind him Luke sobbed. He heard Evelyn shouting at her brother to keep going, but he'd lost his nerve. The boy was frozen. Fighting against every instinct, Eddie inched backwards instead of forwards. His bare foot touched something—Luke's arm or hand or head.

Luke shrieked "Something's in here! Something touched me! Oh God something's got me!"

"It's me!" shouted Eddie. He wanted to turn around but there was no room. He could barely turn his head. "Grab my ankle, Luke! Grab my ankle and I'll pull you. Come on!"

Evelyn took up the cry. "Grab his ankle, Luke. Just keep going!"

A hand clamped around Eddie's ankle. "You got me," called Eddie. "Let's go!" Eddie began to slither forward again. It was harder now with Luke dragging on him. Eddie had to quash the urge to kick out and get free.

They crawled. The darkness was agony. Eddie's mind battered against the cage of his skull, desperate for light. It conjured gibbering phantasms, mocking laughter. He ignored the voice that said it wasn't Luke but Mummer Ben clutching his ankle, the money-digger grinning in the dark, delighted to have a visitor. A visitor he would never let leave.

Then Eddie glimpsed a faint slash of light. At first he thought it was another hallucination. But the slash persisted. The Devil's Smile. It was the exit!

"I see it!" he called. "The way out. It's just ahead!" He redoubled his pace, yanking Luke along behind him. "Keep going! It's there, the way out!"

"I see it!" cried Luke. "I see it!" And then the passage opened slightly, enough for Eddie to get off his belly and onto his hands and knees. He scrambled more quickly now, not caring how the ground barked his shins and bashed his knees. Then he could stand, first hunched and then upright. The slash was there! A moment later Eddie squeezed out of the tunnel and into the chamber with the pool. He was out!

He turned and grabbed for Luke, who wormed his way out and then toppled over onto him. Then Evelyn emerged out of the darkness and back into the world.

Eddie didn't remember crossing the pool, or scrambling up the damp wall, or pelting across the gritty floor of the cave mouth. All he remembered was bursting into the warmth and light of a June day. Sun poured from the sky as if from a golden dipper. The children drank it, rolled in it, bathed in it. Eddie sucked in air and spun in circles, arms outstretched, reveling in space. Space and air and light!

And then the three children wrapped their arms around each other and touched their heads together. They cried and laughed and pounded each other's shoulders. They were dazzled by their foolishness, awestruck by their blessed luck. They grinned and wept into one another's faces. They breathed each other's breaths, mingling their terror and relief. They couldn't stop holding one another. They were out. They'd made it. They were alive.

22

PALMYRA, 1884
THE HAUNTED MAN

The sun was gone by the time Edward returned to Jim's shack. It was the end of his first day in Palmyra. He flung his overcoat and jacket across a chair. He lit a pair of lanterns, rolled up his sleeves, and started a fire in the stove, glad for the light and the heat.

Back outside, he fetched water from the communal pump. The handle squeaked as he worked the lever. The commons stood empty around him; folks must be tending to their suppers. Bucket full, he hauled the heavy container back to the shack. Tongues of water slopped over the rim and licked his trousers.

Inside, he poured water into a basin. He rinsed his hands and scrubbed his face and neck. The cold, clean water stung like a slap.

He sat and unlaced his boots. With a sigh of pleasure he freed his stocking feet. He wriggled his toes and stretched out his legs to the stove. A pair of warm Turkish slippers waited in a trunk, but he felt no rush to lift his bones from the chair. He'd had a long, trying day. It was a pleasure just to sit.

The big toe of his left foot peeked from a newly-worn hole in his stockings. Damn. He wondered if Jim had needle and thread, and if his own fingers remembered how to darn. It had been ages since he'd had to do his own mending.

His stomach complained of hunger. Edward wasn't sure what to do about supper. Jim's larder seemed poorly provisioned. He supposed he could walk into town and get a meal at a public house or hotel. Or he could trouble Tante V for another bowl of stew. And perhaps she had a pastry or two. A generous slice of pie would be worth more of her prattling about Old Bill.

But he wasn't ready to get back into his boots just yet. He slouched in the chair and let the stove's heat seep into his soles.

The sack that held his father's seeing stones sat on the table; he'd put them back after flinging them at the door. He lifted the bag and touched the stones through the fabric. "I found the place where my father dug you up," he told them. "I should take you back there and bury you again. What do you say to that?"

A knock sounded.

Edward yelped and dropped the sack. For a moment he was certain his father stood outside, belt in hand to whip Eddie for his cheek. Beetles and worms would crawl across Pop's moldering face. His clothes would be rags, but his hands would be cold and hard and strong.

"Don't be a fool," Edward scolded himself. He rose and peered out the window. He could just barely make out a woman in the dooryard, a basket in her left hand. Curious, Edward opened the door.

"Hello Edward."

Edward recognized her at once—Evelyn Forrest. When Edward had last seen her, Evelyn had been a mischievous elven-year old. Now she was a woman grown. She wore a simple wool dress and a blue shawl trimmed with squirrel fur. She was as tall as him, her brown eyes level with his.

After their ordeal in the cave, Edward, Evelyn, and her brother Luke had struck up a friendship. Edward had often snuck away from the Bottoms to play with Evelyn and Luke at their farmhouse, or meet them at the creek or somewhere in the woods. They'd been boon companions, bonded by their harrowing adventure—that is, until Mrs. Coffin had taken Edward to Boston.

"Evelyn! How good to see you! Please, come in." As he drew Evelyn into the cabin he blushed at the state of the place. His overcoat and jacket hung lazily across a chair, and his dirt-crusted boots stood dumbly in the middle of the floor. A bucket, basin, and wash cloth cluttered the table. He tucked his left foot under his right to hide the hole in his stocking. "I wasn't expecting company."

"I can see," teased Evelyn.

He cleared the table and gestured for Evelyn to sit. He kicked his boots under the bed and fished his slippers from a trunk. As he slid them on, he looked for something to offer her. Jim's only provisions were rock-hard biscuits and a half-empty bottle of whiskey.

Evelyn tapped the basket she'd carried. "We heard you'd come back to Palmyra, so Mama put up a few things to welcome you home." Beneath a checked cloth was a loaf of brown bread, a Mason jar of blackberry preserves, and another of pickles. There was also a plate of cold chicken and a clay jug. Edward lifted the jug from the basket.

"Home-pressed cider," said Evelyn. "Mama remembered how much you used to like it."

Edward pulled the cork and smelled the tart scent. Memories rushed over him—meals he'd taken at the Forrest table, tucked between Evelyn and Luke like a mismatched sibling. "Will you join me?"

"Yes, all right."

He fetched a pair of tin cups, discretely inspecting them to ensure they were clean, then poured. He handed her a cup and then raised his own. "To E and E."

Evelyn smiled. "To E and E." They drank. The cider was cool and sweet, with the faintest tang of alcohol, but Edward barely tasted it. He was bashful in Evelyn's presence. The bossy, skinny girl in his memory had grown into a young woman. Her oval face was ruddy from the October wind, her sharp cheekbones practically aglow.

Lively brown eyes sparked with intelligence. Her hands were strong and weathered from farm work, yet deft and graceful. She had a wide nose, and her nostrils crinkled when she sipped her cider. Her black hair, which had always been in pigtails when he was a boy, was bound in a red kerchief. When she looked at him over the rim of her cup and smiled, blood rushed to Edward's heart. She was, frankly, lovely.

They traded polite questions: How was the trip from Boston? How are your parents? Have you begun your great excavation in the fens? How goes the school year? The exchange was stilted. Edward found himself treading the waters of formality, unable to change course. They had grown up together, survived the cave together, exchanged pages and pages of correspondence—why did he feel so awkward sitting across from her? He sensed the landmass of their friendship just beneath his thrashing feet. If only he could get purchase.

"I came by your place today," he said. "No one was home."

Evelyn's smile faltered. "We were out in the woods. Looking for Cassie."

"I'm terribly sorry for what's happened. How is Henrietta?" Henrietta was Evelyn's older sister. She lived up the road from the Forrest farm with her husband, Duke. It was Henrietta and Duke's child who had been taken.

"One moment she's frantic, wanting to dash through the forest at all hours of the day and night. The next moment, a melancholy overwhelms her, and she can't do more than sit by a window wrapped in a blanket. Waiting."

"How awful. I'll do what I can to help."

Evelyn reached across the table and squeezed his hand. "Thank you, Edward. I'm sorry you've come home in such terrible circumstances. For us and for your brother."

"Speaking of which, I met your sheriff today," said Edward. "Sheriff Cole. He's convinced Jim is guilty. I fear what might happen if Cole catches him."

"He's not *our* sheriff," said Evelyn. "When Cassie went missing, that man couldn't be bothered to raise a search. It wasn't until Becky Deaver was also taken that he organized his posse."

"What?"

"That's how it is," said Evelyn. "We can't count on the law, so we look out for ourselves."

Her "we" meant Palmyra's Negros. "Not just yourselves," said Edward. "I'm here to help. What can I do?"

"Some of our neighbors are gathering for a search tomorrow morning. Can you come?"

"Certainly."

"It will be early. We're going out at first light. Mama will give you a good meal afterward. She'll be pleased to see you. Luke as well."

"I'll be there."

Evelyn made to get up from the table. Edward leapt up and pulled out her chair. "Do you have to go?"

"Yes. Dad gets anxious when I'm out after dark." She tapped the basket of provisions. "But you should be able to make a good supper from this."

"I will. Please thank your mother for me."

Evelyn went to the door and then paused. "Before Jim vanished, he asked me to keep something for him," she said. "Now that you're here, I think you should have it."

"Oh?" Edward was surprised to hear that Evelyn and Jim associated. As a boy, Jim had sometimes joined Edward on his visits to the Forrest farm, but he'd always held himself aloof, as if friendship with Negros was beneath him. "What is it?"

"I'm not sure. It's something in a box. I haven't looked inside. You can take it tomorrow." As she crossed the threshold she looked back over her shoulder. "I'm pleased to see you, Edward. It's been too long."

23

Edward supped from Evelyn's basket. The roast chicken was tender and well-seasoned, the pickles sour and crunchy. He tore hunks of brown bread from the loaf and slathered them with sweet blackberry jam. He washed it all down with cider.

Belly content, he added more wood to the stove, then sat up with Cooper's novel "The Deerslayer." As a boy he'd delighted in the exploits of the woodsman Natty Bumppo and his Indian companion Chingachgook. Cooper set the book in the Otsego region of New York State, less than eighty miles east of here, the first frontier of a fledgling nation. Reading the novel while on the doorstep of its setting drew Edward deeply into the story. He roamed with Bumppo through thickly timbered forests across the spine of the Alleghenies, longrifle in hand, senses alert for bear, wolf, and Indian.

He read until the pages blurred and his head nodded. He changed into night clothes and climbed into his brother's bed, ignoring the voice that wondered when the blankets had last been laundered. God he was tired!

Yet once beneath the covers, sleep proved difficult to catch. The straw mattress was cold and lumpy. Birch logs hissed and popped as they burned in the wood stove. Autumn wind thumped against the window panes and troubled the eaves. The roof creaked its complaints. Edward missed the solidity of his brownstone on Boylston Street—this rattletrap shack might fall down around his ears.

A gust rattled the flimsy door latch. Edward thought of the ruffians who'd attacked him this morning. Would they really have stripped him naked? Gelded him? He saw himself writhing on the forest floor, blood spilling from a gash between his legs, his manhood chucked into the woods for vermin to devour. What if those lads wanted revenge? What if a mob of Palmyrans decided one Drake was good as another and paid him a night visit?

Edward threw aside the blankets. He lugged his heavy trunks to the door and stacked them in a barricade. If someone tried to burst in, the trunks would hold them off while he girded himself. He found a cleaver among Jim's utensils and laid it on the floor by the bed.

He returned to bed and punched the bolster into a more comfortable shape. He glanced at his trunks by the door. He'd brought with him a small bottle of a patent medicine—Dr. Pemberton's Nervous Cure. Made from an extract of poppies, a drop or two would soothe his mind and send him into a deep restful sleep.

Best not. He had to rise early to help Evelyn search, and the nervous cure often left him foggy and dull-witted. So he tried to convince himself the night noises outside were soothing, that Jim's shack was an upstate Walden where he might meet his true self in nature's solitude.

Moonlight silvered the rafters overhead. The knotholes and nail heads above him formed familiar constellations. He knew every crack and contour, the grain of every board, yet he had become a stranger beneath this roof. His life in Boston had cleaved him from this place as if with a hatchet; he was surprised to find the wound still ached. He turned on his side and curled into himself, small and vulnerable, as if he was turning back into a ten-year-old boy.

24

Edward woke before dawn and dressed in the dark. Outside, he pulled his coat tightly around him. The other shacks in the Bottoms were silent. They slouched against one another in the pre-dawn chill. He walked an hour to Evelyn's place.

As he came down the lane that led to the Forrest farm, pale light brushed the horizon. The farmhouse came into view. It was a plain, timber-frame four-square, two stories tall. As a boy, Edward had thought the farmhouse large and magnificent. His own family's shack could've fit neatly in the parlor. The Forrests had furnished their rooms from the Sears and Roebucks catalogue: a stuffed armchair, a cushioned sofa, a glass-fronted hutch to hold glazed tableware, and a thick, soft rug where you could lay in front of the fireplace with a book.

Now he saw how the front porch sagged, and that the shutters on the second story needed replacing. It was no match for Beacon Hill or Boylston Street. Even so, the old place felt more welcoming than Boston ever had.

Edward had enmeshed himself with the Forrests following the incident at the cave. After he'd helped Evelyn pluck Luke from the passages behind the Devil's Smile, the Forrest siblings had insisted Edward come home with them. He must've been quite a sight for Evelyn's mother—a ragged white urchin from the Bottoms, barefoot and filthy from crawling through the cave. When Evelyn tearfully confessed what they'd done, Mrs. Forrest had paled with fright and then shook with anger. Eddie expected her to whip the three of them then and there.

But instead of beating the children, she'd washed and fed them. She'd taken especial care with him, wiping his face and neck with warm water and soap, and tending gently to the scratches on his hands and bare feet. Then she'd stuffed him full of food—cornbread, molasses, hard-boiled eggs, bacon, hot tea. After that day, he'd become a regular presence at the Forrest place. He'd played with Luke and Evelyn in the barn and the pasture, and taken many meals with the family at the long table, seated between his friends like an adopted brother. More than once he wished he could've lived with them.

Of the Forrests' seven children, only Evelyn and Luke still lived at home. The eldest, Joe, had moved to Pennsylvania after returning from the war against the Slave Powers. Harrison, who also had fought for the Union, was a clerk for the War Department in Washington, DC. Louis worked as a railroad steward, and Robert was a merchant sailor whose home port was Philadelphia. Henrietta, Evelyn's older sister, was married and lived up the road with her husband and five children—four, now that Cassie had gone missing.

Yellow lamp light leaked from the curtained windows. Edward mounted the porch, careful to avoid a rickety stair. Evelyn Forrest opened to his knock. She wore a gingham housedress. Her hair was tied up in a kerchief. Unsure of how to greet her, Edward doffed his hat.

Evelyn laughed and embraced him. He returned her embrace and caught the scent of her, cinnamon and pepper. It woke his blood and roused something beyond affection in him.

As if sensing this impulse, a sharp-muzzled border collie thrust its head through the door and showed Edward its teeth. Edward lurched backwards.

"That's Dickens," said Evelyn. "He won't bite—unless I tell him to."

"I'll mind my manners."

Dickens sniffed Edward's hand and allowed him inside. Mabel Forrest, Evelyn's mother, appeared from the kitchen. Her hair had gone grey, and her face was wrinkled as a winter apple. She walked with a loping gait that favored her left side, but her embrace was as firm as her daughter's. "Eddie Drake, back in Palmyra. You've grown up." She assessed the cut of his clothes. "My, you strike a dapper figure!"

He returned the basket Evelyn had brought him yesterday, and presented her with a bottle of brandy he'd brought from Boston—not appropriate to the hour nor the situation, but the only gift he had. "Good morning, Mrs. Forrest. You look very well. Thank you for the food. It was quite thoughtful of you."

She batted him on the arm. "Eddie, you needn't be so stiff with us!"

Abashed, he stowed his gloves inside his hat and hung his coat on a peg. Evelyn's mother took his arm and led him to the parlor. She stowed away the basket and the brandy. "Mr. Forrest and Luke are out in the pasture," she said. "One of our cows took ill, so they're checkin' up on her." Her husband John was a dairyman and cow breeder. His bovine stock were prodigious producers of milk and cheese. Buyers from as far as Cleveland, Ohio came to purchase Forrest calves. "Have you eaten?"

"No ma'am."

"I got coffee brewin' and a batch of rolls just out the oven."

Edward was installed in an armchair and plied with coffee and buttered rolls. Mrs. Forrest and Evelyn sat on a sofa and watched him eat. "Well, well," said Mrs. Forrest. "How many years it been since you come by here?"

"Sixteen, I believe."

"Too long. I remember when that woman took you away."

"Mrs. Coffin."

"Coffin, that's right. Eddie, you made a hole in your mother's life when you left."

"You knew my mother?"

"Of a certainty. You was over here often enough, I thought it right to let her know."

Edward was stunned. He'd been careful to hide his relationship with Evelyn and Luke. Pop would've beaten him bloody for associating with Negroes. His mother had never once mentioned that she and Mrs. Forrest knew each other. "How did...how did the two of you communicate?"

"Carefully. Theresa and I met when your father weren't around. Sometimes we saw each other in town. We kept meeting even after you left. She and I made up stories about you, what you might be doing."

"You did?"

"Sure we did. Theresa missed you terrible. She must've wrote a stack of letters ten feet high."

Edward shifted in the chair. "It was she who sent me away."

"Now Eddie, you got to understand. Your mother did what she did out of love. It broke her heart to send you off, but she knew you'd have opportunities in Boston—great and grand things she could never give you herself. And more than that. She knew you'd be safe."

Edward sipped his coffee. Mrs. Forrest might be correct, but the wound still ached.

"We thought to see you back here when Theresa passed," said Mrs. Forrest.

Her tone was neutral, but Edward heard the rebuke. Shame bloomed in his cheeks. "I was overseas at the time."

"Mother," said Evelyn.

"Yes alright. I'll let you two converse a bit. I got another batch of rolls to tend to. We got folks coming over for the search." Mrs. Forrest returned to her kitchen.

Edward sat in awkward silence, not sure what to say. Then he remembered he'd brought a gift for Evelyn. "I have something for you." He went to his coat, took a small wrapped package from a pocket, and presented it to her.

Surprised, Evelyn removed the brown paper wrapper, careful not to tear it so it could be used later. Inside was a box of stationery: a dozen cream-colored envelopes and twice as many sheets of writing paper. The paper was thick and decadent, the edges crisp and precisely cut.

"From Crane and Co.," said Edward. "Just a token of my affection, and to thank you for your correspondence."

"It's beautiful," said Evelyn. She brushed an envelope with her fingertips. "I suppose the paper I've been using wasn't good enough for you? Too rough on your citified hands?"

Edward paled. "Not at all! Your paper is quite satisfactory."

"Satisfactory?" Evelyn arched an eyebrow.

"More than satisfactory! What I mean to say is, whether your paper is plain or luxurious makes no matter. It's the words I cherish." Then he saw the laughter in her eyes. She was teasing him. "You're not insulted?"

"Of course not. It's a lovely gift. So lovely I may save it for special occasions. I wouldn't want to waste it on you."

"No. Scraps of butcher paper will do. Or birch bark with a few words scraped on it."

"Short words," said Evelyn. "So as not to tax your comprehension."

Before he could retort, heavy boots clattered through the back door.

"That'll be the men from the pasture," said Mrs. Forrest, emerging from her kitchen. A moment later, John Forrest and his son Luke came through to the living room. On spotting Edward, Luke strode forward and embraced him in a manly crush of arms. Luke smelled of sweat and clover and cold autumn air. He'd grown—he was a head taller than Edward, his face fuller, his shoulders and arms thick from farm work. His coal-black hair sprang from his head, adding to his height. Boyish merriment danced in his eyes.

Luke held Edward at arm's length. He tugged at Edward's brocade cravat. "Eddie Drake! By God, look at them clothes. Someone's disguised you as a gentleman. Long as you don't open your mouth, you might fool 'em!"

Edward laughed and clapped Luke's shoulder. "What about you? You look big enough to wrestle a bull!"

"Oh, I have. More than once."

"He certainly smells like a bull," said Evelyn. Luke swatted at his sister.

John Forrest, Evelyn's father, was tall like his son but lean. His hair was going white. He moved with rheumatic stiffness, but he remained as straight-backed and flinty as Edward remembered. The Forrest patriarch had made him nervous as a boy. Sixteen years had done nothing to change that.

"Hello, sir."

"Hello Eddie. Been a long time." They shook hands solemnly. And suddenly Edward remembered his purpose here—not to give Evelyn a gift or visit with her and Luke, but to search for a child snatched from her family. The air of pleasant reunion leaked out of him.

Presently several Negro men from neighboring farms arrived, including Cassie Brown's father, Duke. The men carried hunting rifles and shotguns. They looked surprised to see a white man in the parlor. When Edward was introduced as the youngest brother of Jim Drake, consternation flicked across their faces.

Mrs. Forrest and Evelyn went among their guests to serve coffee and rolls. The men clumped in two's and three's. There were murmured plans about the search, but also talk of the coming harvest, and chores being left undone. They knew the Brown and Forrest families needed help, but how many more days could they give? Their own needs grew with every hour they were away from their work.

Edward found himself on the periphery, a cup in one hand and a plate in the other. He stood awkwardly, unsure of what to do with himself. Then a Negro sidled over, a short round man in dungaree overalls and clunky boots. He'd removed his hat when he'd come in, revealing a bald head fringed with greying hair like a monk's tonsure. He introduced himself as Willy Hudson. For a long moment Willy studied Edward.

"I spoke with your brother once," he said at last. "Big Jim."

"Oh? What did you speak about?"

Willy glanced at the others and pitched his voice lower. "I asked after the spirit of my sister, Hattie. She lived in Delaware. Worked as a seamstress in a factory. There was a fire and she got burned up."

"My God, how terrible!"

Willy nodded. "Thing is, I'd lent her some money. Ten dollars. She promised to pay me back but she never did. I knew it was a risk to loan her money because her husband Joe's a gambler. Their whole lives together, Joe spent everything she ever got. I asked Hattie to pay me back a little at a time from her wages. Some months she sent a nickel or two. Some months nothin' at all. I tried to be patient with her. My wife was angry that I'd sent so much money in the first place. She figured Joe would piss it away on dice and cards, and she never let up about it. So the last letter I ever sent to Hattie, I said some things. Hurtful things. Then the fire took her."

Willy clutched the brim of his hat. "I felt awful about the way I'd left it between us. My heart was sick. I couldn't sleep. Didn't feel right in my skin."

"So you went to my brother?"

Willy nodded. "He got these stones. One black and one white. When I visited, he set them out in front of me. Said the stones gave him the far-sight. That he could see into the afterlife and speak to the dead. He let 'em set there on the table, quiet and still. Your brother asked if I wanted to touch 'em. No I did not. You got to be careful with such-like."

"Mmm."

"Then he put the stones in a sack and looked inside. He whispered her name. 'Hattie. Hattie. You're brother's here. Hattie, come speak to him.' Oh, it made me shiver to hear him call to her. And then she started speakin' through him. Why did I come? What did I want?"

Willy closed his eyes. "I told her I was sorry. Sorry for what I wrote, sorry for bein' so cross. She was my baby sister. I was supposed to watch over her, protect her. And the last words she ever had from me was 'Get me my damn money or I'll never speak to you again.'"

Willy's voice hitched. "I tell you without shame, I wept in front of your brother. Like a little baby I wept. But I felt her presence. Swear to God, I felt like she stood beside me, her hand on my shoulder. I was so glad to tell her I was sorry, and to know she heard me."

Edward said nothing. He'd witnessed such scenes a hundred times when his father ran the same grift. He'd come to understand that what his father had done was a species of the talking cure, a relief valve for feelings of grief, guilt, and shame that swelled in the psyche. But the same effect could be achieved without the trappings of magic stones and invisible spirits.

"Anyhow, I know there's folks who think your brother's the child-stealer. Prob'ly some in this room. But I don't." Willy shrugged. "Jus' wanted to say that to you."

"Thank you, Mr. Hudson."

At that moment, Mr. Forrest raised his voice. "Alright now. Alright men. It's time to do our business. Head on out to the fence line and we'll get sorted." He handed his cup and plate to his wife. Other men passed their plates along to Evelyn.

Mr. Forrest gestured to Edward to come over to him.

"I'm ready to help," said Edward.

"Well now, I was thinkin' you ought to stay here with Evelyn and the missus. A male presence would steady 'em."

"Stay behind? But I came to search."

Mr. Forrest glanced around the room. "I don't know that it's wise."

"Surely you need every able-bodied man."

"I'll be plain, Eddie. A lot of folks think your brother snatched them girls. How would it look to have you out there?"

"It would look like I'm trying to help."

Mr. Forrest rubbed his cheek.

"Let him come," said Willy Hudson.

Mr. Forrest cleared his throat. He looked to Duke Brown, Cassie's father. The man nodded.

"I'm searching too," said Evelyn.

"Now hold on," said Mr. Forrest. "Edward's a grown man. If he insists on comin', I can't stop him. But you're stayin' here. Mother wants a bit of company."

"Then she can sit with Mrs. Putney down the lane."

"No."

"But why? Cassie's my niece, Daddy. We have to do everything we can to find her! And I won't hinder you one moment. I can walk as long and as far as anyone in this room. My eyes are sharp. Let me help."

Mr. Forrest tilted his head toward his wife. Mrs. Forrest moved in to take her daughter's hand.

"Evelyn should come with us," said Edward. His statement stopped the room. Mr. Forrest glared. Edward stiffened his resolve. "I understand your hesitation, sir, but a child's in danger and the woods are deep. Surely, we could use her."

Mr. Forrest scowled, unaccustomed to being gainsaid in his own living room.

"Go ahead John," said Mrs. Forrest. "Let her go with you. I'll be fine here."

Mr. Forrest grumbled, then pulled Edward closer. "I'm taskin' you with keepin' an eye on her. And bring the dog."

"Certainly."

"Then let's be gone."

The group bundled out the door. As Edward passed Evelyn, she squeezed his hand.

25

The searchers trooped across the Forrests' cow pasture. They passed through a gate in the fence into a narrow strip of yellowing meadow. Drooping stalks of thistle and goldenrod stroked their pantlegs. Beyond the meadow the woods waited.

Mr. Forrest pressed an old revolver into Edward's hand. The gun was dull and heavy, the barrel long and straight. Edward held it uncertainly. His only experience with firearms was a decrepit Remington that Pop had unearthed on one of his digs. His father had cleaned and oiled the rifle until it could fire again. When he was a boy, Edward had shot a woodchuck with it. Then he'd watched in sorrow and regret as the beast whimpered and twitched in the dirt until it died. He'd never touched a gun after that.

The elder Forrest checked the loads, then gave Edward brief instructions on pulling back the hammer before firing the weapon. "You can use it as a signal if you find Cassie or the Deaver girl," said Mr. Forrest.

"And ensure no harm comes to your daughter," thought Edward. He slipped the pistol in an overcoat pocket. It rested awkwardly against his body.

Mr. Forrest arranged the searchers into a picket line, each person separated by five yards or so. Evelyn was on Edward's left. No one was on his right. "Keep your eyes sharp," called Mr. Forrest. "Stay abreast of the line as we move forward. If you see or hear something, sound a cry or fire a shot and we'll all converge."

The woods were gloomy in the day's early light. Tattered rags of brown and gold hung from maple and oak. Stands of white birch poked from earth like exposed bone. Dickens the dog raced ahead of the picket, tail high, the joy of an outing undiminished by the humans' somber mood. The dog passed through the trees and vanished.

The picket moved out. As Edward walked, he wondered what terrors poor Cassie Brown and Becky Deaver might be suffering. Were the girls even still alive?

Edward rarely prayed. His own boyhood cries to the Lord had been ignored, so he'd long ago turned away from asking heaven's intercession. Now he found himself fumbling for words to send up to God, that some strength or solace might be transmitted by grace into the heart of Cassie and Becky, Palmyra's missing children.

After walking for a couple of hours, Edward sat on a tree stump to rest. He rubbed his eyes and wished for a hot cup of tea. He was tired and hungry. He wondered how long they might search. Overhead, the sky was the color of used dishwater. Cold fingers of wind pinched his cheeks. The farmers who'd gathered in the Forrests' living room had murmured of a difficult winter forecast by their almanacs. Snow could be on the ground before Hallow's Eve, and they still had work to do in their fields and barns. How many days could they spare for a search that was likely to be fruitless?

Edward heard a rustling behind him. As he turned, a shape darted towards him. It was Dickens. The dog leapt on the stump and sat next to Edward, panting happily. Edward stroked the dog's shaggy coat. Evelyn emerged a moment later. Edward stood and brushed at his trousers. "Have you found anything?"

"Dickens startled some pheasants and chased a deer," she said, "but otherwise nothing. This is grim work."

"Frustrating too," said Edward. "I already crisscrossed these woods yesterday. I feel helpless."

Evelyn toed the ground. "Are you sure we're helpless?"

"What do you mean?"

"I've been thinking about the last time children went missing, when we were young. Your father found them with his peep stones. I know he only found their bodies, but at least it was *something*. Might the stones be of use again? And perhaps this time we could find the girls alive? Do you know how the peep stones work, Edward? Did your father teach you?"

Evelyn blushed as she spoke. Edward understood her embarrassment; she was a teacher, an educated woman who had trained to rid her students of ignorance and superstition. Yet she had just asked if he could conjure the children like a genie.

"There was nothing to teach, Evelyn. My father was a fraud. The stones were just a prop."

"Then how did he find the bodies?"

Edward chewed his lip. How much should he confess to her? If he told her that a hallucination had led him to the corpses, she might think him mad. So he would tell her a little, but not all.

"I found the bodies, not my father. Pop was with me, and he took the credit, but it was me who led him. Without me, he would've blundered through the woods like we're doing now."

"*You* found those children?"

"Yes."

"All three? And they were dead?" Shock and pity replaced Evelyn's embarrassment. "Oh, Edward! How terrible that must've been. You were just a little boy." She put a hand to his cheek. Her palm was warm.

"It was terrible," he said, leaning in to her. Unbidden, the memory of Katie Cooper's corpse came into his memory; the jewels of snow across her brow, and the lead weight of her body as he lifted her from her nest of tree roots. He covered Evelyn's hand with his.

"But Edward, how did you do it?"

"What do you mean?"

"Your family has a...reputation for peculiar abilities. Your father claimed to speak to the dead. So does Jim. And now you tell me *you* found those children. Could all of that just be coincidence?"

Edward released her hand and stepped back. "Certainly it could."

"But how was it done? Was it a feeling you had? Some kind of guide or pull? Like a magnet or a compass?"

"I'm not a clock to be wound up, Evelyn."

"Of course not. But Cassie is out there somewhere." Evelyn's eyes roved the horizon, desperate and anxious. "I'm at my wits end. The whole family's going mad with fear." She bit her lip. Tears gathered in her eyes. "I know I must sound foolish to you, but if there's some talent you could draw on, some gift that would help us...I'm sorry to goad you, but it's my niece out there. We need to bring her home."

Edward took a clean handkerchief from a pocket and wiped Evelyn's tears. He thought of Mrs. Coffin, and how she insisted he had a gift. Madame Corbeau had spoken of his 'spirit organ,' an aspect of his psyche that connected him to the dead. And Tante V said his family was haunted by a terrible spirit, a spirit who was responsible for taking the very children he was searching for. *Could* he do something?

Edward frowned. One might as well try to summon nyads and dryads to help, or call on leprechauns and pixies. If he proposed such a plan to Evelyn, she would be repulsed by such nonsense. Spiritualism was no different.

Speaking calmly, Edward said "All I can do is the same as anyone else. I can walk these woods. I can search with my eyes and ears."

Evelyn wrung her hands. "I fear it's useless. My bones tell me we're too late."

Edward took the risk of embracing her. She rested her head in the crook of his shoulder. Her warm breath touched his neck. Perhaps he'd been wrong to insist she join the search. This was grim work. He was about to suggest they go back to her house when she spoke.

"But I won't give up. You're right, Edward. Let's do what's in our power to help. We must try."

"Alright," said Edward. "That's what we'll do."

26

Edward and Evelyn abandoned the picket line to search together. They marched in attentive silence, scanning the woods and taking comfort in each another's presence. Dickens loped ahead, snuffling leaves and dashing among brush and bramble.

They came to a clearing. Five white men in winter coats and heavy boots smoked cheroots and passed a flask. They carried rifles. Goodword, the old tanner Edward had rescued from a tree, stood among them. As one, the men turned to Edward and Evelyn. Their looks were unfriendly, their faces ruddy from the cold and liquor.

"Mr. Goodword," said Edward neutrally. "Are you out here searching for the children?"

Goodword ignored Edward's question. His eyes were faded blue, like a pond beneath a scrim of ice.

"What's it to you?" asked one of the men. He wore a bristly black mustache. His cheeks glowed like a furnace. He hawked and spit on the ground. "And why is a white man strollin' round with a nigger?"

Edward flushed with anger, but Evelyn spoke first. "We're

looking for Cassie Brown and Becky Deaver. My kin and some neighbors are out here with us."

"Guess it beats workin'," said the mustachioed man. "You might as well pound drums and dance in circles for all the good it'll do."

"Mind your tongue," said Edward.

"Who the hell are you to tell me that?"

"He's a Drake," said Goodword.

At this intelligence the men shifted position, encompassing Edward and Evelyn in a half circle. "That so? You kin to Big Jim?"

"He's my brother."

"More trash from the Bottoms," said the man. "Shoulda known. I'll wager if we find Becky, we'll find Big Jim. Then we can put a bullet in him and be done with it."

"My brother's done nothing wrong," said Edward.

"Drakes been findin' dead kids for years," said Goodword.

"So they have," said the man. "My Dad always thought your father got away with murder. I'll be damned if I let his son."

"I reckon this one's here to help Big Jim escape," said Goodword.

Rifles that had been pointed at the ground now leveled at Edward.

"Fuckin' Drakes," said the man. "Nothin' but troublemakers. Maybe someone should make trouble for you."

Dickens growled. Edward stepped in front of Evelyn. He slipped his right hand into his coat pocket and grasped the revolver. His thumb found the hammer.

John and Luke Forrest strode into the clearing. The elder Forrest's rifle wasn't pointed at anyone in particular, but it was ready. Luke had a shotgun. He planted his feet and stood next to his father, the big bores of the twin barrels ready to spray buckshot.

"Archie Smith," said John Forrest, addressing the mustachioed man. "I see you're out here too. Any sign of my granddaughter or the Deaver child?"

The man considered John Forrest and his son. Edward could almost hear him calculating the odds of a fight.

Archie Smith tossed the rump end of his cigar to the ground and mashed it with his boot. "No sign of the Deaver child. As for your granddaughter, I wasn't lookin'." He stomped from the clearing. The others followed, except Goodword.

"I knew your father for what he was," said the tanner. "A rascal full of hocus pocus. So's your brother. He thinks he smarter than everyone else. He laughs behind his hand while he pretends to talk to ghosts. Big Jim's a liar and a thief. I expect you're no better."

"I'm no liar and no thief. And I don't spit on people who come to my aid."

"A waste of mouth water, that was. You should pack your things and go. This town'll be rid of Drakes one way or another. It's only one of you that needs to swing, but we've rope enough for two."

"Here now!" cried Luke. "Ain't no call for that kinda talk."

Edward stepped chest to chest with Goodword. "You daren't lay a hand on me or my brother. You hear me?"

"Farewell, thief. I'll see you around." The old man turned his back on Edward and sauntered out of the clearing.

Edward's blood boiled. He thought of going after Goodword, of punching him in his head and knocking him to the dirt. How many threats might Goodword make with a boot on his back and a pistol in his ear? Before he could pursue the man, Evelyn snatched his hand. Her face was ashen, her eyes wide. "Let's go. Now."

27

"You two nearly got yourselves kilt!" barked Mr. Forrest. The quartet marched back to the farmhouse. "I told both of you to keep outta this. Told both of you to stay home! Shoulda' trusted my own judgement. Where's your goddam *sense*, Eddie? You're a white man so you think you can stick your nose in wherever you want and never suffer for it, but then you drag my Evelyn into it? Just like that goddamn cave when you was kids. Y'ain't learned *nothin'* since!" He carried on in this vein for some time.

Edward, his own emotions taut, held his tongue and endured the scolding. Luke nudged him and rolled his eyes in sympathy.

As they approached the farm, Mr. Forrest stopped in the lane. "We ain't gonna speak about this to Mother. Not a goddam word. We searched the woods and that's all. You understand?" His children nodded.

"And you?" He pointed a finger at Edward.

"Yes sir," said Edward.

Mrs. Forrest had a meal waiting: roast chicken, mashed potatoes with butter, roasted red beets, and hot tea and coffee. The mood at the table was somber. Edward, preoccupied by the danger he and Evelyn had escaped, filled his belly but tasted nothing.

After the meal, Evelyn plucked Edward's sleeve. "I'll show you what Jim asked me to hold for him." She led him outside to a shed that stood near the cow barn. Dickens the dog accompanied them. Edward had left his coat inside. He hugged himself against the deepening chill. "What is this mysterious item?"

"I'm not sure. It's in a box, and the box is wrapped in burlap. I never opened it. I had it in my bedroom for a few nights, but it made me uneasy so I moved it."

"Uneasy?"

Evelyn ducked her head in embarrassment. "It gave me nightmares. I stashed it in the chicken coop, but then the hens stopped laying, so I put it in the shed."

"And you don't know what it is?"

"Jim never told me. I presume it's something to do with his vocation."

Edward scoffed. "Play-acting as a medium is not a vocation."

"It's not play-acting. He helps people."

"Not you too, Evelyn. You support his nonsense?"

"Why do you dismiss him?"

"Because he's a fraud. He should've taken up a trade instead of fooling with the peep stones. I could've gotten him a job on my excavation crew in Boston if he couldn't find work around here."

"You think Jim wants to dig out a swamp while his baby brother bosses him around?"

"It's a tidal estuary, not a swamp."

Evelyn rolled her eyes at his pedantry. "Jim's ambitious. He wants to be more than a ditch digger."

"What's wrong with digging ditches?"

"You tell me—how often do your hands touch a shovel? Jim's doing the best he can with what he has. He wasn't given the same chances as you."

Edward opened his mouth to protest, then closed it again. She was right. He and Jim's fortunes had diverged the moment Mrs. Coffin took him to Boston. Even so, he didn't like Evelyn taking his brother's side. "Just what is your relationship with Jim?"

"I wouldn't call it a relationship. We speak now and then is all. Sometimes he comes to help with the haying. Mama fixes him a basket of food once in a while."

"I see." Jim had also been a presence at the Forrest farm as a boy, though not as frequent as Edward. In fact, Edward hadn't wanted Jim to know about Evelyn and Luke at all—he feared Jim would snitch to Pop, then smirk while Pop beat the hell out of Edward. But Jim had kept the secret. It was one good thing in his childhood that Jim hadn't tried to wreck. Perhaps Jim had also found some solace with Evelyn and her family. Edward disliked that notion.

Evelyn opened the shed door. Cobwebs hung limply from the low roof. Shovels, rakes, and an old scythe leaned against a wall of pine boards. A plow rested on the floor. A dead rat splayed in a corner. "It's there," she said, pointing to a shelf.

Careful not to snare cobwebs in his hair, Edward stepped inside and took down a large burlap-wrapped bundle. He removed the burlap to reveal an ungainly wooden box with a brass catch. He undid the catch. Inside was a book, as big and cumbersome as a church Bible. The leather cover had no title. He reached to take it out.

"Please don't," said Evelyn.

"Why not?"

"I don't like that thing. It's...unwholesome."

Edward, who had some experience with unwholesome sensations, didn't feel a thing. It was just an old book.

"Don't make that face at me, Edward. I know I'm being foolish. Just leave it alone for now. You can take it with you when you go."

"If you say so." He latched the lid and wrapped the box in its sacking, then carried the bundle to the house. Evelyn asked him leave it on the porch.

Inside, Edward rinsed his hands and accepted a cup of coffee. Mrs. Forrest also served raspberry cobbler, the last fruit of the season from her patch out back. There was fresh cream to pour on top. They sat in the parlor with their desserts. Mrs. Forrest took the opportunity to brag on her grandbabies—fourteen at last count. There was a moment of awkward silence for Cassie, her missing grandbaby. Mrs. Forrest moved past it by displaying for Edward a sheaf of her grandchildren's drawings. He murmured approvingly over childish scrawls and awkward stick figures. Mrs. Forrest sighed and said she wished for grandchildren in her own house, if only someone weren't so choosy.

Edward caught the look that passed between Mrs. Forrest and her daughter. Wanting to spare Evelyn, Edward turned the subject toward the dairy farm. Now it was Luke's turn to boast; last year had been the best ever in production and income, and Luke had ambitions to expand the breeding operation. As Luke talked, Edward wondered if Luke might agree to a small private investment of capital. He wanted to help his old friend. At the same time, it would give Edward a reason to visit with Evelyn and the family. He wondered how to raise the subject.

After dessert, Edward helped clear the dishes. Luke offered a ride in the wagon. Edward accepted; it would save him another long walk. Mrs. Forrest assembled another basket for him; leftover chicken, rye bread, a pot of butter, a hunk of hard cheese, and a jug of cider. She suggested Evelyn ride along, as Edward might appreciate a woman's hand in getting the victuals sorted.

"Don't tarry," ordered Mr. Forrest, giving Edward a hard look. "It ain't a picnic." He motioned for Luke to bring the shotgun.

Edward and the Forrest siblings arrived at Jim's cabin in full dark. The moon had cleared the treetops, but a skein of gray clouds hid its light. A cold wind blew down on them. The trio descended from the cart and stood before the shabby domicile. It sagged like an old man half asleep.

"I'll help you get these tidbits squared away," said Evelyn. "Then Luke and I should get back before Dad has a conniption."

Edward opened the door and screamed.

A body hung from a rope in the middle of the cabin.

28

The body twisted in a short, gruesome arc. Blood pooled on the floor. It was a raccoon, strung up and eviscerated. Its guts, yellowed and stinking, hung in ropy coils from a gash in its belly.

Edward staggered. For a terrible moment he'd thought Jim had been caught and murdered, the corpse delivered to the cabin to tell Edward his quest was over. But it was just an animal. He stepped inside and nearly slipped in the slick of blood. The raccoon's eyes bulged. Its needle teeth were bared in a final scream. Then Luke was beside him, knife in hand. He cut down the raccoon and flung the carcass into the woods.

Whoever butchered the animal had also ransacked the cabin. Edward's trunks were overturned, his clothes flung willy nilly. Shirts, trousers, and undergarments draped the room. The table was upside down. Jim's pots and plates had been dumped off their shelf.

"You can't stay here," said Evelyn. "It's not safe."

"I won't be driven off!"

"It must've been the men in the woods," said Evelyn. "What if they come back?"

"I can protect myself." Edward brandished the pistol he'd borrowed from Mr. Forrest. A roaring anger drowned out Evelyn's prudence. Let them come. He would welcome them with thunder and death.

Edward told Evelyn and Luke to return home, but the siblings insisted on helping clean up. Luke scrubbed the floor with water and lye, then sluiced the gory mess out into the dooryard. Edward and Evelyn set the cabin to rights—standing up the table, replacing items on the shelf, folding Edward's clothes and returning them to the trunks.

When the work was done, they rinsed their hands in clean water from the pump. Then Edward took the cider from the basket. He popped the cork, drank straight from the jug, and passed it around. The drink braced him, but it couldn't wash the bitter anger from his mouth.

Evelyn again asked Edward to come to the farmhouse, but Edward refused. "Then bar your door," she insisted. "And keep my father's gun close to hand."

With that, the Forrests departed. In the quiet that followed, Edward realized Jim's seeing stones were missing. He searched under the bed and up in the loft. He double-checked his own trunks, wondering if Evelyn had tucked the stones among his shirts and trousers. The stones were gone. Whoever ransacked the cabin must've stolen them.

"Good riddance," muttered Edward. The damn things had brought nothing but trouble to the Drake family. Let their mischief fall on the thief's head now.

Edward lit candles and a lantern. A crimson stain blotched the floor despite Luke's efforts with brush and soap. The cabin was marked by blood. But unlike the doorposts of the Jews in Egypt, this blood was no protection against death.

Who had done it? Was it Goodword, with his grudge against the Drakes? Or those men with the rifles who had threatened him and Evelyn today? Or the lads from the woods yesterday? Too many people in Palmyra wished him ill. Now that his anger had cooled, he wondered if he should've gone with Evelyn and Luke. Too late now; it would be just as dangerous to travel after sundown as to hunker down here. But he didn't have to hunker by himself.

He crossed the commons and knocked on Tante V's door. Sherman the dog greeted Edward with a wet and inquisitive nose in his crotch. Edward squawked.

"That's good manners for a hound," observed Tante V. "Though I'm glad people just shake hands."

He told her of the dead raccoon and the ransacking.

Tante V grimaced. "Things gettin' outta hand, Eddie. Maybe you ought to stay here. I got a bedroll you can use—and my husband's old .22 rifle if it comes to that."

"I'm armed already. But might I borrow Sherman for the night? Would he stay with me?" The beast thumped its tail on the floor.

"I b'live he would," said Tante V. "Go ahead and take him. And if I hear a commotion, I'll come runnin'."

Edward walked the enormous animal back to Jim's place. Tante V sent him with Sherman's wool blanket, shaggy with hair and smelling of dog. Edward spread the blanket by the stove. Sherman nosed around the cabin, paying particular attention to the bloodstain. Then he sniffed at the chicken on the table.

"Like chicken, do you?" Edward wasn't above a little bribery. He plucked meat from the bones and heaped it on a tin plate. Sherman snarfed the morsels in a few mouthfuls, licked the plate, and settled on his blanket with a satisfied "ronk."

"Good boy," said Edward. He patted the beast's great head. "Now if anyone breaks in, remember who fed you."

Once again he shoved the heaviest of his trunks against the door. It wouldn't stop a determined intruder, but it would give Edward a precious second or two. He placed the revolver on the table within easy reach of his hand.

Edward sat in a chair. He felt wrung out and anxious. The last two days had been exceedingly difficult. Wanting some relief, he rummaged in one of his trunks and withdrew a soft velvet bag. Inside was a small brown bottle of Dr. Pemberton's Nervous Cure. Pemberton was a London manufacturer of patent medicines. A drop or two of this liquid, made from an extract of poppies, would soothe his mind give him a bit of peace.

Edward was embarrassed to be a customer of Dr. Pemberton's. Patent medicines and elixirs belonged in the same category as Mesmerism and spiritualism: quack treatments for the anxieties of the modern age.

But Pemberton was no quack. Edward had first come upon the stuff when he was a boy, snooping among the effects on Mrs. Coffin's dressing table. The tiny brown bottle had caught his eye—it looked like a fairy potion. He'd tipped a glistening drop onto his finger and licked.

The taste was so bitter he'd nearly gagged. But moments later a pleasant sensation came him, as if warm, invisible hands held him just off the ground. He'd wobbled downstairs to the parlor and sat in a patch of sun that poured through a mullioned window. Motes of dust slipped through the beams. He'd tracked them like an astronomer tracks the orbits of tiny planets.

As he'd sat drenched in sun, Edward had felt an unfamiliar sensation—peace. He'd almost forgotten what it was like. In Mrs. Coffin's house he'd endured homesickness and loneliness. He was exhausted by daily performances for Mrs. Coffin, who'd squeezed him for every drop she could get of her dead sister Lilith. And lately she had begun to invite her friends, who pressed him for messages from their own departed.

But this potion had washed away all that. It lay him down in green pastures and anointed him with oil, like that psalm his mother cherished. Under the liquid's influence he was no longer a banished son, nor an alien interloper, nor the unwilling conduit of the dead. He was breath and water, translucent and still.

Eventually the potion had worn off. Edward had made several more visits to Mrs. Coffin's dresser, until one afternoon the bottle was gone. It wasn't until he had his own pocket money and his own apartment that he'd reacquainted himself with Dr. Pemberton's cure.

Here in the shack, Edward placed a single drop on his tongue. He didn't want to knock himself out, just sand down the edges of his anxiety. The drop filled his mouth with familiar bitterness. He sat in the chair and breathed. For half an hour he sat perfectly still, bathed in a warm, pleasant calm.

When the sensation left him, he sipped cider to wet his dry mouth and considered the little bottle. Should he take another dose? Three or four drops would send him into a deep sleep. Surely he'd earned a good night's rest.

But no. He needed to be watchful in case of attack. And he still had one task ahead of him. He put the bottle away and turned his attention to the box Evelyn had given him, with the strange book inside.

He set the box on the table. As he did, he became aware of how dark the shack had gotten. Edward lit all the lamps and candles he could find, which weren't many. He arranged the lights in a half circle on his brother's rickety table. The flames strained feebly against the gloom. He built a fire in the wood stove and left the grate open, adding its scant orange glow to the room. He wished for his electric lamps back home, and the clean strong light they threw.

He removed the book and centered it within the meager oval of incandescence. The book was old and heavy. Its amber leather cover was sticky, as if coated in pitch. Earlier today Evelyn had said the book unsettled her. Edward had dismissed her remark as womanish hysteria. Now that he was alone with it, he had to admit the book unsettled him as well.

He opened the cover and leafed through the pages. The paper was thick. Oils from many fingers had leeched into the fibers, leaving whorls and striations. Some pages were speckled with black mold. Others were stained brown with dirt—or blood? Edward turned the moist, pulpy pages with distaste, wiping his fingers on his trousers as he went.

The book was written in an angular, cuneiform script that ran from margin to margin. Edward could make no sense of it. Might it be Sumerian? Egyptian? Or perhaps a cipher system meant to thwart any reader who lacked the key?

Drawings were interspersed among the text: A knife and a chalice. A severed goat's head with mesmerizing eyes. Constellations of stars from no sky Edward had ever stood beneath. An infant with its belly slit, bleeding on a slab of stone adorned with hideous markings.

Good Christ, why did Jim want this thing? What did his brother hope to learn from such a foul tome?

Shadows gathered around him. The room softened. The sharp planes of the walls and floor warped, suddenly pliable as melting wax. Tumorous shapes gathered in the eaves like hives of albino wasps. Sherman the dog whined.

Edward wanted to shut the book, but a strange impulse drove him. He turned a page. There, drawn in careful detail, were a pair of stones. One was ink black. The other was white, bisected with jagged quartz crystals. Edward recognized them. His father's seeing stones. "How?" he gasped.

A groan came from deep under the house, fathoms deep, as if a leviathan rose from unsounded depths, boring through magma and mantle to breach the surface and vomit its madness upon the world. Sherman howled, a high mournful sound. The candles and lantern blew out, one after another, extinguished by fetid puffs of air. The flames in the stove guttered and died, leaving him in darkness. A voice whispered *Come in my sweet. Come in come in.*

Edward shrieked and swept the book off the table.

Fumbling in the dark, he found a candle. His hand trembled as he relit the wick. He burned the tips of his fingers but he didn't care—he wanted light! He snatched the book as if it was a serpent and shut it in its box. He wrapped the box in its sacking, then carried it outside and buried it beneath the wood pile.

29

The next morning Edward found Tante V stooped among her squash and pumpkins in her back garden. He'd brought Sherman with him. The dog trotted happily to his mistress.

Tante V bent and took the dog's great head in her hands. "Oh, I missed you last night, you beast! Oh, I missed you, yes!" The dog licked her face.

Then Tante V regarded her great-nephew. "You all right, Eddie? You look poorly."

Indeed he did. His hair stood in wild tangles and his face was pale.

"I had a strange evening. May I speak with you?"

Inside her cabin, Edward accepted a tin cup of hot coffee. He gulped the strong, bitter brew. Tante V dunked day-old bread into her own cup and munched. Sherman settled himself on Edward's boots.

"That story you told me, about Etienne Cloud and his daughter, Lizbet," said Edward. "You said William Jongold owned a book—a book he cherished above all things. Your granny called it 'the creeping book.' Do you know what happened to it?"

"Nope. Granny Lizbet never said. I figure it was burned up in the fire that took Jongold's house."

"Might Etienne have kept it? Or given it to Lizbet?"

"No! Granny Lizbet always said that book was a foul thing. She wouldn't want it."

"Perhaps Etienne buried it. Which means someone else could have dug it up."

Tante V shrugged. "I suppose. Why you fixed on that book all of a sudden?"

"I think—and I understand how impossible this sounds—I think I have the creeping book."

Tante V lifted an eyebrow. "That so? Yesterday you rolled your eyes when I told you of Old Bill. Now you think you got his book? Did somethin' happen, Eddie?"

Edward sipped his coffee. After he'd stuffed the box with the book under the woodpile, he'd returned to the shack. He'd sat up for a while, waiting to see if any more auditory or visual hallucinations occurred. None had. Eventually he'd gone to bed, assuming that the strange experience had been triggered by the opiates in the nerve cure. Perhaps he'd taken more than he thought, or the batch in the bottle was unusually potent. Whatever the reason, he wasn't going to discuss the experience with his aunt.

Instead, he told Tante V how Jim had entrusted the book to Evelyn Forrest, who in turn had given it to him. "It occurred to me that perhaps Goodword found the book," he said. "The man's constantly digging for treasure. Maybe he unearthed it. And then Jim took it. Remember after we rescued Goodword from those ruffians? Goodword called Jim a thief. He said Jim had stolen from him."

Tante V sucked her teeth. "That's possible. And now that I think on it, I recall Goodword once came to speak with your father about a book. You was just a boy at the time. Goodword didn't show his face much 'round the Bottoms, but your father had a reputation for secret knowledge. Maybe Goodword came across the book and thought your father could learn him somethin'."

"Secret knowledge," said Edward. An idea was forming in his mind about the book and the seeing stones. Pop had dug up the stones from the foundations of an old house. Edward himself had walked among those foundations yesterday. Could that have been William Jongold's place?

"The old man your great-grandmother served—he lived in Palmyra. Where was the house?"

Tante V waved a hand. "Over yonder by the old orchard—the one near that cave. The orchard was Jongold's. His house was nearby. You can still see the foundation stones. But I don't go there."

Edward nodded. The creeping book had belonged to William Jongold. Might the stones also be his? Were they connected somehow?

"If Goodword found Old Bill's book, he's had it for years and years," said Tante V. "Why would Jim steal it now?"

Edward traced the rim of his cup with a finger. "Maybe Jim thought a strange old book would be a good prop for his schemes. Or perhaps the seeing stones and the book are linked, and Jim hoped to decipher that link. I prefer the former explanation—it's more rational. But lately I wonder if the rational holds much sway with our family."

"Don't matter," said Tante V. "You need to burn that book. Take it to the woods, build a fire, and burn it. Burn it to ash, then scatter the ashes."

Edward blanched. He had no love for the thing, but book-burning repelled him. Books were the closest thing in his life to sacred objects. You might as well ask a pastor to set fire to a church. Also, to destroy the book was to admit it had power. Edward didn't want to admit any such thing. "I've secured it in a safe place. I'll think on what to do with it later."

"Later? What you gonna do now?"

Edward ran his hands through his hair. "Keep looking for Jim and the girls. That's why I'm here." This would be his third day of searching. Would it be as fruitless as the first two?

"If I was you, Eddie, I think I'd get gone. Jim don't want to be found. He's smart enough not to stick around after what happened. He could be on his way to California for all you know."

"Perhaps. But there's still Evelyn's niece and the Deaver child."

"I suppose. But it ain't safe for you here."

That was becoming more and more clear to Edward, but he didn't want to abandon Evelyn. "I think I should give it at least another day."

"Do what you think is right," said Tante V. "But be careful, Eddie."

"I will, Auntie."

He returned to Jim's shack and tried to put himself together as best he could—a clean shirt and trousers, a quick shave, and a perfunctory tussle with his unruly hair. Then he set off for town. He wanted to telegram Fred. He didn't have much to report, but likely Fred would want an update.

Back outside, he strode briskly through the Bottoms. As he crossed the weedy commons, a group of children trailed him like leaves in a gust. They tossed questions as they followed.

"Where you from, mister?"

"I'm from here."

"Where you goin'?"

"To the telegraph office."

"I seen you come outta Big Jim's house."

"It's my house too. I'm Jim's brother."

At this intelligence, the children drew closer. "You come to hunt the bogeyman?"

Edward stopped. "Hunt the what?"

A boy in faded overalls, perhaps twelve, spoke up. "The bogeyman. He steals children out their beds."

"He can fly," said a girl. She flapped her hands. "He can fly like a crow."

"Naw. He crawls under the ground, then comes up through the floor to snatch you."

"Who told you this?" asked Edward.

The oldest boy shrugged; it was just known. "Mr. Jim said he was gonna drive the bogeyman away, but he's gone now. And we ain't allowed in the woods no more."

"There's no bogeyman," said Edward. "It's just a story."

"So who took them kids?"

Edward frowned. "I don't know," he said. "But it wasn't a ghost or a bogey, because there are no such things. A man has done this. And he could do it again, so mind your folks and stay close to home."

30

Leaving the children behind, Edward followed a well-worn path through the dense thicket of pine and maple trees that separated the Bottoms from Palmyra's village center. Gold and amber leaves rustled overhead. Their fallen brethren shushed and crackled beneath his boots. Grey squirrels and mottled chipmunks flitted among the underbrush.

The path emptied onto a dirt lane that took him to an alley between a boarding house and the mercantile. Edward emerged from the alley on to Main Street. The sidewalk was red brick now; it had been creaky plank boards in his childhood. Carts and buggies rattled on the cobbled road. New businesses had gone up: a dress maker, a dentist, and a restaurant—signs of the prosperity that had flowed into northwestern New York, first from the canal and then from the railroads.

Some things hadn't changed. One block north, the same four churches dominated the corners of Main and Canandaigua Streets— Presbyterian, Baptist, Episcopal, and Congregational. The crosses atop their spires threw cruciform shadows in the late-morning sun.

Edward had been baptized in the Congregational church, but the

Drakes hadn't congregated much. Pop had preferred the itinerant preachers who pitched tents in a meadow or fallow field. Pop never missed a revival, and he always brought his wife and children along.

As a child, those meetings had intrigued and frightened Edward. All the rules he knew were tossed aside. Whites and Negros, men and women, all mingled freely beneath sagging sheets of mildewed canvas without regard to color, sex, or station.

As the preachers prowled a makeshift pulpit and cranked up their oratory, a charge coursed through the tent, leaping from person to person like a jolt of electricity. It raised the downy hair on Edward's neck and arms.

Men wept like babies as they cried out their sins. Ladies abandoned their modesty to run up and down the aisles, carried away by the Holy Spirit. The praise songs tipped from solemn to ecstatic. Women swung their hips and bosoms as they clapped their hands. Men churned the ground with their feet. Often the gift of tongues swept the tent, a clattering babble that poured forth from the mouths of the people.

And rising above the noise and commotion, the preacher's voice whip-cracked over their heads. "Woe to the sinner!" he cried, and penitents toppled to the ground as if struck by lightning. They flopped in the dirt and moaned for God's mercy.

Not Pop. Edward remembered his father as pillar of stillness. He didn't dance or sing or stomp. He only stood and watched. He fixed his attention on the preachers as they paced the boards—not to receive the Gospel, but to learn techniques of manipulation and excitation that he could weave into his own spiritualist schemes.

A pedestrian eased past Edward, shaking him from his memory. He realized he'd been blocking the way. "Padron me," said Edward. He hadn't meant to wool-gather in public. Nor did like to think about his father. Such thoughts dredged up rusting hulks of resentment and hurt. Better not to trouble those waters just now.

He turned left on the sidewalk toward the telegraph office.

Inside, he was surprised to learn that a message waited for him. It was from Fred. The telegram read:

Any progress?

"No, no goddam progress." He crumpled the message and tossed it into a wastepaper basket, rankled by Fred's perfunctory tone. He sent a reply—Nothing yet—then exited the office.

Outside, a notice was pasted to the wall. It advertised a reward of twenty dollars for the capture of Big Jim Drake. The notice included a drawing. As a young man, Jim had favored their father, who'd had a handsome face with high cheekbones and a rascal's charming air. This drawing showed a dull lummox with an ape's brow, piggish eyes, and rude lips curled in a snarl.

The drawing insulted Edward. His brother might be a charlatan and a brawler, but he wasn't an animal. Making sure no one was watching, he tore the paper from the wall, crumpled it, and tossed it to the ground. A gust blew it into the road.

You shouldn't have done that.

Edward whipped his head around. Who had spoken? A mule cart rolled down Main Street, its wagon heaped with old furniture. From between the slats of a rocking chair Edward glimpsed an elderly man in a top hat on the opposite sidewalk. A young girl stood beside him. Had the old man seen what he'd done?

Then the cart passed and Edward got a better look.

Mr. Jangles stood across the street. He grinned at Edward as if delighted to meet him in the thoroughfare. The girl at his side was Katie Cooper. Mr. Jangles had a hand clamped around her mouth. With his free hand, Mr. Jangles pointed to the notice.

I hadn't figured you for a litterbug.

The words skittered into Edward's ears with frightening clarity. "You're not real," he said.

Oh but I am.

"You're just a story. Granny Lizbet made you up."

That obstinate cunt hadn't the wit to invent someone like me. She cost me a great deal. And now I'll have it back. From you.

Cold terror engulfed Edward, as if he'd plunged through rotten ice on a frozen pond.

Mr. Jangles titled his head toward Katie Cooper. The girl's eyes were wide with horror.

You see this little one? She tried to warn you away. I've since corrected her.

"This isn't happening. This isn't happening." Edward's teeth chattered in his head. His hands and feet went numb.

There's a girl in the woods. She waits for you to find her.

"Not again," moaned Edward. "I can't go through that again!" Mr. Jangles was a just a story—a foolish family myth! So why could he see him in broad daylight? How could hear his voice so clearly?

From behind, a hand touched Edward's shoulder. Edward shrieked and spun around. A rabbity man with round eyeglasses stared at him. "Mr. Drake? Mr. Edward Drake?"

"Who are you?" gasped Edward.

"My name is Henry Hyde," said the man. "Might we speak in private? My office is just over there." Gently he clasped Edward's shoulder. "Are you well, sir?"

Edward glanced back across the street. Mr. Jangles touched the brim of his hat and sauntered away, dragging Katie with him. A wagon rolled past, obscuring the specter. The wagon's wheels rolled over the wanted notice, mashing Jim's image into the cobblestones.

31

Henry Hyde led Edward to a print shop, which occupied the first floor of a three-story building on Main Street. When Hyde opened the door, the liquid-metal odor of ink rushed out and watered Edward's eyes. A board listed prices for print services: cards, pamphlets, bills, and advertisements. A bundle of broadsheets was stacked by the door.

Hyde ushered Edward to wooden chair in front of a work table busy with pens, pencils, and paste. Edward was embarrassed to be attended to like an invalid, but he was glad to sit. Hyde's shop was warm and clean.

"May I offer you tea?" asked Hyde. "The leaves are just steeping now." A china pot steamed on a round-topped table with a curvaceous cabriole leg. Next to it, a copper pot sat on a hot charcoal brazier.

"Yes, thank you," said Edward. A slug of Tante V's steady might be better, but tea would be welcome.

As Hyde busied himself with cups and saucers, Edward looked out the shop's plate-glass window. An old-fashioned top hot bobbed along the thoroughfare, but it wasn't Mr. Jangles—just some white-haired fellow on an errand.

Edward tucked his hands beneath his armpits. "It's the nervous cure," he muttered. A trace of the medicine must've lingered in his system. When combined with the anxiety of the search, the threats against his life, that awful dead raccoon, all of it had pressed on his nerves and left him susceptible to hallucinations. Yes, that was it.

"I'm pleased I spotted you," said Hyde. The man was small and slender. He wore a printer's apron over a white shirt and starched collar. Black and blue ink blotched the apron, but his shirtsleeves were spotless. His thin brown hair was combed and oiled, his mustache trimmed. Round silver spectacles fronted moist, protuberant eyes.

"I'd heard you arrived in Palmyra," said Hyde. "I presumed a smartly-dressed gentleman would be Mr. Edward Drake, so I ventured to introduce myself. And I can see your resemblance to Jim."

"You know my brother?"

"Oh yes. Quite well."

Edward couldn't conceive any kind of relationship between Jim and this fellow. He waited for Hyde to elaborate, but Hyde's attention was split between a pocket watch and the teapot. An arabesque of white steam curled from the pot's spout.

"Does Jim...work for you?" asked Edward.

"Not as such, no."

"Then how are you acquainted?"

"Ten seconds if you please." Hyde raised a finger. "There we are." The printer replaced his watch and poured amber liquid into two cups. He moved like a salamander, quick and darting. "Sugar?"

"Normally no, but I think I shall."

Hyde dropped a sugar cube into the cup and handed it to his guest, along with a delicate little spoon. Edward chased the cube with the spoon until the sugar dissolved. He sipped. The tea was delicious. He took another sip, savoring the hot sweetness in his mouth. Warmth spread through his chest and belly, restoring his own vital heat. He sipped again. The cold and the fear receded.

"Good, isn't it?" said Hyde, lifting his own cup. "Brooke Bond. I have it imported from..."

"From Manchester, England," said Edward. "I know it well. Now, Mr. Hyde, why did you want to speak to me? And how do you know my brother?"

"I publish a journal called *The Seeker*. Perhaps you've heard of it?"

"No."

"Oh? I thought Jim might have mentioned it. *The Seeker* is devoted to the phenomenon of spiritualism; that is, to communication between the living and the dead. I have hundreds of subscribers."

Good Christ. Another spiritualist. Edward masked his chagrin with a sip of tea.

Hyde went on. "Surely you're aware, Mr. Drake, that man has a limited understanding of the invisible forces that govern our lives. We see through a glass darkly and all that. But in recent years we have acquired marvelous knowledge about electricity, wireless communication, magnetism—and communion with the dead. I am convinced that as our knowledge grows, we shall learn that all these phenomena are but limbs of the same tree, with a unifying principle at the root."

Edward had heard similar theories in Mrs. Coffin's parlor. They were nonsense. Electricity and magnetism were physical forces. They might be invisible, but you could test them and measure their effects on material objects. Spiritualism was driven entirely by fantasy. Edward was grateful to this fellow for the tea, but irritated to have fallen in with yet another fabulist.

"What does your journal have to do with Jim?" asked Edward. "Is my brother a subscriber? Is there an unpaid bill?"

"Your brother is a dedicated reader, but I have never once charged him for an issue. Why would I? We're partners."

"Partners? In business?"

"Indeed. There's a growing appetite for spirit communication among the public. Spiritualist societies have sprung up in cities across the United States and Europe."

"I'm aware," said Edward. "What does this have to do with Jim?"

Hyde told Edward of his plans for a lecture tour, in which Jim would demonstrate, both in public and private, his ability to speak with the dead. Hyde would act as Jim's agent to arrange travel, promote events, and manage accounts.

"Was this Jim's idea?" asked Edward.

"It was mine," said Hyde. "Your brother was most eager when I proposed it. We've been planning for weeks. Sadly, our work was interrupted when Jim discovered the body of Liza Ames. The townsfolk reacted...poorly."

"They tried to murder him, Mr. Hyde. This venture seems ill-advised, even without Jim's present trouble."

Hyde raised an eyebrow. "Jim said you'd react this way."

"Did he?"

"He mentioned you live in Boston, as a ward of Tilda Coffin. She's a well-known patroness of mediums. I hoped you might introduce us—she could open many doors. Jim said not to bother. He said you'd dismiss our plans."

"He's correct. Jim's backwoods hocus-pocus might amuse farmers and shopkeepers, but in Boston you'd be tossed out on your ears."

Hyde stiffened. "I do not trifle with 'backwoods hocus pocus.' I have significant experience with mediums. Some are imperfect vessels, their organs of reception coarse. Others are earnest but deluded—they mistake their own imaginations for transmissions from the departed. Several are frauds, exploiting bereavement and human curiosity for their own gain."

"Into which category do you place my brother?"

"Into a category I have yet to enumerate. Your brother, in my considered opinion, is a man of profound psychic abilities. His organs of perception are highly attuned to emanations from the dead."

"Is that so?"

"It is. I have watched him work with others—and experienced for myself—his aptitude at calling forth spirits from across the corporeal divide."

"Table rappings and bogus incantations, you mean?"

"No, none of that," said Hyde. "There are no ghostly knocks nor shuddering tables. There are no phosphorescent lights or gauzy figures processing across darkened rooms. He is a vessel for pure rapport between those in the physical world and those in the great beyond. He's aided in his work by a pair of magnificent stones—a family heirloom, I understand."

"Come, Mr. Hyde. Don't tell me he's bamboozled you with those peep stones."

"Not bamboozled, sir. Your brother has a legitimate talent. And he has the right pedigree."

Edward frowned. There was no pedigree for a child born in the Bottoms. "What do you mean by that? Do you mock him?"

"No! Western New York is a wellspring of ethereal force. This region has produced mediums of exceptional ability, from Andrew Jackson Davis to the Fox sisters. And you'll recall all those years ago that a Mr. Joseph Smith spoke with angels on a hill—right here in Palmyra. Currents of invisible power converge in this region."

"Currents of delusion certainly converge here."

Hyde ignored this. "In addition, your brother's humble background will burnish his appeal. People drawn by his rural character will be surprised and delighted to hear eloquent speech from the mouth of an...mmm... ." Hyde fumbled to a stop. "How might I put this without giving offense?"

"From the mouth of a shanty-dwelling hick," said Edward.

Hyde blushed. "Let us say that your brother's roughness makes for a novel attraction."

"So you wish to display him like one of Barnum's oddities?"

"Certainly not! Jim Drake is no sideshow grotesque. He's a skillful medium. He calls forth grief and sorrow, and then excises them like a surgeon cutting out a tumor. I've watched grown men weep in his arms. Seekers come away transformed, with their hearts lighter, their burdens of grief laid aside."

For a moment Edward was drawn back to Mrs. Coffin's parlor, where wealthy men and women had gathered to hear an impoverished child speak messages from the dead. Some had wept, and expressed sincere thanks. Several had watched with naked skepticism. A few had remarked on the dog-like ability of the lower classes to be trained up for japery and tricks. His brother would respond poorly to such condescension; there was nothing ethereal about Jim's fists.

"And then there's the tale of how Jim found those children, which you know," said Hyde.

"Children? It was only Liza Ames he found."

"No, not recently. When he was a boy. The spirits guided Jim to the three children who were murdered all those years ago. A terrible tragedy to be sure, but also proof of his abilities."

Edward set down his tea cup with a clang. Hyde winced. "*He* discovered?" cried Edward. "You're mistaken, Mr. Hyde. I found those bodies."

"Yes, you accompanied your father and brother. But Jim led you."

"Jim was never there! He had nothing to do with it."

Hyde shrugged. "Jim said you'd dispute this."

Edward stood. "Another successful prophecy. Perhaps Jim should add fortune-telling to his repertoire."

"Mr. Drake, have I offended you?"

"This whole business offends me! Your scheme is ridiculous. Jim shall not take part. I intend to find him and remove him from Palmyra. Do you know where he is?"

"I don't," said Hyde anxiously. "I thought he might come to me for refuge, but he hasn't. I'm frightened for him, Mr. Drake. With Liza Ames dead and Becky Deaver and that Negro child missing, the town is on edge. And with the rumors of the how the Ames girl was interfered with…" Hyde shivered. "If a mob were to catch him, things would go poorly for Jim."

"They would. Yet you yourself have encouraged my brother in his delusions. You, Mr. Hyde, bear a measure of responsibility for his troubles. Good day." Edward made for the door.

"A moment, please!" Hyde rose from his chair and scuttled into a back office. He returned with a neatly folded broadsheet, which he pressed into Edward's hands. "The latest edition of my journal. Complimentary, of course. If you peruse it, you might find your attitude changed."

Edward wanted to fling the journal in Henry Hyde's face, but his habit of decorum prevailed. He would wait until he was home and then throw it in the fire.

32

Edward left Hyde's shop and strode down Main Street, his mind a cloud of wasps. He batted the stinging thoughts that swarmed him: Jim's demented scheme with Henry Hyde; the troubling appearance of Mr. Jangles and Katie Cooper; the specter's promise that another body waited for him in the woods. Did that mean Cassie Brown or Becky Deaver had been murdered? Was Mr. Jangles laying a trap for him as Tante V insisted?

"No goddammit! Mr. Jangles isn't real!"

Edward realized he'd spoken aloud. Embarrassment bloomed in his cheeks. A shopkeeper sweeping in front of his store glanced at Edward and retreated inside. A mother with her little girl, coming towards him along the sidewalk, crossed to the other side of the street. She clutched her child as if Edward might snatch the girl and run howling into the woods.

Edward stopped. He'd been barreling along the sidewalk, talking aloud like a lunatic. He wasn't even wearing his hat, just strangling the brim in one hand. He took several deep breaths, smoothed the brim of his hat, and seated it properly on his head. He tucked Hyde's broadsheet under one arm and took up a more regular pace, his gaze fixed on the middle distance. Just another pedestrian on a morning errand.

A heavy hand clapped his shoulder and spun him around. Sheriff Cole. The lawman spit a brown globule of tobacco into the street. "Edward Drake. You looked peaked—as if you'd seen a ghost. How goes your search for Big Jim? Is he lurking in Hyde's print shop?"

"I haven't seen my brother."

"I know it. Word is you ran into a bit of trouble the other day—an altercation with some Palmyra lads. I thought I told you to keep your head down."

"They attacked *me*, Sheriff. I was beaten and threatened with a knife. They ought to be arrested."

"For boys bein' boys? Naw. I heard an old hag chased 'em off for you."

"My great-aunt, if you please," said Edward. He resented Cole's smirk and decided to see if he could remove it. "You're well informed about me. It's a shame you have no intelligence about my brother. And nothing about Becky Deaver or Cassie Brown. How long have they been missing, Sheriff? More than a week. I wonder how much confidence Palmyra has in you."

Cole's face darkened. "You daren't chastise me. I been out in the woods for days on end. I haven't slept for more than two hours a night since them girls vanished."

"Yet here we are, idly passing the time on Main Street. Where's your urgency?"

Cole slammed Edward against a storefront. He shoved a forearm into Edward's throat. "I am overtopped with urgency! It fills me so excessive it might cause me to break your neck. I won't have my efforts denigrated by a mincing peacock in a silk hat." He grabbed Edward's lapels and shoved him roughly down the sidewalk. "Move along. Move now before I do something you regret."

Edward stumbled away. He felt Cole's eyes boring hotly into his back; he wondered if a fist or a bullet might follow.

In Boston he'd learned the skill of audacity, using his wit to draw figurative blood in salons and parlors. But Palmyra was not Beacon Hill. Frontier roots clung deep in this village. Behind the veneer of prosperity—a rail depot, church spires, a bicycle in a shop window—these people lived on the knife's edge of calamity. They hunched in fear of bank repossession, too much rain or not enough, sick livestock, cruel disease. And stolen children.

There was no appeal to the capricious forces that buffeted them, and no recourse for injury delivered by unseen hands. But if a man did them harm? Here was a blow they could return, and blood they could draw. Edward understood now that the longer he stayed in Palmyra, the greater the risk to his own person. He had to find Jim and the children if he could, and then be gone.

33
BOSTON, 1876
THE HAUNTED CHILD

Stephen the butler dimmed the lamps in Mrs. Coffin's parlor, cloaking the room in murky twilight. He processed solemnly across the carpet, bowed to his mistress and her guests, and closed the door behind him.

Edward Drake, sixteen years old, sat at the head of a long mahogany table. Seven faces, pale and curious, stared at him from their seats. Mrs. Coffin was there, and the widow Greenwood, along with a judge, a painter, a physician, and a young couple who had come all the way from New Bedford for this séance.

Edward shifted uncomfortably in his chair; Mrs. Coffin kept the parlor overwarm. He itched beneath his wool vest and formal jacket. A drop of sweat ran from his armpit down his ribs. His starched collar pinched. He regarded the assembled faces with distaste. They stared at him like greedy little birds, eager to pluck bits of spiritualist pap from his gullet. He wished he could scatter them with a wave of his hands.

A scritching sound came from the shadows. Mr. Jangles leaned insouciantly in a corner, picking idly at Mrs. Coffin's rosette wallpaper with a dirty fingernail. Edward stilled a tremor at the sight of him.

The specter had troubled him regularly over the past five years he'd spent in Mrs. Coffin's house. He typically appeared on evenings such as this; all these assembled minds, concentrating on their dead, drew Mr. Jangles like a crow to carrion. He would hover among the guests and transmit to Edward collops of intelligence about their departed loved ones—a memory, a snatch of song, an image from their lives. Edward served these morsels to Mrs. Coffin and her guests and watched them gorge.

But lately Edward didn't need Mr. Jangles. After so many performances, he knew what these seekers wanted—some hint that their cherished dead could still be reached, that love bridged the chasm of death, that the cords of affection were unsevered.

Take the young couple from New Bedford, Lewis and Violet Howland. Earlier, Mrs. Coffin had told him their twin sons Owen and Theo, age three, had recently died of pneumonia. All evening he'd watched the couple move stiffly around the parlor, as if their limbs were dry sticks. You didn't require spiritual power to see they were shattered by their loss. Now at the table, Lewis stared mutely at the polished teak, tugging a lock of hair. Violet's trembling smile was a papier-mâché mask over an abyss of pain. Edward could have these two weeping in his arms without any help from Mr. Jangles.

But as sorry as he felt for the young couple, he didn't want to speak to them. He was sick of being made to perform. He was weary of the grief these strangers heaped upon him. A dull pain throbbed in his head. Mrs. Coffin and Mr. Jangles were two halves of a vise that squeezed his skull until he feared it would break open. He wanted to be free of both of them.

Mrs. Coffin cleared her throat, the signal for Edward to commence. Edward sat in silence. What if he refused? If he denied her, what would she do? Cut off Fred's seminary tuition for sure. Perhaps throw Edward into the street. Where would he go? Not home. Not back to Pop.

Mrs. Coffin's face was hard. She sensed his recalcitrance. She did not like to be thwarted, particularly when guests were present. "Begin."

Edward bowed his head. Forcing himself to speak calmly, he instructed her guests to clasp hands in communion. Violet Howland, the grieving young mother, was on Edward's right. Her slender fingers were cold in his palm.

Mr. Jangles sauntered out of his corner to lurk among the guests, a devilish gleam in his eye. He hovered behind Alice Greenwood, a widow and a regular attendee at these performances. Her husband, a ship's captain, had died at sea. Edward had heard Mrs. Greenwood talk about him a thousand times. He could clear her off the list easily.

"Captain Greenwood is here with us tonight."

"Oh!" exclaimed his widow. Her expression brightened as she fixed her eyes on Edward. "Does he have a word for me?"

Mr. Jangles stared at Edward.

The fool sailed his schooner onto a reef and damned everyone aboard to a miserable death. Sixty souls lost their lives because of him. He bore the weight of every one of them as he drowned.

Edward wouldn't speak of such a terrible thing to the old woman, even in his resentment at having to perform. He recalled overhearing Mrs. Greenwood talk of scrimshaw pipe her husband had treasured. It sat in his study, untouched for years. "The Captain's pipe. It grows dusty. You might clean it for him."

"Oh? He would know I did it?"

"He would, and he would cherish you for it." Edward didn't know if it was true, but it didn't matter. Mrs. Greenwood seemed content.

Judge Poole leaned forward, blocking the widow. He was jowly and bewhiskered. "Can you tell me what's become of my dog Pepper? She's run away and I'm terribly worried."

Edward glanced at the Howlands—here they were, mourning the loss of their sons, and this man was worried about a pet?

Mr. Jangles caught Edward's eye.

A pack of urchin boys found that dog in an alley. They pelted it with rocks and bricks. The stupid beast fled into the street and was crushed by a wagon. Its head burst like a melon.

Edward grimaced. He didn't know if Mr. Jangles was telling the truth, but the story made him sick. And he would not relate such a story here.

Instead, he assured the judge that Pepper was happy and well. He invented a story about how a family in Roxbury had found the dog and taken her in. Pepper had acres of farmland on which to run. The dog brought comfort to a little girl stricken with polio. "She holds Pepper in her arms and strokes her soft fur," said Edward. "Pepper kisses her cheek and makes her laugh."

The judge beamed. "Such a good dog. A fine and gentle creature. Perhaps I should travel to Roxbury... ."

Mr. Jangles sneered.

Then it was another guest's turn, and another. And always Mr. Jangles spoke of suffering and pain. The specter's eyes burned. He bored into Edward's skull, using horror like an awl to widen a channel into Edward's mind.

A greasy stain appeared on the parlor floor. It grew into a slick of inky black, like oil seeping up from a hidden well. Edward had never seen this before. What did it mean? The slick turned in a nauseating spiral, as if agitated by invisible currents. Sounds leaked out; weeping and curses, screams of terror, buzzing incantations. The dead wailed, and their woe assailed Edward's ears.

No one else in the parlor saw the slick or heard the cries. Edward's heart pounded against his rib. Panic creeped along his nerves. Was he going mad?

And then Mr. Jangles stalked over to Violet Howland. He licked his lips and flared his nostrils as if savoring her pain. The grieving woman waited for a word from Edward. Her anguish was raw on her face, more intimate than if she was naked.

"I see two boys," said Edward, "two fine and handsome boys." He felt sorry for Mrs. Howland. She was lovely and distraught. He wanted to comfort her.

Violet's fingernails bit into Edward's palm. "My babies. Are they well?"

Now Mr. Jangles showed Edward images: a pair of twins toddled along a cold, barren hillside. Ghoulish creatures descended on them and stripped the clothes from their backs. The creatures pinched the boys' naked skin, pulled their hair, and drove them like hogs along a blood-soaked path toward a tree of pain. The twins wailed for their mother. Their terror and confusion were awful.

"They're holding hands," said Edward, struggling to concoct a pleasant fiction, struggling to get through this trial. "Theo and Owen. Bathed in light, warm and safe. The boys hear you when you speak to them. They know Mummy loves them. They know Mummy misses them."

A thought oozed from Mr. Jangles.

Such a good liar. You've lied to them all evening.

"Please, tell me more," begged Violet. Tears traced the hollows of her cheeks. Next to Violet, her husband Lewis gaped.

I'm opening you, Edward. Opening you to serve me.

What did that mean? A salty bead of sweat stung his eye. He fumbled for more story to invent. "I sense a...female presence. Watching over them. An aunt?"

My mother," said Violet. "It must be my mother. She passed away last year."

"Yes, that's it. Granny's with them. She holds the boys and sings to them. They nestle in her arms."

Mr. Jangles sent a different vision. An old woman in a nightdress, mouth hanging dumbly, wandered barefoot and deranged along a stony cliff above a gibbering sea, her mind blasted apart by madness.

I've groomed you, Edward. Cultivated you. It's taken years. And now, at last, you'll bear fruit.

For what? thought Edward. For what?

The babies screamed. Theo and Owen screamed and no one could help them. They would scream in an eternity of pain and terror. The maelstrom in the floor widened, a mouth opening to swallow Edward.

Tonight I break you open. Tonight I master you. You'll come back home with me. We have unfinished business, you and I.

Edward felt fingers inside his head clutching at him. He let go of the hands he held. He needed to get out of this room. He needed to get away from Mr. Jangles. He was done. "Forgive me, but I can't to do this anymore."

"Oh, couldn't you?" pleaded Violet. She plucked at his hand. "Just another few minutes?"

From the far end of the table, Mrs. Coffin clucked. "Come now, Edward."

"I'm sorry, I can't go on." Clammy sweat trickled down his back. He felt feverish. He turned his head away from Mr. Jangles' grinning face. Panic bubbled in his throat.

"We haven't finished," said Mrs. Coffin. "I haven't had *my* turn."

We'll need children. Three sweet children.

"Not again," whispered Edward. "Oh please, not again." The babies screamed. They wouldn't stop. "Mum, I can't...if you please, I don't..." He tugged his collar. God he needed air. He needed to run.

Run all you want. You can't escape me.

It was true. He might flee Mrs. Coffin, but he could never escape Mr. Jangles.

Mrs. Coffin rapped the table with her knuckles. "Carry on, Edward. At once."

Broken boy. I'll carry you back to Palmyra. We'll take the children together. You'll do my will!

"You can't make me!" screamed Edward. He snatched up a heavy ceramic bowl from the center of the table and struck it against his forehead. A sunburst exploded behind his eyes. Voices shouted. Edward struck himself again. Pain rang in his skull, but the ringing drowned out the cries of the dead. Blood sluiced down his forehead into his eyes. Through the blood, Mr. Jangles gaped in alarm.

Stop that!

"You won't have me!" Edward lifted the heavy bowl above his head, held it trembling at arm's length, then crashed it down on his skull. The bowl shattered. Edward tottered in his chair, neck and spine buckling. He tasted blood. With a broken shard he slashed his chest, his belly, his wrist. Here was his escape.

Then hands were on him, pulling him away from the table, wresting jagged pottery from his grasp. Something soft pressed against his forehead. A scarf bound the slash on his wrist. Voices echoed around him. Someone shouted for a doctor.

Blackness crept in from the edges of Edward's perception. The vortex on the floor closed on itself, shrinking away.

"Shut it!" cried Edward. "For God's sake lock him out! Shut it tight!"

And then darkness.

34
PALMYRA, 1884
THE HAUNTED MAN

A banging startled Edward awake. He leapt from bed and grabbed clumsily for the gun he'd laid on the floor. Sherman, who had spent another night with Edward, was already on his feet. The dog growled a warning. Daylight streamed into the one-room cabin. Disoriented and raw-nerved, Edward pointed the pistol at the door.

"Who's there?"

"Mr. Drake, may I speak with you?" The voice belonged to Henry Hyde, the spiritualist publisher.

Edward was in no mood for visitors. After the Sheriff had thrown him up against a wall and threatened to break his neck, Edward had gone back to the woods to continue his search. He'd spent a frustrating day poking his head into old grain silos, a foreman's shack by the railroad tracks, and any number of scratchy thickets and hollow tree trunks. He'd come home cold, filthy, and exhausted. And no closer to finding the children or his brother.

Now he glanced at his watch. 7:42 a.m.

"Go away, Mr. Hyde. It's too early for ethereal discourse."

"I have urgent news!"

Grumbling, Edward set down the gun and picked up a looking glass. His hair was in a frightful state, and his cheeks and chin needed shaving. His clothes were sweaty and rumpled; he'd have to change. "A moment, please!"

He splashed his cheeks with witch hazel tonic to wake himself, then dressed perfunctorily and tamped down his hair with a brush. He slid the trunk from the door. Henry Hyde stood in the dooryard. His shiny shoes tapped impatiently among weeds and pine needles.

"What news, Mr. Hyde?"

"A search party spotted your brother last night!"

Edward yanked the man into the cabin. Hyde drew himself up at the sight of Sherman. The dog inspected the publisher with a judicious nose.

"What have you heard?" demanded Edward.

Hyde said Jim had been seen near Wiborn Cut, a gorge near the railroad tracks. Edward knew this place; it was just three or four miles outside of town. He'd searched the gorge himself two days ago.

"The sheriff's had men and dogs out all night," said Hyde. "They aim to run your brother down."

Edward shook the man's hand. "Thank you, Mr. Hyde—you've done me a good service. I must ask you for another: If Jim should come to you, would you hide him?"

"I'll tuck him out of sight. And you?"

"I'm going to look for him."

"Be warned—armed men are scouring the woods. They may not scruple about which Drake they shoot."

"I know it," said Edward.

Hyde scurried away. Edward kept a reserve of cash in a hidden compartment in one of his trunks. Whoever had ransacked his belongings hadn't discovered it. He added the cash to his wallet. If he found Jim, they would light out immediately for Boston; the cash would pay their way. As for his trunks, Edward would have to send for them later.

Perhaps he and Jim could hop a freight car heading east. When they reached Syracuse or Utica, they could risk a Boston-bound passenger train. He would pay for a private compartment.

And once in Boston? He would put up Jim in a rented room near his own apartment. Then they would have a little time to think about what to do next—but not much. If Sheriff Cole really had eyes on Edward, he would soon know Edward was gone. Authorities in Boston would be wired. The law would gather its power to catch the fugitive.

Perhaps Mrs. Coffin would take in his brother? The authorities would tread more lightly on Beacon Hill. But would Mrs. Coffin harbor Jim? He wasn't sure.

He set these questions aside—escape was the first priority. Edward put a loaf of rye bread and the jug of cider in a sack. He and Jim would have to travel on foot to get out of the county. The bread and cider would provide a little nourishment. He slipped the revolver into his coat pocket.

The morning was cold, but the rising sun was clear and bright. He walked Sherman back to Tante V's place and told her briefly of Hyde's news.

"Maybe my dog ought to help you track your brother," she said.

"No Auntie. If I find Jim, we're leaving Palmyra right away. The dog would be an impediment. Keep Sherman with you. And keep a sharp eye out for Jim. Maybe he'll come through here."

"I'll watch for him. You watch yourself, Eddie—I got a feelin' Old Bill is tightenin' his snare."

Edward, more worried about the sheriff and his vigilantes, made no comment.

"If this our farewell," said Tante V, "I'm pleased I got to see you all grown up." She embraced him.

Edward returned the embrace. "Thank you for your hospitality, Auntie. If our paths don't cross again, I promise to write."

"You do that."

Wiborn Cut was a shallow gorge that ran for nearly a mile through the woods, having been carved out of the earth by a glacier thousands of years ago. Edward sped to the place where the gorge was at its widest—perhaps thirty feet from one bank to the other. The slope there was slightly less precipitous than elsewhere. At the top of the gorge, Edward looked around for signs of his brother or his brother's pursuers. Seeing nothing, he eased his way down, grasping at roots and rocky outcrops for handholds.

A shallow stream ran along the bottom of the gorge. Someone had dropped a log across the water as a makeshift bridge. Edward navigated the log with much arm-waving. As a barefoot boy he would have scampered across like a squirrel, but he congratulated himself for reaching the other side with dry shoes.

The far bank was a narrow spit of sand, clear of vegetation. The remains of a fire littered the bank. Boot prints and dog tracks marked the ground. Jim had been here, and so had a search party. But Edward was alone now.

He put down the sack with the bread and cider and walked along the stream, wondering if his brother had doubled back on his pursuers. He found nothing. Edward retrieved his sack, crossed the log, and scurried back up out of the gorge. The climb left his hands grimy. He wiped them with a handkerchief.

Now what? He inventoried childhood landmarks where Jim might hide. Two or three came to mind. Edward resolved to check them one by one, though he suspected his search would be futile. If Jim hadn't fled Palmyra by now, he must have an excellent hiding place.

Edward walked to a waterfall on Red Creek where a mill once stood. He searched among the brick foundations of the mill and investigated a moldering old cellar. Nothing. He hiked up Indian Hill and wandered among a stand of pine that crowned its top. The woods below were ablaze in maroon, gold, and orange. Somewhere beneath those colors his brother ran from men and dogs. But where?

Edward descended. He traveled along game trails and old

logging paths. Hour mounted on hour. He helped himself to the bread and cider. Noon came and went. The urgency that had driven him from the cabin this morning devolved into frustration. He searched rotely, compelled more by duty than hope.

Now and then he heard men shouting and dogs braying; the sheriff's search party. He took care to avoid them. A pack of angry men wouldn't hesitate to throw any Drake they caught into jail—or just shoot him where he stood.

As the sun traversed the far horizon, Edward abandoned the pretense that the cider and bread were for his brother. He emptied the jug with a long, deep pull. His head spun from the alcohol in the fermented juice. His mood was as sour as the drink. He muttered a curse, and then flung the empty jug with a hard overarm throw. It shattered against a tree trunk. Instantly he regretted the outburst. The jug belonged to Mrs. Forrest, and she'd done nothing to deserve broken crockery. He'd have to compensate her.

Edward munched the loaf of bread, the only food he'd eaten all day. He trailed crumbs through the forest like a boy in a fairy story, the gruesome Germanic kind where children were tormented and murdered.

He sensed a malevolent intelligence in these woods. It lurked among the leaves and boughs. It toyed with him, teased him, caught him up in a cruel game of its own devising. He didn't want to play anymore. He held out his arms.

"Olly olly oxen free!" he called, invoking the spell that summoned hiders to the seeker. "Olly olly oxen free!"

No hiders emerged.

"Very well," he muttered. He started back toward the Bottoms, frustrated and footsore. He would check with Tante V to see if Jim had come through. If not, perhaps he would borrow her dog after all. He'd have Sherman sniff Jim's clothes and see if the beast could track him. The thought of more searching dismayed him. How long could this go on?

Dead leaves crackled nearby, disturbed by furtive footsteps. A twig snapped beneath a boot. Edward paused—perhaps his spell had summoned someone after all. "Jim! Is it you?"

A tall figure slipped behind a maple tree.

"Jim! It's Eddie."

The figure moved away, drawing Edward after him. "Goddam it, I'm here to help you!"

Then Edward saw a pale hand clutch the tree trunk. Long fingers stained the bark like lichen. A face peeked from behind the tree, sallow skin stretched tautly over sharp cheekbones. Fever burned in the gristly orbs of his green eyes.

"Not you," whispered Edward.

Mr. Jangles grinned. The smell of old tobacco wafted from the folds of his soot-colored coat.

"You're not real."

A thread seemed to stretch from the ghoul to Edward. A glistening drop of thought slid across this thread like spider venom and leached into Edward's mind.

Come with me. I have something to show you.

Edward wanted to run in the other direction, but a terrible sense of inevitability took hold of him. He couldn't run from this apparition, nor dismiss it with logic. This was his fate. It could not be escaped. Heavily he lifted one shoe and then the other. He followed Mr. Jangles through the trees.

Becky Deaver was propped against an elm. Her dark hair was plaited in braids. She wore a brown cotton dress and polished black shoes. Becky's hands rested in her lap as if she sat at a school bench, awaiting instruction. There would be no more school days for this child. Her face was chalk white. Flecks of red clay were caught in her braids. Cruel purple marks around her neck showed where a cord or belt had strangled the life from her.

Edward shivered. "So cold," he whispered. "You must be so cold out here in the woods with no coat."

Mr. Jangles loomed nearby.

The way is made ready, Edward. The pieces fall into place. We'll meet again soon.

Mr. Jangles vanished. Edward's head rang like a cracked bell. What did that mean? What pieces? Why would they meet again? He snatched up a rock and flung it where Mr. Jangles had stood. "Go to hell!" he shouted. "Go to hell where you belong and leave me be!"

Then he turned to Becky Deaver. "I'm sorry, child." His voice broke. Tears wet his cheeks. "I'm sorry I couldn't save you. I couldn't save *any* of you."

As he wept over the girl, he waited for her eyes to open. They would be grey and flat, like tarnished lamps lit with rancid oil. Her lips would part. With a raven's voice she would denounce him as a feckless fool and damn him for failing her. For failing all of Palmyra's murdered children. But Becky Deaver was still and silent, her corpse condemnation enough.

Edward stumbled away, clutching his head. "What do I do?" he cried. "What do I do?"

"What have you done?" said a voice.

35

Sherriff Cole stepped into view, his rifle pointed at Edward. "What have you done? Is that Becky Deaver?"

"I found her like this," said Edward. His anguish turned to alarm.

The sheriff bulled past Edward and knelt by the child. He touched her neck with a finger, feeling for a pulse they both knew was absent.

"I heard a voice," said Cole. "Someone yelled 'Olly olly oxen free.'"

"I did," said Edward, realizing how foolish and strange he must appear.

"Is this a game to you?"

"No game."

"I have to take her to town. Her folks will want her. At least they can have a proper burial now."

Edward nodded.

"And you," said Cole. "You're under arrest."

"Me? I didn't harm her. I only came across her moments ago."

"So you say. We'll sort it out at the jail."

Edward stepped back. "If you lock me up, they'll come for me like they did Jim."

Cole didn't dispute this. "Go on," he said. "Pick up the body."

"What?"

"I can't carry her and keep my rifle on you at the same time. Pick her up."

"She's *dead*. I don't want to touch her."

"I don't care what you want. Pick her up."

"I refuse."

Cole aimed his rifle. "Do as I say or I'll put a bullet through your knee. That'll keep you here while I take her back to town. Then I can collect you later."

"You're insane!" cried Edward.

"I'm the law. Now pick her up!"

Panic slithered along Edward's nerves. He was in very bad trouble. He thought of the revolver in his coat pocket, but Cole's finger was already on the trigger of his own weapon. Cole would shoot him dead if he drew a gun.

He turned to the corpse. Becky Deaver lay indifferent to the conflict that swirled around her. Edward bent and lifted the child. She was surprisingly heavy. A desperate idea came to him. "Forgive me," he whispered. He took two steps forward and flung her body at the sheriff.

"Christ!" shouted Cole. The corpse struck him square in the chest. He stumbled backward. Edward crashed into the man with his shoulder, knocking Cole to the ground. He snatched up the rifle and dashed away swift as a deer.

"Stop goddamn you! Edward Drake, come back!"

Edward ignored the commands. "I have the gun, he has the girl. I have the gun, he has the girl. He won't chase me because I have the gun and he has the girl." The refrain played in his head like a mad calliope as he pelted through the woods.

His panic drove him like a steam engine. The brushy ground rolled beneath him as if on rails. He heard no sounds of pursuit, only his breath in his ears and the pounding of his feet. He dodged tree trunks and leapt over stones and clinging brush, running faster than he'd ever run in his life.

But soon the engine of panic ran down. His legs grew dull and heavy. A stitch needled his side. The cold autumn air resisted him. He fetched up against a moss-covered boulder and looked back the way he'd come. He counted ten breaths, then twenty, expecting to see Sheriff Cole trundling over the horizon. Edward raised the rifle. He would shoot if necessary.

Cole did not appear.

"He let me go," thought Edward. He sucked great gusts of cold air into his lungs. "He let me go to bring the Deaver girl home."

But pursuit would come. Of that, Edward had no doubt. He jogged on, this time choosing a direction. The Forrest farm was nearby. He knew he shouldn't drag the Forrests further into his troubles, but he needed to tell someone what had happened, to make sure they understood that he hadn't hurt Becky Deaver. They would believe him. Evelyn would believe him. And then what?

"I should leave," he said aloud. "I'm sorry, Jim. I'm sorry, Cassie. I'll tell the Forrests, and then I have to go." A terrible sense of failure mixed with his despair. He'd come all this way and helped no one. Not his brother. Not Cassie Brown. Not Becky Deaver.

"You're useless," he told himself. He crossed a shallow creek, pausing only to drop the rifle in the water before moving on.

Edward thought it best to avoid the lane that fronted the Forrest farm. Instead, he swung in a wide arc through the woods to the pasture where the family's cows grazed. He stood in the shadows of birch and maple that edged the pasture. A dozen or so cows stood in the field, cropping clover. The barn stood at the far side.

He watched for several minutes, then stepped out into the open. He climbed a rail fence, his movements awkward and ungainly, and then walked carefully across the field. Several of the cows ambled toward him, curious about the human in their midst. They nosed his hands and his pockets.

"Easy now, easy now," he said, as much to himself as to the animals. He stepped gingerly among them, keenly aware of their bulk, their odor, their trampling hooves.

Once he was free, he sped toward the barn. Evelyn stood in the yard, absently scattering feed for chickens. She wore unlaced boots and an unbuttoned coat over her apron and house dress. Her face was drawn and anxious, her movements jerky. She looked up and saw him. She dropped the basket of feed. Chickens swarmed the grain.

"Edward! Where did you come from?"

With a few words he explained what had happened.

"Dear God," she said. "Oh dear God." The blood drained from her face. Edward guessed she was thinking of her niece, that Becky Deaver's murder meant doom for Cassie as well.

"Evelyn," he said. "I need to get out of Palmyra. I just came to tell you how sorry I am I couldn't help. But I have to go now."

Evelyn shook her head. "Not yet you can't. You better come with me."

36

Evelyn led him through the back door of the house and into a mud room. Work boots cluttered the floor. Coats hung on pegs. A short passage connected the mud room to the kitchen. Edward smelled potato soup and fresh-baked biscuits. Mrs. Forrest dithered by the stove, her face drawn and anxious. She dipped her head to Edward but didn't speak. He followed Evelyn through to the dining room. A voice said "Well well. Look who's here."

Edward staggered. It was his father. Pop had come back from the dead.

But it wasn't his father. It was Jim. His fugitive brother sat at the Forrests' dining table, a bowl of soup and a plate of biscuits in front of him. Jim sopped the broth with a biscuit and ate it in one mouthful. Then he stood.

Jim Drake was six foot three, with slabs of muscle in his shoulders and chest. He was handsome like Pop, with sharp cheekbones and an easy grin. His brown eyes gleamed with sardonic intelligence. Yet Jim looked worn. Hunger had hollowed his face. A scraggly beard speckled his cheeks and throat. He wore a filthy coat over bib overalls and a sweat-stained wool shirt. The overalls were nearly worn through at the knees, the hems ragged. Dirt and red clay were embedded beneath his fingernails. He smelled in desperate need of a bath.

Jim wiped his mouth with the back of his hand. "Hello Eddie. That's a fine suit. Never seen a Drake look so dapper." Jim's tone was complimentary, but Edward heard the mockery beneath it, like a glistening trail of slime.

"Haven't seen you for ages," Jim said. "How many years has it been?"

"A long time," croaked Edward. He didn't know what to do: embrace Jim or slap him for all the trouble he'd caused. Instead, he turned to Evelyn.

"He arrived an hour ago," she said. "He was hungry. Cold. Luke took the wagon to go and find you to let you know."

"Did you hear, Eddie?" said Jim. "The good citizens of Palmyra tried to hang me after I found Liza Ames. And when they couldn't string me up, they tried to burn me alive."

"I heard."

"Been livin' rough ever since. Had men and dogs on my heels for days and days. Finally, I threw myself on the mercy of the Forrests." Jim held out a hand to Evelyn. She took it. Jealousy coiled around Edward's heart.

"Pop wouldn't approve," said Jim. "He'd turn in his grave to see one of his sons humble himself to a...to a Forrest. But even Pop couldn't deny they're good Christians. Puttin' themselves at risk to aid a fugitive."

"We know you've done nothing wrong," said Evelyn.

"My best advocate. Too bad no one believes you."

Evelyn squeezed Jim's hand, then broke contact. "I'll leave you two to talk."

Edward saw how Jim watched Evelyn depart, as if he was parched and she a cool drink.

"Where have you been?" asked Edward, drawing Jim's attention away from her. "And how did all this happen?"

"Let's go outside."

They passed Mrs. Forrest on their way through the kitchen. "The soup was delicious," said Jim. Mrs. Forrest only nodded. Her hands trembled as she worked.

Outside, Jim took a battered cheroot from a pocket and struck a match against a rough board to light the cigar.

"Good God, there's no time for a smoke," said Edward. "We need to get out of here." He outlined his plan to get them to Boston. Once there, Edward would retain lawyers to defend them. Thomas Connelly would know a good firm. And Mrs. Coffin could be persuaded to hire Pinkerton agents. They could be dispatched to Palmyra to search for Cassie Brown, and perhaps find the true killer. With some detective work and a little luck, Cassie could still be saved and Jim proved innocent.

"We can be quit of all this," said Edward. "But we have to go *now*." He touched the wallet in his breast pocket, stuffed with cash for their escape. Luke could hide them in a wagon, take them to Syracuse. They could board a train there and stack up the miles between themselves and Palmyra.

Jim raised an eyebrow. He puffed on the cheroot like a man with all the time in the world. "I'm not leavin'," said Jim. "I need to clear my name."

"That's just what I've proposed! With lawyers and detectives, we could..."

"No lawyers. No detectives."

"Then how?"

Jim's only response was an exhalation of white smoke.

"What are you up to, Jim? Do you know who the killer is?"

"I got my suspicions."

"Good Christ, why didn't you say so? Tell me now! We'll clear this up and be done with it!"

"I'll clear it up myself. You needn't get involved."

"Too late—I'm involved up to my neck! I found the Deaver girl, and then Sheriff Cole found me. I escaped him, and now I'm a fugitive like you."

"What'd you say? The Deaver girl's dead?"

Edward nodded.

Jim's powerful shoulders sagged. "I hoped I might save her. I'm sorry I couldn't."

"Cassie's still out there," said Edward. "It might not be too late." He pointed to the Forrest's house. "Evelyn's family is right here. Tell them what you know and let them bring her home. We can help if you want, though I think it's wiser we leave."

Jim gnawed the cheroot. Edward sensed him calculating, like a gambler watching the next card come out of the deck. At last he said "No need to involve them. Nor you. It's best if I handle this myself."

"Goddamit, Jim! Why are you so being so mulish about this?"

"Because this is my opportunity!"

"Opportunity? For what?"

"I got plans, little brother."

Suddenly Edward understood. "Oh, Jim. Not that speaking tour—the one Henry Hyde's arranging. You want to find the killer so you can drum up publicity. Is that it?"

Jim shrugged.

Edward felt sick. "You're going to risk our lives—Cassie's life—for a fraud?"

Jim squared up to Edward, eyes wide and nostrils flaring. "You daren't call me a fraud. People come to me, grieving over loved ones they've lost. With my seeing stones I give 'em comfort. I give 'em peace."

"You give them tricks and make-believe."

"The hell I do. Folks weep with joy when I bring them messages from their dead. They wring my hands in gratitude. I have a talent, Eddie."

"Spare me," scoffed Edward. "It's horseshit. You lie to those people. You lie to yourself."

"I've never lied!"

"No? What about that story you told Henry Hyde."

"What story?"

"That *you* found the children, sixteen years ago. You were never there."

Jim shrugged. "He told you, huh?" If he was embarrassed at being caught out, he didn't show it. "Well, maybe I embellished. It comes with the job. And so what? Pop was there, and the seeing stones guided him. Now I have the stones."

"The stones had nothing to do with it."

"Oh? Then how did Pop find those bodies?"

"He didn't. I did."

"You? You didn't do nothin.' Pop said..."

"It doesn't matter what Pop said. I found the bodies. Me."

"How? With the stones?"

"No, not the stones."

"Then how?"

Edward looked away.

"Just what I thought," scoffed Jim. "Little Eddie, makin' up stories so you can feel big."

"It was a ghost. A ghost showed me." Edward blushed; he hadn't meant to confess this to Jim.

"A ghost?"

Edward waited for Jim's mocking laughter. It was sure to come, just like when they were boys. But Jim didn't laugh. "Let me guess, Eddie—was this ghost an old man? Did he have long scraggly hair and green eyes? Does he wear an old top hat?"

Edward staggered. "You know about him?"

"Old Bill? Sure I do."

"How? Have you...seen him?"

"Seen him? Eddie, he ain't real. Tante V used to tell me about him when we were kids. I'd sneak over to her cabin for a bite to eat, and she'd tell me stories. Then I'd come back and tell the stories to you and Fred. But I made 'em scarier. Scared the hell outta the both of you."

For a moment Edward was back in his childhood bed, he and Jim and Fred jumbled together in the dark beneath their blankets. Jim *had* told them stories, wrapping his siblings in the quilts of his imagination, his voice low and whispery so as not to wake their father.

"Sometimes I'd tell you how Old Bill would stand at the window while you slept. He'd look down at you, his hands like claws, itchin' to snatch you up and carry you away. You'd cry out, 'Don't let him get me!'"

Edward trembled.

"But you never called him Old Bill. You gave him a funny name. The Jangly Man, or some such."

"Mr. Jangles," said Edward.

"That's it. Oh Eddie, you shook like a dog in a thunderstorm whenever I talked Mr. Jangles. Hell, the only time Mama ever whipped me was 'cause one night I scared you so bad, you wouldn't go to sleep. You just cried and cried."

"You made him up?" asked Edward.

"Tante V made him up. I improved on him. Good Christ, Eddie, you still troubled by those tales? I knew I was a good talker, but damn!"

"Why did you do that to me?"

"'Cause I hated you, Eddie. I loved you and hated you at the same time; it was all mixed up inside me. And when I scared you, you held tight to me."

Jim extinguished the cheroot against the sole of a boot and tucked the stub in his coat. "Then you were gone. The Coffin woman took you. Couple years later, she sent Fred to seminary. And me? What did I get? Nothin'. You two rode off on that old lady's money and left me behind. Left me alone with Pop."

"And even then, when there was no one else around, Pop *still* wouldn't take me treasure-hunting. He said I fouled up the stones with my thick head. Not like you. He said you had some kind of gift that made the stones work better. A gift I didn't have."

"It wasn't a gift."

"No? It took you away from here. Made you rich." He fingered the collar of Edward's coat. "I see the old lady's money in the cut of your suit, smell it in your powders and colognes. All I see on me are rags. All I smell on me are sweat and dirt and shit. Is that all I get?"

"No, Jim. You could have more. I can give you more."

"I don't need anything from you. I'll make my own way when I can catch the killer. But I'll do it myself."

"Jim..."

"No, Eddie. This is for me to do, and for me to get somethin' from. If you want to help me so bad, go back to the cabin and get my stones. Bring 'em here to me. Will you?"

"I can't."

Jim glared. "Can't or won't?"

"Someone stole them. They're gone."

"Who stole 'em?" Jim loomed over his brother, fists clenched.

"I don't know. And it doesn't matter. The stones are nothing."

"No, Eddie. Without those stones, *I'm* nothing. Don't you get it?"

Edward grabbed Jim's shoulders. They were hard as oak. Edward wanted to shake Jim loose from the roots of this nonsense, slap his face, pound some sense into his head. "Don't *you* get it? We're in danger of our lives. And there's a girl in danger of hers. If you know who took Cassie, let's tell someone and then get gone. You'll still be the hero. You'll still get your due."

Jim shrugged out of Edward's grip. "No. I'll help Cassie myself. You go. But first, send Evelyn out here. She's holdin' something for me. I'll collect it and be on my way."

"The book," said Edward. "Evelyn gave it to me for safekeeping. I've hidden it."

"Goddammit!" cried Jim. "God fucking dammit, Eddie! Why have you got to interfere with me? Where is it?"

Edward ignored the question. "That book belonged to Goodword. Did you take it from him?"

"I tried to buy it off him, but he wouldn't sell. So, yes, I took it."

"Why?"

Jim crossed his arms and said nothing.

"Why, Jim?"

"Because the book and the stones are connected somehow. They go together. I want to figure out how. I want to see what it might get me."

Edward didn't like this notion, but an idea had come to him. "I'll wager it was Goodword who broke into our house. He wanted the book back. When he couldn't find it, he took the stones."

"That old sneak. He'll get what's comin' to him. Tell me where you hid the book."

"Not unless we leave Palmyra together."

"No, Eddie! I already told you I'm not goin' anywhere with you!"

"And I already told you, we've got to get out of here. Both of our necks are on the line."

"So go back to Boston," said Jim. "Hide behind your lawyers and detectives and Coffin's money. Let me do my work. I'll find where you hid the book—you ain't as clever as you think. Then I'll get the stones from Goodword and rescue little Cassie. I can fix everything."

"Jim…"

"Enough talk. Time for you to go." Jim grabbed Edward and shoved him towards the road, as if ejecting a drunk from a tavern. Edward dug in with his bootheels. Jim wrapped Edward in a bear hug to lift him bodily off the ground. Edward broke Jim's grip.

He relished the look of surprise on Jim's face. Edward's boxing had put some strength into his body. He lifted dumbbells and did press ups and pull ups. He had iron in his back and shoulders now, no longer a runty boy easily subdued.

Jim made a fist with his left hand. With his right, he pointed down the lane. "Get outta here, Eddie, or I'll knock you flat. You don't want to test me."

But Edward did. He stripped off his coat and raised his fists.

"Suit y'self," said Jim. He threw a left hook, lazy and confident. Edward ducked and fired three quick jabs into his brother's kidneys. Jim gasped in surprise and pain. Edward struck him with an uppercut, snapping Jim's head back. Edward grinned savagely. Jim recovered himself, spit blood into the dirt, then launched at Edward.

The brothers collided. Hot breath blasted from their lungs. They growled as they fought. Jim was bigger and stronger, but Edward was nimbler. He practically danced around his brother, pounding Jim's broad frame while slipping counter-punches. He popped Jim in the chin with a deft right cross. Jim staggered.

Edward wound up for the *coup de grace*, then stumbled in the rutted lane. Jim flung a hard, graceless haymaker that struck Edward near his right eye. Edward's consciousness flickered. Jim followed with two big blows to the ribs. Edward's lungs drew tight as if constricted by barrel hoops. He bent double and gasped for air.

Jim reared back, his left fist blotting the sky.

"He's gonna kill me," thought Edward.

The fist crashed down. Stars burst in Edward's skull, then darkness swept them away.

37

"Edward. Edward!"

A sharp slap stung him. Edward sat up and gasped. Pain throbbed through his head and body. Why was he on the dirty ground? Who had hit him with a sledgehammer?

Evelyn put a hand to his cheek. Edward leaned into the cup of her palm. He could rest here.

Then Mr. Forrest came into view. "What happened? Where's Jim?"

Edward pushed himself off the ground, groaning as he did. He picked up his coat and brushed dirt from it. "He's gone. I tried to convince him to leave Palmyra with me, but he wouldn't. Then we fought."

"You fought? Why?"

Edward shrugged; they were brothers. He probed the right side of his face. He felt swelling, and tasted blood in his mouth. His ribs hurt to breath. He hoped he'd given as good as he got.

"Jim knows who snatched the children," said Edward, his words somewhat mushy through his throbbing jaw. "But he wouldn't tell me. He's got some scheme to catch the perpetrator himself." He didn't speak of the publicity and self-promotion that motivated Jim. It was too shameful.

Mr. Forrest grabbed Edward's arm. "What about my grandbaby? Does he know where she is?"

"I don't think so. But if he catches the villain…"

"We'll make him talk," said Mr. Forrest.

Edward took a handkerchief from his pocket and discretely spit into it. Red blood stained the white silk.

"I've more grim news," he said. "I found Becky Deaver's body in the woods. She was murdered."

Mr. Forrest crossed himself. "Where is she?" he asked.

"Sheriff Cole came upon me with her corpse," said Edward. "He wanted to arrest me, take me to the jail. I fled. He has her body."

"Oh goddam," said Mr. Forrest, rubbing his forehead. "You didn't harm that child," he said, half a question and half a statement.

"No. But I feared that if Cole took me to jail, I wouldn't come out."

"You might be right about that. What are we to do with you?"

Before Edward could reply, Luke came barreling down the lane in the cart. "White men are comin'! They got guns!"

"Holy hell," muttered Mr. Forrest.

"They're looking for me," said Edward. "I must go."

"Where?" cried Evelyn.

"I don't know. Into the woods. I'll find a place to hide."

"We can hide you," she said.

"No. I won't bring trouble down on you."

"Too late," said Luke, clattering to a stop. "Trouble'll be here any minute. I passed them in the lane, but they're coming fast."

Evelyn turned on her heel, seeking a hiding place. She grabbed Edward's hand and led him to the barn. Inside was dim and shadowy. Odors of manure and straw crowded Edward's nostrils. Cow pens ran along both sides of the barn. Toward the far end was a loft with bundles of golden hay.

"The loft," said Edward. He could burrow into the hay and hide.

"Not there. Follow me."

She led him down the line of cow stalls and stopped at the one farthest from the barn doors. She lifted a latch and opened the wooden gate. "In here. Get toward the back. Luke, help me bring in the cows. Dad, go and check on Ma." The Forrests dashed away.

Edward stood in the stall, eyes on the open barn doors. What was Evelyn doing? A long minute passed. Edward's head and chest thudded with pain. He spit on the ground. More blood. He ground it into the dirt with his shoe. Presently he heard cow bells clanging. Evelyn, a switch in her hand, drove the animals into the barn. One by one, the cows slotted themselves into their pens.

Evelyn steered a particularly large cow into the stall where Edward waited. The cow was glossy black with a thick white stripe around her middle. The beast moved slowly, even as Evelyn prodded her hindquarters. "Move back," called Evelyn.

Edward retreated to the far wall of the pen. It was littered with straw and smelled of cowhide and dirt. He drew himself up tight as the animal lumbered in. The cow regarded Edward with an inscrutable black eye, then turned away from him. Her belly was oddly distended.

"This is Bee," said Evelyn. "She's very gentle."

"Is something wrong with her?"

"She's got a stomach ailment. Now get down."

"In here? It's filthy."

"Stop being such a dandy and get down!"

"I'm not a dandy," said Edward. "Just fastidious."

Once he was on the ground, back pressed against the wall and knees drawn to his chest, Evelyn pitched straw over him. The dry stalks pricked his hands and face. Chaff wormed down his collar and irritated his neck and back. Flecks got in his eyes and up his nose. Evelyn didn't stop until he was entirely covered.

"Keep still," she ordered. He heard her pat the cow. "Lay down, Bee. Go on."

"What if this animal tramples me?" hissed Edward.

"She won't. The worst she'll do is pass wind."

Then Evelyn was out of the pen. Edward heard the gate latch. The barn doors banged shut. He was alone with the cows. The animals chuffed and grunted as they settled in their straw. Bee the cow shuffled about uneasily. There was a blurt and then a noxious odor that watered Edward's eyes; Evelyn's forecast had proved true.

The animal slowly levered itself to the ground, an operation that required more grunting and venting of gas. The smell was awful. He sensed her heavy shanks teetering towards him. He inched further back against the wall.

At last the cow touched down. Her rump pressed familiarly against his body, as if they were an old married couple. Heat and odor radiated through the straw. Edward found it hard to breath. He feared he might suffocate—done in by a gassy heifer instead of a vigilante sheriff. He shifted uncomfortably, unable to find relief from the itchy straw and his aching head and ribs.

Voices came from outside the barn. Then the doors swung open. Edward willed himself to be still. It was thoughtless of him to have come back here. Thoughtless and stupid. And now he'd endangered the Forrests.

"Have your look, but I told you he ain't here." It was Mr. Forrest. He sounded angry.

Edward heard Sheriff Cole give orders. "The hayloft. Get up there and pitch about with that fork. Don't be gentle." Edward blessed Evelyn's cleverness in steering him away from that hiding place.

Boots passed in front of the stall. Wood creaked as someone ascended a ladder.

"Check these pens," commanded Cole.

Edward, barely breathing, reached carefully into his coat pocket and grasped the pistol he carried.

"Don't spook my cows," said Mr. Forrest. "I don't want soured milk."

"If we find a Drake here, you'll have more than sour milk to worry about," said Cole.

Stall doors swung open. Agitated cows grunted and lowed. How many men were in the barn? If he was discovered, could he fight his way free?

Mr. Forrest said "Edward ain't been here since yesterday."

"But he's been here. You ought to be more careful who you associate with, John Forrest."

"I'll associate with whoever I please. This is my property. You don't even have no warrant."

"I don't need a warrant to search a nigger barn."

A deputy moved methodically down the row of stalls. A glowing lantern rose and dipped, illuminating dark corners. Edward's stall was the last of the row. He breathed silently and shallowly. Straw tickled his lips and nose.

"Edward's committed no crime," said Mr. Forrest.

"Oh? Then why did I find him with a dead child? First the father, then Big Jim, and now the runt. It's time somethin' was done about these Drakes."

"Ain't nobody up in the loft!" called a voice.

"Then get on down here," said Cole.

Edward's pen swung open. Yellow light washed over the straw. He kept utterly still. Bee the cow heaved herself upright with a grunt. As she did, she let fly with another noxious barrage.

"Gaah, what a stink!" said a voice. "What the hell's wrong with that one?"

"She's gassy is all," said Mr. Forrest.

The light swung away and the pen door slammed closed. "Good God, smells like somethin' died inside her."

Edward, rigid beneath the straw, held his breath.

"You've had your look," said Mr. Forrest. "You can go now."

A dangerous silence fell over the barn. Edward pictured the tableau: Cole and a handful white men, hastily deputized. They would be agitated and unsatisfied, their objective thwarted. A defiant Negro ordering them out would not sit well. Might it come to violence? Fists or gunshots? Edward would not stand to have Mr. Forrest harmed nor his family abused. If he must, he would spring up from his hiding place and kill those men. He clutched the revolver in a sweaty palm.

"You listen now," growled Cole. "If I get word that a Drake rested his head here, I'll be back. And I'll burn this whole fuckin' place to the ground."

Boots scuffled and scraped across the plank floor. Hinges on the wide barn doors creaked. Edward wanted to leap up from the hay and gun down the sheriff. But he mastered his fury and kept himself hidden. He counted to ten in his head, then twenty. When he was sure that the men had departed, he extricated himself from his hiding place. He brushed himself off, letting time pass, letting the armed men depart.

When two minutes ticked by, he stepped out of the pen, pausing only to pat the malodorous cow. He scuttled to the barn door and eased it open to find Evelyn just outside.

"Come on," she whispered.

They made their way across the barnyard and through the back door of the house.

The Forrest clan was gathered in the parlor. As one, they turned to look at him. Mr. Forrest was stone-faced, anger baking from him like a stove. Mrs. Forrest twisted a handkerchief in her lap. Her eyes were wet. Luke clutched his shotgun and watched out the window.

Edward stood awkwardly as Evelyn brushed him down and picked flecks of straw from his coat and long hair. He wanted to strip off his waistcoat and shirt and douse himself in buckets of water, but he knew a bath wasn't forthcoming.

"Thank you," he said to the Forrests. "I'm deeply, deeply sorry for the danger I've put you in."

Mr. Forrest glared and said nothing.

"Armed men in our house," said Mrs. Forrest. "Neighbors threatening us with guns. It ain't right."

"What will you do?" asked Evelyn.

"I think I know where Jim's headed. I'll find him. I'll make him tell me what he knows. And I'll get your granddaughter."

"I'll gather Cassie's father Duke and some men," said Mr. Forrest. "Get word back to us quick as you can."

"I will," said Edward. And then he was gone.

38

Edward sped through the gloaming to Goodword's tannery. Jim wanted his stones back; surely that's where he was headed. Edward had to get there first. If he got the stones, he'd have leverage to compel Jim to reveal who the child-stealer was. Edward could share that intelligence with the Forrests. In the meantime, he and Jim would get as far from Palmyra as they could.

If Goodword did have the seeing stones, the old coot wasn't likely to relinquish them. Edward thought he might have to take them by force. That was fine with him.

By the time he reached the tannery the sun was gone. Edward hid behind a maple and spied on Goodword's house. The dwelling was a relic of the region's frontier days. It was built from notched pine logs, the gaps chinked with clay and straw. It had a sod roof, the turves hacked by hand from the ground.

No smoke rose from the chimney. No lantern light spilled through the cabin's narrow windows, which had been cut into the logs and glazed with leaded glass.

Edward hopped a low fence and crossed to the cabin. Foul odors of dung and urine lingered in the old curing pits. The yard was bare of grass, the ground hard and compacted by years of Goodword's tramping. Shovels and picks leaned against the side of the cabin like laborers at a bar after a day's work. A small plot of beans and pumpkins grew near an old stone well. Weathered boards covered the well's mouth.

Edward pressed his ear to Goodword's door. Silence. The door swung inward with a push. Rusty hinges squealed. Gingerly, Edward stuck his head inside. He smelled woodsmoke and unwashed clothes. Goodword had few furnishings: table, chair, bed, and a chest. An unlit lantern and an old Bible rested on the chest. A stack of firewood leaned against one wall.

Nerves singing, Edward stepped inside and pushed the door shut behind him. It was hard to see. He let his eyes adjust, then removed the Bible and lantern to search the chest. He found shirts and trousers, patched and mended many times over, alongside socks and long johns. At the bottom of the chest he found a deck of old cards. Naked women, breasts and buttocks exposed, were painted on each card. The deck was grimy with use. Edward dropped the cards in the chest and wiped his hands on his coat.

He rummaged a shelf nailed to one wall, but found only flour, corn meal, and a jug of mash whiskey.

"Get out!" sang his brain. "Get out get out!" But surely Goodword had taken the stones. They must be here somewhere. He bent on one knee by Goodword's bed and stuck an arm between the frame and the straw tick mattress. He got a splinter for his troubles but nothing else. He found old boots and dust under the bed.

In the fireplace a Dutch oven hung in the hearth. He lifted the black lid and saw half a pan of biscuits. Fieldstones flagged the fireplace floor. Edward noticed discoloration around the edges of one of the stones. Curious, he took a knife from the shelf and pried up a flat rectangle of rock, revealing a small dry hole. Inside the hole was a latched wooden box.

He took the box from the hole and opened it. He expected to see the felt bag that held the seeing stones. Instead he found a few scraps of fabric. It took him a moment to understand what he looked at: a child's undergarments and stockings. He nearly flung the box aside in revulsion. Goodword was the child stealer!

The door creaked open.

"I knew you was a thief." Goodword stood in the doorway. The old man clutched a shovel, the long handle held across his chest. His hands were big and knuckley. Edward fumbled the revolver from his coat and pointed it at the tanner. "Stay where you are!" he cried. "Put down the shovel."

Goodword looked impassively at the gun, then did as Edward commanded. "You're a thief just like your brother."

"And I know what you are!" Edward shook the box with its gruesome evidence. "You're a murderer!"

"You don't know nothin'."

"Cassie Brown. Did you take her? Where is she?"

Goodword didn't speak.

"The sheds," said Edward. "You must be keeping her in one of the tanning sheds."

"I ain't."

"We'll see." Holding the revolver on Goodword, Edward ordered the man to the first of the two sheds on the property. A padlock secured the door. Calmly, as if starting a day's work, Goodword fished out a key and undid the lock. He swung open the door, releasing a cloud of stink that made Edward retch. Goodword chuckled, a dry rasping sound.

"Go inside and stand against the back wall," ordered Edward. When Goodword had complied, Edward stepped across the threshold. The shed was long and narrow with a dirt floor. A line of iron hooks hung from the rafters, ugly and rusted with gore. A few old cow hides lay heaped against one wall. Otherwise the shed was empty. Edward prodded the hides with a toe.

"Cassie! Are you here?"

No response.

"Told ya," said Goodword.

They repeated the pantomime at the second shed. Edward found old tools, a wheelbarrow, and scraps of lumber, but no child. His frustration mounted. Goodword must be the perpetrator! They exited the shed and stood in the yard.

"You're a wanted man," said Goodword. "Wanted for child murder."

"Where is she? Where's the girl?"

"Another feckless Drake—always seekin', never findin'."

Edward brandished the gun in Goodword's face. "Where is she!?!"

"You don't frighten me. Not you nor Big Jim. The law will have him. And it'll have you, too. They'll hang you both from the bandstand. Crows'll pluck the eyes right out of your head."

Edward shook with frustration. Nothing in his experience had prepared him to hold a man at gunpoint. Should he march Goodword to town? Could he convince anyone of the man's guilt before a mob fell on *him*?

"Be gone," said Goodword. "Go hide until the dogs track you down. I'm gonna have my supper." The tanner walked toward his cabin.

"Stop!" shouted Edward. Goodword ignored him. "Stop, damn you!" Edward thumbed back the hammer. "I'll shoot if I have to."

Quick as a snake, Goodword snatched up a shovel that leaned against his house. He turned and charged at Edward, the shovel held high over his head.

"Stop!"

Goodword came on, feet pounding, teeth bared. Edward pulled the trigger. The gun clicked impotently. He tried again. Nothing.

The old man swung.

Edward threw an arm over his head. The flat of the shovel struck his elbow. The bone sang a high song of pain. Edward's hand went numb and he dropped the gun.

The old man reared back to swing again. Edward charged him and wrapped his arms around Goodword's waist. Wiry and fierce,

Goodword writhed in Edward's grasp. Edward's superior weight bowled him over. But Goodword twisted his hips as they fell and landed on top of Edward. His strong, callused hands locked around Edward's throat.

Edward pulled at the man's wrists, but Goodword's grip was too strong. He squeezed Edward's windpipe with his thumbs. It hurt so much! Edward tried to cry out, but he couldn't draw breath.

"You should'a let me be," said Goodword.

A sound rose in Edward's ears: the frantic thud of his own heart. He punched and slapped at Goodword, but the man held on.

"Sneaking thief. Jus' like your brother. This is what you get."

Goodword's thumbs bore into Edward's windpipe. A grey mist crept in at the corners of his vision. Edward groped in the dirt with one hand. His fingers found the gun.

"I'll dig you a hole. Dig it so deep no one'll ever find you."

Edward swung his arm in a hard desperate arc. The gun struck Goodword's temple. The man's eyes rolled up in his head but his hands continued to choke.

Edward swung again. With the second blow, Goodword slumped sideways, his grip broken. Edward sucked in great gouts of air. Pain etched each breath, as if he inhaled shards of glass. The bellows of his lungs opened and closed, opened and closed. Edward rolled on his side. Tears pricked the corners of his eyes. He coughed and gagged, harsh barks that stabbed his throat and skull.

He lay still for a dozen breaths. Finally his vision cleared and his breathing grew less painful. Clumsily he rose to his feet and touched his throat. The flesh was sore and tender.

Goodword lay insensate on the ground, eyes closed. Blood ran from the side of his head. His narrow chest rose and fell, so he wasn't dead. Edward clutched the revolver in his right hand. Bits of skin and white hair stuck to the metal. Why hadn't it fired? Had he been carrying a defective gun this whole time?

"Goddamn, Eddie," said a voice. "Two fights in one day. I ought to call you the Boston Brawler." Jim stepped from the shadows. "You all right?"

"How long were standing there?" wheezed Edward. "He almost killed me!"

"Got here just as you knocked him cold. That was a helluva hit."

"You're here to get your stones?"

"The stones and the girl."

"The girl? You knew it was Goodword?"

"I had my suspicions. Been tryin' to follow him around while I was on the run, to see if he'd lead me to the kids." Jim picked up the box that Edward had taken from its hiding place. He looked inside and shook his head in disgust.

"Cassie," said Edward. "If we find her, our names are clear."

Jim pointed to the sheds. "In there?"

"No, I already looked."

Jim checked the curing pits. They were empty. He tapped a stubbled cheek. "Goodword's a money digger. Dug a maze of tunnels underneath Palmyra. I know 'cause I hid in a few of 'em."

Edward's spirit sank. They were so close—they could save a child's life and exonerate themselves. But network of underground tunnels? How long would that take to search? Could they even find them all? And what of the poor child, hidden away in the dark? "What do we do, Jim?"

"If I was Goodword, I'd want to keep my captives close by."

"I already searched his cabin and the sheds."

Jim walked to the well. It was a ring of stacked stone, perhaps waist high, covered by old planks. He pushed the boards aside. "It's dry!"

A ladder leaned against the side of Goodword's cabin. Jim slotted it down into the well. "Just the right height," he said. Then Jim went over the side and climbed down.

Edward glanced at Goodword. The man was prostrate. Ragged breath whistled from his nostrils but he was still unconscious. Edward snatched up the shovel Goodword had attacked him with and hurried to the well. The ladder touched a clay bed perhaps ten feet down. Jim had vanished from sight.

"There's a tunnel down here." Jim's voice echoed up the stone cylinder.

Edward tapped an anxious foot. At last he saw a dim form wriggle into view. Jim, on his hands and knees, backed out from a narrow opening at the base of the well.

"Did you find her?"

Jim came up the ladder. Red clay matted his hair and stained his palms and knees. "There's no one down there. But I found these." He clutched the neck of a familiar felt bag.

The goddam seeing stones. And now Jim had them, leaving Edward with no leverage. But that was the least of his concerns. "No child? You're sure?"

"I'm sure. The tunnel's pitch dark, but it don't go too far back. Wasn't nothing there but my stones."

Edward yanked at his hair in frustration. Now what?

Jim tapped him on the shoulder and pointed. Goodword was gone.

39

"Goddammit, Eddie. I told you to let me handle this. Now it's all gone to shit."

"Me? This is your fault—if you'd told me it was Goodword, we could've taken him together!"

"I never asked for your help. You thought you knew better, so you stuck your nose in!"

"Shut up and listen to me!" hissed Edward. "Goodword's probably on his way to get Cassie Brown right now. We need to tell the Forrests. They're gathering men. Then we need to get the hell out of here."

Jim scowled. "Guess I got no choice now. But first I want the book."

"To hell with the book!" said Edward.

"I'm gettin' it. You can tell the Forrests."

Edward was reluctant to let his brother slip out of his sight again. "Fine. We get the book and then go tell the Forrests. And then we leave here!"

They put the box with the evidence of Goodword's crimes back in the hole by the fireplace; they would tell the Forrests where to find it. With great care they set off through the woods to Jim's shack. As they slipped among the trees, Jim continued to curse Edward for his meddling. Edward gritted his teeth and ignored it as best he could.

Quickly the brothers arrived at the outskirts of the Bottoms. They hid behind a tree and assessed the situation. For once, Edward was thankful his misanthrope father had built the cabin so close to the woods, and so far away from the other houses on the commons. Edward feared Sheriff Cole might've posted deputies around the Drake cabin, but he saw no sentries, nor anyone for that matter. All the little shanties were buttoned up tight, as if against a coming storm.

"The book," whispered Jim. "Where'd you hide it?"

"This way," Edward huffed. They dashed to the shack and removed the burlap-wrapped bundle from the woodpile.

"I've got a little money hidden inside," said Jim. He tipped his head toward the house.

"No! I've money enough for both of us."

Jim ignored Edward and slipped into the cabin. Edward followed. The cabin was dim and cold. Jim put the stones and the book on the table, and then went to a corner by the stove and began to pry up a loose board.

Edward placed the useless gun on a shelf and stood over the book and the stones. A dim glow surrounded the objects, as if a diabolic current illuminated them. As a boy, Edward had caught the sun in a glass lens. He'd concentrated the light into a beam that set fire to dry grass and dead leaves. He sensed a similar property here, as if the stones and the book could somehow interact and concentrate infernal energies.

Edward rejected etherealism. For many years he had refused to acknowledge occult forces. Yet here in the dark, in the presence of these loathsome artifacts, his refusal crumbled. The book and the stones terrified him.

"We have to go," said Edward. "We have to go now."

Jim came to his brother, stuffing a few bills into his pocket. He reached for his treasured possessions.

"Please," said Edward. "Leave them."

The door burst open. Sheriff Cole leaped into the cabin with a hunter's swiftness. He struck Jim in the head with his rifle. Jim toppled senseless to the floor.

"I'll be havin' you both," said Cole. "Carry your brother outside."

Edward, stunned by Cole's arrival and attack, only gaped.

Cole jammed the rifle in Edward's belly. "Do as I say or I'll blow your guts all over this shithole."

Mind reeling, Edward went to Jim. His brother was unconscious but breathing. Blood trickled from the side of Jim's head. Edward got his hands under Jim's arms and dragged his bulk gracelessly across the floor and outside. Cole followed. A cart and horse waited in the yard.

"Put him in," commanded Cole.

"It's Goodword," said Edward. "Goodword's the child stealer, not Jim. We found evidence! We..."

"Shut up."

Faces peeked from doors and windows, scantly illuminated by candles and lanterns. Tante V came out of her house, Sherman at her side. She gasped at the sight of Jim in the dirt.

"He dead?" she called.

Cole spit on the ground, then raised his voice to carry across the Bottoms. "He ain't dead. He's under arrest. And I'll clap irons on anyone who interferes with me. Get back inside. Now!"

"Eddie, you all right?" asked Tante V.

"Goodword is the child stealer!" called Edward. "There's evidence in his cabin! Tell the Forrests!"

Cole slammed the rifle into Edward's side. Sherman snarled and bared his teeth. Cole pointed his rifle. "Secure that fuckin dog before I put a bullet in him!" Tante V grabbed Sherman by the neck and dragged him back into her house.

Gasping with pain, Edward hauled Jim into the back of the cart.

God he was heavy! Grunting and straining, he managed to load him gracelessly into the wagon. He lay Jim's body next to a bundled tarp. Then Cole manacled Edward's wrists and sat him in the wagon's front bench. A length of chain ran through an iron ring bolted to the footrest. Cole locked the chain to Edward's manacles, securing him to the wagon.

Cole went back into Jim's cabin and returned with the seeing stones and the book. He tossed both into the bed, then climbed in next to Edward and took the reins. A click of his tongue set the horse in motion. The cart trundled out of the Bottoms.

We are well and truly done, thought Edward. In his mind's eye a mob of men waited for them at the village green, torches and rope in hand. He and Jim would be pulled from the wagon. Their heads would be smashed, their ribs staved. They'd be strung up in the same bandstand where Fourth of July speeches were delivered, left to dangle from a beam until they strangled to death.

But Sheriff Cole did not drive to town. He steered the cart down an old logger's track, taking his captives away from Palmyra and into the forest. The sheriff's attention seemed fixed on a distant point.

What did Cole intend? To administer the final punishment himself? Cole could shoot the brothers in the back and claim they tried to flee, or slit their throats and say the Drakes had come at him with knives. Cole could make up any lie he wanted and no one in Palmyra would question him—at least, no one in authority. Mrs. Coffin would surely raise a fuss, but what would it matter? He and Jim would be dead.

"Where are we going?"

Cole punched Edward in the face, a hard blow that rattled his teeth and set his head ringing. "That's partial payment for the trouble you've caused me. We'll settle the full bill directly."

Anger coursed through Edward, overwhelming his fear and despair. If Cole meant to murder them, Edward resolved to draw some of the sheriff's blood before he died. He sat in his manacles and gathered his courage.

40

The tarp rustled. Edward turned, assuming it was Jim, but his brother was still unconscious. Something moved beneath the waxed cloth. Cole reached back and pulled aside a corner. Underneath was a Negro girl, bound and gagged. Her face was streaked with dirt and red clay. She whimpered behind her gag. Her eyes pleaded with Edward for help.

Realization crashed down on Edward like a toppled oak. "That's Cassie Brown. You took her."

"Took 'em all," said Cole. He addressed the girl. "Lay quiet, child. We're almost through." He draped the tarp back over her face.

"But Goodword—I found evidence in his cabin."

"Yes, the undergarments," said Cole. "I gave those to him, the dirty old man. He let me use his tunnels to hide the children I took, and he wanted somethin' in return. Besides, if I ever needed a scapegoat other than Big Jim, them undergarments would be evidence enough to send Goodword to the gallows. But I got your brother back. That's much better. I'll see to it Big Jim takes the blame when all this is done."

Edward knew with sickening certainty that the horror of this night would mount and mount. "Was it you, fifteen years ago, who killed those three children?"

"It was. But I never meant to kill Katie Cooper. That was an accident."

Katie Cooper was the first corpse Edward had found as a boy. Her ghost had appeared to him here in Palmyra, both alone and in the presence of Mr. Jangles. "Accident? You strangled her to death."

"And Lord, I'm sorry for it. I loved that girl. Still do. I made a terrible mistake. And tonight, at last, I'll set it right."

"You can't set right a murder."

"No? *He* says he can bring her back—if I help him. He'll restore her to me just as she was."

"Who says?"

"If I was to bring her back, I would be redeemed. Sometimes I feel Katie's spirit hovering near me, pure and sweet, urging me on to help restore her. You believe that?"

"No. I don't believe in spirits."

Cole spit into the road. "Don't lie. You can see the dead. *He* told me you could. That's why you're part of this."

"Who told you?"

Cole touched the air with one hand, as if feeling for an edge or a seam. "The boundary between this world and the next is thin—thin enough to pass through and back again. *He* knows how to do it."

"Who?!?"

"His given name is William Jongold. You call him 'Mr. Jangles.' That name amuses him. He likes how it makes you tremble."

Edward felt himself coming loose from reality. "How could you know that?"

"He's waiting for us," said Cole. "Just up ahead. We'll perform a ceremony from his book, and my Katie will return."

Cole meant the creeping book. It lay next to Jim in the wagon. Its leather cover glistened like the skin of a poisonous toad. "What do you know of that thing?" asked Edward.

"I know it's a book of power. Goodword dug it up many years

ago. I was seventeen at the time. I worked at his tannery back then, and he showed it to me. The moment I saw that book, it aroused a great curiosity in me."

"Goodword couldn't make sense of it, but he could see I was taken with it. He let me study it. In exchange, I had to help him with his money-diggin'. The fool didn't realize he'd already dug up a treasure beyond price."

"I sat with the book day after day, puzzling over it—more than I ever did with a school book. The symbols on the pages seemed to sink their roots in my head. I was desperate to understand what they meant."

"That's when I started to hear *his* voice. It come to me in dreams. It was faint at first, but the more I studied the book, the clearer the dream-words came. The voice told me the book belonged to him. If I helped him, he would teach me its secrets. And he spoke to me about Katie. He knew what was in my heart; he knew I wanted her. He helped me work up my nerve to go to her."

"To violate her. Murder her."

Cole punched Edward again, a vicious shot that nearly knocked him out of the wagon. "Shut your mouth. I loved that girl. Murder wasn't my intention."

Cole spoke of how, in the spring and summer of his seventeenth year, he had spied on Katie when she walked to school or did chores around her family's place. He talked to her when she played at the creek with other children. Now and then, when no one else could see, he gave her little presents: peppermints, daisies, a flame-bright feather from a cardinal. He was patient and careful in his courtship.

As summer passed into autumn and autumn into winter, the dream-voice told him he'd been patient enough. He could take her for his own. One February day he followed her after school, staying well out of sight. Katie walked with two other girls, all of them bundled against the cold. He knew the place where she would depart from them, and the lonely track across a meadow she'd take to get home.

That's where he came upon her. He smiled and said he'd found a litter of kittens. A wild dog had killed the mother, but the babies were still alive. Would she like to see them? Would she help him care for them? He knew Katie would want to hold those soft kittens in her hands, hear them mew, nurse them with a rag dipped in warm milk. She was gentle and kind; of course she would help.

He led her to his barn. There were no kittens. Just a blanket laid across some straw.

"I took her as a husband takes a wife," said Cole. "I made her mine. But she didn't understand. She cried and said she would tell on me. I got angry and confused. She wouldn't stop crying. I put my hands on her mouth and throat to quiet her. Her pulse fluttered fluttered like a moth in my hands. I squeezed tight to catch it. Then it went still. She was gone."

"When I realized what I'd done, my heart broke. I wept over her. My tears splashed her face and wet her hair. I stayed with her until she went cold. Then I carried her into the woods. I knew of a tunnel Goodword had dug. I hid her beneath the frozen ground."

"I thought I might keep her there. The cold would preserve her just as she was, and I could visit with her. But that night *he* came to me in my sleep. He told me what to do; to leave her body in the woods, arrange her hair just so and put her hands in her lap. I obeyed because he promised he could undo what I done. He could restore her to me. But you had to find her body."

Edward, groggy with pain, couldn't follow Cole's logic. "Why me? What did I have to do with it?"

"I suppose he was courting you, like the way I courted Katie. Or maybe he was breaking you, like a rider breaks a horse. He needed to shock you open, to get inside your head."

"But why?" demanded Edward. "To what end?"

"'Cause you and I are his instruments. We serve him in our particular ways. I'm the hunter, stealthy and silent. I catch the children he needs. You'll serve him in another way—a way that I can't because I don't have your talent."

Edward struggled to understand. "I found three bodies that winter; Katie's and two others. Did you kill them as well?"

"I did."

"And you laid their corpses in the woods?"

"As he instructed, yes."

"But then you stopped," said Edward. "The murders stopped for fifteen years."

"Oh, I never stopped," said Cole. "But our plans were interrupted because my father ran me out of Palmyra. He found the mementos I kept from Katie and the others. I think he'd been suspicious of me for some time. It was stupid to have keepsakes, I know, but I liked to sit with them, hold them. They soothed me."

"When my Dad found them, he dragged me into the yard and beat me with a rod. Beat me so bad he nearly killed me. Then he fetched his rifle. Stuck the barrel in my face while I bled in the dirt. He told me I could leave Palmyra and never come back, or get a load of birdshot through the eye. So I left."

"Why didn't he turn you in?"

"The old man said he didn't want his name ruined. You believe that? As if he had any kinda name. Truth is, he was scared he'd be shunned or driven off if folks learned it was his son who took those girls. Dad never liked me anyway. My mother died in childbed, and Dad always blamed me for it. He was happy to cast me out."

Cole reached across and touched a bruise on Edward's cheek, one he himself had raised. Edward jerked away. "We're alike, you'n I," said Cole. "Your father beat you. Mine beat me. And we was both chosen by *him*. Chosen for what we can do."

"We're nothing alike!" spat Edward.

"It don't please me to say I'm akin to Bottoms trash, but there it is. We each got our talents, and *he'll* put them to use."

Cole said that after he was driven off, he wandered west. He crossed the Alleghenies and crept toward the great wild plains. He found work where he could, and stole when he couldn't. And now and again, when the urge fell on him, he took a child.

With the mysterious book no longer in his possession, Cole said the voice in his head fell silent. But he cherished Katie's memory, and he clung to the promise the voice had made—how she might be restored to him. He vowed to return to Palmyra one day and see that the promise was kept.

In the meantime, he worked odd jobs: a mill hand, a fruit picker, a railroad bull. He never stayed long in one place. When it was time to move on, he traveled west. In Kansas, he joined the army and made war on the Plains Indians.

"That was somethin'," said Cole. "We called the Indians savages, but we met their savagery with our own. We matched it and exceeded it."

He spoke of cannon shot that shredded red men and horses and left them screaming in the dirt. Indian villages set afire, those who couldn't flee burned alive. How he dashed a baby's head against a rock under the approving eye of an Army captain. How he took his turn with a captured native woman, and after they had their fill of her, how they cut off her teats and fed them to dogs.

Edward turned away, sickened by the man's recitation.

"Then I got word my Dad died. I quit the army and came home. That was a year and a half ago. I got a job as a deputy. When the old sheriff retired, I stepped into his place. Goodword still had the book, so I took up with it again—and I didn't have to dig any fuckin' tunnels this time. And just like before, *his* voice come back in my dreams."

"It was faint at first. Barely even a whisper, and hard to understand. But the more time I spent with the book, the clearer his voice became in my dreams. He still needed me because his work wasn't finished. He presented me with a deal—I'd help him achieve his aim. In exchange, he would bring my Katie back. It was my chance to make it right with her."

"Sheriff, this is madness," said Edward. "Do you hear yourself? Katie's dead. Nothing can bring her back. And there's no ghost making bargains with you."

"There is, Edward Drake. There is and you know him. And tonight you'll serve him as you were meant to."

Terror coursed through Edward. The man was insane, and Edward was in his power. He turned his wrists in their manacles, tested the strength of the chain that secured him to the wagon. The manacles were tight, the chain implacable.

"It was me that put the body of Liza Ames in Big Jim's path," said Cole, sounding pleased. "I knew your brother would snatch her up so he could tell everyone how his peep stones had led him to her. I was waiting for him when he strutted into town with Liza in his arms. Big Jim the spirit man! Hero of the hour. Thinkin' he was gonna be praised. I knocked that grin off his face when I clapped cuffs on him. Liza Ames was bait for Jim. And Jim was bait for you."

"Bait?"

"Oh yes. I needed to get you to Palmyra. I figured if your brother was in jail, you'd have to come to his aid."

"And what of the mob that came for Jim? Was that part of your plan?"

Cole chuckled, almost apologetic. "I'll admit it wasn't. Nor him escaping. That caused me some trouble. Things were touch-and-go for a while. But now the matter has resolved to my satisfaction."

"If you put Liza Ames in my brother's path, did you put Becky Deaver in mine?"

"Now you're catchin' on."

"To what purpose?"

"*He* said I should. It had somethin' to do with opening you. I was gonna bring you to him at that moment. Jim was still on the loose, so I figured I'd better collect you while I could. But you surprised me by flinging her corpse. That was cold-blooded. I underestimated you."

"But you underestimated me," continued Cole. "You thought you could escape, but I tracked you down. You and Big Jim. I knew you'd find your brother—I told you, the first day we met. And now I've got you both, so we can proceed."

Cole reached back and stroked the shivering bundle beneath the tarp. "All that's required is a sacrifice."

"Please," begged Edward. "Please, you need to stop. None of this is real. That's a girl, not a sacrifice. Katie can't be restored to you. For God's sake, Sheriff, you're lost in a delusion."

"You're the one's deluded. You refuse to see what's right in front of you. Tonight the scales will fall from your eyes. You'll see the truth."

Edward trembled, setting his iron chains ringing. If he wasn't locked to the wagon he would run screaming into the woods. He was going to die. So would Cassie. So would Jim. All of this death spurred by ghost-haunted lunacy.

As the wagon rolled through the dark, Edward saw a figure flit among the trees. A young girl, barefoot in the cold, illuminated by a pale radiance from an unseen source. Katie Cooper. Her face was drawn in despair. Her throat throbbed with purple bruises.

A thought leapt from her, leaden with regret.

You should have fled when I told you. Now it's too late.

41

Cole drove to a hilly place of ridges and drumlins. The sheriff halted the cart in front of a cave. Edward recognized it. He'd searched here for Jim not three days ago. Inside the cave was the Devil's Smile.

Overhead, the moon was clear and brightly cold. A few faint stars speckled the dark, silent and vastly removed from the human horror below.

Cole jumped down from the driver's seat. He grabbed Jim by his boots and pulled him off the wagon bed. Edward heard his brother's body hit the ground. Jim groaned. The sheriff bound Jim's hands and feet with rope. Then he unshackled Edward from the cart and removed the manacles. For a moment Edward thought of dashing away, but he doubted he could outrun Cole this time. And he couldn't abandon his brother or Cassie.

"You'll find kindling and logs in the cave," said Cole. "Build a fire. Make it big."

"Build it yourself," snapped Edward. Exhausted and at the end of all hope, he wouldn't do the sheriff's bidding.

Cole took a clasp knife from his pocket and freed the blade. He pulled aside the tarp that covered Cassie. "Do as you're told or I'll carve up this child's face. First her ears, then her lips, then her nose. She'll be alive the whole time. You ever hear someone scream as their face gets cut away? I promise you won't forget the sound." Cassie whimpered behind her gag.

Edward did as he was told. Just inside the cave he found a pile of kindling and a neat stack of firewood. He heaped kindling on the dry, sandy floor and set the wood around it. He worked clumsily, his movements graceless.

Around him, the cave stretched into darkness. Dank air wafted from the pool at the bottom of the drop.

Cole gave Edward a match. Edward struck it against the sole of his shoe and set the tip to the dry twigs and bark. The fire caught, and soon orange and yellow flames drove at the shadows. Under directions from the sheriff, Edward piled on more wood until the fire roared.

Then Cole ordered Edward to drag Jim into the cave and lay him by the fire. Edward obeyed, then knelt by his brother. Jim's chest rose and fell, and his eyes fluttered beneath their lids, but he did not wake. An ugly purple bruise clotted the side of his face where Cole had struck him with the rifle.

The sheriff carried the creeping book and the seeing stones into the cave and set them on the ground. Then he brought in Cassie Brown, still bound and gagged. Cole made the child kneel and then stood behind her. He held his knife to her throat. Cole swayed, his eyes distant. He looked like a man who has entered a room and then forgotten his errand.

A presence emerged from the shadowed recess of the cave, sidling forward across the sandy grit. Mr. Jangles oozed into the firelight, a tumor vomited up from the throat of the earth. He bowed mockingly, and grinned a grin that split his face like rotten fruit.

The hour had come.

42

Look at me, Edward.

Mr. Jangles' voice shivered in Edward's head. His words formed blisters of frost on Edward's brain.

Broken boy. Tonight, at last, you'll perform the task for which I've prepared you.

"No. I want nothing to do with you. I never have."

But I want you, Edward. Your ancestor murdered me but a mile from here. Burned my home to the ground. Thwarted my ambition. Now you'll make recompense.

"Why me? You've already made Cole your puppet."

Mr. Jangles sneered. *He snatches children and chokes the life from them, but he cannot see their spirits, nor the aperture through which they pass. His perception is limited. But not yours, Edward. I've watched your family for generations, waiting for one like you. I hoped your father or your brothers might serve, but they were too thick-skulled. Not you. I sensed your potency the moment you slid from between your mother's legs.*

Ever since you were a child you saw me—saw me more clearly than any of your miserable relations. So I nurtured you, opened a channel in you that there might be perfect understanding between us. Because one day I knew you would serve.

The specter reached out with a yellow-nailed finger as if to stroke Edward's cheek. Edward leaned away from the creature's touch. "I rejected you."

Yet here you are.

"What do you want from me?"

The specter rubbed two fingertips together, a sound like beetles crawling over a desiccated corpse.

The boundary between life and death is thin. The living recoil from this boundary, terrified at how easily they might slip through. They won't see it. They blind themselves to it. But not you.

Grains of sand on the cave floor trembled. A tiny hole opened in the ground, sucking away the sand as if through a funnel. The hole grew wider, a sphincter unclenching. A greasy slick welled up like an oil seep. The slick turned in revolting circles.

Edward had seen this once before, in Mrs. Coffin's parlor. Deep booms echoed from the aperture, like the slow grinding of tectonic plates. Whispers leaked from its mouth, a catechism of despair. The swirling slick widened, spreading toward Sheriff Cole and his captive. It licked at Cassie Brown's knees, threatening to swallow her, but neither the girl nor the sheriff noticed.

You see, Edward, how dull they are? The passage is right there and they are ignorant of it. That's why I need you. There are many paths to the land of the dead, but this one serves a particular purpose—my purpose.

"What does it have to do with me?"

Mr. Jangles snapped his fingers at the sheriff.

"He wants you to go through," said Cole. "When I kill this child, her soul will rise from her body and be drawn through an opening into the spirit world. You are to follow the child through the opening. Follow her through."

"He wanted me to follow," said Cole, "but I can't see the way." Cole struck his skull with the hard heel of his palm. "He tried to show me, but my eyes are blind to it. You can see it, Edward Drake. He told me you can see it clearly. And you can go through."

"Go through? What happens if I do?"

"Pick up the stones," ordered Cole. "Look through them."

Reluctantly, Edward took the stones. They buzzed in his hands like wasps. He brought them to his eyes and gasped—they were translucent. Or at least partly. He could see the cave around him, the flickering fire, the ghoulish figure of Mr. Jangles. The aperture on the floor glowed with an eerie light. Through the stones he could see it was the mouth of a tunnel.

Cole cut the rope that bound Cassie Brown's wrists. He ordered the child to pick up the creeping book and hold it out before him. The girl did as ordered. The book snapped open of its own accord.

"Read," said Cole to Edward.

Edward peered at the pages through the smoky lens of the stones. The symbols on the paper were unintelligible. Then came a sensation, as if slimy threads reached out from the book. The threads passed through the stones and wormed into his tear ducts. They slithered along his nerves to nestle in the folds of his brain. Edward gagged.

Yes, sighed Mr. Jangles. *Your spirit organ; so subtle, so fine. For years I've nurtured it, cultivated it. And tonight, it shall bear fruit.*

Understanding dripped along the threads into Edward's mind. The symbols in the book were an ancient language, an unhuman language, older than the Earth and caked in layers of malice and desire. And Edward could read them. Terrible comprehension poured into him. Here were words of power that would allow a living person to cross over into the realms of the dead, to slip through a passage not as a soul, but in a corporeal body.

You will cross over, said Mr. Jangles. *You will cross over and find me waiting. And then you will guide me back.*

"Back? But you're here."

No. What you see is my shade, which I project into this world. My soul resides on the other side. And when you cross over, you can restore me. I shall breathe air, drink wine, feel the earth beneath my feet. I will take my place among the living.

Edward had no intention of doing any such thing, even if it was possible. But if the specter wanted something from him, perhaps he could bargain.

"If I'm the one you need, set the girl free."

Three pure souls must open the way. Liza Ames and Becky Deaver have passed through already. This child will be the third. She must die.

"Then I want no part of this. I won't help you."

Mr. Jangles flicked his fingers at Cole again.

"If you don't do as he says, I'll kill the girl anyhow. I'll kill your brother next. Then I'll snatch up that Forrest bitch and bring her here. I'll slit her throat and you'll watch her die. Then I'll catch three more children and we'll start over. I'll stack corpses around you like cordwood until you obey."

Edward moaned.

"It's the only way," said Cole.

You have no choice, Edward. Do as I command.

The aperture on the cave floor writhed and shimmered. Was it truly a passage to the lands of the dead? Could he go through? And what of the cost? If he did as Mr. Jangles wanted, Cassie would die. If he didn't, Cassie would still die. So would Jim. So might others. Should he sacrifice the girl's life to save the others? Should he try to fight Cole?

Or was all of this just some illusion? What if the madness he'd held at bay had finally overwhelmed him, and all of this was a ghastly pantomime performed in the shadows of his cracked and broken mind?

It's real, Eddie.

The words where a whisper in his ear. It wasn't Mr. Jangles.

This is real, said the voice. *But you mustn't do as Old Bill says. He wants to trick you. You pass over, and he waits on the other side. He'll strip your soul from your body and enter you like an empty vessel. He'll use your body to carry himself back to the land of the living. And when he's used you up, he'll use the book to take another body, and another, on and on forever.*

Edward didn't understand the source of this voice, yet the words rang true. But what was he to do? Could he overpower the sheriff before Cole slit the girl's throat? No. The knife was a hair's breadth from the child's artery; one jerk and Cassie's blood would spill all over the ground.

Then what about himself? He was the fulcrum—without him, Mr. Jangles had no leverage. If he removed himself, could he thwart the specter?

He measured the length of the cave. The precipice was just a handful of yards away. He could dash to the edge and throw himself over the side the before anyone could stop him. He would plunge into the pool and fall upon the jagged teeth of the stalagmites. Surely that would finish him. And then Mr. Jangles would have nothing.

Be smart! hissed the strange voice. *You know what Cole wants. Use that!*

Mr. Jangles pointed at Edward. *It is time.*

The ghastly hole in the cave floor bubbled. Cole touched the blade to Cassie's throat.

Mr. Jangles spoke. *After Cole strikes, you will see the child's spirit leave her body and be drawn into the aperture. Follow her through! You know the consequences if you don't.*

"Wait!" cried Edward. "Please. Give me a moment to prepare myself."

Cole stood over the child like Abraham over Isaac.

Edward stilled his trembling. He drew a deep breath. For a decade or more he had clung to his spiritualist denials like a man on the side of a cliff. It was time to let go. It was time to acknowledge this strange and terrible truth: Mr. Jangles was real. Ghosts were real. And Edward could see them, hear them, communicate with them. It seemed pure madness, but if he was to survive this night, if Cassie was to survive, he must accept it. He could see no other way out.

Mr. Jangles said he'd opened him? Very well. He would be open.

He would embrace the strangeness within him and use it—but not to serve this malicious spirit.

He remembered Tante V's story about her grandmother, the young woman who had been tormented by William Jongold. He knew it was she who had spoken in his ear. His great-grandmother, Lizbet Cloud.

"Granny Lizbet, will you help me?"

What did you say? growled Mr. Jangles.

"Please, Granny Lizbet."

And she was there, bent and aged. Her hair was white, her skin wrinkled, most of her teeth gone from her head. He recognized her long nose and high forehead; it was the same as his father's, and the same he saw in the looking glass. Her right hand went to a small cloth pouch that hung around her neck. As she touched it, her eyes gleamed. There was strength in the old woman.

I can help. But you must be quick.

"Silence him," said Edward, pointing to Mr. Jangles. "Don't let him speak to Cole."

What is she doing here? snarled the specter.

The aged spirit flew at Mr. Jangles. Their ghostly forms tangled and whirled like sparring cats. The air blurred with the force of their struggle.

Edward turned to Cole. For a moment he was back in Mrs. Coffin's parlor, the alien boy with a strange talent, the focus of eager supplicants who yearned for Edward to stanch their grief. An idea came to him.

"Cole," he said softly. "Katie is here."

The sheriff gasped. "What? Where?"

"Right here among us." And she was there by Edward's side, her face composed, her necklace of bruises shimmering faintly in the firelight.

Cole jerked his head around. "Where? I want to see her!"

"Do you want her back?"

"Yes!"

"You caused her terrible pain," said Edward. "You hurt her."

"I didn't want to. I didn't mean to! I'm so sorry my darling!"

"She can forgive you. And she can return to you. But you must atone."

"I'll do it. Anything!"

"A sacrifice is required."

"Oh yes," said Cole. He pressed his knife to Cassie Brown's throat. Cassie cried out.

"Not her!" cried Edward. "She means nothing to you. If you would truly atone, you yourself must bear the cost." Edward held out the seeing stones to Cole. "These will reveal Katie to you. If you look through the stones, you'll see her again as she was, pure and gentle and alive. And she'll be yours, forever." This was a lie; Edward had no intention of giving Katie to Cole.

"Yes! Give me the stones!"

"I will. But first, the sacrifice. You must put out your eyes."

"What?"

"Your eyes of flesh blind you to the spirit world. You know they do. You said so yourself. If you wish to see Katie, if you wish to have her back, you must remove the eyes that blind you."

"My eyes? I can't do that."

Edward pretended to listen to a voice. "No? Katie weeps to hear you say so. She thought you were true."

An image flicked in his mind, a memory sent from Katie. "You made her a daisy chain once, didn't you? You draped it around her neck. You called her your flower."

Behind him, the air flashed and shimmered. Lizbet Cloud had clasped a wrinkled hand over the specter's mouth.

Faster, boy.

In front of him, Cole wavered. "*He* told me he'd restore Katie to me if I served him. *He* promised me."

"He lies," said Edward. "Mr. Jangles wants to keep her for himself, a sweet little girl he can violate and torment as he likes." He didn't know if this was true, but he had to make Cole believe it.

"Don't you say that!"

"Why has he never allowed her to speak to you? He could, if he wanted. He lied to you. He tricked you, Sheriff, just as you tricked me."

Cole pointed the knife at Edward. His knuckles were white against the handle. "You're the fucking liar! I should cut your heart out. But I can't. *He* says you're needed. You're the key."

"Yes. I'm *his* key. I'll open *his* door. And when I do, he won't need you any longer. He'll cast you aside. Me as well. You've made the wrong bargain."

Katie Cooper took Edward's hand. He felt a tiny mote of pressure against his palm.

"She's right here," cajoled Edward. "She longs for you to see her again. Oh how she longs for it. Will you atone for what you've done to her?"

"My eyes," said Cole. "I can't..."

Edward addressed the little spirit. "I'm sorry, Katie. The price is too steep. He won't pay it. He's going to abandon you to Mr. Jangles." He turned to the sheriff. "Say your farewells, Cole. She's fading now. Your chance to make things right is slipping away. You'll never see her again. She'll belong to *him*, and he'll use her as he likes."

"No! Tell her to come back!"

"Then do it," commanded Edward.

"Katie..."

"Do it!"

Cole dropped the knife. He made spears of his fingers and plunged them with sickening force into his sockets. He screamed as he plucked out twin orbs of gristle. Blood streamed down his face. "Katie! See what I done for you! Where are you, Katie?"

Give him the stones. Katie's voice whispered in Edward's ear. The ghostly figure concentrated her will to brighten and become more visible.

Edward put the stones into Cole's outstretched palms. Cole put them to his bloody sockets and gasped.

"Oh my God! You're there! Sweet Katie, I see you!"

The girl padded across the sandy floor, careful to avoid the swirling aperture, and made her way into the cave. Her form brightened and faded, brightened and faded. Her face was fierce.

"Go to her," said Edward.

Cole staggered forward, blood streaming down his face, his hands slick with ichor. He held the stones to his gaping sockets like spectacles. Katie ran deeper into the cave. Cole rushed after her. "Wait for me, little one! I'm coming! I'm coming!" Then came a shriek.

A cauldron of bats exploded from the cave. Flying bodies swarmed the chamber. Chattering squeals echoed against the walls. Leathery wings flicked through Edward's hair. Tiny claws raked his cheeks. He threw his hands over his head and dived to the ground, covering Cassie's body with his own.

The cloud of bats vanished into the night. Edward looked up. Mr. Jangles stood over him, his face a rictus of hate. Lizbet Cloud was gone. Mr. Jangles bent toward him, mouth agape as if to swallow him whole.

Edward rolled away from Cassie. He snatched the creeping book and threw it onto the fire. The pages caught at once. The flames ate greedily into the book. The oil-stained leather writhed as if in pain.

Mr. Jangles howled in rage and despair. Edward screamed into the specter's face. "Burn you bastard! Burn forever! Burn burn burn!"

The specter wavered and vanished. The roiling aperture on the cave floor clenched like a fist and faded into nothingness. A hush fell over the cave.

Edward stumbled back to Cassie Brown. The girl, legs still bound, whimpered and drew away from him.

"You're all right now, Cassie. You're all right. I'm a friend of your aunty Evelyn. I'll take you home." Edward found the sheriff's knife. He willed his hands to be steady as he cut away the ropes.

The girl wept. "Please don't hurt me, mister. I know you're a witch but please don't hurt me."

"I'm not a witch, child. And you're safe now. I'm going to take you home. Just sit still a minute. Rub your ankles and wrists. You need to get your circulation back."

Cassie pulled her knees tight to her chest and rocked back and forth. "Don't let him get me. Don't let him get me."

"I won't. He's gone. You're safe now."

Then Edward went to his brother, still prone. Jim was awake. His eyes were wide, pupils like pinpricks. "Eddie...what in hell happened? You spoke to someone...someone who wasn't there. And Cole...you made him..."

"It's done, Jim."

Edward cut Jim's bonds and helped him to stand. The brothers sagged against one another. Jim used a booted foot to grind the eyes Cole had plucked from his head into the gritty sand.

Slowly, Edward felt reality knit itself around him, like the healing of a break in a bone. A terrible force had been poised to leap into this world, but the bulwark had been restored. And now he had to get them out of here.

But first he had to see. He took a long stick from the fire. Using it as a torch, he walked into the darkness of the cave. He saw marks at the precipice where boots had slipped in the sand. He craned his neck over the edge and held out the burning branch. Down below, a body lay crumpled among the stalagmites in the shallow pool. Sheriff Cole. The body did not move.

For a moment, Katie Cooper stood beside him.

I can go now. Truly go. Thank you.

Then Katie Cooper was gone. So was Lizbet Cloud. And Mr. Jangles. Only the living remained, battered and heartsick but alive.

43

Edward and Jim kicked apart the fire until it was just scattered coals that glowed redly in the dark. Like eyes, thought Edward. The thought made him retch. Jim took Cassie Brown's hand and led her from the cave. The three survivors climbed into Cole's wagon, Cassie sandwiched between the Drake brothers. The girl shivered. Edward draped his coat over the child's narrow shoulders.

As they rolled down the rutted track, hooves sounded in the distance. Torches and lanterns pricked the dark. Was it a search party? Or a hanging party? Jim set Cole's rifle across his lap.

Edward, exhausted and on the verge of collapse, wasn't prepared to face a mob. His mind was scraped raw, his senses brutalized. He wanted to curl up and sleep for a thousand years. But he sat up straight in the cart and summoned the little courage he had left.

Jim spoke to the girl. "You'll tell them it was Cole who took you?"

Cassie looked back and forth between the two white strangers. Tears streaked her dirty face. "I wanna go home. I want my mama."

"You'll be home soon. There's people comin'. You'll tell them it was Cole that took you, and us that helped you?"

The girl nodded. She hunched deeper into Edward's warm coat.

"Good girl," said Edward. But he doubted the truth would shield them from Palmyra's wrath. The approaching men would take Cassie and then hang Edward and Jim from the nearest tree—if they didn't just shoot them dead.

As the party drew near, Jim lifted the rifle. Edward steeled himself for whatever was to come.

A wagon halted. Someone lifted a lantern. Tante V sat in the driver's seat next to Luke and Evelyn, their faces splashed with yellow light.

"Eddie, I knew you was in distress," called Tante V. "I brought help."

Evelyn shouted "Cassie!" She sprang from the seat and scooped her niece into her arms. The child cried "Take me home, Auntie. I wanna go home!"

Edward climbed down from the wagon, trembling with relief. Tante V embraced him. She rubbed his back and shushed him like a baby.

"It was Granny Lizbet," whispered Tante V. "I heard her voice. She told me where to find you."

Luke wrapped his sister and niece in a blanket. They gave the child water to sip and wiped her face. Very briefly, Edward explained that the sheriff had kidnapped the child.

"Where's Cole now?" asked Luke.

Edward looked away. "He fell into the chasm in the cave. He'd dead."

A murmur of consternation passed through the party; there would be an accounting for the sheriff's death.

"Me and Evelyn'll take Cassie to her parents," said Luke. "Eddie and Jim, you might want to get out of here."

Luke was right, but Edward was weary to his bones. An anvil of exhaustion sat on his brow and made it hard to keep his eyes open.

"Where would you go?" asked Tante V. "I heard there's men on every road in and out of Palmyra. At the train depot too."

"Back to the woods, I guess," said Jim. "I know a few hiding spots."

"We shouldn't have to hide!" shouted Edward. "We saved Cassie. *We* did, Jim! They should be carrying us on their goddam shoulders! They should pin medals on us!" Tears streamed down his cheeks. His body shook. He raised a fist and shook it at the night sky. "They should parade us down Canandaigua Street! They should..."

Edward swayed. His vision blurred. He toppled unconscious to the ground.

44

Edward woke someplace dim and cold. For a terrifying moment he thought he'd slipped through the passage to the lands of the dead. Then he heard a snore. Jim lay slumped at a table, his head cradled in one arm.

They were in Jim's shack. Edward was wrapped in blankets in the bed. He sat up and rubbed his eyes against a haze of fatigue. The stove was out and the cabin frigid.

Edward untangled himself. His clothes felt greasy and mulched down around him. He slipped shoes on his feet to cross the cold boards and draped a blanket over Jim's shoulders. The last thing he remembered, they had just left the cave with Cassie Brown and run into the Forrests and Tante V. They must've brought him here.

Edward bent to the stove and fussed with kindling and matches. He and Jim needed heat. Edward snapped a match against the rough grate. The sulphur tip flared to life. The tiny pinprick of light revealed Mr. Jangles, crouched like a panther in the loft.

The specter leapt down without a sound. His face was poisonous with hate.

He's coming for you. I've led him to you.

Edward stood. The match fell to the floor and sputtered out, but he could see Mr. Jangles' sallow skin in the creeping dawn light.

He'll see that you hang, Edward Drake. And in that moment when your neck snaps and your spirit slips loose, I'll be waiting.

"No."

I could've brought them back, my wife and daughter. That's all I wanted. Lizbet could have helped me. If only she'd cooperated, I could've had my family again. But that bitch dared oppose me!

And now you, Edward. I could've lived again, but you've burned my book. You've left me with nothing but revenge. It's a shallow draught and bitter, but I'll drink it to the dregs as you writhe and choke at the end of a noose. There are many paths to the lands of the dead, and I know them all. When your soul leaves your body I'll be waiting. And I'll carry you to hell.

Outside, people shouted. "They're comin'! They're comin'!" Jim startled awake and leapt to his feet.

Mr. Jangles vanished. Edward gaped dumbly at empty space where the specter had stood.

Jim opened the door. The purplish dark was yielding to timorous daylight. Dozens of men poured into Grover's Circle, some in wagons, some on horseback. All were armed. The noise of their arrival set the Bottoms abuzz. Tante V rushed from her house in a dressing gown, Sherman at her heels. She came and stood with her great-nephews. Other denizens of the Bottoms watched from windows and dooryards.

"That's Dale Oberston," said Jim, gesturing to a skinny, bearded man in the lead wagon. "He was Cole's deputy. Guess he's Sheriff now."

The wagon halted. Oberston stood on the seat. He pulled a pistol from a holster. "Jim and Edward Drake, you're under arrest. You best come quietly."

"What charges?" demanded Edward.

"Kidnapping and murder."

"We saved the girl—*we* saved Cassie Brown! Cole was the kidnapper. Ask Cassie. She'll tell you."

"The Negro child's not right in her head," said Oberston. "She's full of wild tales that don't make sense. And where's Cole? He ain't to be found."

"He fell into the pool at the bottom of the cave," said Edward. "You can see for yourself."

"We searched the cave and the pool. Nobody's there."

"That can't be! I heard him fall. I saw him at the bottom!"

"He ain't down there," said Obertson. "But we found blood in the sand, and the sheriff's hat. Looks to me like foul play."

Jim spat on the ground.

"They ain't done nothin' wrong!" cried Tante V.

Oberston tipped his head at the posse he'd brought. "Bring 'em in."

The men dismounted. Sherman braced his paws, hackles raised. He growled low in his throat, a dangerous sound. The deputies brandished rifles and shotguns.

"Please," cried Edward. He couldn't bear to see more blood spilled.

"Stand down!" demanded Oberston. "Stand down and come quiet!"

"Hang them child-killing bastards!" called a man.

A chunk of stone sailed through the air and hit Edward in the chest. Jim picked it up and flung it back. More brickbats flew.

"Sons of bitches!" shouted Tante V.

My God, thought Edward. We're not even going to make it to a cell. They'll kill us right here. They'll kill us in cold blood.

"Do not resist!" shouted Sheriff Oberston. "Do not resist!"

Men drew closer. Sherman snapped his jaws, white foam spraying. Someone aimed a kick at the dog. Tante V clawed at the attacker's face. Hands reached for Edward and Jim. A rifle bolt clacked. Pistols cocked.

"Edward Draaaaake!"

A shriek pierced the dawn. A hideous figure stumbled from the shadows and lurched across the commons. Sheriff Cole. Gore streaked his face. His empty sockets gaped in his skull. His clothes were tattered. Raw bone was visible through a rip in Cole's trousers.

"Holy Christ," gasped Oberston. "Sheriff...are you all right?"

The sheriff turned in a limping circle. "Edward Draaaaake!" he screeched. "Where are you?" He held out his arms, imploring. His hands were scored and grated.

Edward realized Cole must've climbed from the pit. He boggled at the mania that drove the man.

"Where'd she go?" cried Cole. "Where's my Katie?!"

The Bottoms was absolutely still.

"Edward Draaaaaake!"

"I'm here," choked Edward.

The blind man spun toward the sound of Edward's voice. He limped forward. Men gave way, opening a space between Cole and Edward. Cole stopped four or five paces from him.

"I lost the stones," cried Cole. "I lost the stones when I fell. You got to help me! Help me see her again! Help me see my Katie."

"You'll never see her again. You killed her."

Cole moaned, a piteous sound. He pointed to his gaping sockets. "The sacrifice. I made the sacrifice for her. It hurt so much, but I did it!"

"She's gone because you killed her," said Edward.

"It was an accident. I never meant to hurt my darlin'."

"Then what of Emily Stone? Liza Ames? Becky Deaver? All the others. They weren't accidents. You killed all of them and they won't ever come back."

Cole swayed like a rotten branch in a hard wind. "I don't give a fuck about them! I want my Katie."

"Sheriff!" called Oberston. "Sheriff, what in hell happened?"

Cole ignored the deputy. "Edward Drake, you got to help me!"

"No," said Edward. "You should be punished."

"But my sacrifice...I did as you said. I atoned!"

"There's no atonement for what you did."

"You won't help me?"

"I won't."

Cole hung his head. He sobbed, his bullish shoulders quaking. Everyone stood immobile, as if gripped by a spell. Then Cole stiffened his spine and lifted his head, regaining a measure of his old authority. "Fuck you, then. I'll find her myself."

Cole drew his revolver, pointed it in Edward's direction, and fired four shots. The spell broke. People shouted and scattered. Hot pain punched Edward and he fell backwards. A deputy also fell, a bright spray of blood jetting from one leg.

Then Cole put the gun to his temple. Bone and brain burst from his head in a gruesome firework. Cries of horror drowned the echo of the gunshot. From his perch in the wagon, Deputy Oberston vomited. Cole's body fell sideways. Blood poured from his skull. Edward, on the ground, stared into Cole's mangled face. His own blood pooled with the sheriff's in the dirt.

The child stealer was dead.

45

Jim and Tante V carried Edward into the cabin and laid him on Jim's bed. Tante V pressed a rag to his chest. Men loaded the stricken deputy into a wagon, frantically wrapping his leg with a makeshift tourniquet. The deputy screamed in pain as they raced him away.

Oberston detailed five men to guard the Drake house. "Do not move from this place," he ordered Jim. "These men'll shoot you down if you try to flee."

"Where we gonna go when my brother's got a bullet in him?" snarled Jim.

Oberston had no reply. He ordered other men to collect Sheriff Cole's body. When it was done, three bloody smears marked the weedy dooryard.

Edward lay in a haze of pain and shock. A ball of fire burned in his chest. He'd been shot just below his left collarbone. Tante V told Jim to set water to boil while she fetched her birthing kit and a jug of steady.

She returned quickly with a jug and a battered valise. Tante V drew a pair of shears from the valise and cut away Edward's jacket and shirt. Edward felt the cold metal against his bare skin. He caught a glimpse of the wound; raw and ugly, sheened with dark blood. He smelled burnt cotton and gun powder.

"Good Christ, I'm shot. I'm shot!"

"Hang on, *cher*," said Tante V. "You'll be all right." The fear on her face belied her words.

"My trunk," he gasped. "Little brown bottle. For the pain." Jim brought the nerve cure, made from the oil of poppies.

"Just a drop," instructed Tante V. "I don't know what's in that."

Edward accepted the dose, which blunted his agony slightly. Tante V dabbed the wound with her liquor and a clean cloth.

"Bullet didn't go through," she said. "It's gonna have to come out." She took slim metal tweezers from her bag and dropped them in the boiling water. She poured liquor over her hands, rubbing them back and forth. She gestured to Jim. "You hold him down."

"Wait!" cried Edward. "I thought you were just a midwife."

Tante V scoffed. "Not first time I've taken lead out of a body. Jimmy, you hold him still."

Jim draped himself across Edward's legs and held down his brother's arms. Edward could feel his brother's strength. He wondered if it would be enough. Tante V's face loomed over him. She slipped one of Edward's leather belts into his mouth. "You'll want to bite down."

Then dull metal fingers dug through meat and muscle. Edward screamed through clenched teeth. He fought against his brother, wanting his limbs free to strike at the pain that bored through him.

"Keep him still!" cried Tante V.

Jim's grip was fierce. Edward bit the leather until he thought his teeth might shatter. A shaft of fire lanced him as the Tante V probed inside the wound. He roared in his throat. Finally he heard metal clang against metal—a dull bit of lead clunked into a pan.

"I think I got it all," she said. "You lucky, Eddie. An inch to the right and the bullet would've struck your heart."

Edward spit the belt onto the floor and whimpered. He didn't feel lucky. Pain boiled in his chest. His blood dripped on the floor.

With swift movements Tante V cleaned the wound, then sutured it with black thread. She bound it with a compress. "Keep it clean and it won't fester. You'll have a scar, though." She helped Edward sip some cider.

"Thank you," he croaked. Then, very gently, he turned to his brother. "Now what?"

Jim shrugged. "Now we wait."

46

Edward carried a novel into his study. He wore satin pajamas and a tartan dressing gown. He luxuriated in the liquid smoothness of the satin against his skin—even the scar on his chest.

He poured a brandy at the sideboard and then eased into his leather armchair. Mrs. Penney had prepared a fire. The flames gnawed the dry wood. Firelight winked from the crystal chandelier. With a toe he traced a whirling motif on the Turkish rug. God, he'd missed his apartment! And hot baths. And his books.

A precarious heap of correspondence waited on his writing desk. It would keep. After the horrors of Palmyra, he decided he'd earned a few days' indulgence: good meals, clean sheets, and long languorous sleeps.

He sipped the sweet, syrupy brandy. Wilkie Collins' novel *The Moonstone* lay in his lap. He would open it soon. No need to rush. It was a pleasure just to sit and let the brandy warm him from within and the fire from without.

Click.

Edward blinked. Had he dozed off? The light in the parlor seemed wrong.

Click.

The fire sputtered in the grate. The electric lamps flickered in their sconces. Someone climbed the back stairs with slow, heavy steps. Edward smelled rotten leaves and rank mud.

Click.

He wanted to stand up to see who it was, but the wings of the armchair clutched him. His body felt weighted with lead.

Click.

And then Everett Cole stood before him. The left side of the sheriff's head was gone. Yellowed tendons flexed the white bones of his jaw. Brain matter glistened. The seeing stones plugged Cole's empty sockets like bungs in a barrel. Firelight flickered across the veins of quartz in the white stone. The black stone stared unblinking.

You're a liar, Edward Drake.

Edward wanted to scream. He tried to leap up from the chair and run pell-mell out to Boylston Street, but his limbs were frozen. He was trapped. He could not move.

You said I would see Katie. All I see is horror.

Cole flicked the stones in his sockets with a dirty fingernail.

Click.

I'm in hell, Edward. Hell is real. Real as you and me. And it's terrible beyond anything I imagined.

"You deserve it."

Ain't no one deserve this.

Cole grimaced, his grey teeth clenched in agony. A keening leaked from his throat like water burning in a copper kettle.

Edward pressed his hands against his ears until the sound died away.

My only comfort is that you'll be here too. For what you did to me.

"No."

Soon enough you'll be here. But first I can show you.

With a gelatinous pop, Cole plucked the stones from his sockets.

You'll see for yourself.

Cole reached forward, one stone in each hand. He meant to press them into Edward's head and puncture his eyes like grapes. Then all the terrors of the dead would be revealed to him.

"Don't!" cried Edward. He scrunched into the sweaty leather of the chair, drawing his limbs around him for protection.

My eyes are gone but I can't stop seeing. The visions never stop, only come and come and come until I go mad and still they pour over me. Can you imagine what's that's like, to never be able to close your eyes? To never stop seeing?

"Please, no."

Now you'll learn.

Twin needles of pain pierced his skull. Edward screamed.

47

Click.

Edward sat up and grimaced. His gunshot wound throbbed. Sweat sheened his body.

Click.

It was mid-morning. He wasn't in Boston. He was still in Jim's bed, in the shack in Palmyra. Boston was hundreds of miles away. He touched his eyes. The orbs were flesh, not stone.

Click.

Jim and Fred sat at the table. They stared curiously at their brother. "You OK, Eddie?"

"A dream. I had a dream."

Fred fetched a pitcher. He poured soft cider into a tin cup and helped Edward sip.

"When did you get here?" Edward asked.

"Yesterday afternoon. Your friend Thomas Connelly is also here. He's staying at the boarding house. I understand he's representing you in a legal capacity."

Click.

Edward pushed the cup away and looked for the source of that sound. It was Jim. His brother held the seeing stones in his right hand. He rotated one stone around the other, as if they were tiny moons in the orbit of his palm. The stones clicked as they passed. Pop had toyed with the stones in just the same way.

"Goddammit, Jim! Where did you get those?"

"Language," scolded Fred.

"Mornin' Eddie," said Jim. "I let you have the bed on account of your wound. I slept here at the table. It was very uncomfortable." He put a hand to his lower back and grimaced. "Fred bunked down with Tante V, as you can see by the dog hair on his clothes."

"Did you hear me? I asked you..."

"In the cave. I went back and found 'em. I thought I might have to climb down into that pool, but they was right near the edge. Cole must've dropped my stones before he fell."

"Jim, get rid of them."

Jim raised an eyebrow. He passed his left hand over his right and then made a fist, hiding the stones within one big hand. He knocked his fist against the table and then opened it—the stones had vanished. Jim made a little show of searching for them. He picked up Fred's hat from the table, shook it once or twice, and then pulled the stones from it.

"Very clever," said Edward. "But sleight of hand is not what I mean. They're dangerous and you should be quit of them."

"These are my seeing stones," said Jim. "These stones give the gift of far-sight. With these stones I uncover hidden treasure. I see through the veil between this life and the next. I find what is lost."

Edward recognized Pop's patter, spoken like an incantation whenever a supplicant came to him. Jim had matched Pop's timbre and intonation perfectly. Edward shivered.

"So you mean to go forward with your scheme," he said. "You and Hyde and your speaking tour."

"Indeed I do. With these stones, I can see what no other man can." Jim held the stones to his eyes like a pair of spectacles.

"Not your eyes!" shouted Edward. A book lay on the bed next to him. He snatched it up and flung it at Jim. The quick movement set his wound afire. The book struck his brother's hands and sent the stones scattering.

"What the hell?" yelled Jim. He snatched up the stones and stormed to the bed. "Damn you Eddie, I ought to slap you silly."

"Never do that again! Those stones are diabolic."

"Diabolic?" Jim snorted. "Fred, you bring any holy water? Maybe if a reverend blessed them, Eddie would calm down."

"Don't play the fool, Jim. They're tied to Mr. Jangles somehow. To Old Bill and his book. For God's sake, get rid of them!"

Jim opened his mouth to reply, but Fred spoke first. "Stop it, both of you. Eddie, did I hear you say 'Old Bill'?"

Edward blushed. "Yes."

"You mean that haunt Jim used to tell us about?"

"Eddie sees him," said Jim. "Talks to him, even."

"Jim!"

Fred frowned. "Is that so?"

Edward fussed with the bedclothes. He couldn't look Fred in the eye. "I know it sounds mad, but yes. I've seen Old Bill."

Fred puffed his cheeks. "Lord, what a family. One brother fancies himself a medium and the other sees things that aren't there."

Jim spoke up. "'We look not to the things that are seen, but to the things that are unseen. For the things that are seen are transient, but the things that are unseen are eternal.'"

Edward couldn't believe what he'd heard. Had Jim just quoted the Bible? At Fred?

"From Paul's epistle to the Corinthians," said Fred. "And don't quote scripture out of context as evidence for spooks and apparitions."

"I can read the Bible just as well as the next man," said Jim, "and it says what it says. Eddie, look at Fred there. How he sits in judgement over you and me. He believes himself untroubled by ghosts."

"Of course I am."

"Then tell me—does Charlotte ever speak to you?"

Edward gasped. Jim had just invoked the name of Fred's dead daughter. Edward recalled the memorial in Fred's parlor: the photograph, the lock of hair, the withered carnation. Fred's wife Cicely still wore mourning black.

Fred rounded on Jim. "What did you say?"

"Your Charlotte has passed on," said Jim. "But sometimes you feel her nearby. Isn't that so?"

"Why would you ask such a thing?" A corona of anger bristled around Fred.

"You hear her footsteps as she wanders through the house. You hear her voice in the silence of your sleepless hours. Does she ever call out to you?"

"Stop it," growled Fred.

"You glimpse her from the corner of your eye when you walk into a room. Your heart bursts with gladness, but when you rush to greet her, she's gone."

"Be quiet!"

"When the sun goes down, and night grows long, you can't help but think how lonely she must be," said Jim, "buried in her grave under the ground."

Fred turned away, but not before Edward saw the wetness on his cheeks. "Shut your damn mouth!"

"You miss how she used to climb into your lap and nestle in your arms. She whispers 'Daddy I'm here. Why won't you hold me, Daddy?'"

"For God's sake, leave him be," pleaded Edward.

"Do you hear her, Fred? Do you see her?"

Fred cried out like a wounded animal. Edward had never heard such a sound—as if something rusting and jagged had been pulled from his chest. Jim went to Fred and opened his arms. Edward thought Fred would clobber him. Instead he grabbed Jim fiercely. He pressed his face into the well of Jim's shoulder and bawled.

"Why was she taken from me? Why, Jim? Oh God, how I miss her."

Jim wrapped his strong arms across Fred's back. "She knows, Fred. Charlotte knows. She feels your love. It gives her comfort. And she's at peace, brother. She rests in the arms of the Lord. She wants you to be at peace as well."

Edward saw how tightly Fred gripped Jim. He wanted to go to his brothers and join their embrace, but his wound and his habit of distance held him apart. He wept by himself.

Fred cried for a time. As he did, Jim glanced at Edward and raised an eyebrow. Edward caught his meaning: Jim might not see ghosts, but he could evoke them in others.

The three men remained in tableau until Fred's weeping subsided and the two brothers separated. Jim returned to his place at the table. Fred drew a handkerchief from his pocket and dabbed his eyes. Edward watched his two older brothers, waiting for one of them to do something. They sat in silence for a time, listening to the fire grumble in its grate.

"Fred, you can go back to your family," said Jim at last. "You don't have to fret for me or Eddie. We'll be all right. Eddie's lawyer's here—he'll look in on us. And Tante V and the Forrests are feedin' us up."

That last part was certainly true. The little cabin was crowded with plates and pans; cold ham, chicken broth, roast potatoes, pickled beets, pumpkin pie, blueberry cobbler, corn bread, apple tarts, and jugs of cider. Edward could only eat sparingly, but Jim had gorged. The hollowness in his cheeks had filled out, and his face was no longer gaunt.

Fred nodded. "You do seem in good hands. Perhaps I will return to Rochester." He bustled around the cabin for a few minutes, gathering this and that. Then he went to Edward and clasped his hand. "You'll go home soon? To Boston?"

"As soon as I'm fit to travel."

"Come see us on your way back, will you?"

"I will."

"You did well, Eddie. You saved Cassie's life. And your brother's. I'm proud of you."

Edward blushed. Fred's praise was nearly as discomfiting as his tears.

Fred spoke to Jim. "If your speaking tour takes you through Rochester, come stop at my place. The children have already met one of their uncles. As a matter of fact, they can't stop talking about him. I'm sure they'd like to meet another."

"Be warned," said Edward. "They'll expect nickels."

"Then I'll bring dimes," said Jim.

Fred embraced Jim once again, and then he was out the door. In his absence, Edward and Jim suffered an awkward silence. Jim returned the book Edward had thrown at him, then warmed up a bit of broth for Edward to sip.

Edward sensed that an offer had been extended, a way for the Drake brothers to re-enter each other's lives. Edward didn't know if the offer would be accepted; old resentments and years of distance couldn't be bridged in a single afternoon. But a plank had been laid across the fissure. If they were thoughtful and careful, they might widen and strengthen it into something more durable.

Jim returned to the table. He took up the stones again and practiced his disappearing trick. He passed the stones silently from hand to hand, first the black and then the white. They winked out of existence in one palm and appeared in the other.

How easily the eye can be fooled, thought Edward. He knew the stones hadn't vanished; it was merely the deftness of his brother's hands, and a mind willing see the impossible as possible.

Such thoughts put him in mind of Mr. Jangles. Had everything that happened in the cave truly been orchestrated by a malicious spirit? Were there doorways to the lands of the dead? Could they be opened and crossed through? Had the ghost of his ancestor appeared in the cave to help him? Edward didn't want to believe any of it. But if he didn't, how could he trust anything that he saw, or heard, or felt?

One thing was certain; not a single ghost had appeared to him since Cole's suicide. Edward hoped Mr. Jangles and the rest were gone for good, and that he could ignore such questions forever.

48

Evelyn Forrest and her mother were visiting Boston at Edward's invitation. They had spent the morning strolling the Public Gardens. The dogwoods were in bloom, their white and pink petals unfurled to drink the springtime sun. Elm and oak arrayed themselves in verdant green. Edward and the ladies had picnicked in the park, ignoring the looks of other picnickers seeing a white man in the company of two Negro women. Then they'd strolled to the section of the Emerald Necklace that Edward oversaw. The marsh was now filled with dirt and crushed stone. Pyramids of soil stood ready to be spread. Grass seed would follow, along with willow saplings, rose bushes, and a wildflower meadow.

On his return to Boston last fall, Edward had found his position with Mr. Olmsted still open, and he had taken up the work at the Fens with a good will—with no repeat of nervous fevers or malicious apparitions.

He also took up regular correspondence with Evelyn and Luke over that autumn and winter, and had returned several times to Palmyra. Luke had accepted his offer to invest in an expansion of the Forrest dairy, so he'd journeyed to the farm in the name of business.

Of course, it was also a chance to visit with Evelyn, to hear the playful teasing in her voice as they conversed, to admire her figure as she reached for a bowl on a high shelf, even link his arm with hers as they skated on a frozen pond. He felt a bond growing between them, one that might take a different, fuller course than friendship.

But such a course was fraught. Did Evelyn share his feelings? If she did, would either of them be willing to risk the approbation that would spring from racial mingling? Massachusetts had repealed its miscegenation laws some forty years ago, but abstract legal protection would not protect them from social scorn or physical attack. Even Mrs. Coffin, an abolitionist, suffragette, and Unitarian, might find it hard to countenance an actual union of White and Negro within her own sphere. And so, Edward moved carefully, cautiously. And regardless of any social restraints, Edward's first task was to discover if Evelyn might share his affections. As of yet, he hadn't mustered the courage to ask her directly. So, he wrote his letters and made his trips and delighted in her correspondence and company.

One visit to Palmyra had been required. A judge from the county seat in Lyons, New York, had been dispatched to hold an inquest into the kidnappings and murders in Palmyra. Edward had been summoned to testify in front of Judge Elijah Bainbridge Sampson. Thomas Adams had accompanied him.

Evidence had been recovered from Cole's home—items taken from the victims. Ribbons and bits of clothing. Locks of hair. Undergarments.

Similar evidence had been recovered from Goodword's cabin, though the man himself was missing. He'd been named a conspirator, and a warrant for his arrest had been issued.

Edward thought such evidence should be sufficient, but Judge Sampson had still questioned him closely about the actions of Cole, and how he and Jim had escaped with the child. Edward had answered each question as directly as he could—leaving out all mention of Mr. Jangles and the other spirits in the cave. Despite the clarity of his testimony, he could sense that Sampson wasn't satisfied. As the inquest proceeded, Edward wondered if he might somehow be found responsible and sent to jail.

Jim testified as well. The judge probed Jim closely about his activities as a spirit medium, and made no secret that he regarded Jim as a rascal and a fraud. But Jim was not on trial for claiming to speak with the dead.

The most convincing testimony had come from Cassie Brown, the girl who'd been kidnapped. Cassie, with her mother and father standing on either side, related the tale of her capture and imprisonment. Cole had crept into her room in the middle of night and stolen her from her bed, and then hidden her in a tunnel under the ground until bringing her to the cave.

In a clear, high voice, she answered each of Sampson's questions, including the most damning: Who was it who had taken her?

"Sherriff Cole," said Cassie. And when Sampson pressed her, the child affirmed again the identity of the kidnapper. Edward admired Cassie's courage under the scrutiny of the judge, and silently blessed the girl.

The day after the inquest, Edward was at the Forrest farm when the word came: the judge found no cause to bring charges against Edward and Jim. The Forrests had thrown the Drake brothers an impromptu feast to celebrate.

Now, in Boston, Edward checked his pocket watch. Mrs. Coffin expected them for supper. He and his guests were in Copley Square, one of his favorite spots in the city. He'd just taken them through Copley Library. They had toured Bates Hall, the majestic barrel-vaulted reading room, as well as the courtyard of the McKim building, its bubbling fountain and colonnade arches seemingly plucked from an Italian *palazzo*. He wanted to show them more, but it wouldn't do to be late to Beacon Hill.

49

Supper was a roast of beef with gravy *au jus*, carrots julienne, and baked potatoes. The roast was tender and succulent, the potatoes new. Edward, however, was too anxious to enjoy the food. He was desperate for these three women to form good impressions of one another, but a brittle silence hung over the dining table. Mrs. Forrest seemed particularly ill at ease. Unaccustomed to being served, she sat stiffly upright, unsure how to interact with Stephen, the Negro butler, as he set her meal in front of her.

Edward tried to spur the conversation. He ventured several topics, including the weather (very pleasant), the latest trends in landscaping and horticulture (rather dull to everyone but himself), and Boston's recently elected mayor, one Hugh O'Brien. O'Brien was the first Irish Catholic to hold the job. So far, he had proved thrifty, sober, and free of scandal—good for the city but bad for conversation. And a blow to Edward's wallet—he'd bet Thomas Connelly that O'Brien would never get elected, and was now poorer by five dollars.

Evelyn rescued the meal by enquiring about Mrs. Coffin's suffrage work. Here was a subject on which his benefactress could speak for days. When Evelyn spoke of her admiration for the writings of Mary Wollstonecraft and Lucretia Mott, a torrent of mutual enthusiasm carried the conversation into a lively and active channel. Edward relaxed and turned his attention to the roast.

After the meal, Mrs. Coffin escorted her guests to the parlor. She installed Evelyn and her mother in comfortable chairs and summoned herbal teas and poppy-seed cakes. Then she plucked Edward's sleeve and drew him to a corner.

"Well, Mum, Evelyn is a friend to your cause," he said. "You might draft her as a foot soldier."

"I suppose," said Mrs. Coffin. "She's very well behaved. But Edward, I don't quite understand your association with these…persons."

Edward opened his mouth to explain all that the Forrests had done for him, but Mrs. Coffin shushed him. She had a more pressing matter. "Edward, look at this. A friend mailed it to me." She handed Edward a strip of newsprint, which had been snipped from a Chicago broadsheet.

Edward scanned it. "A rural *savant* of spiritualism, his rough-hewn appearance belying a subtle grasp of ethereal links between this world and the beyond…held a packed house spellbound…opened a channel between the living and the dead…a reputation sprung from gruesome events that terrorized a village in a remote corner of western New York…."

The column was about Jim. Edward and his eldest brother had kept up a sporadic correspondence since Henry Hyde had taken Jim on tour, but Edward didn't have much sense of how his brother was being received. Here was praise from a presumably skeptical reporter.

"That could be you!" said Mrs. Coffin, tapping the paper. "A celebrated spiritualist. It should be you, not him."

"I don't want to be a celebrated spiritualist."

"Look at the praise being heaped on him, when you and I both know he's a rascal. Just like your father. I knew it the moment I set eyes on James Drake. I said to myself 'Tilda, this one's a rascal and you'll get no satisfaction from him.' And I was right. *You* were the one with talent!"

"Mum..."

"Edward, you would earn ten times the acclaim if only you'd embrace your gift."

Edward closed his eyes and took a deep breath. Here it was again; Mrs. Coffin's relentless needling for him to serve as her medium. Edward had not told her what he'd experienced in the cave; such a confession would only encourage her.

Ever since that night, he had grudgingly come to accept that some kind of phenomenon had occurred. How else to account for all that he'd experienced? Yet even as he acknowledged that *something* had occurred, he refused to name it, refused to give it his attention. He simply carved out a chamber in his mind, unconnected to any other aspect of his life, and stored the experience away. He could grapple with it later. Or never.

He hadn't been afflicted by spirits since those terrible hours, for which he was grateful. He hoped that the grisly climax—the burning of the book, Cole's death, and his own gunshot wound—had cauterized the part of him that gave form and voice to ghosts. He wanted all of it to be done.

Edward glanced at Evelyn and Mrs. Forrest. They sipped their tea. Evelyn raised an eyebrow—Was everything all right?

He wanted to return to them, but Mrs. Coffin sidled closer. "You needn't make a spectacle," she said. "It could just be you and me, as it was when you were a boy. Just the two of us, cosseted together in a quiet room. Wouldn't it be dear?"

"No, Mum. Never again."

Mrs. Coffin drew more breath to press her appeal, but was interrupted by Stephen's appearance in the doorway. The butler announced that Madame Corbeau had arrived. The medium wished to speak to Mr. Edward Drake.

Edward scowled. "Mum, why did you invite *her*?"

"I didn't. She must have come of her own accord."

"Called by the spirits, I'm sure. Are you roping me into another séance?"

"I do not 'rope,' Edward. I had nothing to do with her arrival. Send her away if you like."

Despite her protestations, Edward wasn't sure he believed her. Stephen stood in silent attendance; if he was in cahoots with his mistress, Edward couldn't tell.

"I'll speak to her privately. May I use your sitting room?"

"You may."

Edward made his apologies to Evelyn and her mother. "Forgive me, but I must step away for a moment."

"Edward, what is it?" asked Evelyn.

"There's a small matter to attend to. I won't be long." He misliked abandoning his guests, but a strange impulse pricked him.

50

Edward climbed the stairs to Mrs. Coffin's sitting room, a private space just off her bedroom. A desk with neatly arranged correspondence stood near a window that looked out on Louisburg square. The sash was a quarter open. May's soft breath stirred the muslin curtains. A vase of fresh-cut lilacs perfumed the chamber.

Catty-corner to the window hung Manet's "My Garden, the bench." One could sit on a plump divan on the opposite wall and contemplate the painting's bright, soothing scene from a Versailles garden.

Edward was not soothed. He paced in a tight orbit on the Oriental rug. Presently he heard footsteps. Stephen escorted Madame Corbeau into the sitting room and left the pair alone.

For this visit, Madame Corbeau had replaced her garish medium's costume with a simple dress of blue and white check. A faded kerchief wrapped her auburn hair. She might be a merchant's wife rather than a renowned speaker to the dead. Even her French accent seemed less pronounced.

"Thank you for seeing me, *Monsieur* Drake."

Edward gestured to the divan. At her invitation, he sat stiffly beside her. Their knees, which did not touch, formed the apex of a triangle.

"I understand you saved a child," said Madame Corbeau.

"Did the spirits inform you?"

"Just a newspaper from Rochester, *Monsieur*. But I sense you've experienced a profound psychic event."

Edward made a non-committal noise.

"When I was young, and my spirit organ began to flower," said Corbeau, "I was frightened. I wondered if I might be a lunatic, or an instrument of the devil. But I could not deny my talent. Rather than fight or ignore it, I worked to develop and strengthen my gift. And as my skill and understanding increased, I grew less afraid for my sanity, or for the disposition of my soul. I made peace with my abilities, however strange they were."

"Is that why you've come? To convince me to accept my 'abilities'? I suppose you can recommend a series of exercises. Perhaps there's an instructional pamphlet? *Madame*, how much has Mrs. Coffin paid you for this?"

"*Non, monsieur.* After our last encounter I never wanted to see you again. The spirit who attached himself to you was terrible. *Une bête diabolique.* I still feel sick in my belly when I think of that day."

"Then why?"

"Because of her." The medium took Edward's hands. Her fingers were icy cold. Edward gasped.

Someone else was in the room with them. An elderly woman stood by the door, a knitted shawl drawn tightly around her stooped shoulders. Sunlight from the window passed through her as if through parchment.

"She would not let me alone," said Corbeau. "She wants someone to know. She wants you to know. She tried to reach out to you, but you have closed yourself to her."

Edward recognized the apparition. Lizbet Cloud. Granny Lizbet. She had helped him in the cave.

"She's been keeping watch over your family," said Madame Corbeau. "For a very long time she's stood guard, knowing that William Jongold would seek revenge against her kin."

Invisible hands squeezed Edward's lungs. He didn't want this. But just as in the cave, he was forced to accept the truth of it. And he had to accept another truth: Without Lizbet Cloud, things might have gone very differently. With a reluctant nod he acknowledged the spirit. "Thank you," he said.

Lizbet Cloud returned his nod, but her expression was troubled.

"She's carried a burden for many years, *Monsieur*. It weighs her down, and keeps her spirit from being free. Will you help her?"

"Me? What can I do?"

"You can see what she would show you."

Granny Lizbet raised an arthritic hand and clasped a small pouch that hung around her neck. Mrs. Coffin's sitting room fell away.

51

She had to walk past his study many times a day. She didn't like to go by it, even with the door closed. A foulness seeped out from under the door. The floor was softer there, or stickier, like spilled molasses that grasped the soles of your feet. It could trap you and leave you helpless for what waited on the other side.

Master Jongold raped her in the study. He'd been raping her since she turned thirteen. She was sixteen now.

She'd become adept at hiding the master's predations from her mother and father. She knew it was shameful; she saw the suspicion in her father's eyes when Master Jongold spoke to her or put a proprietary hand on her arm. Her father warned her not to be alone with the master, to stay near her mother when she worked in the house. And she tried.

But he was the master. If he chose, he could command her mother and father to watch while he violated her. Jongold preferred discretion. If the mood took him, he sent her mother into town on an errand, and tasked his father with some work in the orchard or smithy, leaving her alone with him in that giant old manse.

What he did in that room was awful. Yet there was something

else about the master's study, a vileness that compounded his crimes against her. Now and then she heard things from the study; chittering sounds that made her think of giant insects, mandibles quivering as they buzzed and plotted. Once, as she passed the room with an armload of stove wood, she'd heard a rasping voice call out "Come in, my sweet, come in come in!" She'd screamed and run out of the house, and wouldn't go back inside for the rest of the day.

This day was a cold and dreary October afternoon. Master Jongold brooded over his books in the study. Earlier he had dispatched her father to Rochester to sell a crop of apples from the orchard. Her mother he sent to town with a long list of errands. The old house was silent and still. She kept to the kitchen, feeding the stove, making bread, stirring a pumpkin soup. Pretending it wouldn't happen today.

She tried to sing against the stillness of the house as she punched and kneaded a mound of dough. The song, which her father's family had brought from France to the new world, sounded flat and dull in her ears. Her hands were clumsy and cold. Her belly ached in terrible anticipation. Her body knew the truth of what was to come even if she herself wouldn't admit it.

Her hand went to her chest. A small pouch of blue silk was pinned beneath her blouse. She fingered the little bag and tried to draw courage from it. Papa had made it for her two years ago. He called it *'L'aile de Gabriel'*—Gabriel's wing—a talisman of angelic protection. It was the strongest he knew how to make. She'd watched him lay out its ingredients on a piece of clean linen: a sliver of magnetic lodestone, a nugget of a midnight-black crystal, dried leaves of cinquefoil, and petals of morning glory.

He'd lit two candles and set a small bowl of powdered incense to smolder. Then her father prayed over the ingredients in his native French, his words sonorous and so much more confident that his halting, accented English. He prayed with his Bible in hand. Papa was illiterate, but he knew the psalms of blessing and protection by heart.

When he'd finished praying, he leaned down and blew on the minerals and plants to charge them with his breath. He sprinkled them with drops of oil. He passed his hands over them three times.

As Lizbet sat and watched, the smoke from the incense made her woozy. The objects on the linen shimmered in the light of the candles. She understood her father was pouring his intent into the lodestone, the crystal, the cinquefoil, the morning glory. He imbued these objects with his will, his strength, his protection. He wanted to keep her safe when he couldn't be at her side.

With gentle care he placed the items onto a small square of blue silk. He blew out the candles and snuffed the incense. Then he shaped the silk into a little pouch and sewed it shut with strong thread. He instructed Lizbet to wear Gabriel's Wing close to her body at all times.

"I will, Papa." Her love for him brimmed and spilled over the cup of her heart. But her love was mixed with sorrow; the thing he sought to protect her from had already happened, was happening still.

She touched the pouch, here in Jongold's kitchen. Whatever power might be in the little bag, Master Jongold had overwhelmed it long ago. Yet she kept the talisman and cherished it for what it was—a sign of her father's love.

The master called "Come here, Lizbet. I've something to show you."

Lizbet clutched the pouch, pressed it hard against her skin. She didn't want to go to him. She pretended not to have heard. But he called again, putting steel in his voice.

He'd never hit her, but he had other ways to bend her to his will. If Lizbet disobeyed or struggled against him, he reminded her of her father's secret. If she ever told anyone what he did to her, he would summon the authorities to come and take her father. He would be hung for his crime, and she would be to blame.

When he called a third time, she went to him. But first she dropped a small, sharp knife into the pocket of her apron.

The study was dusty. Candles and lamps threw flickering light against the spines of heavy books and curious instruments. A fire burned in the hearth. Behind the clean scent of burning pine logs she smelled rot, something old and moldering in the walls. Or inside the master.

Master Jongold sat upright in a hard-backed chair behind his desk. A half-eaten meal of bloody roast sat near to hand. She thought she saw a cockroach scurry off the plate and slip out of sight. Next to the plate rested a pair of stones, one dark, one white.

Master Jongold had a book in his desk. The creeping book. The one he cherished above all others. The one that frightened her just to look on it.

Master Jongold moistened a finger with a slimy pink tongue and turned a page. Behind her, the door creaked closed of its own accord. She hated that sound, hated what it meant.

Master Jongold spoke to her of his long study, his quest for hidden knowledge. He had discovered many things, secret things that gave him power over the natural world. As he talked, she felt the floor twist beneath her, as if the ground had grown unsteady. She didn't understand much of what he said. Hadn't he power enough? He had money. Servants attended him. He could sit in the comfort of his grand home all the day long while others saw to his needs. What more could he want?

"Now see here," said Jongold. "My greatest discovery." He rose from his chair and thrust the book into her hands. He held the stones in front of her eyes. The words before her were unrecognizable, but images poured into her mind through the stones. She saw Jongold's gnarled old hands pull a baby from between a woman's legs. Her legs. The life cord trailed from the baby's belly. The infant squalled, its face wrinkled, its mouth wide. A beautiful baby.

And then a knife slashed the newborn's neck. Red blood sluiced from the tiny vessel of its body. Master Jongold, naked, bathed in the blood, covering his brow, his face, his arms and chest. And then he walked out to the little graveyard behind the house, where his wife and daughter were buried. He began to dig in the earth.

The blood from the infant dripped off Master Jongold's hands and into the soil of the graves. The dirt trembled. Pale fingers sprouted up from the ground. Master Jongold dug deeper, exposing a bare white arm, a shoulder. And then a face, hideous and leering, emerged from the dirt and licked the infant's blood from Jongold's skin. Jongold's wife, long dead but somehow called back.

Lizbet recoiled from this vision. She dropped the book and kicked it away from her.

Jongold gathered the book and placed it in an iron strongbox, and rested the stones on his desk. He spoke to her of the loss of his wife and daughter. How his sorrow weighed him with invisible chains and brought him terrible pain. But behind his testimony of grief, Lizbet heard something else; a bold, proud, lustful ambition to break nature's laws. Love did not drive him; dominion did.

He told Lizbet how she would help him. Lizbet would be the instrument that let him overmaster death and draw back those he had lost. But first, a sacrifice must be made. To regain his family, he must sacrifice a child of his own blood. So he would put a baby in her, and use it to resurrect his beloveds.

"We'll dare great things, you and I."

Then he was on her, quick as a scuttling crab. His hands were pincers, his arms and legs grasping claws. She fought back. She gouged and bit and pushed, but the master was clever and cruel and strong. He kicked her legs out from under her and drove her to the floor. He lay on top of her and tore her undergarments away.

"No!" she screamed. "No!"

His violation was sharp and brutal.

At last he rolled off her and got to his feet. He buckled his trousers. She lay on the floor and tried to cover herself with her torn garments.

"Dry your tears, girl. Perhaps you can't comprehend it just now, but you shall play a role in the most audacious act the human mind can conceive: the overthrow of death itself! Does it not fire your imagination, stoke your ambition? Think on it as the child quickens inside you. And weep not for the little one taking root inside you. You'll have others, as many as you like."

The sight of his face, flush with triumph, lanced her heart and burst open the membrane where she stored up all his predations against her and her family. Anger roared through her. She was finished with his cruelty. Gabriel's Wing blazed against her skin like a hot coal.

She took the knife from her apron and slashed his leg. The blade sliced his Achilles cord and he toppled, howling. He knocked a lamp to the floor, spilling fire across the rug.

And then she was on him, thrusting and stabbing. A chorus of voices gibbered and howled. Strange shadows slithered up from cracks between the floor boards to hoot and bellow.

She plunged the knife into his chest, his belly, his groin. His blood, hot and red, covered her hands, her arms, her face.

"Goddamm you no!" he screamed.

She screamed back, roaring into his face. She slashed his cheeks and his throat. His cries died away, replaced by a pathetic burbling. Bubbles of blood percolated from his lips.

With a final shriek she plunged the knife into his heart.

The strange shadows faded. The chorus of voices fell silent, replaced by a growling in her ears. It was the growl of the fire as it spread to drapes, to the books in their rows on lacquered shelves. She rested on her calves. The fire licked the walls and the ceiling. The rug where Jongold lay began to burn. With an effort she yanked the knife from his chest.

She stood, knife in one bloody hand. Her limbs felt draped in lead. Smoke filled her lungs. She staggered to the study door, flung it open, and limped out into the hall.

Tendrils of fire followed. Vines of orange and red spread across carpets, clung to baseboards, and climbed dry wooden walls. She smelled burning flesh; the fire feasted on Jongold's corpse.

She stumbled onto the porch. Etienne Cloud jumped down from a wagon, having returned from his task. He cried out at the sight of his daughter covered in blood, knife in hand. He ran to the porch and caught Lizbet as she fell. Flickering flames scampered onto the porch.

He carried her to the cottage by the orchard where they lived. He lay her on her bed, and then dashed back to the house. She curled up beneath her blankets. Soon she heard other voices; the smoke and flames had attracted men from nearby farms. They were trying to fight the fire.

Then her mother was there, cradling her. She wept as her mother undressed her, washed Jongold's blood from her skin. She clutched the talisman tightly to her. Her mother tore her blood-soaked clothes into strips and burned them in the stove. She dropped the knife into the outhouse.

Sometime later her father returned. He reeked of smoke and sweat. His face and clothes were coated with ash. "*Tout et parti*," he wheezed. "Fire got the whole house." He had an iron strongbox in his hands. "This was the only thing I could save." Inside was the creeping book.

Lizbet recoiled. "Take it away! Hide it away forever!"

Her father kneeled in front of her. She saw the fear in his eyes.

"I'll bury it, *cher*. But you must get hold of yourself. *Les fermier* will ask what happened. You tell 'em he was drunk. You was workin' in the kitchen all day and he was in his study with his dram. You smelled smoke. You went to the study and saw him passed out, fire all 'round. Too late to save him. You barely made it out. *Oui?*"

She understood. She had to lie save her life. To save her parents. But she feared there would be no saving any of them.

———

Jongold had no known relatives, and no will was found among the few effects that survived the fire. But one thing that did survive was a parchment, recovered from a strongbox. It was a wanted notice for Etienne Cloud. Etienne was already under suspicion for the death of William Jongold and the burning of his property. Now here was proof that the foreigner was a criminal. Someone tipped Etienne that men were coming for him. He fled in the night. He told his wife and daughter to stay in Palmyra—that he would send for them when he found someplace safe.

Lizbet's parting from her father was grievous, made more so because it seemed as if Jongold had his revenge. His threat to break up the family had been made good, and Lizbet was to blame. She had committed the worst of all sins—thou shall not kill—and her father bore the punishment. She wanted to go with him, but Lizbet had been sorely injured by Jongold's attack. She bled from the womb, and it wouldn't stop. Etienne told her to get well, and that he would see her soon.

For many days she bled. She grew pale and weak. At last, a doctor came up from Canandaigua to treat her. He managed to stop the bleeding. And when Lizbet recovered, the doctor took her and her mother as house servants.

The doctor soon regretted it. The spirit of William Jongold followed Lizbet. She called him Old Bill, and he wreaked what little mischief he could in her life; breaking dishes, slamming doors, knocking on walls at all hours of the night, and infesting the dreams of the physician and his wife and children.

Less than three months after she'd left, Lizbet Cloud was back in Palmyra. The doctor had sent her away. But she was no longer Lizbet Cloud. She was Lizbet Cooper, wife of a laborer named Nathan Cooper. She and Nat built a house on the only land they could afford—in the Bottoms—and began a life together. She gave birth to her first child, a girl named Mercy. And always she waited for a word from her father. She and her mother had not heard from him since the parting. She'd returned to Palmyra in hopes that a message from her father would find her there. It never came.

But Old Bill was always present, his anger unchecked, his

vengeance a flame that burned without ceasing. He stalked her, watched her, waiting for his chance. He would wait as long as it took.

———

Edward blinked. He was in Mrs. Coffin's study, holding hands with Madame Corbeau. He felt woozy, as if awakened from a stupor. Lizbet Cloud's memories had been so potent he could smell the smoke of the burning house, taste ash on his lips, and feel the pain of Jongold's violation inside him. Tears tracked his cheeks.

The ghost of Lizbet Cloud stood at the door. Her own wrinkled cheeks were wet. Edward wished he could go to her and wipe her tears with his handkerchief.

Lizbet Cloud worried the pouch with her fingers. Then Edward heard her voice, raspy and rough with her father's Quebecois accent.

Never have I told the truth. Not to my husband, not to my children, not to my gran-children. I shut it inside me. Most folks thought my father killed Jongold and set the fire to cover it up. I let them believe it.

"What happened to your parents?"

Nat and I brought my mother home to Palmyra.

"And your father? Etienne?"

He died. He died trying to cross a river to escape agents of the law.

Edward felt her grief, but Lizbet wasn't finished.

You need to know something else. My first-born child. That baby was not from my Nat.

Dread filled Edward's belly. "The rape. Jongold put a baby in you. Surely you didn't keep his child. There are ways... ."

I know there are ways. I thought on it, but I could not end the life that quickened inside me. So I birthed Jongold's baby. A girl. She looked like me, not him, thank God. I swaddled her and nursed her at my breast. Nat knew the child weren't his—the man could count. But he let it be. He never asked questions, just loved that girl with all his heart.

I feared I might hate the child, because of what she came from. But I didn't. She was innocent, just a baby who needed her mama. She was faultless. So I poured my love into her, poured it in like an antidote. And I named her Mercy. That's what she was. And that's what I needed.

Edward remembered Tante V's bible, with the family tree written on the frontispiece. Mercy was Lizbet's first child. And the line from Mercy carried down through the generations in a thread that tied directly to Edward.

"No," said Edward.

I'm sorry, cher. Mercy was Jongold's child. And you come from my line and Mercy's line. He is in your blood. Old Bill, he is part of you.

The revelation swamped him like a fetid tide. He struggled to keep his dinner. He looked down at the veins in his wrists, at the blood that flowed through the channels of his body. Jongold's blood was mixed with his own; just a trace now after all these generations, but inside him. He imagined a splinter of foulness riding the courses of his veins, boring its way through his heart, his brain, his eyes, to every fiber and cord of his body. He wanted to slash himself open and pour his blood through a sieve to sift out the foul splinter. He couldn't bear the thought of it inside him! He saw a letter opener on Mrs. Coffin's writing desk and sprang to his feet.

Arrete!

Lizbet Cloud's command rocked his head like a blow. He sat back heavily on the divan.

I know it hurts, dear heart. I know better than anyone. But I bore the pain. Bore it in my heart and bore it in my womb. And I've carried it for a long time; so long, I despaired of ever being quit of it.

But I saw you in the cave. I saw you stand. Old Bill chose you because of the quality of your mind. But he also chose you because he thought you were weak. A runty boy, beaten and bullied, easy to cow. He thought he could break you to his will. He didn't know how strong you are.

She glided forward, this aged and wrinkled ghost. She glided forward and stood over Edward. With her right hand she touched Gabriel's Wing, the talisman her father made. With her left, she put a bony finger to his forehead.

Faintly, like a wisp of smoke, he felt her touch. In it he sensed a weight, immensely heavy, balanced on a fulcrum between him and Lizbet Cloud.

He is in you. But so am I. So is my father. So is my daughter, and her daughters. And your father and your mother and your brothers. You have strength, cher. *Your own and others'. Will you take the burden?*

"What burden?"

He is still out there, Old Bill. He will not quit his vengeance. He wants to cause our family pain. He wants to hurt our people. So someone must watch. Someone must stand against him.

Edward gulped. The unnamed phenomenon he sought to banish could not be kept away. It bled through into his life, would always bleed through. Whatever this thing was, it was part of him.

His eyes slid to the letter opener again. He gauged the sharpness of its long silver blade. With one quick slash across his wrists, he could be free of all of this.

"*Monsieur,*" said Corbeau. She drew his eyes away from the blade. "Do not despair. You simply know a truth that few others comprehend; there are other worlds a hair's breadth from ours. Sometimes things cross over. Dark things. Terrible things. We who know must watch."

Yes, said Lizbet. *Now you know the truth. And it's a hard truth. A heavy truth. But I ask again—will you stand?*

The great weight trembled on its fulcrum. Lizbet Cloud waited. Edward saw the weariness in her face, in the rheumy wet corners of her eyes, in the crook of her neck and the hunch of her back.

"*I've borne it many days. It's held me down, kept me back. I've waited for someone to take it from me. Will it be you?*"

Edward quailed. What strangeness and terror would she pile upon him? His instinct was to shun this woman, turn his head away, nail up yet another bulwark against ethereal incursions. He must reject this madness!

Or must he? All his life he had been like a man on a hill in a raging storm who insisted the wind and weather were illusions. He'd stood soaked and shivering as sleet slashed his face and lightning stabbed down all around, desperate to convince himself that he was dry and safe and well. He is not safe. He is not well. It is time to open his eyes and acknowledge the storm.

But what an acknowledgement! To accept that Mr. Jangles was real, and bound to Edward and his family? That the dead could speak and Edward could hear them? That spirits could slip through the membrane between the living and the dead? What would it mean to live with such beliefs?

He didn't know. What he knew is that for all his life he'd been at war with his own mind. He'd thought the battle was between madness and sanity, but he was wrong. He'd only been warring against the truth—a truth so bizarre and strange he'd nearly destroyed himself rather than accept it.

He didn't know what would happen if he accepted Granny Lizbet's burden. Terrible spirits might afflict him for as long as he lived. But at least he could stop fighting with himself, stop wondering if he was delusional or insane. And he could grant this brave woman peace.

"I'll take it," he said.

Lizbet Cloud exhaled. As she breathed out, Edward felt a yoke settle across his shoulders, heavy and implacable. Its weight grew and grew. It threated to snap his neck and break his spine. He pushed back, testing his strength against it. His legs buckled. His bones shivered. For a terrible moment he thought he'd made a grave mistake.

And then he straightened. The weight did not put him on his knees. It did not break him. He didn't know what to make of this weight, or how it would bear on the course of his life. But he would shoulder the burden and grapple the consequences, whatever they might be. And he would do it as a man of one mind.

"I can bear it, Granny," said Edward. "It's heavy, but I can bear it. And you can be free."

Granny Lizbet's back seemed straighter now, the anguish in her face eased.

My Nat has waited. A long time he's waited. And so have I. Now I can move on and be united with him. I'll see my Mercy again, her and all my children and grand-children. Oh, how precious it will be! Bless you, Edward. Bless you and keep you.

And then she was gone.

Madame Corbeau stood. "The great horror she suffered, and the task she undertook, those things bound her spirit to this world. Now you have set her free."

She squeezed Edward's hands one last time, then went to the door. "*C'est un bon travail, Monsieur.* You've done a good thing. Farewell."

"But wait. What have I done? What have I taken upon myself? What am I meant to do?"

"I cannot say, Edward. It is for you to find out. But remember, you need not do it alone. *Au revoir.*"

52

Luke Forrest was married in June of 1885 to Octavia Hutchins from Macedon, New York. Edward accepted Luke's invitation to the wedding. Fred and Cicely Drake also attended, traveling from Rochester with their children in tow. Jim was invited, but could not attend as he was touring San Francisco.

The Forrests hosted the reception at their farmhouse. The old place burst with people and food and life and noise. Edward was made to feel very welcome by Evelyn's extended family. What's more, Cassie Brown had greeted him shyly and presented him with a white carnation to wear in his lapel. He was pleased to see the child seemed in good health.

Three hours into the reception, Edward felt overwhelmed; he'd eaten too much, drunk too much, danced until his feet ached. He'd chased Fred's children and Evelyn's nieces and nephews around the house and played hide-n-seek with them in the barn. He was hot and full.

He found Evelyn among a clutch of female cousins. "I'm going to take the air," he said in her ear. She nodded and then returned to her conversation, radiant in a simple yellow dress and a garland of daises from the garden.

Edward threaded his way through the crowded farmhouse and out the back door of the mud room. Dickens, who'd been banished to the yard, greeted him with a lively tail and a doggish grin.

"Hello, boy. Shall we walk?"

Edward and the dog strolled through the cow pasture. The air was deliciously cool after the heat of so many bodies. Fresh clover scented the breeze. Bee the cow, a calf beside her, ambled over greet the man and the dog. Edward stroked their noses, then continued across the pasture.

He came to the fence that bounded the Forrest farm. The woods were just beyond. Edward let himself and the dog through a gate. The trees were in full leaf. The greenery was a verdant contrast to the bare branches and carpets of dead leaves among which he'd wandered last autumn in search of Jim and the missing children. He'd suffered strange and terrible things in those woods, things that he didn't like to think on. But the green freshness of a forest should hold no fear for a grown man—should it?

Dickens spotted a squirrel among the roots of a maple and dashed after it. Edward followed, passing beneath the leafy boughs that marked the border of the woods. The air was cooler beneath the trees. Rays of sun scattered across the leaves, which turned up like palms to scoop the light.

As Edward followed Dickens, the beads of perspiration on his forehead turned clammy. A strange silence held sway. Clouds moved overhead, obscuring the sun. The forest darkened.

Something stirred up ahead. Dickens slouched out of the underbrush, tail tucked, ears flat against his skull. The beast came and leaned into Edward's leg, trembling.

A figure appeared.

Here was a guest no one had invited. Cracked lips split to show mossy teeth. Green eyes glittered with malice. Mr. Jangles raised a pale hand, beckoning Edward deeper into the woods. There was something dark in there, something terrible he wanted to show.

Edward went limp. Here was the specter he'd promised to stand against. A part of him hoped he'd banished Mr. Jangles by thwarting him in the cave, burning that hideous book, and saving a child's life.

No. Mr. Jangles was not banished.

A bead of thought leapt across the gap between Edward and the apparition.

We're not finished, you and I.

At Edward's heel, the dog whined.

And then a hand touched him, warm and gentle. Evelyn. She stood next to him. Her eyes were bright, her lips parted in a smile. The garland in her hair carried a faint perfume. Dickens barked once and danced at her feet.

"Edward, were you ever coming back to the reception?"

Mr. Jangles stood in plain view by the trunk of an elm. His suit was ragged at the hems, and discolored from endless days of wandering. One hand rested at his breast, clutching the lapel of his jacket as if he posed for a portrait.

"Evelyn, do you see anyone there?"

Evelyn peered into the woods. "I don't see anyone. Did a guest go wandering?"

"No guest."

Mr. Jangles sneered. *Your miserable ancestor has moved on. She's left you to pay her debt. And I'll have it from you. One way or another, I'll have it.*

No, thought Edward. I'll fight you. I'll thwart you. He cut the air with the sharp edge of his palm, as if severing an umbilicus that stretched between him and the apparition.

Mr. Jangles grinned. *You can't be rid of me so easily. I'm in your blood.*

Then you know I have strength in me, he thought. My own and others'. I'm not alone.

Edward put his back to the grotesque vision, and took Evelyn in his arms. He drew her close, and she responded in kind, molding her body to his. He kissed her fully, pouring all his attention into the act.

When they separated, Evelyn stepped back. "Edward! How dare you!"

Edward blushed and began to stutter an apology.

"And it took you long enough!"

Now Edward laughed, a true and joyous sound. "I've wanted to do that for some time. But I wasn't sure of your feelings toward me."

"Nor mine towards you," said Evelyn. "But I wanted you to kiss me regardless."

"And now that I have?"

Evelyn's mouth worked as she sought for words. She tangled her fingers in knots. "Edward, I...it's all very confusing. My heart tells me one thing, my head another. I want to follow my heart, but there are so many barriers." She touched the pale skin on the back of his hand. "What would my parents say?"

"I suspect your mother has an inkling of my feelings. I've caught looks from her, as if she were measuring me up."

"Truly? I haven't seen any looks."

"I'm quite observant when it comes to you. I'll wager she hasn't yet told your father. When she does, I expect to be chased off with a pitchfork."

"If Ma can be convinced, Pa will come around. But what about your people? Would Mrs. Coffin approve?"

"I hope so. But I can't say for sure."

"I know you have an income from her, Edward. What if she cut you off? Would you risk that?"

"Without hesitation."

"It's not just her to consider. Much of Boston would be against us. Much of Palmyra for that matter. Perhaps the whole world, Edward."

"Not the whole world. Frederick Douglass married that Pitts woman. She's white."

"You and I don't compare with Mr. Douglass. Besides, have you read of the scorn heaped upon him and his new wife? Her own father has disowned her. The Negro press call him a race traitor. They've been threatened with violence, accosted in public. I don't know that I could live like that."

"It would be hard," acknowledged Edward. "But wouldn't it be harder not to risk it, to leave the chance untaken?"

She began to reply but he rushed over her. "Please, listen. My employer Mr. Olmsted has recently been approached by a client. This client has come into some family money; he's purchased an estate outside Paris from an old French viscount. The client wants Mr. Olmsted to refurbish the grounds and gardens of the estate. Mr. Olmsted is already engaged with another project, so he recommended me. I have a commission, Evelyn. A commission to oversee my own design!"

"Oh," said Evelyn. "I'm very happy for you, Edward." The light draining from her expression said otherwise. "And in France, you say? How marvelous. When do you leave?"

"In two weeks."

"I see. I suppose we could take the time apart to examine our feelings."

"We must examine our feelings, but not apart. Come with me, Evelyn. Come with me to Paris! Your school is finished for the summer, and we can return before you start again in the fall."

Evelyn gasped at the boldness of the idea. She clutched his hands as if he were about to fly overseas that very moment. Then her grip loosened.

"It's a pretty dream, Edward. But I'm afraid it could only ever be a dream. Even without the issue of our different races, an unmarried woman can't travel with a man."

"She can with a chaperone. You could bring your mother. Or a maiden aunt if you've got one. If not, I can recruit one of Mrs. Coffin's old busy-bodies. Or Tante V! She'd take some getting used to, and we'd have to do something about her dog…"

"Edward, slow down! I don't even speak French."

"You've a sharp mind. You'll learn."

"I'm just a dairy maid. What business do I have in Paris?"

"Dairy maid? Evelyn, you're a teacher. An educator. You're well-read. Your wit's sharp as a blade. You'll joust with the best of them in the salons and the cafes. You'll have Paris at your feet."

"And what of my family? Think of all the work that needs to be done around here, especially now with Luke leaving. It's just not practical."

"Luke's not leaving. He's bought a house up the lane. He and I are already planning to hire a hand or two for the dairy business. If you're worried about your mother keeping house by herself, we could get a domestic."

"Oh Lord, I can't imagine Ma with a servant. She wouldn't know what to do with one."

"She'd adapt. She'll see what a sloppy housekeeper you've been all these years."

Evelyn smacked his shoulder. Then she waved a hand in front of her face as if to cool a fever. "Edward, do we dare?"

"We should. We must." He took her hand and guided her from the forest back toward the farm. Their fingers twined. When they reached the fence that marked the pasture boundary, Edward took a deep breath. He'd already risked a kiss. He had to risk something more. "Evelyn, if we're to build a life, whether in friendship or something more, there are things you need to know about me. Things I haven't told you."

"What do you mean?"

Edward glanced back at the ghost-haunted woods. Mr. Jangles had vanished, but Edward was certain the specter hovered nearby, like a dark moon in perpetual orbit. "I don't want to speak of it here. If we travel together we can talk at length. About us. About our future. But I want you to know my truth before you make any… permanent decision."

Evelyn traced his brow with her thumb. Her touch was cool and gentle. "Edward, are you ill?"

"No. But there's a mark on me. Or a burden." He frowned. "It's something I have to bear. And I don't know how it will affect my life. Or our lives, if we live them together. Something even beyond the differences of our skin."

"You're serious."

"I am."

Evelyn pondered his words. "You said 'our lives.'"

"I did."

Evelyn nodded. "A burden is lighter if it's shared."

"You don't know what it is. I'm not even sure I do."

"So we'll take a journey," said Evelyn. "You'll tell me what you need to tell me. And then we'll go forward."

"Together?"

"Yes, Edward. Together."

Edward nodded. "Come then. Let's you and I go make our lives." He helped her over the fence, and she helped him in turn.

The End

ACKNOWLEDGMENTS

Thanks to my wife Clare for her support and encouragement. She read many, many drafts and took long walks with me to talk about how to make Edward a more deeply realized character. She also gave me the push (or pushes) I needed to send this out into the world. She is always my first and best reader.

Thanks also to my friend William Ruoto for the excellent cover design and illustration.

Printed in Great Britain
by Amazon